My Father's Sins

What Others Are Saying

"This is a crackerjack mystery novel with a deep and relevant theme."

iUniverse Editorial Review

‡‡‡

"Men and women of the cloth are not often protagonists in fiction anymore, and it's kind of refreshing to see a smart, interesting, charismatic character such as [Father Mike] as the protagonist of a mystery novel. Rains's greatest strength as a writer is at characterization, in fact.... Father Mike...is consistently interesting and believable. A completely well-rounded character."

Writer's Digest Book Awards Review

‡‡‡

"The author is particularly good at describing the lives and behavior of the *hobes* (the homeless) who have names like Juice, Smiley, Gin-Gin, and, most enigmatic of all, Sir.... The author shows real empathy for such characters."

Philip Grosset, "Clerical Detectives"

‡‡‡

"Couldn't put it down!

Great mystery! I had a hard time putting it down. The plot kept growing and growing.

The characters were easy to get to know and either really like—or not. I fell in love with Father Mike. It was nice seeing both sides of him. He was a priest that so many depended on for guidance in their lives....

I hope there is a sequel. I would like to read more about the characters that I've come to know and care about."

Barnes and Noble Reader's Review

My Father's Sins

A Mike Richey Mystery

Dale Osborn Rains

AARTHAVEN PRESS

Book Publishers
www.aarthaven.com

Dale Osborn Rains

Second Edition

This is a work of fiction. All of the characters, names, incidents, organizations, and dialogue in this novel are either the products of the author's imagination or are used fictitiously.

ISBN: 0615683835
ISBN-13: 978-0615683836

TO JOANNE

Thanks beyond measure to my patient wife, and my love of over a quarter century, for reading and rereading my manuscript and for giving me the support I needed to complete
My Father's Sins

[He] will by no means clear the guilty, visiting the sins of the fathers upon their children and their children's children, to the third and the fourth generation.
Exodus 35:6

O*NE*

S IR PULLED his heavy overcoat tighter and wiped his nose with his sleeve to keep the drips from forming icy stalactites down his upper lip. He staggered down Church Street lurching from one shadow to the next. He was more inebriated than usual, but he knew he had to get to St. Christopher's quickly or he would die. He needed the priest. That was for certain.

To say the day had been difficult for Sir would be an understatement. When he had waked up in Slocum Alley and shifted himself out from under his cardboard tent, he gathered his possessions to begin his morning patrol of the city. He struggled over the alley debris to Juice's tent. Juice, so named because of his predilection for cheap orange-colored wine, had been his first friend in Madison.

"Juice, wake up, man. Let's roll."

Sir stood there in silence waiting for some kind of mumbling and grumbling he always heard from Juice's tent. The usual noises, through which the *Yeah, yeah, I'm comin'* was hardly decipherable, failed to materialize.

This was not good. Juice never left on his patrol this early. In fact, Sir always had to wake him from his stupor to get him going in the mornings. Juice's rusty grocery cart was still in place, and the few things he pushed along the street had not been disturbed. There was the old Nancy rag doll in his cart, a toy that had once belonged to his youngest granddaughter, Joy.

Juice never left the alley without Nancy. A decade or so ago a drunk driver had killed Joy—in her parents' own driveway. Juice had been that drunk driver, and Sir had witnessed over and over again Juice's self-flagellations in atonement for his deeply regretted sin. Joy was still clutching Nancy as the EMTs lifted her lifeless body onto the stretcher. The doll was all Juice had left of his only granddaughter. So Juice never went anywhere without Nancy.

Sir grasped Nancy and held the doll close to his breast. *I've got to find Juice*, thought Sir. *I've got to get Nancy to him somehow.* He closed his arms around Nancy, as if she were a warm puppy, and grabbed his own three-wheeled cart and started his search. *I've got to find Juice.*

Sir trudged across the long bedraggled alley that he had shared with Juice for the past six months. Very few other hobes, as they called themselves, ever came to Slocum. The large green Dumpster that shielded the entrance to the alley from the heavily traveled street provided a modicum of privacy for them. But Sir was always eager to get out of the alley every morning to go on patrol.

But he couldn't go on patrol yet. He had to find Juice. He grabbed his cart and bumped it over the rubble, rumbling his way back and forth over the alley—searching—searching. No Juice. "E-y-o-o-o!"

Great horror surged through Sir's heart. Two hobes had been murdered within the last three months. Temporary hobes—or hobos, as they were called—who flew in on the local freight and then quickly flew out again, had been arrested for the murders. Sir sat on the ground, inadvertently splashing himself down into a pile of ice from last night's sleet. But he didn't care. He placed his face in his hands. What if hobos had found Juice. *The police. The police. No.* He couldn't go find a police officer. That was a no-no in the hobe world.

Then a new thought occurred to him. Perhaps Juice had been too drunk to make it back to his cardboard tent and had passed out somewhere along the alley way. So he headed down Slocum toward the street, zigzagging across the alley—almost like a cop grid-searching a crime scene—looking for Juice. He had difficulty pushing his cart off the beaten path, over the rubble, through the accumulated dead leaves, and around piles of broken glass, where some past hobes had thrown their empty wine bottles against the side brick wall just for the hell of it. But he did not find Juice.

Then just before he reached the Dumpster that shielded the alley from the street, he suddenly stopped, the crippled cart almost throwing him to the ground. Juice lay there, a bloody hole in his forehead. An almost full bottle of orange-colored Bowie's Farm lay gripped in Juice's white-knuckled fist. Sir crouched down beside Juice and stroked his head. The blood was dried by now. *Shit*, he thought, tears dribbling down his cheeks.

Juice had been the first hobe he had met when he arrived in Madison. About six months ago now. When he had appeared at the Tyrone Street Bridge, most of the hobes were sitting around drinking or eating in twos or threes, but Juice sat by himself against a concrete piling eating an apple. Sir gravitated to where Juice was and sat down. Not beside him, mind you, but somewhat apart. Neither said anything. Sir started going through his bag—his collection of treasures. Then he heard a grunt. He looked up, and Juice, although saying nothing, offered Sir the apple. Sir smiled the best he could. He took the apple, and the two had become best buddies. And now Juice was dead.

Instinctively Sir dipped his hand into Juice's right coat pocket. Three quarters, a nickel, and four pennies. He immediately shoved the money into his own pocket. Then Juice's other pocket. A scrap of folded paper. The paper, as if it had been torn from some sort of ledger sheet, had been folded into a neat square. He squatted back on his heels and opened the scrap. A word. No, two words written in a scrawled cursive—by a kid, no less. Then Sir read the note: "Yur neckst."

Several seconds passed before the words registered. "Yur neckst," he muttered. *Eyooo*. The thought was driving him crazy. *No. No.* He looked at the note again. *Your next*. What did that mean? *You're next.*

Sir paused again, and clutched his head with both hands. *You're next.* Then a sudden shock wave lurched through his arthritic body. It was for him. He was the hobe most likely to find the body than anyone. It must be for him. He crescendoed the screech. "E-y-ooo," he keened. "It means me."

Sir sat for several minutes, holding his head in his hands, stunned and unable to move. He gradually came to himself and leaned over the body again. He reached down and prised the bottle of Bowie's Farm out of Juice's hand. He retrieved Nancy from the cart, and placed the doll into Juice's hands, forcing the dead man's fingers around the doll. He knelt there for a couple of moments, as if he were praying, before he pulled himself back up.

Sir left his cart, struggled back to Juice's sleeping berth, and grabbed the old refrigerator box Juice had used as a tent. He dragged the box over the rough alley rubble to where Juice was lying, knelt back down beside the body, and reached out with his hand and placed it upon Juice's forehead and muttered, "Rest in peace, Juice." Almost as if he had forgotten how, Sir signed himself with the cross, and then he placed Juice's tent over him as if it were an eternal halo.

When he again struggled to his cart, he didn't look back. *I'm next!* was all that passed through his mind. He charged forward, as fast as he could manage his cart, and bumped it out of the alley and up Church Street to Bosham Alley where he knew three of his friends would be waiting for him.

Marty, Tom-Tom, and Jo were always there this time of day drinking the breakfast they had created from pre-owned coffee grounds and a cheap bottle of Irish whiskey they had rounded up from somewhere. If all went according to ritual, Marty would offer Sir a mug of their alley-made Irish coffee. And Sir would always accept.

But today was different. Jo apparently wasn't home this morning, but Sir asked no questions. He greeted Marty and Tom-Tom with a limp wave of the hand and sat down on a concrete block. Marty handed him his mug of Irish, and they sat and drank for the next quarter hour without saying a word.

He was glad Jo wasn't here. She had flirted fiercely with Sir from the beginning, and at first her behavior flattered him. But his early attraction to her eventually turned to apathy and then to repulsion—partly because he did not appreciate her fervid aggression and partly because his dick had quit working a long time ago.

Marty and Tom-Tom had been around forever, as far as Sir knew. Developing a friendship with them had never been an easy task. For a month or so after Sir had arrived, the two had apparently wanted nothing to do with this interloper. But then everything had changed when Sir brought them each a chicken leg from St. Christopher's Diner, a free dining room especially for hobes. After that Marty and Tom-Tom started going to the diner themselves, and the three of them had become fast friends.

Then, much against protocol, Sir helped himself to another mug of Irish.

Tom-Tom grumbled, "Ya cheap dog."

But Sir continued to drink with only a "harrumph" in reply.

After the third cup and more growling from his hosts, he pulled himself up with the aid of his cart, felt to make sure Juice's Bowie's Farm was in place, and limped his cart out of the alley, ostensibly to go on patrol as he did every day. He had said nothing to his hosts about Juice.

Marty yelled, "And thank you too, ya big ass."

From here Sir would normally go on his first patrol to gather bananas and other too-ripe fruit from the back of Bi-Lo, Publix, and other supermarkets before he parked his cart behind the privet hedges lining the back wall of the building and moved into the Madison City Library to spend a large part of the day. The library was a special gift from God. After reading the daily papers and a couple of news magazines, he would sit for hours either reading the latest novels or re-reading classical favorites—he was almost finished reading *David Copperfield* for about the fifth time—or writing in his pocket-sized notebook. When a librarian or library patron would pass by his carrel, he would automatically slap the notebook closed as if it held all the secrets of the universe.

At around two or three, he would go on his afternoon patrol in the alleys behind bars. By this time of day, the bartenders had made the bar ready for the evening's traffic and had tossed out quarter-filled cans of beer left over from drinkers' tables of the night before. Sometimes he got lucky and found some stronger stuff. Then he would head off to Masters Park to await the supper prepared for him and the other hobes at St. Christopher's Diner.

But Sir didn't go on patrol. No library for him today. He rambled down Church street and turned right at the next light on to Dambers Avenue and then to Masters Park where he stumbled over to a bench—the most secluded bench in the park—next to a large green Dumpster. The bench and the Dumpster were three-quarters surrounded by a small clump of pines that graduated into a thick grove of trees known as Boswell Thicket. He knew he would be alone here. Nobody else wanted to sit next to the reeking Dumpster. *I need to meditate.*

Sir reached into his cart and pulled out the brown bag with Juice's Bowie's Farm, unscrewed the cap and took a deep draught. And another. And another. He was meditating.

When the sun had lumbered into the afternoon sky, Sir reached into his pocket and pulled out his Polo sunglasses and slipped the temples over his ears. He was proud of the sunglasses, but he would have to remember to take them off before he saw the priest again. He had swiped them one evening at the diner when the priest had laid them alongside his plate. He was ashamed to have stolen them, but he wanted a souvenir from the priest. Except he wouldn't think about that now.

He reached into his cart again and pulled out an aged banana he had scuffled from the alley behind the Bi-Lo yesterday. He took a bite, spit it out and threw the rest into the Dumpster. Sir did not litter. He was raised not to litter, and he clung to this discipline still.

As Sir thought of it, he had been reared with many disciplines, not the least of which were studying, punctuality, studying, obedience, studying, church going, and studying. *I beat out Iris Tucker for valedictorian, for crying out loud. What a priss.* Sir was the first in his family to go to college, a major scholarship in English, and then graduate school. *They called me professor once. They called me doctor.* Sir beamed briefly. Just briefly. And suddenly he looked down at the dirty grass in front of him. *My lovely wife. My beautiful son.*

Then, just as suddenly, he reached into his coat pocket and jerked out the crumpled ledger note he had jammed there this morning. He gazed at it as if he had never seen it before. Then even more suddenly he muttered the words, "You're next." *It means me. I'm the target.*

No, that couldn't be so. Why would anybody want to kill Sir? In spite of the unspoken covenant among hobes never to talk to the police, Sir wanted to talk. Sir wanted to tell. Maybe it would be all right to tell the priest. He had never really talked to the priest—only to the hobes. But he would talk now. He stuffed the paper back into his pocket.

Sir relaxed. For a moment, at least.

He took another draught of his Bowie's Farm. He was feeling the whir rather strongly now. The whir always made him more comfortable. It helped him meditate. He reached back into his bag and extracted another over-ripe banana and tried to peel back the skin. He was having some difficulty matching his fingers to the peel but managed to get most of it pulled down. Sir took a large bite and then another, but that was about all he could do. He stood up to throw the remains into the Dumpster and found it difficult to move his feet in the right direction. So he gave up and just dropped the used banana onto the ground—much against his principles, mind you.

It was getting warmer now. Sir didn't know just how long he had been sitting there. But the southern sun appeared to suggest about 3:00 o'clock in the afternoon. He took another draft of Bowie's

Farm. Whether from the sun or the alcohol, he was getting warm now and peeled off his London Fog overcoat. Then his Polo sweater. And finally his Tommy Hilfiger shirt. Sir was a Salvation-Army attired man. But he was not ashamed. He vividly remembered the day the priest took him to the thrift store. The priest allowed him to search through the racks carefully to pick out his clothing item by item. He was pleased with his name-brand finds—all gifts from the priest. The priest was a good man.

This strip act was a ritual he performed every afternoon in the summer but certainly not his usual practice in the middle of a cold January winter. Sir called it his cool-down. With his shirt off, Sir felt skinny. He used to be proud of his muscular physique, but now his muscles sagged like rags. He had once stood proudly tall, but now he was no taller than Rumpelstiltskin when he hunkered down and scuttled about the streets shoving his enfeebled shopping cart. He used to get a charge out of showing off his mermaids—one tattooed on his upper left arm and the other on his right—his muscle girls, he had called them. He had thought of them as signs of his patriotism, since he had spent six years in the United States Navy before he went to college. But the years and the blistering sun had turned his skin into brittle horse's hide, and the mermaids had suffered accordingly.

Maria never did like the mermaids. Maria. He had married the most beautiful girl in the world, and he rued the day he left her to go chasing skirt just to satisfy his dick. A tear came. But that was spilt milk—or water under the bridge—or whatever the clichés were, and there was no reason for him to scoop up that milk or to try to dam up that river now.

Sir took another draught of Bowie's Farm. That was the last of it now. He tossed his head back and shook the bottle to get the last drop, and then lost it on the ground. He curled up on the bench. He had to do some sleeping now, and he closed his eyes.

The nightmare thrust itself into his subconscious. Some strange man draped in black descended upon him with a loud laugh as Sir struggled valiantly to roll himself out of the way. Dark, fly-eyed sunshades covered his eyes. He swooped Sir up from the ground and placed him sitting against the side wall of some building or other. Sir was too drunk or scared or something to resist. Then the man extracted a pistol from somewhere in his clothes and with a loud whoop pulled the trigger.

Crack! Cra-a-a-ck! The detonation filled Sir's ears, brain, and heart with such fear that he flung himself off the park bench with such a thrust that he cracked his head against the Bowie's Farm bottle. The blow stunned him for a moment before he roused himself enough to realize he was still Sir with no bloody punctures through his skull. He wriggled up with the help of the park bench and held his head between both hands. *The shots! The shots!*

Sir abruptly turned and plunged his hand back into his pocket and snagged the crumpled paper. Sir opened it quickly and read again, *Yur neckst.*

Without so much as a further murmur, Sir struggled upright as fast as he could manage. He jerked his clothes back on, grabbed hold of his cart, hobbled it jerkily back to Church Street, and headed down toward St. Christopher's. On crossing the curb at Bulwark, a second wheel flew off the cart. *Shit.* Sir grabbed as much of his stuff as he could get into his pockets, abandoned the cart, and reeled off down Church. *I've got to find the priest.*

He lurched down the street watching every shadow, eying everybody he met, keeping close to the wall, and from time to time sliding into alleys and behind Dumpsters. Sir knew every hiding place on the street. Three short blocks now separated him from the church. Two tight basement stairwells led down under the Slattern and Wells Fargo buildings. No one ever used these stairwells anymore. They had years ago been walled over on the inside, but the hidden stair wells were still good for hobes to move into quickly to get out of the sidewalk traffic and take a leak.

Now he leaned against the wall of the side building and caught a glimpse of something—no, someone! The man! The man in the nightmare. Some strange man draped in black. Sir darted into an alley, but the man kept charging up the street. *It couldn't be!* He waited. It seemed hours instead of moments.

Sir peeked out into the street and the coast seemed clear. He stumbled his way out of the alley and headed as stealthily and steadily as he could manage back down toward St. Christopher's. He crept along for at least two blocks. He could see the spire now. *Beautiful.* He would make it now. Just one more block.

Then he heard it. A shot. Without a moment's hesitation, he dove into the Wells Fargo basement stairwell, just as a rattling, backfiring clunker of a car charged down Church. But Sir was safe now.

TWO

IN SPITE of his well-tailored, black clerical suit and his sleek overcoat, the Reverend Michael Richey, rector of St. Christopher's Episcopal Church and chaplain to the Madison Police Department, ran briskly down Pine Street toward the rectory. He ran not to get out of the snow sooner, but because he had missed his usual 6:00 morning run. Normally he would meet up with his friend, Police Detective Carlos Ruiz, and the two would jog together from St. Christopher's to the Downing Street YMCA for workouts. But this morning he had been startlingly awakened in the small hours and summoned to the Madison Memorial Hospital for a parishioner's emergency. He was eager to get home.

Who's that? An elderly woman sat on the street curb in front of the rectory, her head thrust between her knees, and her arms hugging her legs like a mother with a small child. He slowed his pace to a trot. Mike was not surprised to find her there. Street folk frequently accosted him. He had made friends with most of them in Madison, especially since St. Christopher's had opened the diner—one of the best, Mike was proud to say, in the South Carolina upstate—with free meals offered every evening, five days a week. And it was not unusual for Mike to visit the street people on their own turf.

The woman did not look up. "Hello, Father."

"Hi, Jo." Mike had known Jo from the day St. Christopher's had opened the diner. She was a short woman with grayish, tangled, shoulder-length hair she often wore in a pony tail held together with a rubber band. She always kept her Dumpster-brand clothes neat, if not clean. Today she had pulled her once-red shawl over her head to avoid as much snow as she could. Mike remembered that Jo was Sir's friend from a couple of blocks down from Slocum, where she shared an alley with Marty and Tom-Tom. In fact, Mike had seen Jo and Sir together occasionally—usually at the diner. But he had also seen them together under the Tyrone Street Bridge. Never in a situation that might suggest a sexual attraction, but Mike couldn't help but wonder if the two had a romantic relationship going.

Jo did not stir.

Mike moved closer. "What can I do for you, Jo?"

The old woman looked up. Her large, gray eyes glistened like dew on unmown grass. "Can I talk to you a minute, Father?" the old woman asked. "As the good book says, 'She who follows must also lead.'"

"Of course." Mike didn't know where Jo got such a quotation, and neither did he know what she meant by it. Her misquotations of the bible often peppered her conversations. So he let it go. His 190-pound, six-two frame was a bit too imposing for Jo's pint-sized stature, so he sat down on the curb beside her to try to equalize the conversational interchange. "What did you have on your mind?"

Jo hesitated.

Mike almost sighed. He ran his fingers through his hair and waited. Nothing came. "Are you in trouble, Jo?"

For the first time the old woman turned and looked at him. "Oh, no, Father." Jo paused. "I just wanted to tell you about, uh, uh—" She abruptly aborted the statement.

Mike was accustomed to this hesitancy from hobes. Many of them frequently wanted to confide but often were not able to. "About what, Jo?"

She still sat rigidly with her arms around her knees. "Uh, uh, oh nothing important, I guess."

Mike again ran his fingers through his hair and sighed—audibly this time. "Now, Jo. Would you come all the way here and sit on the curb—for what? Thirty minutes? An hour? In the snow, no less, waiting to talk with me about something that's not important?"

Jo lowered her eyes and began to quiver. "Sir."

Mike put his hand on her shoulder. "Sir? What about Sir?"

Then just as suddenly as she started quivering, she stopped. Jo dried her eyes on her sleeve and looked back at Father Mike as though a brilliant idea was about to emerge. "Tell you what."

"What?" A long pause. Mike understood not to interrupt or Jo would never answer.

"As the good book says, 'Never do today what you can put off until tonight.' Talk to you tonight at the diner," she said.

Mike knew this evasion well. Perhaps Jo would never talk. But this conversation seemed important to her, and he wanted to give her every opportunity. "Sounds fair enough to me." Mike stood. "See you there." He paused for a moment to see if Jo would have second thoughts and resume the conversation. But no second thoughts were forthcoming.

"See ya," Jo said.

"See ya." Mike touched the old woman gently and moved toward the rectory. He pulled the screen door open and turned back to see Jo struggling to get up. But she apparently thought better of it, because she sat down on the curb again.

‡‡‡

MIKE OPENED the front door—deliberately noisily—snap, crackle, bang—to distract Annie from the love of her life—Johann Sebastian Bach. The golden sounds of "Meine Seele erhebet den Herren" rang out from their inherited baby grand piano. Mike called out in his best Ricky Ricardo voice, "Honey, I'm home!"

The piano slowed to a stop, but Mr. Craggles, the family miniature schnauzer, beat Honey to the door, and showered Mike with the kisses he wanted from Annie.

Annie ambled toward him—quite nonchalantly, so Mike thought. "I see you are."

He was hoping she would come charging in, flinging her delicate arms around his brawny neck, and perhaps even swooning so that he could pick her up heroically in his strapping arms and haul her upstairs into the bedroom for a romp. But, of course, that didn't happen.

Oh, well. What the...? Instead he stood there with a little crooked smile on his face looking humbly—or more likely, pitifully—into her lucent, brown eyes. He slowly reached up and began removing his clerical collar.

"Oh, Mike. We can't. Not now. Tim will be home shortly."

Mike took Annie by the shoulders and pecked her gently on the lips. "And where might that young man be?"

Annie responded with a more exuberant kiss. "This is Monday. He went to his Kodokan lesson with Quinton, and Quinton's mother will be dropping him off in," she looked at her watch, "in about fifteen min—"

"Kodokan, huh?" Mike stepped forward and his right foot landed between Annie's feet. He reached around her legs at the back of her knees.

"Like father, like..." He drove his shoulder forward into her upper body and swept her off her feet.

"Okay, Mr. Black Belt! Save your prowess for later."

Mike grinned. "I will!" he said. "I will!" Annie had not said how much later. So he carried her in his powerful arms up the stairs to the master bedroom and laid her gently on the freshly made bed. Mike lay down beside her and offered his most lascivious look. Her shining blond hair, her deep-set eyes, her high intelligence, and her glowing personality made her very beautiful indeed.

Mike's shirt dropped to the floor. He kissed her and she kissed back with a love that had bound them together for sixteen years.

#‡ ‡ ‡

ANNIE PULLED Mike close to her, and her lips caressed his face and then his lips and then his hardened nipples. How she loved this man!

All the years she had loved Mike came swirling back into her consciousness. Annie had loved Mike from the first moment she met him—after an intramural basketball game at the University of the South, or Sewanee as most folk called it. She and her friend Gina had gone to the event to see Jeff, Gina's fiancé, play. One Pi Kappa Phi basketballer—from the team that had unmercifully routed Jeff's Sigma Nus—summarily caught her eye. On his way to the locker room Mike had torn off his soggy jersey, the sweat pouring down his muscular pecs, and Annie thought, *That guy is the sexiest guy I've ever seen.*

"Still am," Mike said as he gently laid his lips on her lips and on her eyes and on her nose and on her throat.

"What?" Annie muttered.

"Still am the sexiest guy you've ever seen," Mike said, caressing her well-swollen breasts.

"What did you say?"

"Still am the sexiest guy you've ever seen."

Annie gave him a silly slap on his lower right cheek. She suddenly realized she had spoken that thought aloud.

Whether that original encounter was the birth of premature love or simply a surge of tantalizing lust she could not say, but it was the beginning of everything. But even if it had been a simple surge of lust, it quickly grew into love. Mike was the gentlest, most empathetic man she had ever known.

And intelligent. The two of them had vied for first place in their graduating class. But she had won, of course, with a straight 4.00

15

grade point average to Mike's mere 3.98. *What a loser!* Mike had sworn he could never forgive her for this, so he married her instead.

Annie and Gina had hurried over to console Jeff and the Sigma Nus, and then Annie looked up. She felt herself redden as she stared squarely into the face of the young man who was the apparent hero of the evening. Mike had rushed up behind Jeff, ostensibly to shake hands with the captain of the losing team, and found himself shaking hands with Annie instead.

"Hi, I'm Mike Richey," he had said.

"I'm Annie—Annie Leigh," she stammered.

Annie and Mike took over the immediate conversation, and Gina and Jeff found themselves ignored for the next quarter hour or so.

Mike had been a bit slower in catching on to this love thing than Annie. It was Annie who made the first move. Mike hadn't been in his dorm room when she called, so she left a message:

> *Hi Mike, This is Annie Leigh from after the basketball game the other day. I'm doing a story for the Alpha Delta Pi newsletter about the Pi Kapp Journey of Hope bike ride next summer, and somebody told me you were the best source. Could you give me a call please? My extension is 2022. Bye.*

Annie had never been one to allow a formality to stand in her way. She had wondered, however, if an assertive woman would turn Mike off, but she was willing to take that chance. Mike, according to Annie's sources, had signed up for the Push America bicycle ride from San Francisco to Washington to raise both awareness and money to aid in enhancing the quality of life for people with disabilities.

Mike did call her back. And without much resistance, he went with her to the Alpha Delta Pi formal the following Saturday evening. And the rest, as they say, was history. And history, as they say, did not stand still. Mike pinned her at the beginning of their senior year and gave her a diamond for Christmas.

The first few years of their marriage, they had struggled financially. After seminary for him and law school for her, Mike had been called to little St. John's Around-the-Corner in Marsburg, Tennessee, and Annie took a position with Fred Q. Bugle, Esquire—yes, Bugle was his real name—a local attorney who, from Annie's perspective, was not altogether happy about hiring a woman rookie for his firm. She had always believed that the firm hired her because they could get her much cheaper than they could get a man. Annie wasn't altogether pleased with the position, but she and Mike had to pay back student loans somehow.

They also had struggled several years with fertility problems. The two tried and prayed, and finally in their sixth year of marriage they were able to conceive and bear a son. Tim was born almost nine months to the day that they moved in to their new rectory in Wardell, South Carolina. When Annie was able to go back to work, she chose teaching rather than law in order to have more time to spend with Tim. The stress relief seemed to open up a whole new world for them. Tim was the apple of his father's eye, and Annie knew he wanted to do for Tim what his own father had never done for him. Mike had told her that often.

Annie loved Mike now far more than she had sixteen years ago. And the two now—at this time in this bower—blended together like the harmony of two violins playing a Fredric Chopin nocturne. A smile crept upon Annie's lips, and she knew, *Yes—this is just fine. Just fine.*

After the final exhilarating moment, Annie looked up and kissed Mike gently on the lips. She laid her head on his naked shoulder, and they luxuriated in each other's company. And for a moment they almost drifted into blessed unconsciousness.

"Mom! Dad!" Tim came rumbling up the stairs, as ten-year-old boys have a tendency to do. "Mom! Dad!"

The startled parents quickly ejected themselves from the bed and clambered to don their robes.

Tim clambered into the bedroom, whose door his parents in their haste had forgotten to close. He came with the enthusiasm of Mr. Craggles on his way for his mile-long walk with Hans and Bailey, his two doggy friends from across the street. "Mom! Dad! Guess what!"

Annie looked at Tim as if she were seeing him for the first time. He looked so much like Mike, a handsome boy of stocky build and somewhat large for his age. The boy had both the intelligence and the heart of his parents. Annie smiled.

Tim obviously had some good news now. "Guess what!"

"What?" his parents said in unison.

"I threw Quinton twice today, and he threw me only once."

Aaah, that competitive spirit. "That's great," said Annie. *His father all over again.*

"Wish I could have been there." Mike pulled his son up close to him and gave him a bear-like hug.

"Now," Annie said, kissing him on the forehead, "go take your shower and do your homework while Dad and I finish getting ready. You can go with us to the diner this evening."

"Can I?" Tim asked.

Annie knew how much Tim loved going to the diner. His father's spirit of compassion had become a real component of Tim's own personality. Tim had been a large part of the diner for the past three years, and he really got a great deal of pleasure serving and talking with the street folks who came there. So Annie was eager to reaffirm her offer. "Absolutely."

♯♯♯

MIKE TURNED on the shower, and Tim's short life passed through his mind. He had been in the delivery room when Tim had moved gracefully into this beautiful and brilliant world. He had held him close as Annie recovered from the delivery, and the two had bonded almost immediately. They had been almost inseparable since. When Tim was younger, he had often gone with Mike to work—

carrying his "case," as he called his make-shift attaché, created from an old CD carrier. Mike kept a fairly large library of Dr. Seuss, Maurice Sindak, Ezra Jack Keats, and Robert McCloskey, books that Tim devoured over and over again.

Mike had vowed that, unlike his own father, he would always be there for his son. Until Mike was ten, his father and he had been exceedingly close. They had fished together, camped together, and hiked together. He and his father had played catch together, even when his father was ready to collapse from exhaustion from a hard work day. Then it had all suddenly and incomprehensibly and brutally come to an end.

Mike quickly dried himself and slipped into a clean clerical suit. "Sweetheart, I'm going on down to the diner to help June get set up."

"Okay." Annie appeared at the door. "Oh, Mike."

Mike turned around and grinned. He reached up and started to take off his clerical collar. "Yes?"

"Oh, Mike. Cut it out. Here!" she said, shoving his damp and wrinkled clerical suit into his arms. "Cleaners!"

"Now?"

Annie leaned forward and gave Mike a peck on the cheek and didn't say another word. She put her arms around his waist and pivoted both of them around in one big whirl and stepped back into the bedroom.

Mike fished in the pockets of the wadded up suit. "Oh, Annie. Did you take my sunglasses out of my inside coat pocket? Can't find them."

"Haven't seen them, sweetheart. You don't suppose Tim might have borrowed them for some reason."

"Don't think he would have without asking. I'll check with him this evening at the diner. I certainly won't need them tonight. See you." Mike turned and jogged down the stairs and into the basement garage. He took off in his two-year-old Toyota Camry.

✝✝✝

ANNIE FINISHED her shower, slung on her robe, and strode downstairs on her way to the kitchen to make tuna salad for Tim. He always wanted a bite of something to eat after his Kodokan lesson. She pulled several items from the fridge. No tuna. She sighed. *Aaah. Bi-Lo, here I come.* She returned the items to their customary places. *Tomorrow. Not now!* She pulled out a resealed package of boloney. *Sandwiches?* She looked to see if she had enough bread and condiments. "Tim!" she called. "Would boloney sandwiches be okay?" She pulled out the mustard and ketchup. "Tim!" she called again. *He must be in the bathroom.*

Annie finished her fridge chores and went to check on her son. She knocked on Tim's bedroom door. "Tim?" Again there was no answer. She turned the knob and peeked in. Tim was not in the room. Dirty Kodokan uniform on the floor. Books open on the desk. Desk light on. Annie walked over to the closed bathroom door.

"Tim?" She knocked. "Tim?" She waited a moment, but only a moment, and flung the door open. "Tim?"

Towels on the floor. Shower curtain soggy.

Annie's chin quivered uncontrollably. She suddenly thought of Dwanna. When Annie was a child, Dwanna, one of her friends at school, had been picked up by a child snatcher from the street in front of her house. Dwanna had been found the following day wandering around on a country road in tears and tatters. The abductor had never been found. The memory of that time had made Annie cautious—perhaps inordinately so—with Tim. She rushed from room to room frantically combing the house.

"Timmy, Timmy. Oh, God. Timmy!"

She ran to the bay window and stopped—dead still. She caught a glimpse of her son talking to a strange woman on the sidewalk. *That boy!* How many times had she and Mike warned Tim about talking to strangers when he was alone. The highly sensational news stories of Larry Borg, Linda Murdock, and George Maddux, all abducted children, flashed rapidly through her brain. She shuddered and shouted through the window, "Tim, no!"

Annie tightened her bathrobe sash, rushed out the front door, and lunged down the steps—two at a time. "Timmy!"

Tim looked up, rolled his practiced eyes, and made two syllables out of the word, as pre-teens are so capable of doing. "Mo-om!"

Annie rushed over to Tim and grabbed his hand.

"I just wanted to make sure Jo would be at the diner this evening, Mom."

Shades of you-know-who! Annie looked at the old woman. "Jo! I didn't know that was you. I'm so terribly sorry."

The old woman shrugged and rose from the curb, her long, matted, gray hair fluttering down her back. She managed to straighten her otherwise unstraightenable garments and looked at Annie. "Sorry I distressed you, ma'am."

"Annie," the younger woman corrected.

"Annie, ma'am," Jo replied. "As the good book says, 'She who overstays her welcome should go off and eat worms.' See you at the diner." Jo sauntered off toward St. Christopher's.

"Bye, Jo," Tim called.

Annie started after her. "I'm so sorry, Jo. I wouldn't have hurt your feelings for the world."

The older woman turned the corner onto Church Street.

Annie turned back to Tim, grabbed him by the shoulders and looked him straight in the eyes. "Timothy Michael Richey, don't you ever frighten me like that again!" She paused briefly, and her eyes slowly turned from the harsh scolding discs to the soft loving orbs of motherhood. She pulled Tim close—closer than she had since he was a small child. And she loved him.

"I'm sorry, Mom." Tim took his mother's hand and escorted her back into the house. "How about a boloney sandwich?"

THREE

JUNE ELLERBE plunged her ladle into the soup and poured it gently into the ceramic bowl. "Hi, Smiley," she grinned, handing the soup to the old man—one of her favorite hobes—in front of her.

Smiley nodded. Pleasantly, of course. Smiley was never grumpy, at least in public. He didn't ever say much, but he always had that smile on his face that touched hearts all over the diner. At first June wondered why he smiled so much. He was a man who apparently had no family, no home, and no real friends. But yet he smiled. June had quit wondering and became his friend.

She took a second look at Smiley. He was a proud man who liked to dress up. He strutted different clothes as often as he could dig them up, and he was always on the prowl for something new. June had visions of the old man spending half his day sorting through Dumpsters all over the city, selecting only the best shirts and ties. Only the best trousers and sports coats would do. June had asked Smiley a couple of times where he got them, but he would only grin and say nothing.

"Step back," June said, "and let me see what you're wearing tonight."

Smiley grinned and stood back a couple of steps. Delight filled his ocean-blue eyes, and he strutted his wardrobe as suavely as any top model for Kevin Klein. Tonight he had on a pair of brown trousers, only one small hole that June could see, a striped, dress shirt, a Santa Claus tie that had apparently been tossed out in the trash after Christmas, and a tweed wool blazer. The coat looked new. And he wore the clothes well.

Good for him! "Ni-i-ice!" June's compliment was genuine. "Be sure to get some of that apple cobbler Harlan's got down there at the end of the counter. I made it myself this afternoon." She watched Smiley mosey on down the line for further nourishment.

A movement in front of her brought June back to the moment at hand. "Hi, Gin-Gin. Like your earrings." Then she realized the old woman was alone. "Where's Jo tonight?" Gin-Gin and Jo almost always traveled together, but apparently not this time.

Gin-Gin shrugged but said nothing.

"Want some soup?" June didn't know why the crabby faced woman was called Gin-Gin. The *nom de plume* could have been a diminutive for Virginia, or some such name, but, given the old woman's fetish, it could also refer to her love for cheap gin. She was a strong and agile woman, with gray hair and more wrinkles than necessary at this stage in her life, and she had a proud gait, that is, until demon gin claimed her ability to be proud. She looked the least like a hobe of any of the other hobe women. The Gin-Gin, the third bag lady of the evening, took her tray and shoved it down the counter without even giving June a nod.

"No? Okay, maybe next time." But Gin-Gin's solo appearance still concerned June. "Oh, Gin-Gin," she called out.

Gin-Gin looked up as she passed by the chicken wings. June noticed there was something unusual about Gin-Gin. Her top was the same faded green shirt, at least two sizes too large, that she often wore. The frayed, once-black trousers were the same. Nothing different here. Her brooch. She's lost her brooch. Gin-Gin always wore that old brooch with the cameo stone in the center. Rumor had it that she had inherited the brooch from her mother, but she probably had scratched it out of a trash can somewhere.

"Father Mike wants to see you. He's at that table over there. See him?" Gin-Gin smiled, although smiling was not her forte. Just the mention of the priest's name seemed to bring her pleasure. Without finishing the food line, she took her almost empty tray over to Father Mike's table, where he gave her a hug and took her tray while she sat down.

It was almost closing time when June realized Sir had not come in tonight. An uneasiness gripped her abdomen. She stood there, ladle in hand and mind afar and almost failed to notice the woman standing before her. Then something red roused her.

"Oh, hi, Jo." June carefully looked the old woman over. "That's a beautiful red scarf." She always found something about her guests to compliment.

Jo neither acknowledged June's compliment nor spoke a word. She shoved her tray toward June awaiting her bowl of soup.

"Missed you when Gin-Gin came in."

Jo took the bowl of soup and, instead of moving on down the line as was her wont, she turned and crossed to the opposite end of the hall—the end farthest away from Father Mike and the other hobes—and sat down alone at a table that had not yet been cleaned from its previous use.

That's strange, June thought. But she turned her attention back to the hobes in front of her.

When the last of them had been served, she laid her ladle down and walked over to where the priest was sitting. "Father Mike, have you seen Sir?" Sir had always been prompt for his evening meal. "He hasn't come in tonight, and I'm a bit concerned. Do you know anything about him?"

June recalled her first time she saw Sir. It was about six months ago. He seemed a strange and very shy old man. He never said a word, just took his supper tray and wandered around the dining room until he found a chair close to Father Mike. Father Mike always liked Sir and would converse with him, even though Sir would not talk back. The only word he would say when he greeted the priest was *Fahta*, almost as a grunt.

June had given him the name *Sir*. She and the other diner servers, always out of respect for the men and women they served, addressed them by name. But they didn't know this man's name. He wouldn't tell. So June would say, *Would you like some soup, sir?* And Mary would say, *Would you like some chicken, sir?* And Harlan would say, *Would you like some pie, sir.* So *Sir* stuck. And June had said, *That's his name. Let's call him Sir.*

Mike pressed his lips tightly together and ran his fingers through his hair. "I don't have any idea, June." His face suddenly exhibited a glazed look, as if he were remembering something important. He rose from his chair. "Thanks for calling that to my attention." He wiped his lips and laid his napkin by his plate. "I think I'll go over and chat with Jo for a moment. She may know something about him." June went back to clean up her station and she noticed Mike crossing over to the other end of the room and sitting down across from Jo. It appeared Father Mike was doing the talking and Jo was doing the eating—spooning the soup into her mouth with passion.

✝✝✝

I T HAD begun to grow dark, and a heavy mist hung in the air. The sparse streetlights with their dark and spinning halos and Mike's small, black flashlight provided the only light. He had asked Harlan to come with him. Harlan had turned over his duties on the serving line to Mary, the volunteer serving the entree, and the two men grabbed their overcoats and headed up Church Street. Harlan Jeffries, Mike's Senior Warden—the chief lay person on the vestry, the governing board of the congregation—was one of the three on the vestry who had opposed the diner. He and the other two had been afraid of a riff-raff invasion, and indeed that invasion had come. But after the fact, he had made a 180-degree conversion and had become one of Mike's most ardent supporters. He was a regular volunteer at the diner, and Mike knew he had learned to love the hobes he was there to serve.

Before the men had gone far, they felt a bit of sleet but trudged on. They first went to Slocum Alley where Sir stayed, but they found nothing but a huge cardboard box like those that homeless folk often used as tents. Mike lurched to an abrupt halt. Something was askew. His heart leaped inside him, and he walked closer. "That's strange."

Harlan stared into the darkness of the alley and winced. "What is, Father?"

"The box."

Harlan locked his eyes on the large cardboard shelter that had once been a refrigerator container. "What about the box?"

"The box." For a moment Mike said nothing. "The box is in the wrong place."

"What do you mean the wrong place?"

Mike's veins froze. The dread almost overwhelmed him. "Sir shares the alley with another man. Juice, he calls him. They sleep at the other end of the alley. Neither one of them would leave his box at this end of the alley where other guys could steal it."

Mike had visited Slocum Alley perhaps a dozen times over the past few months. He considered Sir one of his most loyal parishioners, but he had come to know Juice as well. He had tried many times to get Juice to come to the diner but without success. So Mike knew about the boxes. He reached down and jerked the box from its resting place and both men uttered a gasp that seemed to echo all the way back to St. Christopher's. There was a man, panicked eyes staring horrified into the dark, weeping sky.

The dread grew into horror. Mike focused his flashlight and crept closer "It's Juice!"

Then without pause, Mike shouted. "Sir!" He left Harlan to stare into Juice's contorted face and tore down to the other end of the alley searching. Like a mad man Mike howled, "Sir!" He galloped over the alley debris until he came to Sir's tent, evidently undisturbed. He yanked it away and threw it aside. But there was no Sir!

Mike stood there awhile—numb. "Oh, God," he whispered.

He rushed back to Harlan, who stood frozen like the sculptures in Masters Park.

Without a word he knelt down and tenderly closed Juice's eyes. Instinctively he reached into his coat pocket and grasped his small portable ampulla, touched his thumb to the holy oil, and placed the sign of the cross on Juice's forehead and said, "Juice, I anoint you with oil in the Name of the Father, and of the Son, and of the Holy Spirit. Amen."

Father Mike continued the holy rite, and Harlan slowly came out of his stupor in time to repeat the *amen* at the end.

Then Mike reached into his other pocket, removed his cell phone, and punched in 911.

Mike turned with a start. In all the sleet, darkness, and commotion of the past few minutes he hadn't noticed the doll clutched in Juice's hands. What was her name? Nancy. Yes, Nancy. He started to reach for the doll but thought better of it. *Where is Juice's Bowie's Farm?* Juice was never without his orange-colored Bowie's Farm. Would another hobe kill just to get his hands on a bottle of cheap wine? Surely not. But it was obvious to Mike that another hobe had been there at some point, either as murderer or as looter. But why would he have left Juice's other property?

During Mike's chaplaincy with the police, he had learned to look for evidence just as the officers did. And he was getting pretty good at it. He stood and looked around the crime scene to see what he could find before the cops came. Nothing except the box. And evidence of rats that had scoured the alley searching for their livelihood. And a mound of broken glass, where some prior hobes had disposed of their wine bottles against the brick wall. And the usual bird poop scattered around the alley floor. *Hey!* That small white object hidden under the edge of Juice's body? He knelt down to get a closer look, and the object reflected the beam of his flashlight. He struggled with his conscience briefly, and, with a grimace, he reached—in spite of police regulations—to pick it up.

"What are you doing, Father?" Harlan asked.

Mike winced and jerked his hand back. At that moment the strobing, blue lights of two patrol cars intermittently lit up the alley as the cars screeched to an abrupt halt. Four uniformed officers, revolvers and flashlights in hand, alit from the car and rushed to where Mike and Harlan stood, spoke briefly, and went about their business. After surveying the site, they holstered their guns, ordered Mike and Harlan to stay put, called the Major Crime Scene Unit, and went about securing the site.

In fewer than ten minutes, patrol cars aplenty, marked and unmarked alike, avalanched to the mouth of the alley. Officers of every ilk swarmed onto the scene, doing what officers of these ilks do when murder is the focus.

"Mike," Detective Carlos Ruiz greeted the priest. "What are you doing here?"

Carlos was the priest's best friend. He had been on the Madison police force for over fifteen years and had risen, by his own industry, to the rank of detective. He and Mike had first met at the Y in the gym, both of them vigorous exercise buffs and weight trainers with the competitive urge of a couple of Schwarzeneggers.

Before Mike could answer, another detective suddenly accosted him.

"Reverend, what are you doing here?" Chief Detective Jerry Majors, Carlos's investigative superior, stood immediately in front of him. Jerry's inflection insisted that he would rather *the reverend*, as he called him, would find himself somewhere else.

As police chaplain, Mike knew Jerry for what he was—a brilliant police detective, a cut above the other detectives on the force. A cut above many police detectives in South Carolina. Indeed, the state had recently awarded him the title of South Carolina Detective of the Year. He was a big man, both vertically and horizontally. But unlike Carlos he never darkened the door of the Y or any other establishment of the sort. He had never cared much for Mike, and

Mike was fully aware that he thought of the chaplain as more of a nuisance on a call than any real assistance.

"So. Tell us your story, Reverend." Jerry's blustery voice matched his blustery anatomy.

Mike motioned the two detectives over to one corner of the alley, and called for Harlan to join them.

Jerry quickly ordered Harlan to stay put. "No conversing, gentlemen, until after we take your statements down at the station house."

The sleet grew more impelling, and Mike pulled his overcoat tighter.

The chief detective asked again, "So, Reverend, what are you doing here?" This time with a little less chaff in his voice.

Mike relayed the incidence of discovery to the two detectives.

"Do both these hobes live in this alley?" Jerry asked.

Mike flinched. It was one thing for the hobes themselves or their friends to refer to the street people as hobes, but Jerry's use of the term seemed to Mike to be arrogantly derogatory. But he left it untouched. Mike explained to the detectives about Sir's and Juice's places in the alley. About their tents and about their habits.

Jerry stood rigid and stared at Mike as if he couldn't figure out the third line of an eye chart. "I want you to come with me and Detective Ruiz, Reverend."

"What?" It sounded to Mike as if Jerry were making an arrest. He had known Jerry ever since he had become chaplain, but he still had difficulty figuring out just how to take Jerry's gruff manner. "What do you mean?"

"You know all these hobes' hiding places, Reverend. I want you to help us find this Sir hobe. He may very well be in de-e-ep doo doo."

"You're not thinking Sir had anything to do with any of this, are you?" Mike asked.

"We just gotta find him—now!"

"Sure, if I can be of any help. But I'm certain Sir had absolutely nothing to do with this," Mike replied.

The sleet surged down now. The temperature had remained below freezing for at least the last three nights, so the sleet was sticking heavily to the ground.

Jerry ushered Mike and Harlan into the Crown Victoria. He dropped Harlan and Carlos at the station house and ordered Carlos to take Harlan's statement. Jerry and Mike took off to find Sir.

Mike picked up his cell.

"Who ya calling, Reverend?"

Mike continued pushing buttons. "I'm calling Annie. Do you mind?"

"Tell her nothing about what happened tonight. Do you understand, Reverend?"

Mike didn't answer. A click. "Hi, sweetheart. We're having a bit of a problem finding Sir, and I'll have to be here a bit longer." He listened for a moment. "Can't say now. I'll get home as quickly as I can. Apologize to Tim for me, will you? Love you."

Mike pressed the *END* button just as Jerry pulled into Perin Alley. Nothing there. They searched every alley hiding place within twenty blocks, the bridges that attracted hobes, the park Sir habituated, and the Dumpsters that Sir was known to pillage. There was no Sir.

The sleet surged, the ice grew thicker, and Jerry called off the search for the night. He brought Mike back to the station house. "I need to take your statement, Reverend."

Mike slumped his shoulders. He clinched his fists. He shut his eyes. There was no Sir.

FOUR

MIKE JOGGED toward the gym at the Downing Street YMCA five minutes late. He normally met up with Carlos around six in the mornings in front of St. Christopher's, and the two of them would jog together the half mile to the Y to run four miles on the treadmills before hitting the weights. This regimen was so much a part of their day that missing the appointment was unthinkable. Carlos had reneged once, and Mike had jocularly tagged him a big wimp for a good couple of weeks.

Carlos had not shown up at St. Christopher's this morning, and Mike thought he would have to work the treads solo. But when Mike jogged into the Y parking lot he spotted Carlos's Harley-Davidson settled in between a Cadillac Escalade and a Lexus LS. High class bike rider!

It had crossed Mike's mind more than once this morning to renege. Jerry and Carlos had kept him at the station until the small hours, hashing and rehashing the events of the evening before. They had looked at each moment from almost every possibility. They compared Mike's and Harlan's statements, almost sentence by sentence. And it wasn't until three that morning that they were satisfied they had the picture. So Mike was hoping—almost praying—that Carlos would be too tired to make it to the gym today. But God had, for whatever reason, failed to answer those prayers.

Mike plowed through the wall-to-wall aerobic and muscle machines occupying a space that rivaled the Bi-Lo supermarket two blocks up Downing. He spotted Carlos several seconds before Carlos saw him and stood there watching the detective sweat to the tune of some music or other that entered his brain via ear buds that clung to his ears like suction cups against a glass window.

Mike had always admired Carlos. Like Mike, Carlos had been born of Mexican and Anglo parents, and they shared the same dark skin. At six foot three, Carlos was trim and robust. A noticeable scar, the souvenir of an injury he had received in the line of duty, crawled down his right cheek. Carlos's intelligence was undeniable. He had confided to Mike his academic problems in college, but that didn't tell the whole story. Mike was able to see through those exceptionally clever eyes a keenness that would measure up to the best of them. After college he had graduated from the police academy with honors, though he never had told anyone but Mike about it.

At last Carlos spotted Mike, pointed to his wrist watch, and grinned. That grin said it all: *You're late, and you're a wimp.*

Mike acknowledged his wimpship with a grin of his own, threw his backpack with its clothing change on the floor, and joined Carlos on the machine beside him.

After the treads and a liter of Gatorade, the two hit the weights. Mike managed to win the weight challenge—for today, at least. Today was pecs day. On other days they might work on the lats or the quads, but today they worked on pecs. And Mike nosed his way to victory with one more repetition than Carlos was able to conjure up. The loser during any given week had to treat the other to a couple of beers at Sarah's Cafe, the general meeting place for the two friends. Two free Heinekens coming up!

So they sat and sweated and chatted and drank more Gatorade. The chat was mostly about Sir. The police had him first on the list of primary suspects for Juice's murder, and Jerry and Carlos were on the trail. As a police detective, Carlos never admitted aloud any conclusions about guilt or innocence this early in the investigation, but Mike was certain Carlos believed Sir was the perp.

Mike wasn't so sure though. "I know Sir. I just can't believe he did it."

Carlos wiped his brow with his towel. "How long have you known him?"

Mike hesitated. "About six months."

Carlos raised his eyebrows.

That wasn't long, Mike realized. Sir had suddenly appeared on the scene at the diner. Mike had been in deep conversation with Gin-Gin who had a complaint against a police officer whom she accused of a manhandle. Then Mike looked up, and there sat Sir opposite him. "Fahta," he grunted.

"Can you really get to know anybody in six months?"

Mike prided himself on being able to come back with logical answers in soft-core arguments such as this one, but he was now silent. During Mike's three-year friendship with Carlos, the two had often quarreled—in a good-natured manner, of course. In fact, their friendship had begun with an argument—of sorts. Mike had met Carlos at the Y. They happened to be running side-by-side on the treadmill. Mike glanced over to read Carlos's setting, and Carlos sped the machine up a half-mile per hour. Mike followed suit. Carlos elevated his incline, and so did Mike. Carlos noticed Mike's mimicry and sped up again. Carlos elevated and Mike elevated. Again. Again. Again. The thirty-minute beeper signaled the end of the competition, and Mike let out a whoop. "Yesssss!!" he yelled as Carlos groaned. And the two became fast friends.

Carlos had always referred to this contest as *dueling cintas*—dueling treadmills.

Mike had not been surprised that Carlos was a police officer. He had the stereotypical build and the competitive edge that Mike remembered in the officers he had known before. Carlos had admitted to Mike, however, that he had been somewhat shocked that

Mike was a priest. He didn't live up—or down, as the case may be—to the priestly stereotypes he had known. He had told Mike that he had not known many priests or ministers in recent years. Of the few he had known, he had arrested two of them, one for sexual abuse of a minor and the other for financial fraud. He had not seen much good in ministers.

So now, the Gatorade finished, the two replaced their weights and headed for the showers. "Are you going to be free for lunch today?"

"I've got to meet Jerry at 10:00 for an evidence review, but I should be able to meet you at Sarah's about noon."

The spraying water rinsed the sweat from Mike's body and the tension from his soul. This had been a good workout.

✝✝✝

THE MOMENT Carlos stepped out of the shower, his cell phone chimed the ragtime theme from *The Sting*.

"Detective Ruiz?"

"Yes."

"This is Officer Mark Foley. We think we've found Sir."

Carlos turned quickly to Mike and mouthed, "It's Sir."

Mike leaned his ear closer to Carlos's phone.

"Where've you found him?"

"Down in the stairwell next to the Wells Fargo. He's dead."

"Be there *pronto*."

Carlos jumped on his Harley, Mike on the saddle behind him, and took off toward the Wells Fargo Bank. The bike charged forward to the crossing of Church and Lufkin and came to a sudden resting place. An old black Ford Escort appeared from nowhere, bouncing like a football after an incomplete pass, and crashing against the right front fender of the car immediately ahead. Vehicles from all four directions entangled themselves in a snarl that permitted neither progress nor regress for the motorcycle and a dozen automobiles.

"*Mierda*," Carlos shouted. He flew off the Harley like a wren off its perch and lit on the Escort's driver's window.

Within five minutes, crescendoing sirens brought the police—two to get the traffic moving and two to check out the accident. Carlos eventually wove the Harley out of the snarl, and they reached Wells Fargo in less than two minutes. The two men rushed over to the stairwell. The officers on duty parted like the Red Sea to make a passage for Detective Ruiz, and the cops went about their business.

Mike attempted to push through the passel of cops.

"Come on in, Father." Officer Mark Foley stood as a sentry keeping the curious away from the crime scene.

"You here again, Reverend?" Jerry bulged up against Mike to stop his progress.

"Hi, Jerry. Could I see the body? Thought maybe you might need an ID."

Jerry didn't move. "Can't go there, Reverend. They're still doing cop stuff down there. They should be done in a couple of minutes."

Jerry's "couple of minutes" turned out to be a couple of hours, but that was not unusual for police estimates of time.

Mike had always had difficulty waiting. The cashier's line at the supermarket—or the teller's line at the bank—or the interminable line to get through the metal detector at the airport. And this wait was untenable. But he surrendered and leaned against the Wells Fargo wall to suffer the inevitable.

His mind wandered to thoughts of Sir. He had visited Sir on several occasions, both in Slocum and under the Tyrone Street Bridge—the favorite hang-out for most of the hobes in Madison. He knew about Sir's patrols of the city to pick up scraps of food and half-spent bottles of wine. He knew about Sir's breakfast rituals with Tom-Tom and Jo and Marty. He knew about Sir's relaxing time in Masters Park and his reading time at the Madison Public Library. He was certain that Sir had been a valued member of society in his previous life.

He quickly emerged from his mentation when a couple of officers hauled Sir's body up out of the stairwell, and slid it onto the gurney. They fussed over the dead man about a quarter of an hour before Jerry came over to Mike. "It's all yours, Reverend. Do the ID stuff."

Mike scowled. He had been eager to see Sir, but now he was having second thoughts. He was afraid of what he would find—or see—or feel. He could not move.

"Reverend," Jerry prompted.

Mike forced himself out of his hesitancy, plodded over to the gurney, and paused for a couple of seconds. The body was really in pretty good shape, considering how long it had been in the stairwell. With the low recent temperatures, however, the body was in no danger of decomposing. Sir looked like himself, except for the reddish brown blotch in his temple. His thrift-store clothing had been ripped in several places and was inordinately dirty, as if Sir had been shot at the top of the stairs and had tumbled down the steps face forward. His shirt had been ripped from his body on one side and his chest skin had shriveled from either too much sun or too much cold. The body's facial features were locked with brows almost reaching his hairline, his eyes protruding from their sockets, and his mouth contorted like a Greek tragic masque. "It's Sir," Mike stated with as much grace as he could muster. Jerry took due note of the identification.

Mike reached in his coat pocket and retrieved his ampulla. He moistened his thumb with the holy oil and traced a cross on Sir's forehead. "Sir, I anoint you with oil in the Name of the Father, and of the Son, and of the Holy Spirit. Amen."

He placed his hand upon Sir's forehead and said, "Into your hands, O merciful Savior, we commit your servant Sir. Acknowledge, we humbly beseech you, a sheep of your own fold, a lamb of your own flock, a sinner of your own redeeming. Receive him…"

Then Mike stopped. Dead still. He stared at Sir as if he were a banshee.

Carlos placed his hand on Mike's shoulder. "What's the matter, Mike?"

Mike didn't answer. He gawked at the man. His eyes eventually focused, and he made out a blurred, tattooed mermaid on Sir's left bicep. Mike—suddenly—with a crazed frenzy not often seen in the gentle Father Michael Richey, began ripping Sir's shirt off his body like a crazed demoniac. He paused for a moment. A second mermaid abruptly appeared on Sir's right bicep. And then with wild abandon he began pounding Sir on the chest with all the strength he could summon and cried out, "You son of a bitch! You damned son of a bitch!"

With all their strength Carlos and Jerry pulled Mike off the body and jerked him up against the side of the bank wall.

"What in the hell do you think you're doing?" yelled Jerry.

"Mike, snap out of it. Mike!" Carlos overlapped.

A whole crew of cops surrounded Mike against the wall. Then without grace and with great abandon, Mike cried out, "He's my father! He's my fucking father!"

FIVE

IKE WAS furious. He had not seen his father in twenty-eight years, and he hated the man. He hated all those bums in winery row. He hated the world. He wanted to get out of this place—now. He wanted to smother his memories—perhaps at the nearest bar, perhaps tearing his muscles to shreds on the bench press, perhaps driving the Camry to Timbuktu. But he did none of these things. Instead he sat there in Jerry's office spilling his guts.

Mike had been born of happily married parents. Happy, that is, until he was ten, when his father—Michael Basil Richey, Sr.—had abruptly left Mike and his mother, Maria, and fled with Inez, Mike's best friend's mother. Mike had been enraged with his father for not being there to support him in Little League, to bolster him as high school student-body president, and to applaud him as valedictorian of his senior class.

Robert and Inez Grover had lived next door to the Richeys for as long as Mike could remember. But, even though the two families were friends, they normally went their separate ways on social occasions. The Grovers were country clubbers, game hunters, and avid members of the NRA. Inez always ruled the family—her husband and her son. The Richeys were theatergoers and music lovers. It was this difference in interests that caused much surprise, or even shock, among the people of the community, that Basil and Inez would elope and leave their families behind.

Inez's son Bobby was left without a mother, and he and Mike bonded from their common experience. Over the years the buddies did almost everything together: played basketball, sang in the school choir, and went to movies. Their favorite movie was *Star Wars,* a film they must have seen a dozen times. Mike had rooted for Luke Skywalker and Han Solo, but—and Mike always thought it bizarre— Bobby boisterously cheered for Darth Vader, the Dark Side's hero.

As the years passed, the two friends grew their separate ways. Mike dove into his studies with a zeal rarely found in a teenager. Into sports like gymnastics, basketball, weight training, and Kodokan Judo. Kodokan appealed to Mike because it was an art of combat in which the skills of gentleness and agility overcame the strength and aggression of an opponent. And into his church, where his EYC— the Episcopal Youth Community—taught him to love those unfortunate souls who slept in the streets, who lay sick in the basement stairwells, and who died of malnutrition in the alleys. It was this love that drove him to become a priest.

The two mermaids on Basil Richey's arms, vestiges of his time in the Navy, were his father's delight. His father was a muscular man, and he often wore muscle shirts in the evenings to show off either his biceps or his tattoos. Mike never knew which. Those tattoos on Basil's arms brought back visions of his father sitting on the side of the bed telling him bedtime stories. And of his father playing catch with him on lazy Sunday afternoons. And of his father frying fish over an open fire on camping trips to Edisto Beach. But strongest of all was the recollection of his father kissing him goodnight one evening and Mike's never seeing him again.

Sitting in Jerry's office at the station, Mike unloaded these memories of his early childhood and adolescence. He knew that these confessions were perhaps overkill, but, when he started talking, he couldn't stop until he had unburdened himself of the entire story. And the two detectives let him go on. Mike never realized he still had so much resentment and rage stored up in him. He sat trembling like a Quaking Aspen.

Jerry thrust a wilted form into his hands. "Reverend," he said, "you need to sign this."

Mike grabbed the paper with both hands. "What is it?"

"Reverend, we need you to give us a swab."

Mike froze. What was Jerry up to now? "Why, for God's sake?"

"We need to get a DNA sample…"

"Am I a suspect, Detective?"

"…to prove that you really are Basil's son."

Mike winced. He certainly didn't mind ceding his DNA, but this demand seemed to be some sort of veiled accusation. He rubbed his fingers through his hair. "Why would you need to prove that?"

Jerry stared at him as if Mike were a recalcitrant teenager. "Somebody's got to make some decisions here in regard to Basil's body, and we don't want any trouble if we make the wrong decision in somebody's eyes. Okay?"

Mike's anger evolved into frustration. How could he make a decision for Sir—or Basil as he now was? The man was just another stranger to him. *Oh, what the heck!* "Okay, Detective, if that's what you want." And Mike signed the form.

Jerry reached into his desk drawer and withdrew a packet of DNA buccal swabs, selected one. "Wanna open your mouth?"

Mike shrugged but did as instructed. Jerry reached into his mouth with the swab and retrieved what he needed from the right cheek.

"And Reverend, if you do legally prove to be Basil's son, what would you like us to do with his body when we're finished with it?"

A whole new string of emotions filtered through Mike's being, from annoyance to embarrassment to worry. "What about Basil's wife Inez? What if he has other heirs from Inez or whoever else he might have slept with?"

Jerry grimaced. "Let us take care of that part. Okay?"

"Okay. Why don't you go ahead and cremate him. Send me the bill, and after that, I don't care what you do with him."

Carlos flinched. "You don't mean that, Mike."

"Very well. Just save his ashes, and I'll figure out something to do with them." Mike rose. "If that's all, Detectives, I've got to get back to Annie."

"Sit down, Reverend," Jerry ordered. His sudden policeman's voice was highly strident and not one to ignore.

"Yes, Sir!" Mike snarled but obeyed.

Jerry reached into his desk drawer and snatched out a couple of pairs of plastic gloves, tossed one pair over to Mike. "Here, put these on," he growled and slapped the other pair on his own hands.

It was hard for Mike to conceal his pique. He stuttered, and sighed, and stretched the gloves over his large palms. Jerry dug into a plastic Zip Lock evidence bag and pulled out a piece of crumpled paper.

"Look at this." Jerry handed him the evidence. "We found it on the body."

The note, written in number-two pencil lead, appeared to be in a child's hand—half printed, half cursive. A scribbled star substituted for the dot of the *i*: "The sins of the fathers."

"The sins of the fathers." Mike repeated. "What's this?" He pointed toward a somewhat illegible word at the end of the note. "Death?" In the killer's best doctor's handwriting, he had signed the note: *Death*.

"What do you make of it?" Jerry said.

Mike frowned. He ran his gloved hand across the words as if he were attempting to divine the answer. "You have a bible here, by any chance?"

"Hang on," Carlos said, and he left the room.

Mike examined the paper from every angle—carefully. He turned the note over. The paper was ruled as if it had been a part of a ledger sheet or invoice form or something else with spaces for money amounts in dollars and cents.

Carlos was back. "Here." He pushed the bible into Mike's hands.

Mike took the bible and opened it to the book of Exodus and began flipping pages. It took him about five minutes to come up with the verse he was looking for. He pored over it for a couple of seconds. "Look at this." Mike's index finger swiped across the seventh verse of the thirty-fourth chapter. He handed the bible to Jerry. He and Carlos hovered over the passage.

Carlos read aloud,

> *The LORD passed before him, and proclaimed, 'The LORD, the LORD, a God merciful and gracious, slow to anger, and abounding in steadfast love and faithfulness, keeping steadfast love for thousands, forgiving iniquity and transgression and sin, but who will by no means clear the guilty, visiting the sins of the fathers upon their children and their children's children, to the third and the fourth generation.*

"Visiting the sins of the fathers upon their children and their children's children," Carlos repeated. "Meaning what?"

"I wish I knew." Mike clung to the hope that it didn't mean what he thought it might mean. He knew how to interpret the verse in its biblical context. But what the killer meant was another proposition altogether.

Mike peeled off the gloves and flung them onto the desk. He stood up and reached for his cell. "I need to make a couple of calls, if you don't mind, Detective."

Jerry apparently was taken aback by Mike's bluntness. "What're you up to, Reverend?" Jerry said, as if he were not accustomed to this kind of curt.

Mike slowly sighed, as if he had suddenly released a two-hundred-pound barbell. He crossed over to Jerry and placed his hand on Jerry's shoulder. "I'm afraid what's coming up is going to be a rather lengthy ordeal. I need to let a couple of people know where I am."

"Be my guest, Reverend."

Mike walked out the front door of the station, pulling his overcoat tight as the sleet battered his face. He dialed the church, instructed his secretary to reschedule his appointments for the day and then immediately speed-dialed Annie's cell phone. She was probably in fourth period by this time.

"Hey. I'm sorry, darling, but I can't talk right now. I'm in the middle of…"

"They found Sir," Mike said.

There was no sound from Annie's end of the line.

"Annie?"

"Is he okay?"

"He's dead, Annie."

Annie let out an audible gasp. "Where?"

"In the street stairwell at Wells Fargo. I'm at the station house, and I have a few more things to do. Can you get someone to cover for you for the rest of the afternoon? I need you!"

"What?" Annie said. "What's the matter?"

Mike could not answer immediately. He shifted the phone to the other ear and held his breath. "Can't talk on the phone. I'll tell you about it when we get home. Meet me in a couple of hours?"

"Of course, sweetheart."

"See you." Mike pressed the *END* button.

His stomach reeled, like unwashed, oily rags in a spin cycle. He walked back into the station house.

"Gentlemen," Mike said, "I have a possible interpretation of the Exodus passage—and it isn't pretty."

The detectives looked at Mike as if to say, *Go on.*

Mike sat and exhaled at length. "The murderer killed Basil—the father—for some perceived wrong. And…" He dropped his head as if he didn't want to say anything else.

"And?"

"The verse mentioned his children. That's me—I'm his child. It could very well be that I'm the next one on the killer's hit list."

The detectives looked at Mike almost as if he were the culprit.

Carlos eventually broke the silence. "And the children's children." He paused. "I hesitate to continue, Mike, but it could also mean that Tim's life may be in danger."

Mike grimaced and dropped his head.

The next two hours wore slowly. Jerry and Carlos grilled him as if he were the perp. He had to rehash much of what he had already told them. Was there anybody from Mike's early memory who might have waited until now to get even for a wrong, either real or imagined? Was Mike certain he had had no contact with Basil through the years?

And then the question—the ultimate question—that Mike knew was coming and that he dreaded like the pangs of hell.

"Reverend?"

Mike's stomach turned over a half a dozen times.

"Reverend, did you kill your father?"

Mike sobered. All of a sudden his dread, his nausea, his pain left his body. "No, Detective. I did not kill Basil."

Mike stood, and, without a word, he threw his overcoat back on and started out the door.

Carlos followed him. "Let me drive you."

Mike didn't want to converse with Carlos or anyone right now. In fact, he didn't want anybody but Annie. "No thanks, Carlos. I'll walk." Mike tightened his overcoat around him and stepped out into the cold.

Carlos stayed with him. "Are you sure?"

"I need to think."

And he did indeed think. At around eighteen or so he had come to terms with his father's betrayal, or so he thought. But this morning's brush with Basil Richey had opened up old wounds, and his mind flitted from one moment in his life to another, and not without pain.

$$\maltese\maltese\maltese$$

MIKE OPENED the door, and there stood Annie. The eonic embrace broke apart only after Annie had inundated him with a plethora of kisses. Her strokes of his hair soon became caresses of the face and then the fondling of the hand. Her fingers interlaced with his and she whispered, "Come on." And she led him upstairs into the bedroom.

They slipped off their clothes and lay naked on the king-sized bed, where the two had often made ardent love. But today the bed was not for making love but simply for loving. They laced their bare legs together, breasts touching, arms around each other, and Mike told her everything—everything except for the scrap of paper. Tears welled up in her deep brown eyes, drops that made her eyes more beautiful than ever.

The silence was long, like the calm in the eye of a hurricane. Mike turned onto his back. He lay there, his mouth opening and closing in silence, as if he were attempting to conjure up the gumption to say something he did not want to say. Then Mike felt the blood rush to his face. "I hate him!" he shouted. "I hate him," he whispered.

They lay there side by side until the weeping subsided.

"Can we pray about it?" Annie suggested.

The stunned Reverend Michael Basil Richey stopped dead still and answered only after he had glued his mind back together. "I can't pray." Mike leaned his head back on Annie's arm. "Prayer is my business. I've based my life on prayer, but I can't pray now."

"Then I will."

Mike saw her lips moving but heard nothing.

Then—her eyes suddenly jerked open. "You know, he was really trying to tell you who he was."

Mike looked at Annie. He placed his hand delicately on her swollen cheek. "Who? What?"

"Sir. Sir was."

"What do you mean? Sir was what?"

Annie hesitated for a moment. "You thought he was addressing you as a priest when he would say *Fahta*. But I think he was trying to say *I'm your father.* I think he really wanted you to know who he was. And I think, in a way, he was asking your forgiveness."

"Fahta," Mike repeated. That thought seemed to hit Mike like a hammer on the head of a nail. Then he buried his face in Annie's bosom and said nothing more.

Annie stroked his hair. Mike couldn't count the number of times in their marriage that she had stroked his hair. It was an act of love. When the two of them were undergoing pre-marital counseling, the bishop asked them to answer a question. *What small thing,* she had asked, *does the other one do to show love to you?*

Mike had thought a moment. *How small?*

The smallest.

Without another moment's hesitation, Mike said, *She strokes my hair.*

Annie now held him tighter, and the two lay there caressing each other. And they drifted into oblivion.

SIX

THE HARPSICHORD sounds of "Jesu, Joy of Man's Desiring" interrupted Michele Norris on NPR, and Mike reached for his cell. "Hi, sweetie."

"Hi, sweetheart," Annie finally uttered between panting breaths. "Where are you?"

"Just past Simpsonville. Are you okay?"

Annie said nothing for a moment.

"Annie?"

"A car's been circling the block. Passing the rectory every few minutes."

"Hang on!" Mike floored the accelerator and headed for the next exit. "What kind of car?" A U-turn and he would be back on I-385 North headed for home.

"Near as I can tell, it's a black Ford Escort. Old."

The intersection suddenly appeared, and Mike moved over into the right lane and took the exit ramp. His meeting with the bishop would have to wait.

"Mike," Annie said, "Carlos is here. He just drove up."

"You're sure its Carlos?"

"Yes. He's coming up the walk."

Phew. "Thank God for Carlos."

In the next split second, Mike made the decision to go on to Columbia and crossed SC 418 and headed down the ramp back to I-385 South. "Bye, darling. Just make sure Tim is safe. I'll call you back a bit later."

Mike was particularly sensitive now. He and Annie had quarreled for the past three days. Annie had sensed that Mike had not told her the whole story. She had persisted and Mike had resisted. At last he gathered the courage to tell her about the note. The Exodus note about the sins of the fathers. The killer, he told her, was convinced that God had ordered him to take revenge for some perceived wrong Basil had committed. By killing Basil and his children—that meant Mike, and his children's children—that meant Tim, he would be the agent of God in wreaking vengeance on an evil world.

Mike gripped the steering wheel. A foreboding suddenly swept over him, and his eyes glazed. His knuckles paled into a ghost-like whiteness. The one thing he had always promised himself—and God—was never to allow his son to grow up without a father. He had experienced that first hand, and it was no fun.

Mike drove on past the Clinton Exit 2 and merged onto I-26. He glanced into his rear-view mirror. *This can't be. No way that car could be two places at one time. And sixty or so miles apart, at that.* A dozen miles ahead, Mike pulled into a rest stop. Walking into the shelter, he glanced back over his shoulder, and the Escort pulled into the parking lot. *Coincidence. It's got to be coincidence.*

When Mike returned, the Escort was still there. He pulled out onto the Interstate and headed back toward Columbia. No Escort. Finally he allowed himself to drive at leisure.

He drove passed the Columbiana Mall and glanced back. *I think I'm getting paranoid.* The Escort had reappeared. He tried to ignore the car behind him but couldn't. He drove on and the Escort followed, passing the Riverbanks Zoo and turning right onto Assembly Street. The Escort left Assembly at Laurel Street. *Well, that's that, thank God.*

Mike turned left onto Gervais and passed the South Carolina capitol building. On the other side of the state house the traffic was heavy, so he moved slowly around All Saints' Cathedral onto Sumter Street and into the parking lot of the Beinville Diocesan House. He locked the Camry's parking brake and looked around for the Escort. He saw nothing at first—just the bumper-to-bumper traffic on Gervais, stopping and starting with each change of the next traffic light. Two black Ford Escorts passed by within two minutes. And then there was one that appeared to be circling the block. It passed by on Sumter three times within five minutes. The car unsettled him. *Dammit! Keep your cool, Mike Richey!* He knew his unease was irrational, but it was still there nonetheless. Then the Escort turned back onto Gervais and disappeared in about three blocks. Mike waited another five minutes, and the Escort did not reappear.

He glanced at his dash-board clock. He still had thirty minutes or so before his scheduled appointment, so he shifted into drive, pulled back onto Gervais, and turned right onto Main Street. *Ah, a parking space.* He parked directly in front of the State House City News, a feat not often accomplished.

He looked around him carefully—no Escorts in sight—before venturing out of the Camry and into the book and magazine shop. The aroma of stuffy, ancient books greeted him at the door. *Aaah.* He loved that smell. Several customers, scattered about the shop, perused hardbacks, paperbacks, and magazines shelved in rows and racks stretching length-wise from the entrance to the back wall of the store. The narrow aisles could be claustrophobic to some, but to Mike the meager space provided the ambiance of book-heaven. If he just had the time to stay longer. But now he had to limit himself to the racks. Mike paced one aisle after another scanning the magazines, eventually settling on a copy of *Men's Health* to take with him to the bishop's office in the event he had to wait.

He glanced at his watch. *Almost time.* Mike took his magazine and settled in line at the cashier's counter and waited to pay for his purchase. Waiting was not one of Mike's strong points—even in a queue consisting of only three customers. So he lapsed into his people-watch mode, as he often did when he had time to kill. The guy at the head of the line—Mike could swear he had seen him before—a tall, black man with shoulders a yard wide and biceps bursting his tee-shirt sleeves. Then he remembered—University of South Carolina's star quarterback. MVP last season. Satchel Sims, his name was. Mike had seen his picture in the sports pages a dozen times.

He turned his attention to the customer directly in front of him. This guy was the negative counterpart of Satchel. Skinny fellow with pasty skin. Dressed in a black jumpsuit and a large Johnny Cash, fake Stetson, the guy danced back and forth from one foot to the other, like a would-be fakir on a bed of hot coals. A pack of Marlboros poked its head out of the left shirt pocket. Mike thought maybe he had seen this guy before too.

Satchel paid for his *USA Today* and walked out the door. The man in the fake Stetson tossed two pieces of bubble gum onto the counter. As the gum bounced the first time, he pulled a gun—looked like a police Glock—and rammed it into the cashier's face. The peach-faced kid with the USC tee-shirt threw up his hands, his eyes glistening with near-tears, and stuttered. "What do you want, sir?"

The customers in the shop froze.

"Listen exactly to what I tell you." For some reason he didn't say anything further for what seemed like a half minute, his face twitching like the trembling heart of a captive bird. Then, in a surprise move, he quickly turned around, stuck the gun into Mike's face, and cocked the hammer.

Mike's blood rushed through his system a dozen times in three seconds. The killer. The man who had shed Basil's blood, and, because of some sick interpretation of scripture, had vowed to take Mike's life. And then Tim's. This killer had finally caught up with him. This was it. Tim would no longer have a father. If Tim escaped the wild man's fury, who would admire his turtle collections? Who would take him camping—or hiking—or rock climbing? Who would be there to applaud his successes? And Annie. What would happen to Annie?

The Stetson man appeared to show a moment of recognition, and he perused Mike carefully.

The collar. He's staring at my collar.

"A preacher man." He said nothing for a couple of moments. "Don't you try nothing, preacher." He sized up Mike's muscular frame. "You might be strong—you might be strong as a horse—but you ain't strong as this." He waved the gun in Mike's face. "Just don't you try nothing!"

Then just as suddenly as he turned on Mike, the guy turned back and pointed the gun at the college kid. "Put all your money into a paper sack and hand it over."

Mike was not relieved. No one spoke. The USC kid did exactly as he was told.

The Stetson guy charged toward the door, then turned back and flashed the Glock at the other customers who stood agape in the aisles. "Don't you even think about following me!" He turned, charged out the front door, and immediately fell squarely on his face onto the concrete sidewalk.

Mike was the first out the door, and Satchel Sims, the quarterback, was sitting astraddle of the Stetson guy, holding him to the ground. The cops were there in a matter of seconds

SEVEN

JERRY, WITH his perpetually tepid cup of coffee, sat at his old gray desk sorting his evidence cards. Two ancient metal typewriter tables, salvaged from the maintenance barn, served as a sorting board, where he had arranged both Juice's and Sir's cards so he could see everything at a glance. This sorting and resorting was a ritual he always counted on for a spark or two—or sometimes a piercing flame—of inspiration on his cases.

But he had very little room to spread out, as he preferred to do. He scowled. Last year, when he had been promoted to Chief Detective, he was sure he would be moved to the new annex—a chrome and glass building touted as the finest police facility in the state. But it was not to be. He was still here among the scarred desks and gray file cabinets that lined the walls like tall tombstones without inscriptions or flowers. And very little space.

His and Carlos's interrogation of the reverend had raised more questions than it answered. The reverend had seemed so defensive, his story so rehearsed. The alacrity with which he found the insulting biblical passage. The haste with which he interpreted it to point to himself and his son as victims.

And then there were the sunglasses. He picked up the sunglasses from the evidence spread, and examined them again from every possible angle. He measured the width of the sunglasses against his own. Too narrow. He held them up to his own eyes. Not prescription. Jerry had found them under Basil's body, and the prints on the glasses had consisted of several smudges and three prints that clearly matched the reverend's. Jerry had some thinking to do. He leaned back in his chair and closed his eyes.

The sunglasses. His own father's image seeped into his head. His father's sunglasses, worn mostly to cover up his alcohol-induced red eyes made him wince. When Jerry was a kid, he had gone out for the middle school football team, primarily to give himself a legitimate excuse not to go home after school. He often stayed longer than necessary to delay the inevitable. But when he would at last bike home, Pap would meet him at the door, wearing those evil-looking sunglasses, with an equally evil-looking leather belt.

"Whur ya been, boy?" Pap would yell.

"Just been to football practice."

"Like hell ya have." *Whack*. The belt slammed into Jerry's back like an ax on the trunk of a tree.

"Football practice don't last that long. Ya been out doing nasty things. Don't tell me no different." *Whack*.

"Please, Pap!" Jerry refused to cry. He would not give the old man that satisfaction.

His father's nostrils flared and his voice rose into a harsh, raspy falsetto. "Please—please—please." The old man's sarcasm hurt almost as much as the lashes. *Whack*. Pap whimpered like a dying horse, "Wh-i-i-ne, wh-i-i-ne, wh-i-i-ne." *Whack*.

"Pap!"

His father spat out gin-soaked droplets of venom into Jerry's face. "Don't you Pap me, you sneaky little son-of-a-bitch." *Whack*. "I know whur ya been." *Whack*. "Ya been out screwin' some little sixth-grade tart." *Whack*. "That's whur ya been, boy!" *Whack*.

The older and stronger Jerry grew, the more severe the beatings grew. Jerry endured them with anger and a burgeoning resentment. He wished he were dead. Or better still, he wished the old man were dead. That scraggly bearded face, that snaggle-toothed grin with the tobacco juice oozing from both corners—he wanted the old man dead.

By the time he reached eighth grade Jerry had grown larger than Pap. The final thrashing came one day—and Jerry remembered it well—when Pap pulled out the belt, and, before he could issue the first whack, Jerry drew his hard fist back and rammed it into Pap's face. "Don't you ever touch me again, you fucking bastard."

The old man fell to the floor and lay stunned for a moment or so. When Pap came to, he pulled himself off the floor and sat down at the breakfast table. He put his face into his hands and cried. That was the only time Jerry had ever seen his father cry. And for some reason, some feeling, some intuition—Jerry still didn't know why—he looked back over his shoulder and spotted his mom leaning against the door, her face as white as ash, looking as if she could crumple to the floor at any moment. Jerry charged upstairs to his room and lay on his bed. He cried too.

Jerry didn't know how long he had lain there. It couldn't have been long. He heard his bedroom door open and close. His solitude was over. His mom tiptoed into the room and sat down on the bed beside him. "Jerry?"

He turned away from her.

His mother reached over and caressed his cheeks. She kissed him gently and whispered. "Jerry. Son."

He remembered his mom's tender touch when he was a child. Her luxurious lap, her ample bosom, her goodnight prayers. He had always felt safe when her soft lips had given him the last kiss of the night. To Jerry, she was the most beautiful mom in the world. But Jerry didn't move.

"Please, Son. Don't turn away from me."

Jerry thought for a long time. When he was about five or six, the caresses suddenly stopped, and Jerry never knew why. One night she kissed him, and then she never kissed him again. Now the caress was back, and the kiss made him feel loved again. And so he turned back over. He loved his mom. He loved her dearly. But it was hard looking at her now, so he didn't make eye contact.

"I know you didn't mean to do it, but it was your father you hit."

Jerry didn't stir.

"You hit your father. Your own father."

For the first time Jerry looked straight into her eyes.

Mom waited. "Just go down and tell him you're sorry."

Jerry didn't move, but he listened.

"For me. Do it for me. Please."

Jerry closed his eyes.

"That'll make everything all right," she said. "Just tell him you're sorry." After a moment, his mother leaned over and kissed him again on his tear-stained cheek.

He pulled away and turned back over and buried his face in his pillow. Then he heard her get up, walk from the room, and close the door lightly behind her.

Jerry lay there for perhaps half an hour, staring into the emptiness of his small, drab room—almost as drab as his office at the MPD. He could see nothing but the three old photos in sepia hanging slovenly on the floral-papered wall. There was a man in a derby hat and a heavy mustache, a woman with long brown hair gathered around her head like a halo. His paternal grandparents. But then there was a boy—a boy—the saddest boy he'd ever seen. Everywhere Jerry would move in the room, the boy's eyes seemed to follow him.

Jerry cringed and sat up. He couldn't look at that boy any longer. He got up from the bed and made his way over to the window, the only light source he had in the room, paused for a moment, then raised the four-paned sash and propped it up with the cut-off broom handle made for the purpose. He looked out for a long time. Then he moved. He crawled out the window and shimmied down the bare, paint-peeled trellis—once the ladder for thriving Confederate Jasmine—that stood outside his window.

He grabbed his somewhat deflated basketball and shot hoops in his driveway, missing every other shot. *Shoot—whack.* The ball whacking the much-patched, asphalt surface echoed eerily around the otherwise silent neighborhood. *Shoot—whack. Shoot—whack.* An hour passed. *Shoot—whack. Shoot—whack.* The whacks now started to sound too much like the belt strokes against his own flesh.

Jerry threw the ball to the side, jumped on his bike, and headed off. He could not apologize to the bastard. He would not apologize to the bastard. He pedaled to the highway and then to Morristown Boulevard and then to Bantam Street and then to—Jerry suddenly realized he had been traveling in a circle. He was home again. It was late. His watch said eleven o'clock. The lights were still on. What would it hurt to say *I'm sorry*? He would do almost anything to please his mom. He would apologize.

He parked his bike in the garage, opened the door into the den, and heard a whack and a scream that stopped his heart. He dashed into the kitchen just in time to see his father raise his belt again and strike his mother. He ran back into the hallway, grabbed a gun from his father's never-locked gun case, and charged into the kitchen.

"Don't you dare hit her again!" he yelled.

The belt stopped in midair, and Pap turned to see his own Smith and Wesson double-action revolver staring him in the face.

Jerry's mother wiped the blood from her face and stared at her son. "No, Jerry. Don't. Don't. It's not what you think."

Pap stuttered. "Wait, Son."

Jerry's face flushed. "You son-of-a-bitch!" He aimed the gun right at the old man's mid-section.

Pap turned red and then blue and then almost purple. "Give me the gun, you little bastard. Give me the goddamned gun!"

Mom whimpered. "Please, Son. Put the gun down."

Pap reached out his hand to retrieve the gun. "You don't know how to use the goddamned gun, you little wimp."

Jerry cocked the hammer. "Don't come one step closer."

Pap inched nearer. "Give me the goddamned gun, you little bastard!"

Jerry pulled the trigger. The bullet whizzed by Pap's arm, through the cupboard, shattering dishes, and lodged in the wall. "Now. Get out of this house. Now!"

"Ya can't run me outa my own house, you stupid kid!"

"Just watch me." And Jerry cocked the hammer again.

Pap staggered back and fell against the kitchen table and crumpled to the floor.

"Get up and get out of this house. Don't ever come back. Don't ever touch my mother again. Do you hear me?"

Pap made a final desperate plea. "Son?"

"I swear I'll kill you. If I ever see your fool face again, I'll kill you!"

Pap grappled his way up—and fled.

Jerry had seen his father only three times since. And those sunglasses—still hanging from the bridge of his nose—made him appear more sinister than ever. Each time he saw the old man, he had been tempted to grab his MPD-issued handgun and fulfill his promise of over thirty years ago. But reason prevailed.

Those sunglasses. Jerry opened his eyes and picked up the sunglasses. He turned them over and inspected them again—piece by piece. He dropped them back onto the table and blurted aloud, "The reverend murdered the old man." At that moment Jerry sensed a shadow in the doorway. It was Carlos

EIGHT

IKE RUSHED into Bishop Michener's waiting room, as if to make up somehow for the time lost at the book store. The room was void of people. Most often there were at least two or three folks waiting to get a word in with the bishop. Not even Julia, who normally sat at that silly looking, kidney-shaped desk was in her place answering the phone and punching the keys on her keyboard.

Mike hated waiting rooms, mainly because he hated waiting. The doctor, the lawyer, the bishop. But he took his place on the sofa anyway. He started to reach for his new magazine purchase and suddenly realized he must have dropped his copy of *Men's Health* during the commotion at the book store. He shrugged and picked up a copy of the *South Carolina Architectural Journal* from the glass-topped coffee table and looked at the cover. *Yes! Up to date. Good old Julia— keeping the new magazines on top.* He glanced at the table of contents but then threw it back on the stack. He couldn't concentrate.

Mike debated whether or not to knock on the bishop's door but decided it was best to wait. He leaned back against the paisley sofa. It must be some sort of sin to cover furniture with that stuff. He made a mental note to search his bible when he got home for some scripture or other that would prohibit paisley-covered furniture. After all, people did that all the time—finding quotations from the bible to justify their own preconceived biases—religious, political, and otherwise. Why couldn't he?

Then the icon caught his eye—the large Eastern Orthodox illumination hanging over Bishop Michener's office door. That icon was the one thing that set this waiting room apart from other waiting rooms. He recalled the first time he had seen this icon of the Resurrection, and it impressed him immediately. The Lord trampling down the gates of death and simultaneously raising Adam—that potent symbol of humanity—from the dead. Mike gazed on Adam for several moments as if he were mesmerized. If he could only trust in this moment. Suddenly he doubled his fists. *Where is that resurrection now? Where is that hope now?* Then he caught his breath and gradually allowed his fingers to relax.

His eyes drifted down to the nameplate on the door itself. The Right Reverend Barbara Michener. He almost smiled. Such a long title for such a small woman. He had always loved this bishop. She had celebrated the Sacrament of Marriage for Annie and him and then had shepherded him into Holy Orders. This barely five-foot woman could seem quite intimidating to some. A very demanding bishop, she required much of her clergy. Mike almost smiled again—*whatever Barbara wanted, Barbara generally got.* She had been nothing but gracious to Mike. He had admired the way she had taken the high road through some turbulent times for the diocese with a profound faith in God and the *via media* of Anglicanism. She had been a positive, healing influence in the diocese.

"Hi, Father Richey." Julia walked in from the bishop's inner office and took her seat behind the kidney-shaped desk. "Sorry to have kept you waiting."

"Hi, Julia. What's up?"

"The sky, for one."

Mike grinned. Julia always had a different answer for the ritual question every time he came into the office.

"The bishop will be with you shortly. There're some new magazines on the coffee table. Help yourself."

59

"Thanks," he said.

Mike had hardly picked up the magazine again, when the bishop appeared at the door.

"Hi, Mike. Come on in," she said. The bishop held the door for Mike and guided him over to a corner of the huge room—a conversation area with three comfortable, wing-backed chairs surrounding a large round coffee table. A similarly shaped, braided, three-colored rug under the table lent a sense of serenity—especially after the paisley furniture—to the space. Mike had always been glad that Bishop Michener was not the kind of bishop who sat in her high-backed Broyhill throne behind her conference-sized desk to wield her episcopal authority over a shrinking, ashen-faced young priest who had come in for counsel.

The bishop took a chair opposite. As if on cue, Julia entered and placed two cups of extra-strong—the bishop liked it that way— coffee in front of them. Mike had often wondered how many cups of coffee had sat on that brilliantly Windexed table over the years.

"That's okay, Julia," the bishop said. "Please be sure we're not disturbed."

"Certainly, Bishop." And Julia left the room.

The bishop opened the conversation. "Hear you've been through a bit of a mess this afternoon."

Mike nodded. He had called Julia earlier to explain his belated appearance. He and the bishop got through the magazine-shop experience in a couple of paragraphs, and she went straight to the point of the meeting. The bishop had never permitted a lot of small talk in her presence. "Now what's this about you and Sir?"

"You've talked with Harlan, I presume."

"Indeed. Your senior warden has been very helpful in keeping me up to date on this situation. He has given me an abbreviated version of the story, but I'd like to hear it from you. I want you to tell me the story."

Mike knew the bishop was well aware of Sir. She had championed Mike's efforts at St. Christopher's to initiate and maintain the parish's ministry to the homeless. Mike had reported monthly the progress of both the diner and other homeless ministries. But he started at the beginning. It took almost an hour to recount the narrative. The bishop did not interrupt. And he talked about his fears—especially his fear for Tim's life.

The bishop was sympathetic—no, empathetic.

"You know, Bishop, I've got to find this guy before he finds Tim."

"Mike, you are not a detective or a police officer. You don't have the knowledge or the skills to be a detective. You must leave that to the police. You will end up getting both you and Tim murdered. Your life is very precious to God—and to me. You still have many years of God's work to do before you die."

"But Bishop, I've got to do something," Mike protested. "I can't just stand around and allow Tim and me to be the next items on the killer's to-do list. Besides, the Chief Detective thinks I murdered Basil. I've got to prove my innocence."

"Nevertheless, Mike," the bishop responded, "I strongly advise you against doing this."

Mike rubbed his fingers through his hair, an idiosyncrasy he often resorted to when he found himself caught in an unhappy dilemma.

"What I will do," she continued, "indeed what I have done—"

The bishop broke off for a moment and Mike looked up.

"I have talked with your senior warden. Harlan agrees with me on this. I have given my blessing and my warrant for you to take an extended leave of absence from St. Christopher's. This should give you ample time to do whatever you can to keep you and Tim alive until the police do their work. I have a competent young priest—Margaret Seaburg—who will be supplying for you for the duration."

"Thank you, Bishop."

Bishop Michener reached out her hand to extend a blessing to Mike.

But then in mid-blessing Mike stopped her. "Bishop, I want to make a confession."

Bishop Michener paused and looked at Mike for a long time. To Mike it was as if the thought had crossed her mind that he was going to confess to something heinous—perhaps even murder.

But then she asked gently, "A sacramental confession?"

"Yes."

"Of course." The bishop looked at Mike for what seemed a full minute—and she looked kindly. "Let's come over here." She guided Mike past the mega-desk to the opposite end of the room. There, the bishop had set up a small private chapel with its teakwood *prie dieu* facing a beautifully hand-carved crucifix hanging on the opposite wall. The corpus looked down in compassion upon anyone who knelt to pray. She invited Mike to kneel.

Mike knelt. He said a brief silent prayer and crossed himself. Then he said, "Bless me, Mother, for I have sinned."

"The Lord be in your heart and upon your lips that you may truly and humbly confess your sins. In the Name of the Father"—the bishop traced a cross on Mike's forehead—"and of the Son, and of the Holy Spirit."

"Amen."

Mike continued, "I confess to Almighty God, to his Church, and to you, Mother, that I have sinned by my own fault in thought, word, and deed, in things done and left undone, especially the sin of hating my own father. I really hate Basil, Bishop. And I can't stop hating him." Mike recounted his atrocious behavior upon identifying Basil, his bitterness in recalling his youth, and his difficulty in coming to terms with Basil's continued power over him. "I must be honest, Bishop. I don't hate the person who killed Basil—and potentially me and my son—nearly as much as I hate Basil." He paused for a moment. "I've hardly prayed at all since all this happened. I can't pray."

The bishop placed her hand on his shoulder and let Mike weep. She said nothing. But Mike knew the bishop's compassion and was comforted.

When he regained his composure, he continued. "For this sin and all other sins I cannot now remember, I am truly sorry. I pray God to have mercy on me. I firmly intend amendment of life, and I humbly beg forgiveness of God and his Church, and ask you, Mother, for counsel, direction, and absolution."

The bishop waited an eon before she answered. "I know this is going to be hard for you, Mike. You believe you have been betrayed. I don't know Sir's—or Basil's—motives, and I don't understand his actions. But Basil must not be in control. God must be in control, and you've got to let Basil go."

Mike had preached this counsel to others in the pulpit and otherwise since he had been in the ministry. He felt like a hypocrite. "But how can I do that?" Mike had always been on the receiving, not the asking, end of that question.

"As your penance, I want you to celebrate a requiem mass for Basil."

Mike was surprised. No, Mike was shocked. He had never entertained this idea. He had celebrated requiems for other homeless persons over the years. But he could not do this for Basil. That would be like praying the evilest of men into heaven. "I can't do that, Bishop."

The bishop's eyes drew together, and her brow quickly furrowed. "Yes." Her lips pressed together and turned down at the ends. "Yes. You can and you will," the bishop commanded—no, the bishop demanded.

Mike's head reeled. He grew ill. He was on the verge of retching. The bishop took Mike's hand and held it until Mike was able to go on. "But how can I do this when I hate the man so much?"

"Just do it, and we'll see what God does. Now promise me you will do this penance."

All sorts of mutinous notions, like a dozen tennis balls, bounced simultaneously through his brain. He could run away like Jonah. He could renounce his priesthood. He could respond in eighteen other contrary ways. Or, he could just say *yes*. He looked the bishop directly in the eyes. "Yes, Bishop. I will do this penance."

The bishop did not hesitate. "Good." She tightened her grip on Mike's hand. "Our Lord Jesus Christ, who has left power to his Church to absolve all sinners who truly repent and believe in him, of his great mercy forgive you all your offenses; and by his authority committed to me, I absolve you from all your sins." And then she raised her right hand and made the sign of the cross over Mike. "In the Name of the Father, and of the Son, and of the Holy Spirit."

Mike crossed himself. "Amen."

"The Lord has put away all your sins."

"Thanks be to God."

Then the bishop placed her hand on Mike's head and said, "Go in peace, and pray for me, a sinner."

The two stood and the bishop hugged him. "Good-bye, my friend and my son. Go with God. I'll pray for your safety and for Tim's."

Mike stopped in the corridor outside the waiting room, as if he could go no farther. A swell of contradictory emotions gushed through his soul. He felt as if he had been in the presence of God, and yet—and yet—he still hated Basil. How could he be forgiven if he still hated his father? Perhaps, in spite of what he had preached to his congregations over the years, his sin was too great for God to forgive. He leapt down the stairs and out to his Camry, drove onto Gervais, and headed back toward I-26. After about five miles up the Interstate, he glanced in his rear-view mirror and then looked again to be certain he saw what he thought he saw. There was the black Ford Escort.

‡ ‡ ‡

THE ESCORT had departed the Interstate long ago. But the 3:00 southwestern sun beamed mercilessly through Mike's windshield, and the sun visors were not enough to soften the glare of his distress. He automatically reached into his inside coat pocket and grimaced.

He suddenly remembered—he had lost his sunglasses. He sighed. Nevertheless, he charged incautiously west on I-26 to I-385 toward Greenville. He had about seventy-three more miles to go, according to the last mile marker he had passed. He was determined to get back to Madison and put this day behind him.

Mike had never before felt so desolate. He normally would listen to favorite CDs, contemplate his sermon for the following Sunday, or think through a parishioner's problem. But today he missed Annie. He missed Tim. Then he caught himself. He had to think about Basil and his funeral. He wished that he had not given his promise to the bishop that he would offer a funeral mass for Basil. What good would that do? If he did it—and it was back to an *if* now, not a *when*—he would be doing it grudgingly, and he had always thought—and taught—that bitter offerings to God were no offerings at all. And yet, how could he go back on his word to his beloved bishop and the penance she had given him to do?

Mike reached forward and punched the buttons to play an already loaded CD, turned the volume up, and sat back to deafen himself to the rationalizations that zigzagged through his brain. He found himself suddenly bombarded with the Taizé interpretation of the *Kyrie eleison. Lord, have mercy*, it cried. *Lord, have mercy. Christ, have mercy. Lord, have mercy.*

Mike winced. He punched more buttons and eventually found U2's strains of "Window in the Skies," a song he had played over and over again. He sang along with as much vigor as he could muster, but his thoughts continued to drift. He pushed the power button into the off position, as flight attendants are wont to say, then pulled over to the side of the road and stopped. "God!" he cried. "What do you want from me?" He buried his face in his hands.

It was after dark when Mike pulled into his driveway, and he sat there with his head down over the steering wheel. *Kyrie eleison, Christe eleison, Kyrie eleison.*

.

NINE

CARLOS WALKED through the kitchen door at 1814 South Adair Street, crossed to the refrigerator and grabbed a Michelob. He took a long draft and looked around the dark house searching for— for God knew what. Cachorro, his coffee-colored Labradoodle, who had greeted him after work every day for thirteen years? But Cachorro had passed away six months ago. Laura and Rita rushing into the room to give old dad a hug? His daughters were safe at college. Ellen? Ellen—a professor of theater arts at Madison University and the only woman he had ever really loved. Whichever one of them got home first would prepare dinner for the other. Except on Fridays. On Fridays they would treat each other to dinner at the Restaurant-of-the-Week—to be determined by closing their eyes and stabbing the point of a pencil into the restaurant yellow pages. But Ellen was not here and would not be here soon. She had received a generous Fulbright grant to teach theater history for a year at the University of Helsinki. Thank God she would be home for good in a month or so. But he needed her now. God, he hated to be alone in this big house.

He took his beer and wandered into the elongated den of this ranch-style house and leaned back in his La-Z-Boy recliner. He automatically looked at the other La-Z-Boy to his left. But Ellen was not there. He winced. Although it wasn't in the least cold, Carlos thought briefly of throwing a couple of logs on the wide, stone-laid fireplace just for the comfort of a blazing fire. But he quickly abandoned that idea. So he leaned farther back in his chair and absent-mindedly flicked on his forty-two inch, high-definition television set ensconced in a full-wall, black bookcase filled with heavily read books. But he was really in no mood to watch television or read books tonight.

He had taken two or three sips of his Michelob before noticing the game of the year flickering noiselessly. He turned the volume up, and the Clemson-Carolina game from Littlejohn Coliseum blared forth in all its glory. The second half was just starting. For a quarter of an hour or so, Carlos stared into the screen. The game's energy level boosted his mettle for a moment. Lateeshe Bush, Clemson's star forward, dribbled down the court toward the goal and rushed in without opposition. And Mike lifted the ball up and easily dropped it through the basket to a quickening noise throughout the coliseum that lingered in the air for an eon. Carlos jerked to attention. *Mike*, he almost shouted. His eyes dilated. He looked at the replay again and again. Relief swept over him and a sigh gushed from his lungs. Carlos eventually comprehended that the scorer was Lateeshe—not Mike.

But Mike clung to his brain. To hell with Lateeshe Bush. It was Mike that flew back and forth in his head like a bat trapped in its own belfry. Mike was not guilty of this crime, no matter what Jerry thought. He couldn't be guilty. Mike's integrity would not allow him to be guilty.

Carlos got up to retrieve another beer. He reached back into the fridge and pulled out the pimento cheese. Old though it was, he slapped it on two slices of stale, whole-wheat bread and sat back down in his La-Z-Boy.

What if Mike had somehow discovered that Sir was his father *before* the police found the body? There's no doubt he hated the old man. His actions at the crime scene certainly bore witness to that. Beating the corpse with his fists, no less. And Mike had certainly acknowledged the fact. Suppose, when Mike found out, all the perceived wrongs came flooding back into his psyche. Perhaps the only way to kill those memories was to kill the man who created them. Uh-uh. Mike could never do that sort of thing. Not in a million years. Carlos determined to put Mike out of his mind. He couldn't stand the television anymore, so he clicked it off and went back to his sandwich and his beer.

But how could Mike have done it? He certainly knew the difference between Juice and Sir. And Mike was averse to guns. The two had talked about it numerous times. Why would he have...? Hell, he was doing it again. He almost screamed, *Mike, get outa my head!*

The telephone did scream, however. Carlos reached for the receiver and—in a fit of clumsiness not often found in this usually adroit police detective—knocked his Michelob into his lap. "Shit!" He jumped up and the amber liquid drained from his lap onto the carpet. It was all he could do to lift the phone to his ear. "Hello," he finally managed to say.

"Shit?"

"Ellen! Honey! I'm so glad it's you."

"It certainly didn't sound like it."

"Just spilled beer all over the carpet."

He could hear Ellen attempting to suppress her amusement. "What? Beer on that beautiful, antique carpet?"

Carlos understood Ellen's fabricated dismay. The old carpet had really seen its last days. Threadbare in five or six places. Other spills and abuses harkening back to the toddler days of Laura and Rita and the puppy days of Cachorro. "We've gotta get a new carpet."

"First thing when I get home."

"And when'll that be, my love?"

"I've got some good news and some bad news."

"The good news first.. I need some good news right now."

She must have felt Carlos's self-pity, because Ellen took back her bad news. "Oh, it's only good news, sweetheart."

Carlos sounded much like the first grader he had been thirty something years ago. "Tell me."

"I'm coming home earlier than we had planned."

"Yes! *¡Sí!*"

"My classes are heading to Athens on a field trip with the department head to research the ancient Greek theater. For reasons I can't get into right now, the department couldn't get it scheduled for the summer, so they're counting the field trip as their class work for the rest of the term. And I won't be needed."

"*¡Sí! ¡Sí!*"

His last three years with Ellen had been exhilarating. These had been the happiest years of his life. Yet there were the sad times. Perhaps the saddest was realizing the Church would never permit them to marry. Carlos had been a devout Catholic. When he and his wife Dorothy had divorced ten years ago, he knew that the Church would deny its blessing should he ever decide to marry again. But he had thought no more of this injunction until he met Ellen, also a devout Catholic. The two had wanted to marry, but under the circumstances decided it better to cohabit without the benefit of blessing. So they had gradually lost interest in church. That is, until Father Mike came along. He had taught them that God was a god of second chances. "*¡Ah Dios mío!*" There was Mike again penetrating his brain!

Apparently his thoughts had seeped into his further conversation, for Ellen interrupted, "Are you all right, Carlos?"

"I'm fine," he said. "Just tired."

Carlos seldom bored Ellen with his cases, but he had kept her up to date on the Sir situation. She had known Sir well at the diner, so he told her everything. But he would not tell her—yet—that Mike was a suspect.

So they talked about love and Finland and love and the university and love and coming home and love. Carlos missed her. And he would have to go to bed tonight without her.

He hung up the phone and cleaned up the mess on the floor. *But what if Mike is guilty?*

So he went to bed—early for him—and dreamed. A demonic dream. Mike and Sir. Mike was guilty. Nothing was rational. The two men flitted about like two flies at a picnic. Carlos awoke with a start. Then he drifted back into restless unconsciousness.

TEN

MIKE'S ON-AND-OFF wakefulness didn't allow him to anticipate the morning with any degree of readiness. He got up at his usual time and blended his breakfast cereal with three parts Cheerios and one part Heartland Granola. He splashed almond milk into the bowl, swallowed his hastily made coffee, and finished his breakfast in about two minutes.

It was too early to go to the station house. Carlos and Jerry would not be there until at least 8:00. The Y. Mike hadn't been to the Y in nearly a week. He threw on his jogging suit, grabbed his ready-packed backpack, charged out the front door—taking the steps in two bounds—and headed off down Pine into the unusually foggy morning.

Carlos was apparently reneging today, so Mike took to the treadmill alone. His workout was half-hearted. He couldn't get his mind off the bishop's orders. And the rhythm of his treadmill strides seemed to emit the sounds of the Taizé *Kyrie. Lord, have mercy. Christ have mercy. Lord have mercy.* The words of this ancient anthem crescendoed in his head until he could take it no longer. He turned the treadmill speed to four miles an hour—then five—then six. The faster Mike ran, the stronger the chant surged. He reached up and grabbed his temples with both hands and shouted to the far-reaches of the Y, "Stop the music!"

Amidst the wild stares of his fellow exercisers, Mike quickly pressed the stop button and was forced to hang onto the side rails with the grip of Samson to keep from tumbling onto the hard tiled floor. The whole room whirled about him. He struggled off the treadmill and fled the building. He stood on the concrete steps and hung onto the hand rail to keep his balance. Then abruptly a large hand grasped his shoulder. He froze.

"Mike! Are you okay?"

Mike was never so happy to hear someone's voice as he was to hear Carlos's voice at that moment.

"Mike?" Carlos repeated. "Come on. Let's go get into the car."

Mike sat there, the passenger's window down, inhaling deeply. "Where were you this morning?"

"I was delayed at the station house. By the time I got here, you were standing outside swaying in the wind and gasping for breath. What happened?"

"Think I just got a bit hot inside and needed some air. I'm okay now."

"You're sure?"

"I'm fine. Why don't we just go on to the station house? I need to talk to Jerry about Basil's ashes."

‡‡‡

CARLOS ACCOMPANIED Mike into the station. "Just sit here for now. I've got some police stuff to take care of. Jerry's out, but he should be back shortly." He disappeared down the corridor.

Mike hadn't sat there for more than two or three minutes when Jerry and some other officer rushed by him with a handcuffed prisoner in tow.

"Be with you in a second, Reverend," Jerry said.

"I'll be here."

A short frizzy-haired woman sat next to him with an impressively tall, pubescent boy who fidgeted incessantly. They were the only other inhabitants of the room. The exacting glare of the overhead fluorescent lights showed off the boy's acne without mercy. Mike couldn't help but wonder what trouble the boy had gotten himself into. Then he reluctantly picked up a germ-ridden, ragged, two-year-old issue of *Time* and immediately wished he hadn't. *Oh, well. The damage's been done.* He turned to the table of contents and discovered an article on "Weight Lifting: An Old Health Fad Turned New" and began searching for the page number without success. On the whim of some editor or other, *Time* had the untenable habit of refusing to number some pages, so he surrendered and picked up a copy of *People.* He learned a lot from *People*: what movie stars had recently divorced their spouses, what up and coming rock star had been publicly insulted by an American Idol judge, and what ghosts had haunted Marilyn Monroe's home after her demise. *Just what I needed to know*, he cracked to himself. *There must be a sermon in there somewhere.*

About three articles later, he heard, "Reverend!" Jerry called from down the corridor somewhere. So he threw down the *People*, wishing he had his small bottle of anti-bacterial gel to delete the magazine germs from his hands, and headed to Jerry's office.

They spoke no pleasantries. Without being asked, Mike sat down in one of the two visitors' chairs. "Do you still have Basil's ashes?"

Without looking up from his computer, Jerry pressed the intercom button. "Bobbie Jo, will you go into the evidence room and bring in Basil Richey's urn?"

"I'm going to have a funeral." Mike's terse contribution to this non-conversation caught Jerry's immediate attention.

He looked up, his eyes widened, and his brow furrowed. "What?"

"I'm going to give Basil a funeral."

"That's what I thought you said." Jerry looked Mike in the eye and turned on his obstinate personality. "The last time I heard, you wanted us to dispose of the ashes. What's this business about a funeral?"

Mike was reluctant to tell Jerry the truth. He could have made up a story, such as *I wanted to do the right thing* or *I decided to love my father after all*, but Mike had never been one to be political with his answers, so he told the truth. "My bishop ordered me to."

Jerry turned back to his computer. "Well, at least there's some discipline in your religion, Reverend." He pecked exactly three keys on the keyboard before turning back to Mike. "You never know."

The *urn*, when it came, turned out to be a perfectly cubed, six-inch cardboard box. Mike reached out for it.

Jerry grabbed the box. "Hold on there a minute, Reverend."

"What? What's the deal?"

"Two things we gotta accomplish before you can have those ashes." Jerry looked carefully at the box, like a jeweler examining a freshly cut diamond.

"What the...?"

"It's not likely you'll get these today."

"Don't play games with me, Jerry."

"Who's playing games? We have reason to believe that Basil has a widow somewhere, and she—if she exists—will have first crack at these ashes."

Mike didn't know whether to laugh or cry. He had never wanted the ashes. But now—now he wanted those ashes, and he couldn't explain why. A montage danced through his head—a montage of his bishop's voice and the words she spoke and the intensification of the *Kyrie eleison*. He wanted those ashes. He was not about to let Inez—or whoever Basil's current widow may be—get her hands on those ashes.

Mike stood and started out the door. Then he turned back. "Detective?"

"Yep?"

"I'll be back for those ashes." And Mike left the room.

ELEVEN

HIS BREAKFAST of Cheerios and granola tasted extraordinarily good this morning. Mike knew what he had to do. He had to talk to the hobes. He knew the police had already interrogated them, and he knew the police had gotten virtually nothing from them. But they trusted Mike. Perhaps they would talk to him. He threw on his jeans and Cargo jacket, kissed Annie goodbye, forewent his workout, and started walking.

For a moment, Mike remembered his bishop's advice against playing detective, and his conscience pricked briefly. But it was not like she had ordered him not to. It was not like a Godly admonition, he rationalized. He had to do it. So Mike headed toward Slocum Alley.

The alley's appearance had changed considerably. Apparently no new hobes—probably spooked by the murders—had taken up residence there. It had been torn apart by the police during the Crime Scene Investigation. They had removed everything of any significance. Only a few leftovers remained. Pine cones and dead leaves blown in by recent winds covered the ground.

He scanned the debris. Piles of broken glass, a fragment of a faded cemetery wreath, and traces of burned wood and ash—a memorial to where the hobes attempted to keep themselves warm on cold winter nights. Of course, the shiny object he had seen under the edge of Juice's body was no longer there. No cardboard boxes for tents, no crippled shopping carts, and no other signs of recent human life. Wait. There was one sign of recent human life—a scattering of used condoms, indubitably where recent secret trysts had occurred, on the ground below the brick wall of the Slocum building. Nothing worth examining.

Then a thought occurred to him. Basil's grocery cart. Where is that crippled cart—and his notebook he so scrupulously kept when he spent time in the library? Then Mike sighed. *Of course!* No self-respecting hobe would allow accoutrements such as these to remain on the sidewalk for long. Whoever found them first would immediately appropriate them as his own. He sighed again.

Mike moved back down the alleyway toward the entrance where the body had been found. Juice's body, eyes staring into outer space, haunted him. Why had the killer murdered Juice when he was really after Basil? Perhaps he had mistaken Juice for Basil. The two had had the same scruffy beard, the same round face, and the same unkempt, scraggly hair. And it was night. Or perhaps Juice had simply got in the killer's way in his attempt to get to Basil. He had to talk to the hobes.

Mike left Slocum and headed toward Bosham. He was disappointed that this alley too was devoid of hobes, but he wandered in anyway. He crossed over to the fire site, where the three hobes had always drunk their spiked, morning coffee, and wondered if they missed sharing it with Basil. There was no broken glass here, only empty bottles stacked neatly, lying on their sides in seven small pyramids. In the third stack he noticed a strange bottle—a brand he had not heard of before—so he stooped over and picked it up to examine it more closely.

Uh! He abruptly stood erect. The butt of a gun plunged into the small of his back. Mike froze. *The killer!* His fists doubled and his knuckles grew white. He was not afraid—he was angry.

"Hold it, buddy!" The killer shoved the gun deeper into his flesh.

Mike flinched but did not move. He had been through these alleys many times and had never felt threatened. More often than not, at least after his first few visits, the hobes had welcomed him with greetings of *Hello, Father* or *Hi, Padre* or something of the sort. But obviously not this time.

"Whatcha want here, buddy?" The killer snapped.

There was something in that voice. "Is that you, Marty?"

Mike felt the slackening of the piece of scrap iron that had gouged into his back and finally heard it drop to the ground.

"Father Mike!" Marty said. "Oh, Father, I didn't know it was you."

Mike turned around, and Marty stood there quivering. "I didn't know it was you, Father."

Mike put his hand on Marty's shoulder. "It's okay, Marty. No harm done."

"You didn't look like a priest."

Mike had never been to the alleys without his collar. He had wanted always to be recognized as a priest when the hobes were around. "That's okay. That's okay." He wanted to hug Marty, enfold him in his arms, and comfort him like a child. But he knew Marty would never stand for such sloppy sentimentality. "Come on. Let's sit over here." They crossed over to the concrete blocks Marty and his friends had set up as parlor chairs around the unlit fire site.

"I'm glad it was you, Father." Interestingly enough, Marty seemed eager to talk about something. He had never been the gregarious sort. Never told stories over and over like some of his buddies. Never opened his mouth unless he felt he had to.

"What can I do for you, Marty?"

Marty's eyes dampened. "We're all dying, Father."

"Dying?"

"There's a killer after us. We're dying."

As much as Mike had cared for these homeless people, people Jesus would have cared for, this was the first time it had occurred to him that his recent thoughts had been almost entirely vested in his attitude toward Basil. He had not once thought to ask about Juice's remains or his burial. These were God's children, and they were indeed dying—one by one. He was a minister of God, and he had to fight not only for his and his son's lives, but also for Marty's and Jo's and Tom-Tom's and Smiley's—and all the others who needed him.

"I'm trying to find that killer now, Marty." Two hobes had died within the past few days, and there had been other killings within the past year. "Do you mind if I ask you a few questions?"

Marty paused for a moment. Mike knew the police had already queried him repeatedly. But Marty nodded—one nod. He hoped the old man would trust him.

Mike ran his fingers through his hair and hesitated. "On the night Juice was killed, did you hear anything unusual?"

Marty said nothing, and Mike thought perhaps he had run into a stone wall. Then Marty nodded—one nod.

A sigh escaped Mike's lungs. "Did you tell this to the police?"

Marty shook his head—one shake. *No.*

Maybe Mike was on to something here. Marty had admitted that he heard something unusual, but he had not told the police.

"What did you hear?"

Marty didn't respond.

"Can you tell me what you heard?"

Marty shook his head—one shake.

"Why not?"

Marty again didn't respond.

Marty's reticence perturbed Mike, but he couldn't show it if he wanted answers. "Marty, did you see anything unusual that night?"

Marty nodded—one nod.

"Did you tell the police?"

Marty shook his head—one shake.

"Can you tell me what you saw?"

Still Marty did not respond.

Mike sighed and again ran his fingers through his hair. This was going to be a hard bone to gnaw. Marty knew something he had not told the police. But what? The code of silence, no doubt, often found among the street people. He asked a few more unproductive questions, and Mike figured he had better leave it at that for the time being. "Marty? Will there ever be a time when you would be willing to answer these questions?"

Marty started to nod but didn't finish.

Mike waited. But nothing further came. He stood up and put his hand on Marty's arm. "Thanks, Marty. This has been hard for you. God bless you." And he left Marty sitting there with his arms folded and his head down.

Mike didn't know whether he would be any more successful with the other hobes than he was with Marty, but he could try. There were other alleys he could search, but probably the best place to find hobes this time of day was the bridge. The Tyrone Street Bridge crossed the Shawnee River, more of a creek than a river really. Almost all the hobes gathered at the river daily to swap stories and to share sources of food. The hobes didn't often welcome outsiders under the bridge and certainly not the police. Intruders would hear nothing but silence. The hobes would go about their business but would say nothing until the trespasser left. But the hobes had always welcomed Mike. They looked upon him as a friend.

"Hi, Father," they said in different words and with different inflections. Even those who didn't speak beamed broken-toothed smiles.

Some lay back against the concrete bridge pilings eating bananas and apples cribbed from here and there. Others on hands and knees washed underwear in the river's edge. Still others sat in groups of twos and threes puffing on used cigarette and cigar butts and nipping from their bottles of various and sundry liquid refreshments.

Mike grinned and waved.

"Where's your collar, Father?" Jimbo hollered.

"Left it at home today, Jimbo."

Mike went over to sit on the ground by Jimbo's rock-shaped dining table, where he was eating a can of Vienna sausages he had scrounged from somewhere. He rammed his fingers into the can, grabbed a sausage, and offered it to Mike. Mike took the sausage and relished it with a Saltine cracker he picked up from Jimbo's newspaper table cloth. He had learned long ago that to refuse a hobe's hospitality was to refuse the hobe. And he couldn't take that chance.

"Thanks, Jimbo."

Jimbo nodded.

"Jimbo, I'm trying to find the guy who murdered Juice and Sir. I'm not doing this for the police. I'm not working with the police now. I'm doing it for you and me. The murderer killed twice and could easily strike again."

He repeated the plea he had made to Marty. "May I ask you a couple of questions?"

Jimbo stalled. But then he nodded.

Mike reached over and put his hand on Jimbo's shoulder. "Have you heard something among your friends here about seeing or hearing anything unusual on the night Juice was killed?"

Jimbo stalled again. His faded brown eyes widened, and Mike could have sworn he saw a moment's reflection of horror in them. But then the horror quickly disappeared. Jimbo nodded.

"Have you told the police about this?"

Jimbo shook his head.

Mike ran his fingers through his hair and silently took a deep breath. "Will you tell me what you've heard?"

The code of silence re-emerged. "Can't tell you, Father."

And again Mike was stumped. "Can you talk to me later?"

Jimbo said nothing.

"Jimbo? Maybe when we're alone?"

Jimbo looked—one by one—at the hobes around him. A moment of worry creased his forehead. Then he leaned as close to Mike as he could get. And he whispered, "Maybe."

"How about if I come see you in Masters Park? Tomorrow maybe? About this same time? Over by Dumpster three?"

Jimbo shrugged.

Mike felt like he had made some kind of breakthrough. But what? He determined to keep this appointment in hopes that Jimbo would as well. He squeezed the hobe's hand. "Thanks, Jimbo. God bless you."

He said his goodbyes to his other friends and climbed up the river bank to the sidewalk before he pulled out his vibrating phone. "We need to talk to you, Mike. Call me back." Mike waited until he had put some distance between the hobe conclave and himself before punching in Carlos's number.

"We need you back down at the station, Mike. Something important has come up. Can you make it?"

"I'll be there in half an hour."

"I'll pick you up in five minutes."

"That important, huh?"

"That important. Where are you?"

"At the bridge. Tyrone Street."

"See you." Carlos hung up. And within the five minutes, Carlos was there.

TWELVE

MIKE WALKED through the door of the station house, and Jerry called, "Come in here, Reverend." No one spoke any pleasantries. Jerry sat at the computer pounding on the keyboard with two fingers, like a couple of sledge hammers trying to break up a concrete block. "Sit down."

Mike had never been accustomed to following such terse demands, and his ego urged him to turn and leave. *Shit!* But he did sit, and Carlos stood behind him. Jerry didn't look up. He continued to pummel the keyboard. It seemed a quarter of an hour before he quit typing and stared at the monitor for what seemed another five minutes.

Then he reached into his drawer and pulled out a plastic bag that enveloped a pair of gnarled sunglasses. "Ever seen these before, Reverend?"

There they are. Mike ran his fingers through his hair and then reached for the shades. "They look like mine. What about them?"

Jerry took them back and sat for half a minute before he answered. "I'm sure they're yours. They're Polos, Reverend, and they have your prints all over them."

"What about them, Detective? What do they have to do with anything?"

"We found them under Basil's body." Jerry stared into Mike's eyes as if to let those profound words elicit some kind of soul-stirring confession from him. "How do you suppose they got there?"

"I lost those glasses several days ago. I thought Tim had borrowed them, but apparently I was wrong on that count. Maybe I lost them at the diner."

"Several days ago?" Jerry said. "Can you pinpoint the date more precisely?"

"Am I a suspect now, Detective?"

"Can you pinpoint the date, Reverend?"

"Are Basil's prints on them too?"

Jerry leered at Mike. His eyes grew thin, and he knitted his brow and growled, "Tell me, Reverend, exactly what day you lost the glasses."

Mike leaned back in his chair. Jerry was being all too irascible for his taste, but he refused to allow Jerry's temper to distress him. "I'm not certain, Detective. But I believe it was a couple of days before Sir—or Basil—disappeared. What was that—on Monday maybe?"

"You believe, huh?" Jerry replaced the sunglasses in the plastic bag.

Mike fingered his hair and stared back at Jerry. "Do I get my sunglasses back, Detective?"

"Here, have a look at this." Jerry handed Mike what appeared to be a downloaded copy of a newspaper clipping dated a couple of months ago. "Detective Ruiz found this in the archives of the *Charleston Post and Courier*. Check it out. I'm contacting the CPD now to get more details." He went back to typing.

The piece was headlined: *Local Twins Murdered*. Mike glanced up at Jerry, who gazed at the monitor, and then back again to the article. The secondary headline read: *Murderer leaves Bible quotation on bodies*.

A lump the shape of an egg wedged itself into Mike's throat. The piece continued:

A woman called 911 early yesterday morning to report finding her husband's body on the front steps of their home. According to the wife, the husband did not return home the evening before, and she had called neighbors and relatives and co-workers during the night attempting to locate him. She said she had been on her front porch shortly before 3:00 a. m., and she discovered the body around 6:00. The body had apparently been left on the front steps some time between 3:00 and 6:00 that morning.

Shortly thereafter, 911 received another call from the other side of Charleston from a woman who reported that her husband's body had also been found on the front steps of her home. Investigations revealed that the dead men were twin brothers.

Both brothers had a note in child-like handwriting attached to the bodies. It read, "The sins of the fathers."

Mike winced and looked up at Jerry.
"Go on."

It was learned later that this phrase came from a verse from the biblical book of Exodus. Authorities have yet to determine its meaning in the current context.

Mike again looked up at Jerry and then at Carlos.
"Read their names," Carlos insisted.
Jerry finally took his eyes away from the computer monitor and stared at Mike.
Mike looked back at the clipping.

The two men have been identified as Claibourne Richey of 2049 Renola Avenue and Marvin Richey of 4973 Tuttle Drive, both of Charleston.

Mike's heart stopped beating. He stared at the article for perhaps a full sixty seconds before he looked up again.

"Here, read this, Reverend." Jerry handed Mike another printout. "The obituary from the *Post and Courier* archives."

Sweat trickled from Mike's forehead like blood from a newly cut wound. He read on.

> *The brothers were the sons of the late Michael Basil Richey and Inez Claibourne Richey of 4898 Pepperdine Way, Charleston, South Carolina.*

"They're my brothers," Mike stammered. "They're my half brothers. I didn't know they existed." The horror sank into Mike's head, and his brain grew fuzzy and dim. He struggled to look up. "Yes, Inez was the name of the woman my father eloped with. She left her family—Robert Grover and their son Bobby—like Basil left my mother and me."

He abruptly stopped speaking. His eyes zeroed into nothing. Memories of his mother flurried about in his head. For twenty-three years Maria Sanchez Richey had been both mother and father to him. She—the most beautiful mother in the world—had worked as a waitress in Mexican restaurants so he could go to college. She had died shortly after he had graduated from Sewanee—from a staph infection contracted in the hospital where she had gone to be treated for a relatively minor condition.

"Mike, are you okay?" Carlos touched him gently by the shoulder.

"Oh, this…"

Carlos looked at him. "You were saying?"

Mike shook his head. His eyes returned to some semblance of normalcy, and he looked back at the obituary. He read it again. "But—But—It said the *late* Michael Basil Richey. What made them think he was dead?"

"We've done a little prying there," Jerry answered. "According to several sources we've investigated, Basil must have staged his own death. It appears that Inez, Basil's wife, had been named as beneficiary in a life insurance policy of $1,750,000. There was a great deal of circumstantial evidence that Basil had drowned in the Ashley River three years ago, but the body was never found. Apparently there's some dispute as to whether his supposed death was a suicide or not. The insurance will not pay if the death is ruled a suicide."

"Okay," Mike grunted. "And then?"

Carlos continued what Jerry had begun. "Evidently, Basil had lost his job at the College of Charleston, where he was an English professor, allegedly because of alcohol. He apparently drank more and more to the extent that he could no longer do his job, and the College dismissed him in spite of his tenure. The Charleston police had locked him up on several occasions. Within a few months he was dead, or so he led them to believe."

"The shit-ass left his other sons like he left me."

"Could it be," Carlos interjected, "that what Basil did was a last heroic effort to help his family even after he had disappeared?"

"Yeah, yeah," Mike scoffed. "I'm sure he did."

Carlos looked at Jerry. "What has CPD done about the brothers' murders?"

"They came up empty," Jerry said. "No witnesses. No prints. No real evidence of any sort discovered at the site where the bodies were found. They assume the brothers were killed elsewhere and then dumped on the doorsteps, but they've never been able to decide where. The mystery remains unsolved, of course."

"If indeed Basil's murder and his sons' murders were done by the same person," Mike said, "why do you think they were committed so far apart in time? It's been some months since the Charleston murders."

"Don't know," Jerry said. "Could be it took that long for him—or her—to track Basil down. Could be the perp was in prison on another charge during that time. Could be..."

"What is the CPD going to do now, since the bible notes suggest that the three murders are related?" Carlos asked.

"I've talked with them. Since we have the newest body, they said, they're leaving this part up to us. If we should get any meaningful leads, they'll jump in and see if they can make some connections. And then we'll all take it from there."

Then Jerry turned back to Mike. "But we digress." Jerry paused for a moment and looked Mike straight in the eye. "Reverend, let's look at something else just a minute." He reached over and grabbed Carlos's bible, found the book-marked passage, and thrust it into Mike's hands.

"I know. 'Visiting the sins of the fathers upon their children and their children's children, to the third and the fourth generation.' On Basil's children. The two men, who were killed in Charleston were Basil's children." Mike's eyes closed, and he clamped them together like a hand made into a tight fist. "Oh, God!" he prayed, and the blood drained from his face. "Oh, God!" He paused briefly. "This guy means it!"

‡‡‡

MIKE LEFT the station house running. He needed to run. He started off with a jog and graduated to full speed. He didn't know where he was going, and he didn't really care. He ran to the Y and thought about going in but passed it up and headed toward the river. He crossed the Tyrone Street Bridge, and two miles later he stopped at an old deserted church cemetery and sat down on a marble bench in front of the small funeral chapel. He needed Annie. He tried to pray but couldn't.

"Mike!"

Mike froze for a moment and the blood curdled in his veins. Then he turned. "Who invited you?"

"Mike, you've had a tough afternoon. For Jerry to hit you with the possibility—and I say possibility, not probability—that you may be a suspect in Basil's death, and then for you to learn you had two brothers who were murdered in much the same way your father died, is untenable. I ran behind you all the way here. You didn't look back. Thought maybe I could help."

"I don't need your help, Carlos. I need God's help. And God has deserted me." Mike pulled up the front of his tee shirt and mopped his face. How could his life have deteriorated so much in the past couple of weeks?

"Just thought you might need somebody to talk to."

"Wouldn't that be a conflict of interest? You're the cop, Carlos. Isn't it your duty to prove my guilt?"

Carlos sat on the opposite bench. "To hell with that, Mike. You are not guilty. And I'm your friend."

"I didn't want anybody to talk to."

"Let me tell you a story."

"I've had enough stories for one day."

But Carlos went on anyway. "I heard this story when I was a kid in catechism class, and I've never forgotten it."

Mike could do nothing but grimace.

"Once upon a time there was this eighty-year-old couple living alone in the Mississippi delta. One spring the delta had unprecedented rain, and the Mississippi and its tributaries rose and wouldn't stop rising. The water overflowed and covered the entire delta with water flooding many homes up to the eaves. Somehow this old couple managed to climb onto the roof. They were safe there, but they were also stuck there. No food, no blankets, no anything. So they decided to ask God for deliverance. After all, if God could divide the waters of the Red Sea and rescue the Israelites, he could certainly part the waters of this flood and rescue them."

Mike wiped his face again and looked up.

"After a bit, a man in a boat came along and offered them help. But they said, 'No. No. God will deliver us.' A second boat came and then a third, and the old couple responded the same way. No further boats came. It began to get dark, and the two were afraid. They called out again to God. 'God, we trusted in you, and you did not deliver us.' Then they heard a loud voice from—they knew not where. 'I sent three boats after you, and you refused to go. What else can you want of me?"

Mike didn't say anything. He just sat there staring into the wild blue of the cloudless sky.

Carlos started to get up and Mike motioned him back down.

"I'm glad you're here, Carlos. Thanks for caring."

"*Yo no podía hacer otra*—I could do no other."

"I've counseled so many people in horrific straits as a priest. I've heard confessions. I've forgiven sins in the name of God and his Church. And in many ways I've walked in their moccasins. But apparently I cannot hear my own counsel."

"Nor can any of us."

"I have been a happy man with a family and a congregation and a vigorous ministry to the homeless. Now I have no church, and I have no ministry to the street people. My father and two brothers have all been murdered, and my son and I are on some madman's hit list."

"Mike, I know how you feel."

"No, Carlos, you don't."

"Not completely, no. My life has never been threatened in the same way. My two daughters' have never been threatened in the same way. No, I cannot say I can completely empathize with you. But—let me tell you another story."

Mike bowed his head and waited for the inevitable.

"Ten years ago when Dorothy left with Laura and Rita, I thought the apocalypse had come—at least for me. I was not innocent in that breakup. I had had an affair with a young woman officer in the department. I begged Dorothy's forgiveness—a second chance. I was truly sorry—not just sorry I had been caught. But no forgiveness was forthcoming. So she ran off with a man half her age, who was twice as good looking as me, and who made double my salary. She took the girls to Montana—to Montana, for crying out loud. Out of reach of everybody else, and especially me. Although the judge had awarded us joint custody, Dorothy said she never wanted me to see them again. I could have pursued it in court, but I didn't want to drag the girls through such a nasty battle. I stayed in touch the best ways that I could, phone calls, e-mails, visits, and sent much more child support than the judge had ordered me to. My heart was broken." Carlos paused for what seemed to Mike an eon. "You know who got me straightened out?"

Mike looked up at Carlos.

"You did, Mike. Father Michael Richey. The man I trust most in this world. You taught me that God was a god of second chances. That God never gives up on God's people."

Mike said nothing.

"Of course you know what happened, Mike. When time came for the girls to go to college, Laura and Rita both chose Presbyterian College, just down the Interstate a few miles. They chose it not only because it is one of the best colleges in the nation, but also because it was home. It was near their old man. The girls had forgiven me even if Dorothy would not."

Mike dropped his head again and said nothing.

"So I know a little something about losing my family, losing my reputation, and losing my effectiveness. Let me help you, Mike. I want to find this murderer just as much as you do. Now go home and keep yourself safe. Stay healthy for Annie and Tim. Stay healthy for me. Jerry and I can't guarantee to keep you alive if you keep running around helter-skelter alone."

"I'm really glad for your happy ending, Carlos. I truly am." Mike stood and ran his fingers through his hair. "Come on. Let's jog to the rectory."

They crossed the Tyrone Street Bridge and ran passed the Y. They reached 203 Pine Street, and Mike walked up the front steps as Carlos turned to go back to the station house.

Then Mike turned back. "Carlos."

Carlos stopped.

"I'm going to find that mad man if it's the last thing I do."

THIRTEEN

TIM LAY staring at the ceiling and counting the indentions in the base of the light fixture over his bed. His whole universe had shattered before his eyes. Sir, his best hobe friend, was dead, his dad had deserted him, and his mom would not answer his questions. To top it off his parents wouldn't let him go to school or anywhere else for that matter. Nobody would tell him why. He was indeed a boy most miserable.

The day had been long for him. He turned over and closed his eyes again. Tears forced their way through the corners of his eyelids and dampened his pillow. He wanted his dad. His old dad. The dad who would take him to the diner to talk with the hobes. The dad who told him stories and played catch with him. The dad who would tuck him in at night.

But that dad seemed to be gone. His dad wouldn't even talk about Sir. Sir had always been his dad's favorite hobe, and, yet, whenever Tim would mention the old man, his dad seemed to get upset—almost angry. His lips would press together in a tight line, and he would mumble something about how awful it was but then would change the subject—quickly.

His mom was almost as bad. She just didn't understand. He guessed he had been rude. Mom had called it sullen. He had sat in the red-and-white checkered chair in the den, brought his legs up with him, and turned away from everybody. His mom came over to him—probably to scold him again.

"I'm missing school," he said. "I've got that group demo—science class—third period."

"I've made it okay with Ms. Swan," his mother said. "You can make everything up when you get back."

"But I want to do it tomorrow, when I'm supposed to."

Tim had never seen his mom sweat so much. Her forehead. And her eyes. He couldn't tell whether they were sweat drops or tear drops, and they almost made him ashamed. Yet he continued. "And the gymnastics team."

Then his mom yelled. Tim had seldom—perhaps never—heard his mother yell, and it frightened him. "I'm tired of hearing about gymnastics and Kodokan and demonstrations or whatever.

"But Mom—"

"Listen. A killer's loose. You must trust me on this. It would be very wise if you stayed here for now."

The reason didn't seem right to Tim. If the killer was after hobes, what did it have to do with him? "I'm going to my room." He leapt from the checkered chair and charged up the stairs. He stopped and gave one more glance at his mother before he went into his room. He jerked up the sheets and plunged in under the covers. He was still sobbing softly when he heard the bedroom door open. His mother whispered, "Tim." He didn't answer. Then he heard her tiptoeing into the room and felt her lips touch his cheek, but he didn't respond. The gentle steps moved quickly away, and the door closed softly. Tim lay still and eventually cried himself into a fitful sleep.

♯♯♯

TIM DIDN'T know what woke him. Something downstairs. He sat up in bed against the headboard. Voices. Dad was home. He could tell that. He heard his name—twice. Then he heard his mom say something he couldn't understand, and they lowered their voices. He heard his name again. Tim got up slowly and crept out of bed and crossed out the door and stood on the balcony above the stairs. The voices below rose. His mom and dad were arguing—apparently about him.

Tim covered his ears with his palms and shouted. "Mom! Dad!"

His mother suddenly turned and ran up the stairs. "Tim! Timmy. Timmy."

"I'm scared," he cried.

Mr. Craggles sympathized deeply with Tim, and Tim knelt down and gathered the miniature schnauzer into his arms. Mr. Craggles's kisses gathered the tears from his face.

"Come on, sweetheart. Let's go into the den." His mother held his hand tightly and led him and Mr. Craggles down the stairs.

His dad sat on the sofa, and he invited Tim to sit beside him. His mom chose the chair opposite. His dad put his arm around him and pulled him up close to his warm body. Tim felt better now. Maybe Dad would be Dad again. He prayed.

His father kissed Tim gently on the cheek. "Son, your mother and I love you very much. You know that don't you?"

Tim stiffened his back, and his eyes widened. He really didn't know how to answer, but he took the plunge. "Yes, sir."

Then it hit Tim like a bowling ball splattering against the maple-wood pins. He felt the strike in his tummy and in his heart and in his brain. The tears came and he emitted a scream that drained his soul of all stamina. The words came—words he dreaded saying. "Are you—are you and Mom getting a divorce?"

Without waiting for an answer, Tim jerked away from his dad's grasp and headed upstairs toward his bedroom, taking two steps at a time. He flung the door open and lunged onto the bed, face down between the two pillows, and keened like an Irish mother. So many of his friends had divorced parents. They had tried to act cool about it, but Tim knew how much they were hurting. He had caught his friend Jason sobbing uncontrollably in his bedroom when he had gone over for a visit. Jason quit crying and tried to pretend it was something else. But Tim knew better.

The moaning ebbed into silence, and Tim lay there still—still as a corpse. Then he felt the bed move slightly and gentle fingers against his cheek. But Tim did not move.

"Tim?" His mother's voice fell gratingly into his ears. "Sweetheart. Listen to me."

Tim still did not move.

"Dad and I are *not* getting a divorce."

His mother touched him again. This time Tim did not resist. He turned over—face up. His dad stood immediately behind his mom—some kind of smile on his lips, but it didn't look real. His mother moved closer and sat on the edge of the bed. He looked at her, and she brushed the tears from his cheeks. "No, darling. No. Far from it. Was that what you were worried about?"

"So many of my friends' parents are divorced."

"Don't worry about that at all. Dad and I love each other very, very much. We wouldn't consider such a thing."

Tim relaxed slightly. "Then what?"

His dad came around the bed and sat on the other side. He leaned over and took Tim's hand. "Son, do you remember when you got yourself into some real trouble with that bully a couple of years ago? What was his name again?"

"Glen. Glen Mables."

"Glen. Yeah," Mike agreed. "Glen was a lot bigger than you, right?"

"Uh huh." Tim frowned. Why did Dad want to change the subject? He was always changing the subject.

"Tell me what happened again."

"Do I have to?"

"No, you don't have to. But it will help me to help you understand what's going on now. How about it?"

Tim looked away. At last he squeezed his father's hand and looked back into his eyes. "Almost every day Glen would get me on the playground at recess and force me to go behind the school building. He knew I was a P. K."

"Preacher's kid, right?"

"Yeah, right."

"He would light a cigarette. He would hold the lighted end up next to my skin and tell me he would burn a hole in my arm unless I smoked with him."

"Did you smoke with him?"

"Yes sir. I didn't want to, but he made me."

"Then what happened?" Mike asked.

"You know this part, Dad."

"I know. But tell me again."

Tim sighed. He dreaded having to dredge this whole thing up again. "The teacher caught us smoking, and we both had to leave school for three days."

"What happened when you got back in school?"

"Glen lit a cigarette, but I wouldn't smoke with him. He said he'd tell the teacher I did smoke. Then he said he wouldn't tell if I would let him touch—my private parts."

"And how did we solve the problem?"

Tim lay there a long time, all sorts of queries floating around in his brain. What does this have to do with anything? Unless... Unless...? "Dad?" Tim paused. "Is somebody trying to bully you, Dad?"

His dad held his breath and then exhaled slowly. It was a long time before he said anything. "I'm afraid so, Son." His dad swallowed. "The guy who killed Juice—the guy who killed Sir. He's trying to get to me—to bully me—just like Glen tried to get to you. Right now he's in hiding. The police and I have to find him and put him in prison so he won't try to bully anyone else again. Does that make sense?"

"I guess so." Tim lowered his eyes as if he were deep in thought. Then he looked up again. "Dad?"

"What, Son?"

Tim squeezed his father's hand tighter. "But why do I have to stay home from school?" He looked down at the pillow beneath his elbow and punched a small dent into it. "Dad? What's the bully trying to get you to do?" Mike held his breath again. "I can't tell you now, Son. But I will tell you when the time is right. Will you trust me on this?"

Tim nodded and flung his arms around his father. "I love you, Dad."

"I love you too, Son."

Tim lay back on his bed, tears glistening his eyes. His mom caressed him. He felt better somehow, but he didn't know why. Then he sank his head into his pillow and closed his eyes.

FOURTEEN

"I REALLY don't want to do this," Mike said aloud to himself. He clenched his teeth, and his jaw turned to steel. He was in a grumpy mood, and he knew it. These feelings were unbecoming to a man in his best, black clerical suit. But it was no fun sleeping alone. He and Annie had decided that it would be best if she would take Tim and go to her parents' home in Sumter to get him out of the way until this whole thing blew over. So Annie had gotten a substitute to take her sixth grade class, and she and Tim had left yesterday. And he missed them—terribly.

After half an hour's drive, Mike turned onto the Interstate and headed toward Charleston. He had driven the route many times but never in such a foul mood. At the Orangeburg exit he spotted an older, black Ford Escort about three cars behind him. He made no attempt to lose the car but kept it constantly in his sight. At the Charleston city limits the car continued to follow. At the turn onto Meeting Street, the car stayed its course. At the old slave market the Escort had stopped at the traffic light a block behind him. But when he reached the Battery, the Escort had disappeared, and he heaved a sigh of relief. After a half dozen other turns he found himself on Renola Avenue and looked at the address again—2049. Basil Richey's phone on Pepperdine Way had been disconnected, the robotic telephone operator informed him, so Mike headed toward Claibourne Richey's address on Renola. *Let's see.* He was in the 800 block so he still had twelve to go. Every traffic light on the street stopped him, and his veins tensed.

The 1900 block. He slowed down, crossed Pandona, and moved slowly into the 2000 block looking at house numbers on the left side of the street. And there it was. A large cottage-style house with a well-kept lawn. Two Nissans parked in the driveway told him someone was home. Something about the house showed signs of a young couple who intended to move up in the world—not yuppyish by any means, but fresh.

Mike parked the car on the street and crossed up the walk. *I really don't want to do this.* He hesitated at the front steps. This was where they found the body. He walked up the steps to the porch and— hesitantly—rang the doorbell. Mike could not imagine what the conversation might be like when someone came to the door. His mind went through a dozen scenarios, not one of which was satisfactory. And what about the reaction to his sudden appearance? They may not even know that he existed. He could visualize a welcome with open arms—a vision he doubted—and he could visualize having the door slammed in his face—a vision he thought much more likely. It seemed forever before he heard someone stirring inside. A woman in her late twenties opened the door.

"Mrs. Richey?"

"I'm Lorraine Richey," the woman replied, carefully eying his clerical collar. "What can I do for you, Father?"

Lorraine Richey was pretty but not beautiful in the classical sense of the word. She had blond hair—perhaps enhanced a bit from a bottle—blue eyes, and sunburned skin that showed a tendency to go to the beach—or if not the beach, certainly the tanning bed—too often. She wore fresh makeup that said she had something else in mind other than conversing with a priest. Her hourglass figure would lend itself to admiration from most men—priests included.

"Mrs. Richey," he said, "my name is Michael Richey—Michael Basil Richey, Jr. May I come in?"

Silence. Lorraine's complexion rotated from sallow to bright red to a drab shade of gray. She grabbed hold of the doorknob and squeezed it until her knuckles turned white.

Mike began to fear for her safety. "Mrs. Richey? Can I help you?"

Lorraine stared at Mike for what seemed an eternity, although it was probably closer to fifteen seconds, before she said anything else.

"You look just like him," she finally said.

"Who?" Mike asked.

"You look just like—like Clay. Like Clay, my late husband. And Marvin too, of course. They're twins."

"Yes, I know," Mike replied. "I read about them in the paper."

"Yes," she said. "But that must have been two months ago. Why are you here now?"

"I didn't know until yesterday. A friend of mine was looking into the *Post and Courier*'s archives and discovered the news article about Clay's and Marvin's deaths. I need to talk with you, Mrs. Richey."

"Lorraine, please," she said. "Please, Father, come in."

"It's Mike," he corrected, and he walked into the house.

The room, a large, rectangular great-room, a sitting area at one end and a dining space at the other, opened up into a high cathedral ceiling. The drywall-mud-textured walls gave an appealing appearance to the room. Over the hefty fireplace hung Lorraine and Clay's wedding portrait. To the right, a wide hallway, whose walls displayed what appeared to be family photographs, opened into other parts of the house.

"Here, sit in this chair." Lorraine directed him to an overstuffed, easy chair with an oversized ottoman. "This was Clay's chair. I don't have but about a half hour. Judy is coming over shortly."

"Judy?"

"Judy was Marvin's wife. I'm expecting her in about a half hour. We have a hairdressing appointment to make."

This announcement put Mike on notice that Lorraine intended to keep this meeting short.

"Yes," said Mike. "Good, I would like to talk with her too."

Mike sat. Lorraine chose to settle on the matching sofa and drew her legs up into the lotus position.

On the table by Mike's chair stood a photograph of Clay Richey, probably made not long before he died. He picked it up and took a full minute to absorb it. Clay was trim like Mike. His eyes were blue like Mike's. His hair and skin were much lighter—but having been born of Anglo parents, that was understandable—yes, he and Clay did look a lot alike. He set it back on the table, but could hardly take his eyes off it during the conversation.

"I'm so sorry for your loss. I'm sorry I never knew Clay. He was my half brother, and I never knew he existed."

This was not a surprise to Lorraine. "Clay knew there was an older brother somewhere."

Mike raised his eyebrows as if to say, *Yes. Go on.*

"Clay was never able to please Basil, although he spent his entire life trying. Once, when he was small, Clay told me, he and Basil got into a big fight over something Basil perceived as not being good enough. A poor grade on a school essay, I think. *I wish you would be more like Mike!* Basil blurted out. Clay, of course, wanted to know who Mike was, and Basil was forced to admit that he had an older son. As far as I know, the subject never came up again."

Mike fingered his hair. "That puts me in a rather unflattering light for you then, doesn't it?"

"Certainly not," Lorraine answered. "In Clay's eyes, even though he didn't know you, you were the ideal, the one to emulate. So he decided to try to please Basil even harder, hoping to be like you. But he never could satisfy him."

"So, what...?"

Lorraine brushed a twig of hair out of her face before she went on. "After serving in the army for two years, Clay became a college professor like his father. He took his Ph. D. in English at Chapel Hill and taught at The Citadel for the two years before he died."

"Yes, Basil was an English professor. Did that please Basil?"

Lorraine settled back in a more comfortable position. "We'll never know. Basil lost his professorship about five years ago for drug and alcohol abuse. Oh, they said it was for incompetence or insubordination or some such claptrap. But that is so untrue. Basil was a top-notch professor. He received the Professor of the Year award twice for College of Charleston and once for the state. But his addictions grew worse and worse until the department couldn't take it anymore. So he lost his tenure, and he began to drink even more. It finally got to the point that Inez, Clay's mother, couldn't stand him being in the house. Basil left home one day about three years ago and we never saw him again. We don't really know what happened to him. One day he went fishing in the Ashley. He was really into fishing."

"Yes, I remember."

"He went out in his boat, and the next day another boater found his boat with all his fishing gear. There were three fish in the bucket and an empty fifth of Jack Daniels still in the boat. But there was no Basil. Everyone assumed he fell out of the boat and drowned. But his body was never found. But I wasn't so sure…"

Lorraine stood and looked out the window. "Oh, there's Judy now. Good. She's early. We have a few minutes before we have do go."

Lorraine went to the door and called out. "Judy, come on in. I have somebody I want you to meet." Lorraine appeared to be warming up to Mike.

"Just a minute," Judy called back. "I've got to get something out of the trunk." And a couple of moments later, "Eureka!" she shouted. But it took her a few more minutes to get to the door.

Mike used this hiatus to cross to the hallway and peruse the family pictures there. In the midst of the photos stood a tall gun case with glass doors. Mike had never had much use for guns, but the display inside the case attracted his attention. The arrangement was almost artistic. Four hunting rifles, two on each side of the safe, were attached to the back wall leaning diagonally toward the side walls. Between the rifles, in the center of the back wall, hung six Smith and Wesson revolvers positioned so that they formed a circle, almost like an elephant ring in the circus, each elephant's trunk attached to the tail of the elephant in front. A brass star hung in the center of the revolver arrangement.

"Come on in." Lorraine held the door open for Judy.

Mike turned and came back into the room.

"I've got something here for Inez. I'll just put it in the refrig—oh, my God! Marvin!" She stood agape, as if Marvin had suddenly appeared from the dead.

Mike crossed over and held out his hand. "Mike Richey, Judy. I'm Marvin's older brother."

"Oh, my God, Father. I'm so sorry. But you look so much like Marv."

"Mike, please." They touched hands.

Judy was a lot like Lorraine in some ways. After all, identical twins did pick them out. Bottled blond hair, browned skin, blue eyes, same build. But in other ways she was Lorraine's opposite: hair in a single bun neatly nestled on the top of her head, an over-abundance of makeup—reminiscent of Tammy Faye Bakker's—and a bit on the flamboyant side.

Lorraine placed Judy on the sofa next to her.

"You like Inez's gun arrangement?" Lorraine said. "That was the only thing she brought with her from her home when she moved in with Clay and me."

"I've never been very fond of guns. But I do remember that Inez used to like to hunt and shoot skeet."

"So, why are you here, Father… er…Mike?" Judy asked.

"Yesterday I read about Marvin's and Claibourne's deaths in an archived article from the *Post and Courier*. Until then, I didn't know they existed. Their last names raised some curiosity, but when I saw

Basil was their father, I knew who they were. I decided to come and offer my belated condolences in person."

Lorraine interrupted, "I'm glad you did, Mike."

She turned to Judy, "I was just telling Mike about Basil's disappearing act."

"Lorraine, sounds like you don't believe he died that day," Mike said.

Lorraine turned cardinal red. She paused as if she were unsure whether or not to go on. "It's just a hunch, really. Basil was an excellent swimmer and a very experienced boatman. All the evidence left in the boat seemed, to Clay at least, to be too perfect—so perfect, in fact, that it looked as if it were actually set up to make us believe that he was dead."

A long pause. "You're right, Lorraine. He wasn't dead."

Mike heard an audible gasp and an "Oh, my God" from Judy's direction, and Lorraine sat there with glazed eyes. She turned white. She said nothing. A moment passed—no, two moments.

"What do you mean?" Lorraine finally allowed herself to ask.

"About six months ago, Basil showed up on the street in Madison, where my parish is. No one knew it was Basil, of course. I certainly didn't know. I hadn't heard from him since I was ten years old. He eloped with Inez, and I haven't seen him since."

Another "Oh, my God" from Judy.

"I've done a lot of ministry with homeless people, and I saw him on the street several times. But I really got to know him, or at least I thought I did, when he started coming to St. Christopher's Diner. That's the soup kitchen my congregation has set up to serve the homeless. We serve a free dinner five days a week."

"He slept in the street? Oh, my God." It was Judy again.

"Anyway, I had invited him to come eat at St. Christopher's Diner, and he took me up on the invitation right away. He wouldn't tell us his name. In fact, he wouldn't speak at all, at least to us in the diner. The only word I ever heard him speak was something that sounded like *fahta*. Did he have a pronounced speech impediment?"

"Not before he died." Loraine interjected. "Or rather before he disappeared. He was a plain spoken, very articulate speaker and was in constant demand for scholarly speaking engagements all over the country and sometimes abroad."

Mike continued. "I had the feeling he had been in some kind of accident that perhaps affected his speech. He had a major scar on his lower lip and another on his right temple. The accident must have occurred after he left Charleston. But of course he never said anything about it. Anyway, I interpreted *fahta* as *father* and thought he was addressing me as a priest. But I now believe he was trying to tell me that he was my father."

"Sounds logical," Lorraine said.

"I was very fond of Sir, as we at the diner called him. In fact, I was particularly partial to him. I don't know why. I went out of my way to see that he had decent clothes and that he came to the diner every day. But I'm afraid my feelings toward him changed."

"Oh, my God." Judy was on the edge of her seat.

"I was chaplain to the police department in Madison, and I was often called when the police found a victim of a heinous crime on the street. This time it was murder."

"Oh, my God! He's dead after all. Oh, my God! But murder? Oh, my God!"

"Sir's body was found on the sidewalk steps going down to an old basement beside the Wells Fargo Bank."

"Like Clay and Marvin. They were both found on the steps." Lorraine for the first time showed some emotion.

"Oh, my God. Oh, my God! Oh, my God!"

Mike continued, "I went there to anoint the victim. I knelt down over him, placed my hands on his forehead and prayed. Then I saw something I recognized. It was a small tattoo of a mermaid on his left upper arm. In dread, I tore his shirt back on his right shoulder, and there was another mermaid on his right upper arm."

"Oh, my God."

"Yes. We've seen his tattoos," Lorraine interjected.

"That's when I knew it was Basil. And I hated him. I hated him for leaving my mother and me when I was only ten. I hated him for taking away Bobby Grover's mother—Bobby was my best friend. And I'm afraid I still hate him. I'm sorry." In the silence that followed, Lorraine hugged herself tightly with her arms and began to quiver, and Judy sat there agape, like a hyena paused in half laugh.

"But I digress. I came here for another reason as well. On Basil's body the police found a crumpled note in pseudo children's handwriting that read, *The sins of the fathers.*"

"Oh, my God!!"

"You're not toying with us, Mike?"

"The verse continued, 'The sins of the fathers shall be visited upon their children and their children's children.' Apparently the deranged killer believed that Basil had wronged him in some way, and that it was up to him to get even. We believe that the killer interpreted that Exodus passage to mean that it was somehow his sacred duty not only to kill Basil but also to kill Basil's children and Basil's grandchildren. I believe my life is in serious danger and that my son Tim's life is in serious danger."

Both Lorraine and Judy reacted as if Tim Lahaye's rapture were upon them and they had been left behind.

"Oh, my God! The police found the same kind of note on Clay and Marv."

Mike hesitated a moment. "I'm confident that that's why Clay and Marvin were killed. They were Basil's sons."

Lorraine said nothing but turned solid white, in spite of her makeup.

Before Mike could inquire as to Lorraine's well being, a sudden rustling on the stair landing distracted him.

"Hello, Mike." The woman had apparently been standing there during the entire conversation.

Mike stood. "Hello, Miss Inez."

Except for the gray hair and a few wrinkles, Inez looked much the same as when Mike last saw her. She held herself straight and erect like a proud giraffe. Even though she braced herself with a cane, she appeared to Mike to be a strong and agile woman, strong and agile enough to wield a gun handily. It crossed Mike's mind that the cane may very well be for show rather than need.

Then he thought back to the business at hand. Perhaps since she had been deprived of nearly two million in insurance money upon Basil's first death, she could have decided, when she finally located him in Madison, to solve the problem by personally assigning him to the second death—making it appear as if another hobe had gotten enough of him and did him in.

"Pretty as ever, Miss Inez."

"Cut the bullshit, Mike. I was afraid you would show up one day." She started down the stairs with the aid of her chic, ebony cane.

"May I inquire about Bobby, Miss Inez?"

"Bobby?" She acted for a moment as if she had never heard the name before. "Of course, you may inquire." Inez crossed over and made herself comfortable alongside Lorraine, who had re-acquired some of her color. "Bobby."

"Your son, Bobby." Out of the corner of his eye, Mike caught Lorraine and Judy trading rolled eye glances.

"I've not heard from Bobby for awhile."

It appeared to Mike that Inez was evading the question.

She changed the subject. "I see that you've become—a man of the cloth, as they say."

"Indeed I have, as they—say."

"Come. Sit, sit, sit, sit, sit," Inez gave the order as if she might have been clicking her tongue in either disgust or dismay. Mike couldn't really tell which, but he obeyed.

"I see you've come to tell us about Basil."

"Oh, my God! You knew about Basil? Oh, my God!" It was Judy, of course.

Mike looked askance at Inez.

"Oh, oh, oh, oh, oh," she rattled off. "I've startled you." She looked directly at Mike. "You'll have to forgive me, Father. I'm afraid I've sinned."

Now it was time for Lorraine and Judy to look askance at Inez.

"I'm afraid I was eavesdropping from the top of the stairs. Forgive me, Father. Now tell us all about Basil."

Mike started at the beginning and told Inez everything. She interrupted from time to time with the clicking tongue and a *how sad* and a frown or two, but she never seemed surprised or troubled or touched. And she closed her eyes from time to time. Mike thought perhaps she was going to yawn, but she never did. When he finally finished, Inez sat there staring at him as if he were something to be exorcised.

"Miss Inez?"

"Just Inez'll do."

"Inez?" Mike paused for a moment. "Inez, Basil's ashes are still in police custody. When the police release them, I'll deliver them to you for burial or inurnment."

Inez stood and Mike stood with her. She caned herself over to the foot of the stairs as three sets of eyes followed her step by step. On the stair landing, she turned and glowered at Mike. "You can keep his goddamned ashes." At that she turned and climbed the stairs and disappeared behind a closed door.

Mike turned and crossed to the two women. "Well, I believe I've outstayed my welcome."

"Oh, my God, Mike."

"I'm sorry, Mike," Lorraine said. "She's been on a somewhat understated rampage, particularly since she retired from MAVIS. That's the company here in Charleston that makes those upscale tires—for BMW and Mercedes Benz, you know. She was an office manager there for over twenty years. But when all this stuff came up with Basil, she retired—and not entirely on amicable terms."

Mike's lips pressed together into a thin line.

"Oh, my God, Mike. Inez really is not as bad as she sounds. Don't worry about Inez. She's really been like that since day one," Judy managed to say.

Mike crossed to the door and then turned back. "Nevertheless, I need to be going. I'm afraid I've made you miss your hair appointments."

The two women followed him to the door protesting his apology. "Don't worry about that, Mike, "Lorraine said. "We've missed appointments before for far inferior reasons."

They stepped outside.

"I thought you may like to know." Mike hesitated a moment. "Since Inez has refused the ashes, as soon as I get them from the cops, I'll be celebrating a requiem eucharist at St. Christopher's. I'll let you know." He opened the Camry door and started to get in.

Lorraine stopped him." Mike, just for the record, Bobby has been in a mental institution for the past three years."

Mike turned to her, "I'm really not surprised."

He handed the women each a card. "If either of you needs to get in touch with me, please—give me a call." He started to shake hands, but each woman reached up and hugged him with feeling. He got into the Camry and lowered his window to say his last goodbyes.

Lorraine put both her hands on the window base and said, "Father, pray for us."

"Of course. And you for me."

"Mike," Lorraine whispered. "I'm afraid my life may also be in danger."

Mike looked up at her.

"I'm pregnant," she said.

FIFTEEN

A BLAST of ice-cold air hit Mike full in the face the moment he opened the door at Sarah's Cafe. Sarah's was the coldest eating joint in town, and it often took Mike the first quarter of an hour to adjust his internal thermostat. He had once asked Sarah about the indoor climate, and she had told him that Toby, the short-order cook, couldn't, unlike Harry Truman, take the heat of the kitchen and needed the AC to fry the hamburgers to perfection. Toby created the best hamburgers in town, and he didn't want to upset the cook, so Mike never mentioned the discomfort again. He just swore he would wear his overcoat the next time he came to Sarah's, but he never did.

The small cafe had four tables against one wall and three against the other. But most folks liked to sit on round swivel stools at the counter, where they could watch Toby finesse the sandwiches together almost as if he were singing in sign language. Toby kneaded chopped onions into his ball-like hamburger patties and stacked them in pyramids beside the grill. He carved his sugar-cured ham on a per-need basis from a large, roasted ham-bone and laid the slices gracefully on the grilled sourdough bread. He sliced comely slivers from a hoop of extra-sharp cheddar and slipped them neatly between the buns like a sleeping baby between its flannel blankets. Mike viewed Toby's work as a real art form.

Sarah herself—proprietor, manager, cashier, and waitress—stood at Carlos's table ready to take the order. The moment she spied Mike, she hollered out to Toby, "Ham and hoop with onions and pickles and a side of cole slaw!"

Mike grinned. Somehow Sarah knew what he was going to order, even before he did. Or maybe she just placed an order and Mike accepted it without question. He really didn't know. Neither did he care, because he did know that she served the best ham and cheddar in three counties. Mike nodded, and Sarah Edith-Bunkered her way into the kitchen.

Mike sauntered over to Carlos. "Must be off duty." Carlos had already ordered a Heineken for Mike and a Michelob for himself.

"Sometimes I get that way."

Mike sat and they nursed their beers and ate the free tabletop peanuts for the next few minutes without saying much of any significance. The food came in record time. Carlos had ordered a fully loaded cheeseburger—with the hoop cheese and the sweet-potato fries. They mumbled something about how great the food smelled and how wonderful Sarah was, comments that drew broad grins from the owner-server, and then she departed to wait on customers at the counter.

"As much as I enjoy the fellowship of your company and the pleasure of the beer brigade," Carlos finally said, "you must have wanted to talk with me about something. Would it be out of line to ask what?"

Mike cleared his throat and recounted to Carlos the strange events of the past few hours, his meeting his sisters-in-law, the conversation with Inez—*Inez didn't want the goddamned ashes*—and Lorraine's pregnancy. Another task for the police?

Carlos knitted his brow. His eyes stared directly into Mike's. It was apparently the pregnancy that alarmed Carlos most. "Does anyone else know about it?"

"What? The pregnancy? She says not. Judy, her sister-in-law, of course, knows. She was standing there when Lorraine made the confession." Mike took another sip of beer.

"More important, does Inez know?"

"Lorraine says not. But I wouldn't put it past Inez to know everything."

"Does Inez live in the house with Lorraine?"

"Yes."

"Inez must never know about the pregnancy—at least, not yet."

"Could Inez be a suspect then?"

"Let's just say—a person of interest. According to what you've told me, Inez had motive and possibly opportunity. According to Basil's policy, Inez stood to receive half the money and the rest would be divided among Basil's sons."

"What?"

Carlos allowed that statement to rest for a moment. He dabbled with his sandwich for just a moment before he raised his head and looked Mike in the eyes. "That includes you, Mike."

Mike quickly closed his eyes and pressed his lips together in a taut line. He sighed and looked at Carlos again. "Another reason for Jerry to think I'm guilty."

Carlos let that remark go. "She did not get the insurance money the first time around, because there was suspicion of suicide. But now there is no suspicion of suicide. If she got Basil out of the way, and if she got you and Tim out of the way, under the pretense of being murdered by a crazed maniac, she possibly could—and I say *could*—have reason to make another claim on that insurance." He took a sip of his beer and looked back at Mike. "Perhaps—in her mind, at least—she would be able to collect the entire amount for herself."

Mike said nothing, but he raised his eyebrows into two solid arches.

"That's $1,750,000, Mike. That's an odd amount. But apparently the old man was making it easy to divide. Half to Inez and a quarter of a mil for each of the tree sons."

"Hmmm." Mike had completely forgotten his ham and cheddar. "But would she want to kill her own twin sons for an extra three quarters of a million?"

"Don't know, Mike. And we don't know yet where she's been over the past few weeks. That's something we'll have to find out."

"I'll go back and talk to her."

"Not you, Mike."

"What?"

"The police. *Eso no es su trabajo.* That's not your job. In fact, nothing of this is your job."

Mike clenched his teeth but said nothing more.

"We can't—the MPD can't—do anything in Charleston. Out of our jurisdiction. But we're in constant touch with the CPD, and they're going to be more than willing to follow through. They have a stake in this too, you know."

With a scant good-bye, Mike left Sarah's and walked to the rectory for another night of restless sleep.

SIXTEEN

JERRY LURCHED into the Bridgewater Church parking lot like a teenager at the wheel for the first time. In spite of the fact that he was late for Wednesday-evening prayer meeting, he didn't go in immediately. He sat there gazing into the center of the steering wheel with thoughts from the last couple of days crisscrossing his gray cells like aquarium fish, flitting from side to side. The reverend was there. Basil was there. The lady from Charleston was there. He was there. And none of them knew exactly where they were going or why they were going there. The reverend was guilty. No doubt about that. Well, almost no doubt. He didn't have any real evidence—except the sunglasses, of course, and the reverend's beneficiary status—to support his theory. But his hunches almost never lied. All he needed was to find some corroborating evidence. And he *would* do that.

It was almost as if he *wanted* the reverend to be guilty. And yet— no, he didn't. The reverend might be an egotistical semi-pagan, but he was a good friend of Carlos's. And, come to think of it, he had done a pretty good job as chaplain for the men and women on the force. And he really did have a likable personality, if you could get used to it. He guessed he really didn't want him to be guilty. And yet— His stomach brewed acid. He swallowed a couple of Gas-X pills from his stash in the glove compartment.

Jerry clutched the steering wheel so tightly the blood seeped out of his knuckles like the dye in a red shirt soaking in a tub of bleach water. Then he looked up through the windshield and, through the suddenly foggy evening, saw the front façade of the church, a view he had admired many times over. It was a beautiful brick structure with a portico that sported six Georgian columns to support a colossal brick and plaster canopy that over-spread the portico. The sight took the aquarium right out of his mind. This was the way a church was supposed to look.

He looked farther up above the canopy and there stood the steeple—he and Maureen had contributed over five thousand dollars to help build that steeple—with the cross on top. When he looked at it, it took his spirit into the highest heaven, and he liked that feeling. He certainly liked it now, because it made him forget Basil and the reverend and all those other cases he was into.

He looked at his watch—*the time*—*the time*—and abruptly jumped out of the Crown Vic and charged up the steps to the portico, through the gigantic doorway, and into the sanctuary. The preacher was in the midst of reading aloud from the tenth chapter of Matthew in the King James Version.

> *Think not that I am come to send peace on earth. I came not to send peace, but a sword. For I am come to set a man at variance against his father, and the daughter against her mother, and the daughter in law against her mother in law. And a man's foes shall be they of his own household.*

"Je-e-e-sus"—Brother Sam had the habit of stretching out the first syllable—"did not come to bring peace but a sword." The preacher's voice rose in both intensity and volume. Several *amens* rang forth from the congregation. "A sword, I say. In today's terms that would mean a gun. Je-e-e-sus's disciples carried swords. Did you know that?"

Some in the congregation grunted.

"Yes. You remember the Apostle Peter in the Garden of Gethsemane? You remember he pulled out his sword and *shot* off the man's ear." The preacher belted out a boisterous laugh that made even Jerry's blood run cold. But several in the congregation joined in the laughter, whether or not they got the gag.

Jerry looked around before he took his seat. He couldn't see Maureen anywhere. The kids would be in their separate small-group meetings. Mack and Sissy, the fourteen-year-old twins would be with the teenagers' group. Maybe she had to see to Jack, the toddler in the family, to make sure he was properly situated. She would be back in the sanctuary in a minute or so. He sat in the back pew to wait for her.

Somehow or other he wasn't into listening to the preacher tonight. Brother Sam grew louder and louder and congregational *amens* followed suit. But Jerry's thoughts buried themselves deeper and deeper into the reverend's presumed guilt. He admitted that the sunglasses idea was weak. But, if they were indeed the reverend's, how did they get buried under Basil's body. The shot was at close range, so the reverend apparently lay in wait for the right moment. During the commotion, he lost his sunglasses, and Basil's body fell on them. And then there was that insurance policy. *I've got to find more evidence.*

"But Je-e-e-sus!" Brother Sam shouted. "Je-e-e-sus would have done it that way."

As if the preacher knew exactly how Jesus would have done it. Jerry caught himself being a bit skeptical of Brother Sam's thinking.

"He…"

Jerry's cell phone vibrated. Maureen. He went out into the vestibule and answered. "Hey. Where are you?"

"Ya gotta come, Jerry. Mack's been in a bad accident. We're at the ER at Madison Memorial. Come quick."

"Be there!" He shoved the phone back into his pocket, and with yard-long running strides he was back in the Crown Vic, blue lights flashing and siren blasting, accelerating toward Madison Memorial. He hadn't bothered to ask what, how, or when. That would deprive his journey-time of excruciatingly important minutes.

Mack was Jerry and Maureen's first born—his sister, Sissy, coming fifteen minutes later. The twins had been born two months premature, and both had to be kept in the hospital under close supervision. But when Sissy came home, Mack—he had been named after Douglas MacArthur, Jerry's favorite general—had to stay. His lungs were not fully developed, and he had to have breathing assistance for three weeks. Jerry had been eminently happy to have him home. Mack had become Jerry's favorite, although he genuinely tried not to show it.

He had never been a strong boy—good looking, yes; strong, no. The doctors had discovered that Mack suffered from a mild version of hypertrophic cardiomyopathy, a disease of the heart in which a portion of the myocardium, the muscular substance of the heart, is thickened without any obvious cause. This disease is perhaps best known as a leading cause of sudden cardiac death in young athletes. The doctors had been able to keep the HCM under control with a beta blocker, and Mack could live a relatively normal life. Except for one thing—he would never be able to play competitive sports. This pronouncement took Jerry for a psychological concussion. He had always wanted a football player like himself.

Jerry had eventually taken this blow in his stride. So he taught Mack to shoot, to hunt, and to fight—to defend himself, of course, from bullies he knew were there and ready to strike out at the weak kids. He would have to wait for Jack if he was to have his football player.

He surged into the ER parking lot and within seconds he had found his way to Maureen with Sissy and Jack sitting in the surgery waiting room. The moment he touched Maureen, she buried her face in his shoulder and sobbed.

"What? Tell me!" Jerry demanded.

"Mack shot himself."

SEVENTEEN

C ARLOS JERKED awake. He heard a piercing scream that eventually evolved into the shattering ring of the telephone. He rolled over quickly to grab the receiver, and it slipped from his hand like an oversized ice cube. *Shit!* He jumped out of bed like it was afire and retrieved the phone.

"Hello." Carlos tried to sound chipper but, unfortunately, did not.

"Carlos?" Jerry seldom called him by his first name. MPD protocol expected all members of the force to address each other by title, especially on duty.

"Hi, Jerry. What's up?"

"Detective?" Jerry switched back to police formality. "I'm at the hospital—Madison Memorial—and I need you."

"Certainly Chief. Give me thirty minutes for a shave and shower, and I'll be right there."

"I'll meet you on the fourth floor, B Wing nurses' station."

B Wing catered to ICU patients. Carlos and Jerry had visited B Wing on numerous occasions during police investigations. But Jerry's use of *Carlos* said that the call might be of a personal nature. "What's wrong, Chief."

A long pause on Jerry's end of the line. "My son, Mack, had an accident."

Carlos glanced at his watch. Half-past five. Not light yet. "I'll be there in fifteen minutes."

Carlos neither shaved nor showered. He dressed quickly, his tie askew, and charged out to the Crown Victoria and headed toward the hospital. Carlos was relieved that he would not be going to the Y today. Mike had virtually quit the Y since his troubles started. Working out was not a great deal of fun without Mike.

Madison Memorial appeared through his windshield in exactly fourteen minutes, and he found Jerry at the nurses' station. The man looked as if he had been run over by a Caterpillar backhoe. "You okay?"

"Detective, you're out of regulation dress."

"What?"

"The face. The face!"

"Yep. The beard. I got here as quickly as I could. Couldn't work in the razor."

Jerry did not follow through on this line of verbal discipline. The two men walked to the waiting room without further conversation. Jerry clicked off the blaring television set in the empty room and the two sat across from each other. "Mack shot himself last night."

"What?" Carlos pressed his lips together in a tight line.

"In the head. It's a miracle he's still alive. Doctors don't give him much hope."

Carlos sat there, his hands holding up his face. He didn't know what to say. He didn't know what to do. In his capacity as a police officer and a police detective, he had often had to face the families of those who had attempted suicide, and he had handled the situations very well. Now here he was with his superior officer—yes, and someone he cared about—with nothing to say. He reached over and placed his hand gently on Jerry's arm. With the exception of handshakes, this was probably the first time he had ever touched Jerry.

Then he looked into Jerry's eyes. "I'm so sorry, Jerry." To hell with police formalities now. "I'm so terribly sorry." He said nothing else for half a minute. "What can be done for him now?"

"Mack was in surgery almost all night. He's in a coma now. It could go either way. The doctors say that if he comes out of the coma within the next week or so, he has a much greater chance of survival. The prognosis will be a lot better."

Then, probably for the first time since Jerry was a kid, Carlos thought, tears seeped from his eyes. Jerry wiped them away as quickly as they came. "He didn't have to do this, you know."

Carlos sat up. Jerry had seldom mentioned his personal life. When he and Dorothy were together, the two couples had occasionally joined each other for a cookout. Dorothy had never liked Jerry and Maureen. They were beneath her perceived social status. But she reluctantly went along with the cookouts.

But Jerry was talkative this morning. "I tried very hard to be a good father to Mack, because mine was not—to me." Jerry talked about his childhood and his abusive father, a topic, Carlos thought, he probably had told no one until this moment.

The similarities between Jerry and Mike did not escape Carlos.

"Mack has never been a strong child," Jerry continued. "He was born with a congenital heart disease."

Something else Carlos had not known.

"Bullies at school constantly ragged him for not playing sports— they called him *sissy* and physically tormented him. I taught him how to fight so he could defend himself. I didn't realize life had become so unbearable for him." Jerry teared up again.

"Has Brother Argyle been to see you? You know, prayer can do a lot of healing and provide a lot of comfort."

Carlos really didn't have much faith in Brother Argyle. He remembered once, years ago, not long after Dorothy had left, going with Jerry and Maureen to their church. When they drove up to the church, the marquee read in gargantuan block letters, *THE KING JAMES BIBLE IS THE WORD OF GOD*. Not knowing much about either King James or the bible, he couldn't make much sense of the sign. He made a mental note to ask Jerry about this later.

The preacher's sermon had been oddly interesting that day. He titled it *Be Prepared*. Carlos at first thought the preacher was going to discuss the Boy Scouts, but he managed to talk about wise and foolish virgins. The wise had been prepared, and the foolish had been unprepared. How this sermon got turned into a political diatribe supporting a new state legislative bill to authorize teachers and administrators to carry guns in the public schools, he did not know. This was all from the bible—the twenty-fifth chapter of Matthew, he believed it was—the preacher assured the congregation.

As a police officer and an agent of the city of Madison, it was necessary for him to wear a gun. But he agreed with the Police Association's position that the general public carrying firearms was asking for major trouble.

But Brother Argyle was Jerry and Maureen's pastor, and he certainly could pray.

"Brother Sam?" Jerry said. "Yep. Been here all night with us. But…"

"But what?"

"I'll tell you 'but what!'" Maureen burst into the room. She looked no better than Jerry. Tears streaked her face, and her grayish black hair looked like she had been trying for an Afro but failed.

"What's going on?" Jerry said.

Maureen sat down in the chair across the coffee table from Jerry. "Nurses came in and ran me out. They're in there doing whatever nurses do."

Carlos wondered if they would ever get back to Brother Sam again. But to Carlos's surprise, Maureen jumped right back on it, as if she had hoarded her emotions until she could amass no more.

"Brother Sam is a good man," Maureen said. "He prayed with us all night. He prayed for Mack, and he prayed for us. We appreciated that. But before he left, he said something that crushed us."

Maureen sobbed loudly enough to be heard all the way to the nurses' station, for a moment later a nurse stuck her head in the door to see if she could be of any help. Jerry assured her they were fine and moved over behind Maureen. He put his arms around her and kissed her. Carlos raised his eyebrows. He had never seen Jerry show any affection for Maureen.

Jerry looked straight at Carlos. "The preacher left us some parting words of—wisdom."

Carlos detected the sarcasm in Jerry's voice. So he waited. But it seemed forever before Jerry went on.

"He said, 'You'd better pray real hard for Mack to open his eyes. Because if he dies, he'll go straight to hell.'"

Carlos understood immediately what the preacher had said. He had been taught the same thing as a child. Suicide is a mortal sin. When people take their own lives, they have no time to repent. And any unrepented mortal sin would send the soul to hell. He had asked Mike about that once. And Mike had said that God was big enough to see the entire picture and to understand the physical and psychological problems that led up to the terrible act. That God loved enough to fold his arms around both the victim and those who love the victim. That God was merciful enough to forgive every sin—even those committed by someone who did not have the mental or physical ability to repent. Carlos shared Mike's answer with Jerry and Maureen, but neither of them appeared impressed.

A long silence ensued before Jerry stood up. "Detective!" He was back to the formality again.

Carlos reacted professionally and stood up to face the chief.

"Detective Ruiz, I did not ask you here to feed me the reverend's poppycock theology. I asked you to come here because I have a special assignment for you."

"Yes, Chief?" Carlos waited.

"It's obvious I'm going to be tied up for a few days. I am officially putting you in charge of the Detective Division of the Madison Police Department until I am able to return."

Carlos nodded.

"And I will be the sole determiner of when I am able to return. Is that clear, Detective?"

"Yes, Chief."

"You are dismissed, Detective."

Carlos raised his hand in salute. "Thank you, Sir." He turned and crossed to the exit door.

"Detective," Jerry called.

Carlos turned back. "Chief?" He looked closely at Jerry and thought he detected the minutest of smiles on Jerry's face.

"Get rid of that god-awful beard, Detective."

"Thought I was in charge now, Chief."

"God be with you, Carlos."

"And with you too, Jerry."

Carlos, weighted down by a heavy heart, left the hospital determined to make Jerry proud and exercise his new role with as much aplomb as he could muster.

‡‡‡

CARLOS HAD some thinking to do and walked into St. Christopher's. He was not alone. Others had their burdens too. He knelt in the fourth pew and gazed steadily at the altar cross. So many questions inundated his mind. Laura and Rita. What would it be like to lose his children? What if they were in an automobile accident? What if they lay in a hospital bed in a deep coma? And, God forbid, what if they had done what Mack had? The more he thought, the deeper he sank into the Slough of Despond. He crossed himself. He prayed for Mack, for Jerry and Maureen, and for Sissy and Jack. And then he prayed for his daughters.

Carlos left the church and steered the Crown Vic out Highway 18 and two Interstates and eventually found himself at Exit 2. He pulled into the Belk Hall parking lot and called the girls' room. Rita was down in two minutes to let him into the dorm. Carlos held her as if it were the last time he would ever see her. The happy chitchat up the stairs to the third floor lifted him immediately out of the Slough.

They arrived at Room 306, and Rita stopped. "Dad, before you go in, I've got to tell you something."

Carlos's eyes widened. "Uh-oh." It could be anything from the horror of a messy room to something like Laura's got a broken leg.

Before either of them could speak further, the room door opened. "Well! If it isn't the Mexican ladies' man!"

"Mom!" Laura shouted from inside. "You promised to be good."

"Dorothy. What in the hell are you doing here?"

"I've come to see my daughters, if it's all right with you. And what might the fuc—"

"Quit it, Mom."

"And what might the fornicating Mexican, who thinks he's God's gift to women, be here for?"

"Mom!" The two girls shouted in unison.

"That's enough," Rita added.

"Come on in, Dad," Laura said.

And together the girls ushered him into the room.

"I think maybe I should come back another time," Carlos suggested.

"Don't be silly," Laura said.

"Stunning room you've got here." He hoped his admiration of his daughters' dorm-room décor would suddenly make Dorothy disappear. He had moved them into the room at the beginning of the term. He had accompanied them to the Hospice Thrift Store, where they chose everything the room demanded—carpet, paint, curtains, furnishings, a small refrigerator. And in a Cinderella-style miracle, he instantly became chief carpenter and gofer for the duration. When they were finished, the room was fit for a two-page display in *Southern Living*.

"Hey, what else have you done with the closet? Looks good."

But Carlos was called back to reality when Dorothy broke into his head. "You still running around with that little slut, or have you found another one?"

Dorothy was well aware of Carlos's current status. She would have pumped the girls until they told her everything. He sat on the chair arm and tried to pull himself together. "Dorothy," he said, quietly and without a trace of rancor, "her name is Ellen. She is not a slut. And we love each other."

After Mario the tennis pro left her six months after their elopement, Dorothy had stayed in Montana to keep the girls away from Carlos. Rita and Laura had come to Presbyterian College, against the exorbitant protests of their mother. Dorothy had recently followed the girls back to South Carolina, he supposed, to make sure the girls didn't get too close to him.

His ire ignited. "And I might add that my love for Ellen exceeds any love that I have ever had for anyone—except for Rita and Laura."

"Don't you dare bring the girls into this sordid little conversation."

"You know, Dorothy." His choler rose. "The only good thing you ever did in this world was to bring my daughters into it."

Dorothy stood, and without further word she crossed over to Carlos and slapped him in the face. Carlos flinched. He had a momentary urge to respond in kind, but Carlos had never been a man of violence, and he wasn't going to become one now. Instead, he reached up and touched his stinging cheek but said nothing.

"I'm leaving this room, Carlos Ruiz. And when I return, I expect you to be in Madison, South Carolina, catching the crooks under all the bushes—or whatever it is you do there." Dorothy grabbed her purse, strutted from the room in righteous indignation, and slammed the door behind her.

The moment trembled like an electric shock. The girls, stunned by their mother's behavior, sat agape. Then Rita suddenly took off to the bathroom and lost her breakfast, and Laura followed to empathize. Carlos sat there watching the black holes in outer space, wondering what had just occurred. He walked over to the bathroom door and knocked. "Rita, are you okay?"

"We'll be out in a minute, Dad," Laura called back.

Carlos sat and contemplated the Bono poster that hung on the opposite wall.

The girls eventually emerged from the bathroom, a damp washcloth plastered on Rita's face, and crossed over to their father. "Dad?"

Carlos took both girls by the hands and gently squeezed. "I'm sorry. I'm so terribly sorry you had to witness that little exhibition. I shouldn't have barged in on you like this. I didn't know your mother would be here."

"Neither did we," Laura said.

Rita continued, "She was waiting for us in the dining hall when we went down for breakfast this morning."

"Believe us, Dad," Laura said. "She's never like this when we're alone with her."

"I know. I'm afraid I have a tendency to bring out the worst in your mother. I'm sorry."

Trying to extricate himself from the recent scene, Carlos turned to Rita. "You have any need to replenish your breakfast?"

Rita grinned, her recent upchuck forgotten. "Sure. Let's go to Whiteford's."

"Oh, Rita. No. Señor García." The two restaurants bounced back and forth in the conversation like a ping-pong ball. But after further negotiations, Laura deferred to her sister. So she nodded, "Okay."

"Whiteford's it is, then." Carlos thought for a moment. "But what about your mother? What if she comes back while we're gone?"

"Nah. She won't be back for two or three hours. She's gone to Wal-Mart," Rita inserted.

"Wal-Mart? Didn't think your mother ever went to Wal-Mart. Thought she was the Neiman Marcus type."

Laura rolled her eyes. "Dad. She was. Is, I guess. But her financial situation isn't the best right now."

"She goes to Wal-Mart to pray," Rita interjected.

"Pray? Thought she'd quit praying a long time ago. What does she pray for?"

Rita's imitation of her mother was right on the money: "Oh, Lord," she wailed. "Please don't let me die in Wal-Mart."

Carlos laughed—the best laugh he'd had in weeks. "Then let's go."

The three grabbed their cheeseburgers and sat at a table next to the window overlooking Broad Street. The girls talked and Carlos listened. They talked of biology grades, tennis wins, and Alpha Delta Pi. Perhaps a superficial conversation to an eavesdropper, but Carlos genuinely interested himself in the girls—their work and their play. He tried very hard to be a good father.

It was Rita who changed the subject. "Dad, just out of curiosity, why did you pop in today? You've never come without calling ahead."

"Don't get us wrong," Laura said. "We're glad you did, even if you and Mom did have a real blowout."

But your mother started it, the child in Carlos wanted to say but fortunately refrained.

"Dad?" Rita prompted.

Carlos took several bites before he responded. "I know this will sound mushy to you," he began. "Believe it or not, I just needed to see you and feel your hugs and know first hand that you're okay."

The girls looked at each other, the puzzlement obvious in their faces. Then they returned to their dad. "What?"

Carlos told them about Mack. And about Jerry and Maureen. "I would rather die than for anything to happen to either one of you." He swallowed and paused briefly. "Come on. Let's get you back to Belk Hall before your mother returns."

After the brief goodbyes, Carlos headed back toward Madison to catch the crooks under all the bushes—or whatever he did there.

✝✝✝

CARLOS ENTERED Madison singing to himself. He had seen his daughters. They were okay—in spite of their having to deal with Dorothy. Carlos was happy.

He drove up Church Street toward the Bridge and passed Slocum and Bosham and Perin. And was he crazy? He thought he had heard a shot. He pulled over, drew his gun, and ran up Massey Alley. He stopped—dead still. He held his free hand over his eyes to shield them from the brilliant afternoon sun. The silhouette of a lone figure slumped against the side of the Massey Insurance Building. Carlos's blood ran cold. He moved slowly toward Mike—slumped over, face between his knees, sobbing uncontrollably. A small Saturday Night Special dangled from Mike's hand.

Carlos shoved the gun back into its holster and quickly pulled on his plastic gloves. He moved closer. "Hand me the gun, Mike."

Mike didn't look up but held his hand out for Carlos to take the gun.

Carlos examined the gun carefully, and then placed it in a Zip-Lock evidence bag he pulled out of his jacket pocket. "What is this all about, Mike?"

Mike nodded to the far corner of the alley. Carlos rushed over, and there, with blood covering his Tommy Hilfiger shirt, lay Smiley, the hobe who constantly smiled and who always dressed for his audiences. He had served Smiley numerous times at the diner and had grown to love him. The people at the diner had become family for Carlos over the months he and Ellen had volunteered there. A tear emerged from his eye. He knelt down over the body and checked Smiley for any signs of life—nothing. He called in the Crime Scene Investigators and returned to Mike.

Carlos knelt down beside the priest. "Mike?"

Mike said nothing.

"Talk to me, Mike."

Mike said nothing.

"Pull yourself together, Mike. You've got to go with me down to the station house. You know that, don't you?" Carlos's heart sank. He snapped the cuffs on his old friend and lead him to the Crown Vic. Carlos gave the CSI instructions, when they arrived, and got behind the steering wheel and headed down Church.

The two friends faced each other across Carlos's desk. This was the hardest thing Carlos had ever had to do. He sat there looking at Mike and said nothing.

Mike finally broke the silence. He looked up and held his hands up to Carlos. "Do I really have to wear these things, Carlos?"

Carlos said nothing for a long time. "You're not going to try to get away are you, Mike? You know you'll be stopped before you hit the front door."

"You know me, Carlos."

Carlos came around the desk and unlocked the cuffs and sat on the corner of his desk. "Now tell me your story."

Mike, with no reluctance, looked Carlos straight in the eye. "I was going from alley to alley trying to talk to as many hobes as possible. Most of them trust me. I was trying to find out if any of them had heard or seen anything unusual on the night Juice was murdered. I found no one at the first three alleys, but then I spotted Smiley in Massey and went in to talk to him. When I got to him, he was sitting on a concrete block holding a gun. That gun." Mike pointed to the Zip-Lock bag on Carlos's desk.

Carlos picked up the bag and looked at the gun again. "This is a cheapy. One of the infamous Saturday Night Specials." He looked at Mike. "And then?"

"Smiley and I have always had a good relationship. I asked him where he got the gun. *Stole it*, he said. Then I asked him what he was planning to do with the gun. *Kill myself*, he said. I had had similar conversations with other hobes, and not one of them ever actually acted on his threat."

"What did you do then?"

"I asked him why he was going to kill himself, and he said, *I'm scared.* I asked him what he was scared of, and he said the strangest thing."

Carlos lifted his eyebrows.

"Smiley said, *To whip the enemy.* I didn't know what he meant. Then he said that so many hobes were being killed in the city that he had rather beat them to the punch. And then he did something I really wasn't prepared for. He pushed the gun barrel against his temple."

Carlos leaned forward. "What did you do?"

"I asked him to give me the gun, which he refused to do. He simply cocked the hammer and grinned like he had conquered the world. Then I grabbed the gun and there was a tussle. The gun went off and Smiley dropped to the ground. I immediately was hit with the worst remorse possible, and I lost it." Mike teared up again. "And that's when you came in."

"That sounds logical," Carlos said. "But you understand that we've got to treat you as a suspect until the evidence shows otherwise. When Jerry gets back to work, he will want to go over all the evidence himself."

"You can't let him do that, Carlos. You know as well as I do that Jerry wants to prove me guil—Wait a minute. What's with Jerry?"

Carlos raised his eyebrows. He was surprised that Mike hadn't heard. He told Mike about the attempted suicide, and asked him for his prayers.

"I'll be happy to pray." That was it! Mike had just committed himself to pray for the first time since he had discovered Basil. He had to do it now.

Then Carlos's voice interrupted his silence. "I'm going to let you go now, Mike, but you have to understand that you cannot leave the city until all this is cleared up."

Mike said nothing.

"Is that clear, Mike?"

"Very clear. Very clear indeed."

EIGHTEEN

MIKE LEFT the station house at a run and slammed himself into the Camry. The blackened sky only added to his flappable anxiety. The drops of rain that had dampened his hair drained to his forehead like so many drops of sweat. It was several moments later that he realized his hands had crushed themselves into a tight squeeze, forming powerful fists that could have shattered the windshield into thousands of jagged pieces. Tightened lips, furrowed brow, and squinted eyelids made his face ache with the intensity of a rheumatoid flare up.

He had to get his mind off Smiley. He couldn't help but feel somehow responsible for Smiley's death. Maybe he was. Jerry would certainly think so. If he had not struggled with Smiley to take the gun away from him! Maybe he could have eventually talked him out of his self-destructive behavior. But it had happened, and there was nothing he could do about it now.

And there was that damned Ford Escort. It had haunted him for days. The car accident on the way to identify Basil's body. The trip to Columbia to see the bishop. The trek to Charleston to see Inez. Mike shook his head vigorously. *I'm obsessed.* The Escorts were real, but their intent must be a figment of his imagination. He shook his head again. Mike leaned his head back against the headrest and forced himself to relax the taut muscles enough to allow his mind some sort of respite.

A couple of moments later he leaned forward and pulled the shift into drive and headed out to—to God knows where. He eased on to Route 123 toward Easley. But he didn't stop in Easley. He turned left onto Route 86. Mike didn't know where he was going, and he didn't care. At Pickens he moved onto Route 27—back toward Madison, but he skirted Madison and headed up through Clemson and Seneca and on up through the mountains on Route 28 toward Walhalla.

A couple of miles later Mike automatically flicked his eyes to the rear-view mirror. A car. A black car followed three or four vehicles behind. He could not yet determine the make or model. He was being intolerably paranoid. *Forget it. I've got Ford Escorts on the brain.* He turned left onto Taylor Road.

The rain had slowed considerably, but the heavy sky continued to move slowly, almost, Mike thought, like a gigantic funeral canopy dirging its way across the heavens. Then in the rear-view mirror the black car pulled directly behind him. He sped up, and the Escort—yes, it was the Escort—followed suit. He turned left at the next road, and the Escort turned left. The car was getting closer now. *I'm getting out of here!* He pressed the accelerator pedal to the floor and charged up the road at aeronautic speed. A lightning bolt split the heavens, and the rain came down in torrents.

The windshield wipers had a difficult time keeping up with the spattering water on the glass, but Mike bolted ahead anyway. *Uh-oh!* A new vehicle behind him flashed lights like blue streaks of lightning. *A cop.* He sighed heavily, forced himself to pull over onto whatever shoulder the old county road provided. The siren screeched a dire warning, and Mike braced himself for the inevitable.

The cop silenced the siren and pulled up behind the Camry. Watching the cop intently in his rear-view mirror, Mike saw him lean over as if to retrieve something from the glove compartment or from the passenger-side floorboard—Mike couldn't tell which—and sat there another five minutes or so examining the object—a folded paper of some sort—in great detail. Then he played with something on the dashboard for a couple of minutes. With every passing moment, Mike's tension grew exponentially.

The officer folded the paper back to its original shape, and, as if on cue, the rain stopped. He retrieved his ticket pad, exited the patrol car, and headed toward the Camry

Mike lowered his window. "Good afternoon, Officer."

"Good afternoon, sir. May I see your driver's license, automobile registration, and your proof of insurance, sir?"

"Certainly, Officer Meara." In his stint with the MPD, Mike had learned to read police name badges quickly. He handed the documents to the cop.

The officer examined the documents, and then he looked up and examined Mike. "You a preacher, Mr. Richey?" The clerical collar had ratted on him.

"Yes, Officer. I'm rec—" Mike stopped in mid-word, opened his eyes to their limits, and zoomed in on the Escort sauntering by. He could have sworn the driver thumbed his nose at him, but maybe that bit of crudeness was a simple fabrication of his imagination.

"Are you okay, Reverend Richey?"

The cop's concern brought Mike back to the issue at hand. "Oh. Sorry, Officer. I thought I recognized the driver of that Ford Escort that just passed."

Meara couldn't care less about the Ford Escort and was not deterred. "Sir, do you know how fast you were driving this Camry?"

"No, Officer Meara, I really don't. I had something else on my mind at the time."

Meara stared at Mike for a moment. "I think I know you from somewhere, Reverend."

Mike certainly hoped not.

"You're the preacher that goes down to the bridge in Madison to see the bums, aren't you?"

Mike flinched at the word *bums*, but he said nothing.

"I've seen you down there a couple of times when me and my partner went down there to pick a bum up for theft. That was when I worked for the MPD."

Must have been before Mike's chaplaincy. He certainly didn't recognize the man.

"Those bums are all like that, wouldn't you say?"

Mike refused to be complicit to this judgment, and he opened his mouth to refute this base generality.

But Meara jumped back in before Mike uttered. "Now, Reverend. What if one of your beloved bums saw you like this—breaking the law like a common criminal?"

Mike clenched his teeth. During his time with the MPD, he had met all sorts of cops, and he knew this type. *Here comes the sermon.* He knew better than to look directly into the officer's eyes. That might be construed as sassy defiance, and he couldn't afford that. So he looked straight ahead watching the occasional car that passed heading around the next curve.

Indeed the sermon did come. Officer Meara filled the next several minutes scolding Mike for behavior unbecoming to a preacher. He never said a word about the perils of speeding in inclement weather. He eventually ended the homily and handed Mike a slip of paper from his ticket pad.

"Sir," Officer Meara said, "since you're a preacher, I'm just giving you a warning this time. Now see that you behave yourself." The cop handed Mike the warning ticket and swaggered back to the patrol car before Mike could say *thank you* and took off with the speed of a cheetah.

Mike sat there for a couple of minutes, staring at the view around him, before pulling the shift stick into drive and moving on. He recognized nothing. He was lost.

He drove on. Most of the houses on the roadside appeared to be shot-gun hovels or dilapidated mobile homes with no signs of life. So Mike started looking for road markers—numbers, names, anything, but none was visible to the naked eye. After four or five miles, he spotted some sort of roadside sign in the distance. He drove until he could see the placard clearly. It was a square board held to its post with a single nail. The letters were almost completely illegible.

He stopped the car and got out to examine the drooping marker more closely. Maybe it would give Mike a clue as to where he might be. The board used to be yellow with red letters advertising some sort of restaurant that had apparently once graced the countryside. Mike made out the word *Cafe*, above which appeared a faded word—the name of the cafe, perhaps?—that looked like *olo. Olo Cafe?* He traced the letters with his fingers. Perhaps another letter or two once appeared before the word *olo*. At the bottom of the sign he made out the word *miles*. A number he couldn't identify had once immediately preceded it. It couldn't be too far ahead. *Maybe someone still lives around the old restaurant.* Mike got back into the car and headed—he hoped—toward the old Olo Cafe.

Then a wisp of color on the dash hit his consciousness. The orange warning light glared steadily at him with an unblinking eye. He didn't know how long the light might have been on. He quickly shifted his vision to the gas gauge. Empty. No, below empty. The needle drooped down as low as the needle could go below the *E* mark. If he could just make it to the old cafe, maybe there would be a service station of some sort somewhere around.

He slowed the Camry down to keep from wasting the tiniest bit of fuel. He inched ahead. Half a mile. One mile. And then in the distance an old faded sign appeared on an erect pole. *Esso. Esso?* Esso hadn't been around in decades. But maybe—just maybe—some sort of gas might be available.

Mike pulled into the station. The fuel pumps were of the ancient variety—no digital readouts, no credit-card slots, nothing that indicated even a hint of modernity. The station appeared abandoned. The front door boasted a gigantic Yale padlock—he could read the brand name from the car. No one around anywhere. He saw no hope for his belabored gas tank, but he decided to try the pump anyway.

Mike exited the car, removed the gas cap, picked up the nozzle, and pulled the trigger. Nothing. He scowled and replaced the nozzle.

He crossed around to the side of the station. Mike really didn't know what he was looking for. A whom. He was looking for a whom. Maybe there was a person around somewhere. His eyes widened. There behind the station on the side of a mini-mountain stood an old Victorian-type mansion with peeling paint and dilapidated porch. He thought he caught a glimpse of a glowing light bulb hanging naked behind a second-floor window. *Psycho*, he thought. *The Bates house behind the motel.*

Mike started up the hill toward the mansion, and then he stopped. An old man exited the house and shuffled down the hill. He was at least 350 pounds with a long gray beard and wrinkled sunburned skin. But then Mike detected a twinkle in his eyes and a hint of a smile that seemed to suggest he wasn't all bad.

"Hidy, pal," the man said.

"Hidy, yourself," Mike answered.

The man drew closer, and Mike realized that he wasn't as old as he appeared. Probably close to fifty. His rough demeanor might have intimidated a lesser man than Mike.

"How about a gallon or two of gas?" Mike spotted the white patch attached to his shoulder. Floyd, his name was.

The twinkle left Floyd's eyes. Tobacco juice seeped out of the right corner of his mouth. He glared at Mike. "Okay. But it'll cost ya."

"What do you mean it'll cost me?"

"Well," Floyd answered, "the cost of the gas."

"Yes?"

"And a dollar more for making me leave my wife and my dinner to come down here to get you some gas."

"Sorry about that, Floyd. I was out of gas, and this is the only station I've seen for miles." Mike reached into his wallet and drew out a one and handed it to Floyd. "Here's for your trouble."

Floyd stared at the bill for a moment, spat tobacco juice on the ground, and then said, "Wait here." He crumpled the bill into his overalls bib pocket and meandered over to the door. He reached in his pocket, pulled out his key, and fiddled for a couple of seconds with the lock. The door opened, and he walked inside. After some minutes Mike thought Floyd had deserted him, but he leaned against the Camry and waited. Eventually he heard a buzz on the gas pump signaling that Floyd had switched the power on.

Floyd appeared in the doorway. "Go at her."

"Thanks, Floyd."

Mike picked up the nozzle, flipped the lever, and started feeding the gas tank. "Floyd?"

Floyd ambled back to the pump to watch the dollars roll by. "Yup?"

"Floyd, can you tell me how to get back to Route 23?"

"Yup." But he said nothing else.

Mike grimaced. "Let me rephrase. How do I get back to Route 23?"

Floyd walked over and leaned on the gas pump. "Yer at it."

"At it?"

"Up the road here about a quarter. Just on the other side of the old cafe. Ya can't miss it."

The tank filled, but the pump did not click off, and Mike splashed gasoline all over the thigh of his black trousers.

"Sorry about that." Floyd grinned.

Mike reached into his wallet, paid for the gas, and told Floyd to keep the change. "Thanks, Floyd."

"Yup."

Mike got back into the car, started the engine, and eased out, leaving Floyd gazing after him.

In another tenth of a mile, Mike spotted the Solo Cafe. It looked much as he had expected it to look. Windows broken out. Doors sagging open. Roof falling in. And Mike pushed on.

Finding the road was easy enough. Just as he was about to enter the highway, the black Ford Escort whisked by. Mike pulled onto the road behind the Escort and accelerated enough that he could read the license tag number. 726 BEN. *Okay!*

Mike pulled in behind the Escort, and the Escort escalated to 75 mph in this 55 mph zone. The driver knew Mike was behind him, and the faster Mike drove, the faster the killer drove. Mike thought of all the clichés here: the tables are turned, the shoe is on the other foot, the hunter becomes the hunted. But none of them really seemed to fit. He knew that he still was the hunted, but he had to pursue this Escort. He had to find out where it was going.

But then the chase took a different turn. Literally. Up ahead he saw the Escort steer around a steep curve, and Mike, dutifully following, careened around the curve and headed straight toward a husky old oak. The last thing Mike heard was the crashing sound of metal against hardwood.

‡‡‡

MIKE SHOOK his dazed head, not remembering where he was or why he was there. He began to squirm his way out from behind the inflated airbag. The driver's door stood ajar, and he managed to push it open and scramble out. He stood back, and surveyed the damage. He had grazed the front right fender on the old tree, and had plowed through a barbed wire fence and landed directly in Brer Rabbit's briar patch, completely out of sight of the road. No one driving by would see him out here.

The Escort, he remembered. He sat on an antediluvian stump, retrieved his cell phone, and called AAA for a tow truck.

"Give them forty-five minutes to get there," AAA said.

Mike punched in Carlos's number.

"Mike, where you been, buddy. Been trying to get you for the past thirty minutes. Are you okay?"

"I'm fine, Carlos." He said nothing about his accident.

"You had us scared there for awhile. Thought *el viejo asesino* had found you."

"He found me all right. But best of all, I've found him."

"What do you mean?"

"I've got his license tag number."

"You mean from the black Escort?"

"Yeah. He was following me. I got onto a side road and he passed. Then I got behind him and got the tag number."

Carlos seemed strangely skeptical. "And the number?"

"726 BEN."

"Are you sure about that number, Mike?"

"Yeah, I'm sure. You sound a bit cynical."

"Don't mean to."

"Can you dig into it and let me know where I can find this Escort?"

The pause was interminable.

"Carlos, are you still there?"

"Yeah, I'm here, Mike." Another pause. "Mike, I can't help you with that. That's police business, and you know it. It's not only against regulations, but the regulations are there for a reason. You're going to go out there and get yourself killed."

"Carlos."

"Sorry, buddy."

"Thanks for all your great help, Carlos." Mike immediately regretted the sarcasm.

It took another fifteen minutes for the tow truck to show up and another hour before it deposited the Camry securely at Baldwin's Body Shop. The Camry wouldn't be ready for at least a couple of weeks, but Baldwin provided him a loaner, a steel gray Nissan Altima. Maybe this is good. Perhaps he would not be spotted as easily in a different car. After a moment's orientation to the Altima, he drove back to the rectory.

He had to find a way to get that license tag ID.

NINETEEN

THE MORNING opened up with a beautiful blue sky, Carlos's dreaded conversation with Jerry the only cloud hovering over him. It had been three days since the ordeal with Mike and Smiley. He had waited too long. He had to tell Jerry about Mike and the gun. In spite of Jerry's reputation for fairness, he had shown a decided bias against Mike, and he would jump to all the wrong conclusions. Carlos believed Mike's story. Mike was not a killer, and neither was he a liar. He wouldn't have killed Smiley. He *couldn't* have. Not Mike.

Instead of driving toward the station house, he headed the Crown Vic toward Madison Memorial Hospital. He did not want to do this, but duty required it. He drove the twelve blocks, parked on the third garage level, and sat in the car for ten minutes. Only then did he muster the courage to go ahead with his mission.

Carlos walked into the ICU waiting room. The room was stark this morning. For some reason, someone had drawn the blinds over the plate-glass wall that separated the room from the corridor. The almost constantly blaring television set hung lifelessly in the far corner of the room. The room was void of humanity—except for one lone figure with his back to the doorway, reaching for the carafe to fill his Styrofoam cup with the normally potent, black coffee that blended its aroma with the antiseptic smell of the hospital. The figure turned around.

"Mike!"

Mike took a sip of the coffee and pressed his lips together as if he needed a second or two to swallow. "Hi Carlos."

"Hi, yourself." Then he spotted the bruise on Mike's forehead but said nothing.

"Just got here. Nurse has gone in to tell Jerry I'm here." He immediately grabbed another cup for Carlos. "Don't know if he'll want to see me or not."

"He'll see you. Unless there's some crisis with Mack."

Mike handed Carlos his cup and the two sat down on two of the three wing-backed, leather chairs on either side of the large round coffee table.

"Wow. You've got a major knot on that head."

Mike hesitated. "Yup. Bumped it pretty hard." He said nothing about the accident.

Carlos laughed. "What did you do? Run into a glass door?"

"Something like that."

Apparently Mike didn't want to talk about it, so he left it alone. He sipped his coffee. "Mike?" Carlos held his breath for a moment. He was having a difficult time saying what he was about to say. "You know I'm going to have to tell Jerry about you and Smiley and the— the gun."

Mike looked up from his coffee again, his lips pressed into a tight downward arc.

"Mike, I…"

A distinct and careful clearing of the throat issued from the doorway. Jerry walked into the room and stood looking at both men but said nothing.

Carlos didn't know whether Jerry would be official tonight or not, but he took the plunge. "Hi, Jerry."

Jerry's face appeared sterner than usual, but he nodded toward both men. "Detective. Reverend."

Carlos stood up. *Well. That answers that question.*

Jerry crossed to the coffee maker. "What brings the two of you here?" He filled the cup a bit too hastily, and the inordinately hot coffee spilled over the sides and onto his fingers. He emitted a mild expletive and quickly jerked his fingers away from the cup.

"Just wanted to check on you and Mack," Mike said. "Thought maybe I could pray with you." He had committed himself to pray for Mack, and he would.

Jerry failed to acknowledge Mike's offer and turned to Carlos. "No change. Maureen and I sit with him twenty-four-seven. We take four-hour turns. I guess we hope that one of us will be here when he opens his eyes."

Carlos grimaced. Any intention of telling Jerry about Mike and the gun now suddenly disappeared. Jerry looked exhausted. Dark rings around the eyes. Beard a quarter inch long. Hair hastily combed. He couldn't broach the subject now.

Then Carlos had second thoughts. "Chief?" Perhaps he should go ahead and get it over with, regardless of the current situation. He glanced at Mike, and his heart skipped a beat. "Chief…"

Jerry quickly held up his hand and stopped Carlos from going any further. "No. Don't say it, Detective. No police business this morning." It was as if Jerry already knew what Carlos had come to tell him. How long had he been standing in the doorway before announcing his presence?

"Please sit down, Detective. Reverend, sit."

The two did as Jerry had commanded, but Jerry stood behind a third and similar chair, holding his Styrofoam cup as if it were a hot potato.

The conversation that followed surprised Carlos. Jerry wanted to talk. He wanted to talk about baseball and basketball and spring football practice. He wanted to talk about Clint Eastwood and Sylvester Stallone and old John Wayne movies. He wanted to talk about Maddux and Aaron and Sosa. But not a further word about Mack.

Then Jerry abruptly changed the subject again. He interrogated Carlos about his daughters. How were they doing at Presbyterian College? Did they have college boyfriends yet? When would they be home again? He was eager to see them. "Give them my love." All this, completely out of character for Jerry.

Then a sudden turn toward Mike. "Reverend?"

Mike looked up at Jerry, his powerful eyes attempting to penetrate the virtual fog that had always separated the two. He took a deep breath.

"Your son," Jerry continued. "Your son, Tim. I understand he and his mother are in Sumter now."

Mike closed his eyes. "Yes. They're with her parents."

Jerry's mien didn't change. "Wise decision." He looked up at the ceiling for a moment as if he were counting the light fixtures in the room. Then he allowed his gaze to settle back on the two men in front of him. "Gentlemen?"

Carlos had never seen Jerry in this state.

"Gentlemen," he repeated. "Your children are your most valued treasure. Don't ever forget that." He turned and walked to the door.

Carlos looked at Mike. Were they being dismissed?

Then Jerry turned back to them and raised his eyebrows. Several long creases crossed his brow. "Detective. Reverend, come on in and do—whatever it is you do."

An ICU nurse—Catherine Turner, her name tag read—cleared the way into the room and stayed with them. Jerry went over to check his son's wound, caressing the large bandage attached to his forehead. Mack appeared to be in restful sleep. His color was good, and his breathing appeared soft and regular. Carlos had difficulty retaining his composure.

"Okay, Reverend," Jerry said.

Mike reached into his pocket and retrieved his ampulla.

Then suddenly a hysterical sob burst through the doorway. Maureen, perhaps returning from her rest to take a turn at standing sentry, stood looking at Mack as if it were the last time she would ever see him.

Jerry rushed to her, placed his arm around her. "Come on in, sweetheart."

She quickly looked around at the brood of people populating the room. "What's wrong?" she sobbed. "My baby, my Mack. Is he dead?"

"Oh, no! No, honey!"

She broke loose and ran to the hospital bed.

"The reverend here was about to say a prayer for Mack."

"Oh." Maureen turned and looked at Mike, a clear signal of displeasure on her face. "With everybody standing around the bed, I thought…"

Nurse Catherine reached over, put her arm around Maureen, and escorted her gently to the foot of the bed. "It's okay," she whispered. "It's okay."

Carlos had never seen Maureen in this state. He wondered if he and Mike should leave, but that might have a more jarring effect on Jerry and Maureen than continuing on with the healing rite. So he didn't interrupt.

"Now, Reverend!" Jerry commanded.

"Wait!" A lingering pause filled the room with an eerie apprehension. "Jerry, honey. Do you think this is wise?"

Jerry crossed to Maureen and put his arm around her and kissed her lightly on the cheek. "It's okay, sweetheart. We need all the prayers we can get."

"But you heard what Brother Sam said about this man's pagan prayers."

"I know, sweetheart. But just let the reverend do what he has to do and he'll be on his way."

Mike gripped the ampulla tightly, his tortured face revealing an embarrassment not often seen on the priest. "Maureen, I'm sorry. I don't wish to intrude on your grief." He turned to Jerry. "Jerry, if you had rather not—"

"Get on with it, Reverend!"

Mike moved to the bedside and stretched out his hand.

"Jerry, stop him!" Maureen was beside herself. "No." She drew her right fist up to her mouth and closed her eyes, as if she would not watch while Mike cast an evil spell on her son. "But Brother Sam said—"

Carlos moved over and stationed himself beside Mike. His friend needed all the support he could give him.

Jerry put his hand on Maureen's and pulled her up next to him. He held her tight. "Sh-h-h," he whispered. "It's okay. It's okay. It's okay."

Mike reluctantly continued, signing the cross over the small congregation. "Peace to this place and all who are here." He opened his bible. "A reading from the Letter of James."

> *Are any among you sick? They should call for the elders of the church and have them pray over them, anointing them with oil in the name of the Lord. The prayer of faith will save the sick, and the Lord will raise them up; and anyone who has committed sins will be forgiven.*

Mike paused briefly. "Let us pray,"

> *Savior of the world, by your cross and precious blood you have redeemed us. Save us and help us, we humbly beseech you, O Lord.*

Then he turned his attention to Mack. He looked at him with troubled eyes, and Carlos knew he must be thinking of Tim.

Mike opened the ampulla, dipped his thumb into the holy oil and traced a cross on Mack's bandaged wound, his forehead and his hands.

"Mack, a beautiful child of God of whom God is especially fond, I anoint you with oil in the name of the Father, and of the Son, and of the Holy Spirit. Amen."

Mike then placed his hand on Mack's head.

> *As you are outwardly anointed with this holy oil so may our heavenly Father grant you the inward anointing of the Holy Spirit. Of his great mercy, may he forgive you your sins, release you from suffering, and restore you to wholeness and strength. May he deliver you from all evil,*

preserve you in all goodness, and bring you to everlasting life; through Jesus Christ our Lord. Amen.

Carlos noticed the stillness in the room. Even Maureen had calmed down significantly, and Nurse Catherine wiped a brief tear from the corner of her eye. He was glad he had not rushed Mike out of the room.

He reached over and placed his hand on Mike's shoulder, and Mike prayed for all the people in the room by name—for mercy, comfort, strength, and patience. And he ended with the Lord's Prayer in which the little congregation joined. Some of them said *trespasses*, and some of them said *debts*. But, Carlos thought, it didn't matter to Mike. They were praying.

When he had finished, Mike walked over to Maureen and gave her a hug, which she grudgingly accepted. "I'm sorry I distressed you, Maureen," Mike whispered. "I did Mack no harm. He is in the hands of God now. Whether he will receive physical healing or not, I do not know. But this I do know. God will be with him every step of the way. And if those steps should lead to death, God will be there for you and for him. Mack is a beloved child of God, and God will not desert him, whatever some others may have told you."

Silence engulfed the room. Jerry stared at Mack and grimaced. Carlos looked at Mack with compassion. Maureen laid her head on Jerry's shoulder and cried. The nurse crossed herself and moved her lips.

"Goodbye, my friends," Mike said. "Go with God."

Inside the room, no one stirred. The only sound, the ping announcing that Mike's elevator had arrived.

And Mack's eyes fluttered open.

TWENTY

JERRY TURNED the lights on in his office for the first time in seven days. It had been three days since Mack suddenly waked up. This indescribable thrill set him afire, and he could conquer anything now. In fact, he was glad to get back to work.

He sat at his desk carefully sipping the steaming mug of coffee Bobbie Jo had brought him. He looked around the room. Nothing had changed. He didn't know why he had expected anything to change. Wait—it was tidier than usual. *Good for Bobbie Jo.* Then he spotted something atop the filing cabinet. He usually kept a stack of something-or-other there, but the stack was now gone. The thing he saw now was a cube of some sort covered by some kind of towel or something. He crossed over and jerked off the cover and spotted a plain red box. No tag. No markings to identify the box in any way.

The police academy and his own experience had trained Jerry to suspect bombs in unidentified boxes. He crossed to his desk to punch in the bomb-squad number, and then thought better of it. He flicked the intercom switch and yelled to the entire building, "Anybody out there know anything about this damned red box on my filing cabinet?"

He had stirred the hornet's nest. Folks emerged from every cranny, converging on his office like ants on an ant hill. Bobby Jo, Carlos, and—it seemed—a baker's dozen filled his inner sanctum before he could shout them back. He scowled.

"Welcome back, Chief," yelled one. "Good to see you, Chief," yelled another. And a dozen other greetings mingled together into a boisterous din.

"See you found it." Bobbie Jo laughed. She crossed over to the filing cabinet, grabbed the red box, and brought it to the chief's desk. "It's for your…"

Jerry stood confounded. "What?"

"Open it," shouted a bunch of folks.

"Figure you could use a little Christmas about now," shouted another source.

Jerry fumbled his way into the parcel. "What in the heck is this?" He pulled out a cellophane-wrapped package of colorful, square, plastic cases.

"DVDs," someone yelled.

"All Clint Eastwood," another shouted.

"Twelve of them," said still another.

A smile almost crossed Jerry's face. He had seen every Eastwood movie on the large screen and several on the small. Eastwood had provided the subject of many of Jerry's conversations over the years. He straightened up and looked at as many faces as he could get in his line of vision. "Thanks, guys." He couldn't let them see the tears that threatened to swell up inside him. "Thanks a lot."

The card, signed by Bobbie Jo and Carlos and a host of others, read, *Clint welcomes you back, and so do we*. He smiled again—briefly. Then he noticed the last signature on the card. *Mike Richey*. And a bit of King Henry II, of Saint Thomas Beckett fame, coiled up inside him. *Will no one rid me of this meddlesome priest?* Jerry's gruff had returned.

♯♯♯

WHEN HIS office had emptied and the dust had at last settled, he sat down and opened the first report from a stack Bobby Jo had carefully placed in the center of his desk. He went back to his work.

He began plowing through the stack, and, halfway through his second report, Carlos popped back into Jerry's office. "Just wanted to make sure you had all your reports."

Jerry stared at Carlos blankly.

"And, by the way, what's the latest on Mack?"

"Still in the hospital—his own room, now—and mending well." Jerry paused and turned back to the report he had been reading to camouflage a moist eye. He looked back at Carlos. "Mack's mental ability appears to be unimpaired." He paused again. "Thank God."

"That's miraculous."

Jerry jumped in quickly. "Now don't go thinking his recovery—his slow recovery, I might add—had anything to do with the reverend's bookish words."

"How can you say that, Jerry?" This was one of the few times Carlos had broken protocol and had addressed the chief detective by his name at work. "You saw what happened after Father Mike left."

"Coincidence. Coincidence. That's all it was. Coincidence." Jerry squinted his eyes. The thoughts of that evening came flooding back through his brain like the waters of Hurricane Katrina. The doctors and nurses had poured into the room to examine Mack and had ejected the family so that they could confirm Mack's consciousness. Jerry had emerged from the ICU shaken, Maureen close behind, and had collapsed into the thankfully empty waiting room.

Maureen had sat beside her husband. "Thank God. Thank God. Thank God."

"He's just opened his eyes, Maureen," Jerry said. "He's not out of danger yet."

"But it's a start. And thank God for that preacher and his prayers. It was a miracle."

Jerry sat there astounded. It was Maureen who didn't want the prayers in the first place. *Pagan prayers*, she had said. "Do you really believe what just happened had anything to do with the reverend's falderal?"

Maureen sat silently for a moment. "Jerry, did you hear what Reverend Mike said to me after the prayer?"

Jerry rolled his eyes. "I heard it, Maureen."

Maureen pressed her lips together in a taut line. "He said, and I remember it almost word for word, that God will place his hand upon Mack. Whether he would receive physical healing or not, he didn't know. But God will be with him every step of the way. And if those steps should lead to death, God will be there for him and for us. Mack is a beloved child of God, and God will not desert him."

Jerry stood up and crossed to the coffee pot. "I heard it, Maureen! You want some coffee?"

Maureen ignored the question. "No preacher has ever put it like that to me before."

Jerry frowned and released a deep sigh. He felt as if he were talking down to a twelve-year-old. "That's because you've never experienced this sort of thing before."

Maureen mustered her courage. "No, Jerry. Mack is a child of God, whether he takes his own life or not. I believe that, Jerry."

"Maureen."

"It's an answer to prayer."

"Coincidence," Jerry handed Maureen the Styrofoam cup. "It could have been Brother Sam's prayer or anybody else's prayer."

"Yes, it could have been Brother Sam's prayer."

"Or it could have been no prayer at all. The only reason I allowed the reverend to come in there in the first place was to get it over with and get him out of our hair."

"I'm convinced." Maureen raised her eyebrows and looked straight into Jerry's eyes. "I'm going to invite him to come back."

Jerry bristled. Maureen had never been so adamant. He flung his hands into the air, and he turned back to the carafe to pour his own cup of coffee. He sighed and turned back. "Okay—do as you please. But make sure I'm not here when you do."

"Oh, Jerry. Don't be that way. This is your son whose life is on the line here. He needs all the help we can give him."

Jerry glared at her a moment, and, without a word, he charged out of the room, down the corridors, and out to the parking lot. He ended up in the smoking area, although he didn't smoke, and absorbed the second-hand fumes without noticing. Could Maureen be right? Could the reverend's prayers really make a difference? Could God really obey the reverend's demands? No, it couldn't be. *God, help me!*

Jerry looked back at Carlos. "I'm back in charge now, Detective. Let me finish these reports, and I'll get back to you if I have any questions."

Carlos disappeared and Jerry went back to his reading.

The third report dealt with a sordid liaison between the CEO of the Burgundy Company and a woman he had picked up off the street. She had apparently taken the man for a wad. The next involved the killing of a thief in mid-crime in the home of a city councilman. Then the next and the next and the next. And the final report concerned Smiley (surname unknown) and the Reverend Michael Basil Richey, Jr.

Jerry gritted his teeth. *That bastard!* He examined the report meticulously, scrutinizing each paragraph—every sentence— tediously. He read Detective Ruiz's report, the CSI report, and the lab reports. Then he reread them just as carefully as he had the first time. He sat there, his elbows propped on the desk top and his face in his hands. A couple of minutes passed. Then he abruptly pressed the intercom button. "Detective, I need you in my office pronto."

A moment later Carlos poked his head in the door. "What can I do for you, Chief?"

"Come on in, Detective. I'd like to discuss this Smiley/Richey report with you."

"Certainly." Carlos came in and sat down in the chair next to Jerry's desk. "Where would you like to start?"

"Why didn't you tell me about this when it happened?"

"I—"

Jerry flipped his hand at Carlos. "Never mind. I know. *You* were in charge." He glanced again through the report quickly. "Detective, you interrogated the suspect yourself?"

Carlos hesitated. "The suspect?" He hesitated again. "Yes, I did, Detective."

"Was another officer present when you did the interrogation?"

"No, I did it alone."

"Why did you interrogate the suspect alone?"

"I'm aware that we most often interrogate with another officer present. But it is not a requirement of the department."

"Don't lecture me on the regulations of the department, Detective!"

Carlos paused and pressed his lips tightly together. "As we sometimes do, in the absence of significant evidence, I opted to interview Father Richey alone."

"Absence of any significant evidence?"

"Yes!"

"He was holding the murder weapon, for God's sake!" Jerry shouted.

"If the killing was indeed a suicide, then it wasn't a murder weapon. And I believed it was a suicide. Father Mike's story sounded logical."

"Sounded logical? Since when do we accept the story of a suspect just because it sounds logical?"

"But the prints. Father Mike's prints were on the handle only. There were two prints on the trigger—one smudged and the other definitely Smiley's. And Smiley's overlapped the smudged one. I would say there is no real evidence linking Father Mike to the killing."

"But you didn't know that at the time, did you?" Jerry said.

Carlos's customary even temper rose significantly with each interrogatory remark. "Are you interrogating me, Chief Detective? Why don't you call in another officer to witness this interrogation, Chief Detective?"

Jerry rose from his chair, his stature overpowering the room. "Detective Ruiz, you are, as of this moment, off this case. Not just the case of the hobe and the preacher but of every case involving the reverend. Do I make myself clear, Detective?"

Carlos stood and faced Jerry. "Perfectly clear, Chief."

"Now, get out of here. You're dismissed."

Carlos left the room in double time.

The telephone rang. "Chief Detective Jerry Majors here."

Jerry listened for a moment, clamped the telephone down, and pressed the intercom button. "Emergency at the hospital, Bobbie Jo. Don't know when I'll be back."

‡‡‡

"WHAT IN the hell are you doing here, Reverend?" Mike's presence in the ICU waiting room distressed him severely. He had thought the man would have disappeared after he let him say his so-called prayer over Mack. But here he was again pouring his coffee from the carafe like he owned the place.

"I asked him to come, Jerry. And don't you say a word!" Maureen was the only person who could get away with a bit of bossiness with Jerry.

Mike crossed over to the Chief Detective. "I'm sorry, Jerry. I mean no offense to you or to anyone." He turned to Maureen. "Perhaps I'd better go."

Maureen reached over and put her hand on Mike's arm. "Please stay, Reverend Mike."

"But Jer…"

"Jerry will be okay." Maureen looked at Jerry. "He's very stressed right now."

"I really think I'd better go."

Cynicism seeped from both sides of Jerry's mouth. "Stay, Reverend, stay!" He sat down across the waiting room from Maureen and Mike, as if he were totally exhausted. "What's happening with Mack?"

"Thought you'd never ask." The sarcasm was not lost on her husband. Maureen's mien grew softer. "I'm sorry, honey. Didn't mean to stress you more." She turned to Mike. "Please sit, Reverend Mike."

Maureen crossed over to Jerry. "Apparently Mack has developed a staph infection, and right now his fever is inordinately high. He's been a bit delirious."

Jerry's face twitched. His eyes glazed over, and a moment or two later he closed them. "What's happening now?"

"Dr. Wilson and two nurses are in there with him. They've plugged in IVs with antibiotics for the staph. And they're giving him fever reducers."

Jerry opened his eyes. "When can we see him?"

"Don't know yet. Maybe when they come out."

Mike sat there with his elbows on his knees and his face in his hands. Jerry could not look at him. The bastard apparently was praying. *Who does he think he is? Jesus Christ?* Then a pang of remorse hit him in the heart, and he closed his eyes again.

A strong silence lent itself to the next quarter of an hour. Maureen leaned back in the chair, closing her eyes tightly. Jerry sat forward and twiddled his thumbs. Mike still covered his face.

Sudden shuffling noises caused all three to take notice and look through the plate-glass walls into the adjacent corridor. Dr. Wilson left the room and made a beeline to the nurses' station. A couple of minutes later, a nurse followed suit. The three waited in anticipation. Another five minutes passed and the third nurse, Nurse Catherine— the same woman who had been Mack's nurse in the ICU— disappeared in the opposite direction. In about five minutes she returned and came straight to the waiting room carrying what looked like yellow plastic rain ponchos.

"Sorry you had to wait so long," Catherine greeted them.

The three looked at her expectantly.

"I hate to bring you bad news," she continued, "but we can't yet get the temperature down. Right now Mack's temperature stands steady at 104."

Jerry winced. "When can we see him?"

"All three of you can go in briefly—say, five minutes. After that, two of you must leave, and from that point on, only one of you at a time will be allowed in the room until the doctor gives further orders."

Jerry started to move.

"Just a minute, Mr. Majors."

Jerry was a bit miffed that she didn't use his proper police title, but he couldn't allow that to bother him now. So he waited.

"The doctor has established some visitation regulations. You must put on a plastic gown, gloves, and a face mask." She laid the disposable gowns across a chair and turned back to them. "I know this is going to be annoying to you, but using these garments protects Mack from any outside influences that may affect his condition for the worse. They will also protect you from the staph bacteria, and they will keep you from spreading the bacteria to others." She paused briefly. "If you wish, you may go ahead and put them on now."

Without a word they pulled the plastic garments on.

"O, yes," Catherine continued. "You'll notice two large boxes on each side of Mack's door. When you leave the room, you will discard these garments in the left box. When you return to the room, you will select new ones from the batch in the right box. You'll note that the boxes are clearly marked. Do not use the same ones twice. Any questions?"

"Oh, and one more thing." Catherine reached in her pocket and retrieved a large pump bottle of antibacterial gel. "Before you enter the room and after you exit, you must drench your hands in this solution, or else wash your hands with soap in the sink." She went to each of them and pumped sufficient gel into each person's hands. "Mr. Majors. Mrs. Majors. Father Mike."

It suddenly occurred to Jerry that the nurse was preparing the reverend to go into Mack's room. "You aren't going to let the preacher go in, are you? This is a family matter."

Catherine was taken aback. "But I thought…"

"Don't think!" Jerry scolded.

Maureen glared at Jerry. "Reverend Mike's going in, Jerry, whether you like it or not."

Jerry stood amazed. This was the first time in their married life that Maureen had deliberately contradicted him and embarrassed him in public. "Then he can go in without me."

"Just a moment!" Mike almost shouted. Then he turned to the nurse. "Nurse Catherine, I know how embarrassed you must be." He grimaced. "Would you please excuse us?"

The nurse charged out the door like a hundred-meter athlete.

"Jerry and Maureen," Mike continued, "I have caused nothing but strife between you two since I first came to see your son."

"No. No, Reverend Mike," Maureen protested.

"Yes, I have. I really think it best that I go and leave you two alone with your son."

"Reverend, I—"

"I've learned from many years' experience visiting the sick in hospitals and elsewhere that the attitude of those who visit a patient often has a direct impact on the health of the sick person. I would not like to have it on my conscience if we did that to Mack on my account."

The Majorses remained silent.

"Call Brother Argyle. He's your pastor. He can pray. Pray yourselves. Believe me, I have no monopoly on God's ear. All I can do as a priest of the Church is to visit the sick and pray for them as Jesus commanded us. I can offer the sacraments of the Church to those who want them. I will leave now and God be with you."

Mike discarded the yellow plastic gown and headed toward the elevators.

"Reverend?" Jerry held the call button so the door would not close.

Mike stepped out and let the car drop.

"Reverend, we want you to go in with us. *I* want you to go in with us. We want all the positive influence we can get for our son. Will you come and pray?"

Mike hesitated. "Are you sure?"

"Come on, Reverend. Let's get you some yellow clothes on."

TWENTY-ONE

THE RECTORY'S daunting emptiness haunted Mike like the cavernous tunnels of the Roman catacombs. The pit in his stomach twisted to and fro with every move he made. Even Mr. Craggles—the normally bouncing miniature schnauzer and Mike's only source of comfort since Annie's and Tim's departure—straggled into the den, yawning as if his master had interrupted his evening nap far too soon. Mike knelt down for just a moment and scratched Mr. Craggles behind the ears, but his heart foundered. He missed Annie and Tim terribly.

Then his mind turned to thoughts of Mack—and especially Maureen and what he had told her in the ICU. *This I do know. God will be with Mack every step of the way. And if those steps should lead to death, God will be there for him and for you.* Mike's heart turned over. *What a hypocrite I am!* He couldn't take his own counsel. But he couldn't think about that now.

Mike attempted to end Mr. Craggles's therapeutic massage, but the schnauzer would have none of it. He bossy-pawed his master's hand long after the gentle strokes had ceased. He lay down on the carpet, eyes disconsolate, and settled his chin on the toe of Mike's shoe.

Mike gave the dog one final pat, and then ambled into the kitchen. Mr. Craggles followed close behind wiggling his nub of a tail, apparently deciding that his master was worth the interrupted nap. Mike replenished Mr. Craggles's food and water and plopped down at the kitchen table, hoping a two-inch rib-eye would miraculously appear before him. But Jesus dealt in fishes and loaves, not steak and potatoes. So he finally screwed up the gumption to plod to the refrigerator to see what he could find. *Oh, yeah!* Eggs. Milk, cheese, tomatoes, and bacon. An omelet.

He gathered the ingredients in separate bowls, placed the small skillet on the burner, and went to work. Skillfully flipping the solidifying mixture, he slid the omelet onto his plate. He grabbed the butter-and-jam-smeared toast and said grace. After the third bite or so an incandescent notion flashed through his brain. He finished his supper quickly.

Mike didn't bother to clear the table. He shoved his plate out of the way, reached over and nabbed the laptop and Googled *license tag search free*. He came up with the first twenty-five of about 50,000 possible web sites. He clicked on *netsleuth.com*, inserted 726 BEN in the search space, and came up with the name Radgill Richey Hayes. Richey? He leaned back in his chair and stared again at the name. A moment later he reached into his pocket and dragged out his drug-store reading glasses, slapped them on his face, and leaned forward so closely that his nose almost touched the monitor screen. There was that name again: Richey. Radgill Richey Hayes. Home address, 12 Codington Drive, Seneca, South Carolina.

He looked at his watch. Nine-twenty. Too late tonight. Mike shut his computer down, drifted over to the sofa in the den, switched the television on to CNN, and woke up the following morning to Matt Lauer and Savannah Guthrie interviewing Bishop Desmond Tutu. He had not moved. He wasn't sure how the channels got switched from CNN to NBC, but so be it.

After his morning workout at the Y—Carlos was not there—he returned to the rectory, freshened himself up, pulled on his jeans and plaid flannel shirt, and climbed into the Nissan. In spite of Carlos's orders, he drove toward Clemson and then onto Route 123 to

Seneca. The street was not hard to find. It was in a quiet neighborhood, probably one of the oldest neighborhoods in town. It apparently had at one time been a neighborhood of the well-to-do but had since—according to the human evidence populating the lawns and driveways—become home to the middle-class elderly. The lawns of the two-story houses, most of which had been built with variegated brick, had been well-kept through the decades.

Yes! Number twelve, and the Escort, parked in the driveway, gave him pause. Same Escort, same tag number. Mike parked on the street a block away so as not to call attention to himself, and walked back up the block to the front door and rang the doorbell. It was only then the thought occurred to him that somebody in the house might meet him at the door with a drawn weapon. He stepped aside, quite conscious now of the possible danger. He hung back behind the parked Escort, but nobody came to the door. He wasn't sure whether to ring again and was pondering whether or not to go through with this without help from Carlos. He started to punch in Carlos's number, when he heard singing coming from somewhere. Hymns? He followed the sound around the house to a privacy-fenced backyard and peered warily over the top. A sixty-fivish, blue-haired lady knelt in the back flower bed digging away with a trowel and humming "The Old Rugged Cross."

"Good morning," Mike greeted.

She looked up and stood quickly, no arthritic knees here. "Good morning, yourself." She smiled. "What can I do for you?"

"Mrs. Hayes?"

The woman came toward the fence. She raised her eyebrows as if she might have incurred a brief moment of recognition. "Yes. How may I help you?"

"Mrs. Hayes, I'm Mike Richey. May I talk with you a moment?"

"Richey?"

"Yes, ma'am."

"Well, anybody named Richey can't be all bad. I'm not going anywhere." She stepped through the gate and into the driveway. She came out onto the walkway into the full view of two or three lawn keepers and a couple of gossips that populated the block. Mike couldn't blame her.

"May I speak with your husband?" Mike asked.

"Oh, child. I haven't had a husband in ten years. He died with a heart attack mowing the front lawn. He wouldn't use the riding mower. Said it was too boring. He always used the old push mower, and it got to be a bit too much for him."

"I'm sorry for your loss. I was hoping to get to talk with Radgill Richey Hayes."

"You're looking at her."

"You're Radgill Richey Hayes?"

"That's me."

What a let down. Mike was expecting a brawny man with a bit too much weight, sporting a John Deere baseball cap, inch-long hair on his chest and back, and a rifle pointing at Mike's brain or at least resting on the man's left shoulder. So this nice lady was Radgill Richey Hayes.

"Mrs. Hayes, is this your Ford Escort?"

A blank look appeared abruptly in Mrs. Hayes's eyes. Then, just as abruptly, it went away, and she looked directly into Mike's face. The earlier moment of recognition evolved into full cognizance. "Aha!"

"Aha?"

"Aha! You're the young man who tailed me all afternoon yesterday. Thought I'd finally lost you." She looked at Mike more carefully. "But somehow I thought it was a priest in that car."

Mike couldn't find enough words to apologize to Radgill Richey Hayes.

‡‡‡

ASIDE FROM discovering that he and Radgill Richey Hayes had no known ancestral links, he knew no more than he did before his ill-fated journey down Route 28. He pulled into the Sarah's Cafe parking lot but didn't see Carlos's Crown Vic anywhere. Mike grabbed his jacket to ward off Sarah's high-powered AC, found a table, and ordered his customary Heineken. He looked at his watch. Carlos had never been this late before. He waited another ten minutes and picked up his cell to punch in Carlos's number. No signal in Sarah's Cafe. He knew that. He stepped out of the booth to take the cell outside, and Carlos charged into the restaurant like a cop on a mission.

"Sorry about that." Carlos gave no further explanation for his tardy entrance.

"Two Reubens with sweet potato fries coming right up," Sarah snapped with the practiced clip of the old-time waitress.

"Whatcha been up to, Mike? Didn't know you were in the market for new wheels."

"You noticed, huh?"

"Yup. It's my business to notice things." Carlos took a sip of his Diet Coke. "Or it *was* my business."

"What?"

"For reasons I shall not enumerate, Jerry has decided to take me off the case."

Mike scowled. "What?"

"And any case in which you are involved. Jerry seems to think I'm too close to you to be unbiased."

The scowl turned into a long stare. "But…"

"No buts. That's the way he sees it, and that's the way it's going to be." Carlos closed his eyes for a moment. "Now, what was it you wanted to talk to me about?"

Mike told Carlos everything. The tailing, the accident, the license search, Radgill Richey Hayes.

Ten seconds turned into twenty before Carlos spoke. "I owe you an apology, Mike."

Those were the last words Mike expected to hear. *Stay out of police business, Mike. You're gonna get yourself killed, Mike. You're in over your head, Mike.* That was the usual litany, and that was what Mike had braced himself for. But *I owe you an apology, Mike?* He frowned. "You owe me an apology?"

"We knew about Mrs. Hayes, Mike. We already had the license tag number, and we had already traced it to Radgill Richey Hayes. We did a background check on the lady and found absolutely nothing that would, by any stretch of the imagination, link her with any crime whatsoever."

"Why, Carlos? Why didn't you tell me?"

"We wanted you to mind your own business."

"If this isn't my business, I don't know what is. My father's dead. My brothers are dead. My life has been threatened. My son's frightened. I cannot sit still and think that this is none of my business."

Carlos said nothing.

"What else haven't you told me?"

"I don't want to lose my best friend, Mike."

"What else haven't you told me?"

Carlos looked down at his barely touched Reuben and picked at it nervously with his fork. Then he took two heavy breaths and looked back at Mike. "You're determined, aren't you, my friend."

"Some folks might call me stubborn."

Carlos grinned. "Yup."

Mike returned the grin. "You didn't have to agree with me."

"Mike, I tell you what. I can't legally or ethically give you any info regarding this case while it's under investigation. But I am interested in keeping you alive. I want you to come to me when you need me. I will help when I can. I can't guarantee anything. But I won't fight you."

"That's all I ask."

"I cannot speak for Jerry."

They finished their Reubens, speaking only of children and workouts and running and God.

TWENTY-TWO

CARLOS CLOSED out the last file on his computer, locked his office, and headed home. He was exhausted, but he would certainly not allow his exhaustion to interfere with his evening. It was Friday and he expected the girls to come home from college about six or so. The girls' visits were always major events for Carlos. It was easier, of course, when Ellen was home, but he wouldn't allow her absence to slow him down. As was their custom, they would cook out. Carlos was an expert at the grill. They would watch a DVD of his daughters' choice and talk about school and anything else the girls wanted to talk about. And then on Saturday the twins would do whatever it is teenage girls often do on the weekend—go to the mall or whatever. He greatly valued his time with the girls.

Carlos especially looked forward to this visit. Ever since Jerry's lecture in the hospital—*Gentlemen,* Jerry had said, *your children are your most valued treasure. Don't ever forget that*—he had been more concerned about the girls than ever. He had talked to one of them every day since.

The house stood empty and dark. He flipped the light switch. *¡Sí!* The cleaning woman had done her job well. He took the two long-stemmed yellow roses he had purchased on his way home and placed them carefully in their bud vases in the center of the dining table. Each rose had a tag that read,

To my beautiful daughter Rita and *To my beautiful daughter Laura—for the laughter, the brightness, the pleasure, and the love you have brought to me. Dad.*

He stood back and looked at the roses and gave them a nod and a smile. Rita and Laura had not lived here for ten years, since Carlos and Dorothy had split up. So Carlos did everything he could to make them feel at home.

Carlos had come home at noon to prep the Big Green Egg—the smoker-grill he had purchased when Rita and Laura had first moved down from Montana. He regulated the heat at between 200 and 250 degrees and went back into the kitchen. He laid the ribs out on the cutting board and massaged his homemade dry bar-be-cue rub carefully into every crevice of the meat. He covered the ribs with aluminum foil and left them to stand at room temperature for a half hour. Carlos ate his lunch while he waited on the ribs. Then he placed the ribs carefully in the Egg and closed the lid. They would be just right in four or five hours.

Now the clock read 5:03. He checked on the Egg and the beautiful ribs. About another hour to go. He spent the next thirty minutes or so prepping the vegetables. He quickly sliced mushrooms, a couple of zucchinis, an onion, a Japanese eggplant, and multicolored bell peppers and threw them in a Zip-Lock bag. There. He was finished. Everything would be ready when the girls got home around six o'clock or so.

Carlos picked up the *Madison Times*, and sat down in his La-Z-Boy to await the twins' arrival. His fatigue gradually insinuated itself throughout his body, and the newspaper dropped slowly into his lap.

Carlos awoke with a snort. The clock read 7:42. "The ribs," he muttered. He ran out to the Egg and grabbed the ribs up and onto a platter and sighed. *Overdone! Far too overdone.* He sighed again.

The girls! The twins were not there. He ran back into the house, grabbed the phone, and dialed Rita's cell. It rang the required number of times and threw the call over to voice mail. A jolt shot through his body. "Rita, sweetie, when you get this, give your old man a call, will you? I'm worried about you and Laura, honey." He hung up.

Carlos sat and waited for his mind to clear. He picked up the phone again and dialed Laura.

Second ring. "Hi, Dad." Loud rock music hopped in the background.

"Hi, sweetheart." Carlos tried to sound chipper, although he felt anything but. "Got worried about you and Rita, sweetheart. What's up?"

"Oh, Dad. I'm so sorry. Shoulda called you. We stopped over at Andy's place and…"

Andy? Who's Andy? Andy's Place? Sounds like a seedy bar of some kind.

"…and he and Ron had take-out cheeseburger pizza. We just let the time slip up on us."

Carlos's heart sank. He didn't know whether to be angry or thankful. Angry. Angry. He had to choose angry. Never mind the Big Egg. "Who's Andy and Ron?"

"They're roommates at MU."

Yeah. Yeah. Madison University. I got that.

"Andy Swayne and Ron Lassiter. They live in Connaught Hall. We met them last summer when we moved down from Montana. Remember, we stopped at Burger King to eat supper, and they were there. They offered to help us move our stuff into your house."

Uh huh. Carlos remembered the two boys now. But he didn't remember anything else about them. "Laura, I'd like for you and Rita to come on home."

"Not now, Dad. Please. We'd like to stay a while longer."

"Now, Laura."

"Tell you what, Dad. We'll be there before twelve, and then we'll have all day tomorrow to spend with you."

"Now, Laura!"

"No, Dad." And the line went dead.

Carlos slammed down the receiver. He could feel the blood rushing to his face. He shot up from the La-Z-Boy, stormed to his wet bar, and downed a shot of Jim Beam without a chaser. And then another. He paced from the bar to the front door, then back to the bar for another shot. He walked out the door and around the house—once, twice, thrice—and finally he sat down on the front steps.

Call Ellen. Call Ellen. She'll know what to do. She's raised a teenager of her own. Call Ellen.

Carlos got up and charged into the house and picked up the phone. He looked at his watch. *No. Can't do that now. It's only five in the morning there. Can't put this on her in the middle of the night.* He walked through the house again, and on the dining-room table he spotted the two yellow roses. Reflexively, he reached out and knocked both vases to the floor. Then instantly he knelt into the shards of glass, picked up the roses, and held them—held them next to his heart. And cried.

He didn't know how long he had knelt there, but his anger—his fear—had burned up inside him like jalapeño salsa lining the inside of his stomach.

He stood and laid the roses side by side in the center of the table and picked up the phone again. The phone rang at the other end three, four—"Pick up, Ellen. Pick up, please, honey!"—five, six times. No answer. He slammed the receiver down, wrapped his arms around himself, and shivered like the limb of a willow in a storm.

A minute or two passed. He gathered himself together, charged into his bedroom, and shut the door. He really didn't know why he shut the door—there was no one else in the house—but he did. He went to his chest-of-drawers and pulled out his tightest muscle shirt and pulled it over his head, tight over his torso, fully displaying to his advantage his bulging biceps and triceps, his solid pectorals and abdominals. He jerked on his most masculine jeans. He ran out of the house, forgetting to lock the door, jumped onto his red Harley, and headed out to Madison University.

The directory in the Connaught Hall lobby told Carlos where to go. He didn't wait for the elevator but bounded up the stairs, three steps at a time, and stopped at the door. Loud music, giggling and laughing, clinking of glasses. *Dammit!* He beat on the door several times with the side of his right fist. The giggling and laughing abruptly stopped. He beat the door again. He almost shouted, *Police! Open up!* But he refrained.

The music suddenly stopped. He beat on the door one more time. A few seconds later the door timidly cracked open, and a young man, a small pimple between the eyes of an otherwise handsome face, appeared on the other side. With practiced foot, Carlos shoved it through the crack and slammed the door back against the wall with his fist. He stared into the room.

"Dad!" the girls cried out in unison. Tears burst out of their eyes like water from a tap, and, almost in unison, the twins wrapped their arms around themselves and stared at their father as if he were an alien from Jupiter or somewhere.

The furniture had been moved aside, and the rug had been rolled up and placed on the thrift-store sofa. His disheveled daughters stood against the window holding their breath. *Hmmm.* No clothing appeared to be missing, but out of the corner of his eye, he spotted several Bud Lite bottles piled in a corner beside the now-quiet stereo.

"We're dancing, Dad. Just dancing," Rita said. "That's all."

"*¡Llegar a casa ahora!*" Carlos shouted.

"But Dad—"

"Get home now!"

Carlos looked at the boys, standing, like two pitiful puppies, beside the girls. He moved toward them and lifted his massive arms, his tight fists directed toward the boys. If he had intended to intimidate them, he certainly had succeeded.

"No, Dad. Don't. Please don't!"

"Then get home—now!"

Laura looked at her dad as if she had never seen him before. In fact she had never seen *this* dad before. "We're leaving, Dad," Laura said. "But we're not going to your house. We're going back to college where we belong."

The girls gathered their things and headed out. Laura turned back and said, "Call us, Dad, when you feel like apologizing." And they hurried down the stairs.

"We're sorry, Mr. Ruiz," Andy said.

Carlos relaxed his arms and looked more carefully at the two handsome young men.

"Yes, Mr. Ruiz, we're really sorry," Ron added. "We didn't know—"

Carlos's mind dug severely back into the past, and the past revealed itself vividly. At Clemson, when he and his roommate—with similar bunks and similar furniture and similar girls—had done similar things.

His temper roiled again, but he said nothing. He gritted his teeth, he tightened his fists, and he squeezed his lips together like the pages of a book. These boys—Ron and Andy—they did have names after all—doing nothing more than he himself had done when he was at Clemson. Without further comment, his lips softened, his fists unfolded, and his jaw relaxed. "No, boys. Ron and Andy," he said with quiet fortitude. He walked over and placed his hands on the boys' shoulders, almost as if he were offering them absolution. "*I'm sorry.*" And he left the room.

TWENTY-THREE

MIKE SNORTED—not once, but twice—and jerked awake. He sat up in bed as if he had heard a gunshot, and it took a moment to clear his brain. His body crumpled into an impotent collapse last night when he hit the bed. He had followed two false leads and had queried three hobes. He had dropped in on Mack when Jerry was not there to avoid an unpleasantness he did not feel capable of facing right then. It was one o'clock this morning before he got back to the rectory. He had eaten his way through the leftovers in the fridge— which was unusual—had left the dirty dishes in the sink—which was unusual—and had slept until nine this morning—which was certainly unusual.

For the first time in many years, Mike hesitated to rouse himself from the bed. His mind went back to all the possible evidence sources of yesterday, but it continually zipped back to Mack. It had been two weeks since his fever broke, and he had improved so rapidly that the doctors were stunned in disbelief. He now had only a small, patch-bandage over his wound. His mental competence had apparently fully returned. And he had been walking all over the hospital, interacting with other patients, especially the young ones. *Thank God.*

Then he thought of the Y. He had to get back to the Y today. He had missed a week and was as hungry for the sweat as he had been for the turkey sandwich he had thrown together in the small hours of the morning. But he couldn't get up—not right now anyway.

The telephone changed all that.

"Hey, Mike."

"Hey, Carlos. What's up?"

"How about a little brunch at Sarah's—say eleven?"

"When's the last time you've been to the Y?"

"*Siempre*. Forever."

"How about meeting me there in twenty minutes and we'll go to Sarah's afterwards."

Carlos hesitated. "Let me check my—yeah, I think I can manage that."

Mike got there first. It had felt so good running to Downing Street in the slightly warm morning mist. It could have poured waterfalls and he wouldn't have cared. Few people were in the Y this time of the day. Most came early, during lunchtime, or after work. So there was a sense of privacy here that he needed right now.

He wiped down the sidebars and the control buttons, set the level and speed, and started the belt revolving. A moment later he looked up, and Carlos was marching right beside him, pushing the speed button every time Mike did. And so the competition renewed itself. For one brief moment, Mike allowed himself a surge of exuberance. If he could have been happy, he would have been happy now. But his disconsolation overruled his contentment, and the pleasure dampened into a gaunt depression.

After the weights and the showers, the two headed back to town in the Crown Vic, settled into a parking spot adjacent to Sarah's, and walked in to claim their usual table. Mike shivered a bit and wished for his jacket—*oh, what the heck*—and settled down. Sarah was already at the table waiting for them. She repeated the twin orders back to them: "Java. OJ. Omelets with hoop and country ham. Grits.

Biscuits. Coming up." She served the orders post-haste, and left them to their own devices.

They buttered their biscuits, spread them with strawberry jam, and took several bites before either of them said anything.

Mike broke the silence. "What's up?"

"I want to thank you for the prayers for Mack."

Mike held his hand up in an apparent move to protest.

"Anyway, I'm afraid Jerry is still not happy with you."

"I sensed that."

"He's under a great deal of tension now."

And who isn't?

"I know Jerry appreciates your help, whether he says so or not, but he still wants to believe you had something to do with Basil's death and perhaps even Smiley's. It's irrational, I know. Just thought you should know that." Carlos's voice trailed to an almost indecipherable quietness.

Mike looked at Carlos's face and there he detected a worry— perhaps even a feeling of despondence—and he knew Carlos had more to say but didn't want to say it. "And what else?"

Carlos waited. "I've got a problem."

Carlos has a problem. Jerry has a problem. We all have problems. Does somebody want to shoot Carlos in the head? Is somebody trying to eliminate Rita and Laura? Is Jerry trying to frame Carlos for a crime he didn't commit? Carlos has a problem?

"Carlos?" Mike felt like getting up from the table and tearing through the continent nonstop from here to Nome. "Carlos. How can I help you, my friend?"

Little by little, episode by episode, scene by scene, Carlos told Mike the story of Rita and Laura and himself. And of Andy and Ron. "I've—I've never felt so helpless in all my life." That was an arduous admission for this steel-bodied cop.

Mike said nothing.

"I'm desperate, Father Mike."

"Are you asking for absolution, Carlos?"

"Absolution? Have I done anything I need absolution for?"

"I don't know. Have you?"

"Don't play games with me, Mike. I need your help, not your sarcasm."

"I really didn't mean to sound sarcastic, Carlos. That was not my purpose at all." It was difficult to counsel a friend.

The two talked—and ate from time to time—refilling their mugs as needed from the thermal carafe Sarah had left on the table. They talked another half-hour, not always about—or directly about—Carlos's problem. But everything said, every point raised, every question asked eventually led back to Carlos and his daughters.

"At this point," Mike said, "it is not important who's right and who's wrong. Reconciliation must be the priority now. Once that is achieved, you'll be surprised at how so many other things will fall into place."

Carlos lifted the final spoonful of grits to his mouth and looked at Mike.

Mike raised his brows. "That could start with an apology." He wanted to make sure Carlos understood him and kept his eyes on Carlos's eyes.

Carlos lowered his head and nodded.

Mike reached over and touched his friend's hand. "God be with you, Carlos."

Their brunch had long been finished, and Sarah hadn't interrupted once—not even to ask the banal question, *Is everything okay?* That probably was the best thing about coming to Sarah's. She read her patrons with frightening accuracy. When she sensed the customer needed to be hovered over, she was capable of hovering. When she sensed the customer needed to be left alone, she could do that too. She only now appeared to leave the check.

The two moseyed back to the Crown Vic, and Carlos let Mike off at the front steps to the rectory. He climbed the steps and reached for his house key.

"Mike!" Carlos called.

Mike turned around to see Carlos coming toward him on the walkway holding a cube-shaped cardboard box. It looked like the doggy toy Tim stuffed dry dog food in. Mr. Craggles had long had a wonderful time extracting the food from the cube—one ort at the time.

"Sorry, Mike. I almost forgot the main reason for calling you this morning."

Mike raised his eyebrows.

Carlos placed the box in Mike's hand. "Here are Basil's ashes."

TWENTY-FOUR

AT EXACTLY one o'clock in the afternoon on the Monday afterwards, the sexton, Jake Dobbins, swung open the enormous west doors of this once-beautiful, neogothic church. Since the severe change in demographics over the past ten years, the remnant left in this downtown parish had been financially unable to keep the church in good repair, and the façade had deteriorated considerably. Father Mike had made some headway in raising the needed funds since his arrival, but it would take several years and much more money to bring the fabric back to its one-time glory. But Jake went about his business as he had for the last thirty years. Today he was making sure the narthex was presentable for the parishioners and others who would be attending Sir's funeral, and he needed to air out the stuffy old building.

Jake threw open the north door. Time was when he could see across to Masters Park and he could admire the beauty of the flowers and trees and other vegetation. He could hear the sounds of children playing, Little League bats cracking against hard round balls, birds singing their praises to God on early Sunday mornings. But no more. All he could see now across Orca Alley was a drab zoomed-in view of the Bigham Building, a fifteen-story medical-office structure erected ten years ago. Orca Alley was a lane dedicated primarily to trash and garbage pickups, and the occasional street person who made his living digging around in the Dumpsters. The hobes normally did not make their camps in Orca for reasons no one really knew. Jake made a mental note to close and secure this door before the congregation began to arrive.

Along side the north door inside the narthex, a set of steps, akin to the winding stairway in Hitchcock's *Vertigo,* issued into the balcony and then upward still into the bell tower three stories above street level. St. Christopher's choir once sang from the ornate balcony. Every time Jake looked at those stairs, he longed for those days to return. But, because of the years of deterioration, the balcony was no longer used, and a velvet-covered chain now hung across the stairwell to prevent entrance.

Then he threw open the south door with a view to Abel Street. The traffic on Abel was moderately still at this time of day. But he was certain the street would be lined with the cars of those who would come to honor Sir this afternoon. *Good for them!*

Jake turned and crossed back toward the nave. Then something caught his attention—the stairway into the balcony. Something was wrong. The left end of the chain was not even with the right end. *What the—* Although Jake certainly had never used the word *perfectionist* and probably had never heard of it, Jake surely was one. Everything he did at St. Christopher's had to be perfect. He owed that much to God and to Father Mike. And he would never have left an uneven chain across these stairs. Jake took a closer look. The left-end hook had been fastened to the wrong eyescrew. There were two eyescrews attached to the left newel post. The top eyescrew—the original eyescrew—had been placed there before he had come to St Christopher's. Jake had placed the lower eyescrew there himself so the chain would hang evenly. Jake started to replace the chain onto its proper eyescrew and then— *Damn! Somebody's been in the balcony.* He immediately let the chain drop and climbed the stairs to investigate.

✝✝✝

MIKE, VESTED in his alb, white stole, and cope, stood outside the west doors, watching the congregation trickle into the church. There were those parishioners from other congregations Mike had served, who came out of respect for their beloved priest. There were those from St. Christopher's who knew nothing of Sir but who wanted to memorialize Mike's father. Then there were those who knew Sir. Of course there were June and Harlan and Mary and all those others who faithfully served in St. Christopher's Diner. And then there were Gin-Gin and Marty and Tom-Tom and Jimbo and a host of other street folks, who knew Sir and had come to pray for him. By the time the people packed the church, a dozen or more shopping carts littered the sidewalks around St. Christopher's. Everybody was there with the notable exception of Annabel Leigh Richey and Timothy Michael Richey, and Mike's heart crumbled.

Mike carried Basil's urn in his hands. Inez had finally legally released her control over the ashes. Mike remembered Inez's acrimony.

I don't want them, she had insisted. *You can keep his goddamned ashes.*

But surely— Mike had started to reply.

No, Mike. The first five years were good—or relatively so, she said. *But after that my life was one of sheer misery. His drinking grew worse, and we stayed in constant combat. When he was drinking, he often let me know in no uncertain terms that he deeply regretted leaving your mother and you. I grew bitter—still am bitter.*

Miss Inez, I—

Inez pushed her palm toward Mike as if to silence him.

Mike was suddenly jarred from his digression when, out of the corner of his eye, he spotted a black Ford Escort parked about two blocks down Church Street. Not able to keep his eyes off the automobile, he lagged some ten feet behind the procession into the church. Why did he keep thinking about that Escort? Hadn't Radgill Richey Hayes and her Escort been proved innocent? *Okay, Mike. Quit the stupidity. The car could belong to anybody in the congregation.*

Mike turned his attention back to the procession and the beautiful resurrection hymn, *This is the feast of victory for our God. Alleluia! Alleluia! Alleluia.* The thurifer did a 360-degree revolution of the thurible, and the sweet smell of incense filled the nave. The crucifer, who had the awe-inspiring responsibility of bearing the cross of Christ through the midst of the congregation, was flanked on both sides by two torchbearers, who lit the way of the cross with their tall candlesticks.

Mike gazed down the long aisle and was immediately struck by, though he had seen it many dozens of times, the most resplendent stained glass window that adorned the church—the depiction of the Resurrection of Our Lord. Then the large wooden cross hanging above the beautifully appointed altar, the eucharistic candles and fresh flowers, and the paten and chalice that would soon contain the real presence of Christ, seemed to welcome Basil and Mike to the holy altar of God.

The choir and other ministers took their places, and Mike placed the urn, loosely draped with a white veil, on a small table below the chancel steps. He moved around the table to face the altar, took the thurible, and processed around the altar leaving clouds of billowing incense smoke rising as the prayers of the faithful ascended to the heavens. He censed the ministers and the congregation and then the urn with three swings of the thurible. He returned the thurible to the thurifer and turned to face the congregation.

Using the venerable words of *The Book of Common Prayer*, Mike spoke.

> *I am Resurrection and I am Life, says the Lord. Whoever has faith in me shall have life, even though he die. And everyone who has life, and has committed himself to me in faith, shall not die for ever.*

Then Mike glanced up toward the balcony and, for one brief moment, thought he saw a black shadow flash by, but he quickly dismissed it.

O God, whose mercies cannot be numbered: Accept our prayers on behalf of your servant Basil, and grant him an entrance into the land of light and joy, in the fellowship of your saints...

Lectors from the congregation came forward and read the usual biblical lessons for the burial office. A deacon sent from the bishop for the occasion read the Gospel lesson. Father Mike moved toward the pulpit for the homily. He was struck again—as he was every time he preached—with the beautifully carved cherubim and seraphim and hosts of angels singing *holy, holy, holy* that adorned the pulpit's façade. He scaled the short flight of steps and took his place in this grand Victorian-style structure.

Mike paused and looked out over the congregation. He allowed his gaze to venture to every corner of the nave. He searched for Inez. There. There were Lorraine and Judy. No Inez in sight. He allowed his eyes to drift back to his homily manuscript on the pulpit. But still he waited. He looked up again. The people waited expectantly for him to say something. Anything. But Mike's heart trembled. He had never been in this position before. These were his father's ashes before him. His father was a hobe. But nothing came. At last, he crossed himself and spoke, "In the name of the Father, and of the Son, and of the Holy Spirit. Amen."

Mike had worked until three this morning on his homily and was unhappy with what he had written. What could he say about a father whom he hardly knew? A father who had turned his back on his mother? A father who had broken his heart at the age of ten? For a moment he felt weak, as if he were going to collapse. He held on to the sides of the pulpit until his whitened knuckles grew red. He gazed into the congregation again as the people began to rustle uneasily.

"Say somethin', Father!" shouted Tom-Tom.

The homeless folk began to fidget. "Yeah. Say somethin'!" Gin-Gin yelled.

Many in the congregation craned their necks to see where the commotion was coming from.

Then he looked to the left and saw Jerry and Carlos sitting side by side. His mouth ticced involuntarily. He looked to the right and saw Bishop Michener smiling at him. She gave him a reassuring nod, and Mike nodded in return.

"My brothers and sisters in Christ," he began. The rustling slowed down, and he looked back at his manuscript. He paused again, looked up, and abruptly closed the manuscript folder. He briefly noticed a torn piece of paper protruding from the edge of the folder. A note— from the bishop, perhaps? But that could wait. He looked the congregation straight in the eyes. Now was the moment.

"Bless me, my brothers and sisters, for I have sinned." Mike bowed his head.

The rustling started again. He lifted his hand to quieten the crowd, and a great hush fell upon the congregation.

"I have a confession to make to you." He glanced at the smiling bishop. The prelate nodded again.

Mike turned directly to the coterie of two dozen or so homeless men and women who had segregated themselves to the left of the congregation. "I came to St. Christopher's because I loved you."

The rabble began to rumble again. Mike swept his hand over to the hobes. "Yes, you," he shouted above the rattling din. And the rumble quietened. "I loved you as I visited you in your alleys and your card board tents."

Solid silence. Mike heard a service bulletin flutter to the floor of the nave.

"I loved you when you came to St. Christopher's Diner to eat and to chat. I especially loved you when you began to see your friends dying one by one—including Juice and Sir and Smiley. I loved you because our Lord loved you and gave himself for you."

A mockingbird sang his exquisite hymns just outside the Resurrection window.

"I wanted to be like our Lord. I wanted to feed the hungry, give drink to the thirsty, welcome the stranger, clothe the naked, comfort the sick, and visit the prisoners, all as our Lord commanded. In short,

I loved you, and a great many other people in this congregation loved you as well. There was June and there was Harlan and there was my beloved wife Annie. And there was my son—Tim. And there was a host of others—like the angels carved in the façade of this beautiful pulpit."

The hush deepened.

"I loved Gin-Gin and Tom-Tom and Marty and Smiley and all of you wonderful creatures of God. And I loved Sir. Sir was very special to me."

Mike had never seen a congregation so still.

"But the one person I did not, would not, and could not love was Michael Basil Richey, my biological father, the man whose ashes rest here."

There was a slight stir and Mike saw Inez Richey enter the nave and step into the back pew.

"Basil Richey left my mother and me when I was a boy of ten." He glanced at Inez. "And another woman took my mother's place as his wife."

Inez sat motionless.

"I never heard from my father again until six months ago when Sir came to Madison. It was not until Sir's death that I discovered that he was Michael Basil Richey."

The bishop nodded.

"And I went into a formidable rage. I not only disliked him, I hated him. I think I had never really hated anyone before. But I hated Michael Basil Richey."

The mumbling mounted.

"And I hated the woman who took him away from my mother and me."

The dissonance rose to a thousand decibels. Mike looked again at Inez. She sat stone-faced. He again raised his hand for silence, and the noise subsided.

"That was my sin! I am sorry for my sin. I want to love my father, and I want to love my stepmother." Mike paused. "That's strange. I've never thought of her as my stepmother before."

He looked at Inez. No change. He didn't know anything else to say. Mike paused and looked at the bishop. She was still smiling and nodding. He bowed his head.

Mike heard the noise again and he stiffened. It started among the hobes. He could hear them becoming restless. Mike was afraid of a mass exodus. But then he heard more. One clap at first, and then two and three and four and then the whole congregation burst forth in an applause that would awake even Basil and threaten the rafters of the old structure.

It was then he knew—knew for a fact—that he was forgiven.

The applause began to die down, and Mike looked up. There was someone standing. It was Inez. She disappeared through the back door of the nave.

"My brothers and sisters." He adjusted his cope. "I can assure you this day and particularly this moment, there is indeed resurrection and there is life. I failed to understand when Sir's one word to me was *fahta* that he was not addressing me as a priest but was trying to reveal himself to me as my own father and was asking for my forgiveness and love as his son."

Mike stepped down from the pulpit and crossed to Basil's urn. He looked out again upon the entire congregation. "Just as surely as God's children will rise again at the last day to be with our Lord, so do we rise again every time we are forgiven—and every time we forgive."

Father Mike stretched out his hand over the urn and addressed Basil's ashes, "As a priest of Jesus Christ and his Church and as your own son, I forgive you all your sins." Making the sign of the cross over the ashes, he added the powerful Trinitarian formula, "In the name of the Father, and of the Son, and of the Holy Spirit." And the people shouted, "Amen!"

The congregation erupted again into even greater applause than before, an applause that would equal that of the grandest opera at the Met. Mike glanced to the balcony again and saw a brief movement.

Then suddenly Mike felt the blood drain from his body, and he began crumpling down—down toward the chancel steps.

TWENTY-FIVE

MIKE'S EYES abruptly opened. Fuzzy at first, the long unlit fluorescent fixture came into focus. The drab, suspended ceiling opened up nothing to him. Another fluorescent fixture above his headboard shed dim light on the sterile, white room. He knew where he was. He had seen the inside of a hospital room hundreds of times. But he didn't know why he was here. He closed his eyes only to open them again, when he felt the moist warm familiar lips upon his own. Annie brushed her face against his, and Mike felt the gentle tears against his cheek. Ordinarily he would be ready to shed his clerical collar if he had had one on. But not today. His body was in no condition for that.

"Hello, sweetheart." Annie brushed a tear away with her gentle fingers.

"Hi, beautiful." At the moment he gave no thought to where he was—or, for that matter, where he had been.

"Welcome back. We thought we had lost you." Annie rang for the nurse. "They made me promise to call them when you woke up."

Mike closed his eyes.

"May I help you?" the electronic voice responded.

"Mike's awake now."

"A nurse will be right there." A short click on the speaker and the sound shut off.

"What's this all about?" Mike asked.

Annie took his fingers and placed them against his face. *Gauze*, he thought. *A bandage.*

"What's this all about?" he repeated.

"You've been shot. Somebody tried to kill you."

Mike clenched his fists. "Tim! Where's Tim? The guy'll think I'm dead and go after Tim."

Before Annie could answer, two green-scrubbed nurses rushed into the room. Nurse Sharon Potter crossed to the bed, and Nurse Amy Glidemore moved to the other side.

"Glad you're here, Father," Sharon said.

"Should I be glad too?" Mike asked.

The nurses took note of Mike's vital signs as electronically registered by the nurse-on-a-stick and then proceeded with their business, testing Mike's eyesight, his hearing, and performing other vital examinations.

✝✝✝

ANNIE SAT down in the chair beside Mike's hospital bed and thought back on the four days since she and Tim had rushed from her parents' home. About three-thirty in the afternoon, her stomach had suddenly jumped into her throat. She mentioned to her mother her fear that something—she didn't know what—had happened to Mike.

Surely not, her mother said. *It's only natural under these circumstances to be afraid.*

But Annie couldn't let go of it. Mike's secretary answered his office phone and assured her that he was in the church conducting Basil's funeral. Annie had begun to lower her guard, when the phone shook the house with a cruel vibrato. Her mother answered and then passed the receiver on to Annie. It was Carlos. It took about ten minutes to pack, and she and Tim were on their way back to Madison. The Sumter Police Department had generously provided the transportation.

Officer Millard Sparks greeted them at the hospital door. "Hi, Ms. Richey. Sorry about Father Mike."

"Thanks, Officer," she said, holding onto Tim with a vise grip, and they made their way toward the front desk. Carlos intercepted them before they reached the receptionist.

"Hi, Annie. Hi, Tim." He kissed Annie gently on the cheek. "Let's sit over here for a few minutes."

"But I want to see Mike," she pleaded.

"He's in surgery now," Carlos replied. "Been in about two hours now. We'll all have to wait awhile."

Annie could not wait another moment. Her tears had dissipated, but her stomach was in ruins. Carlos maneuvered Annie and Tim over to a small, deserted corner of the waiting room and sat down beside her. She rebuffed his consolations. She really didn't want to be consoled. She wanted to see Mike.

"Officer Collins," he called.

Officer Sara Collins emerged from a trio of officers who were apparently waiting for orders from Detective Ruiz. Carlos stood and escorted her over to Annie. "Officer Collins, this is Annie Richey and her son Tim."

"Ms. Richey," she responded. "Hi, Tim."

Annie nodded.

"Tim has had a hard journey from Sumter and is probably hungry by now. Will you take him to the cafeteria and get him a pizza or hamburger or something?"

"Certainly, sir." She turned to Tim. "Wanta come with me, Tim? I'm hungry too. I didn't have much lunch."

"But I wanta see Dad," Tim said, reluctant to leave his mother.

"Tim, we'll get you in to see him as soon as the doctors will let us. Okay?" Carlos promised.

"But you're a policeman. You could make them let us in."

"I'm afraid it doesn't work that way, Tim. We'll get there as quickly as we can."

"Go on with Officer Collins, Tim. You'll be okay," Annie urged.

"We'll be sure to get you when we're allowed to see your dad," Carlos said.

Tim reluctantly went with Officer Collins. She attempted to take his hand, but he rebuffed her. "I'll be okay."

The officer smiled. "No problem," she assured him as they moved through the exit.

"Carlos," Annie pleaded as soon as Tim was beyond earshot. "What happened? Is Mike going to be okay?"

"I'll be honest with you, Annie. He almost died. And we don't know now what the doctors will find."

The greatest dread filled Annie's psyche. "I can't lose him, Carlos. I can't lose him!"

"I don't believe you will lose him. I can't believe *we'll* lose him."

Annie struggled for words. "Tell me—what—happened, Carlos."

"Mike was celebrating the requiem eucharist. In the homily, he told the congregation that he now felt completely absolved for his hate of Basil."

"Yes. This was hanging over his head like an anvil. The bishop had advised him to do the funeral. She believed the funeral itself would assuage his guilt."

"When he finished the homily, he stepped down from the pulpit and crossed to the body—the ashes—and absolved Basil both as a priest and as Basil's son. The congregation gave Mike a thunderous ovation."

Tears gushed from Annie's eyes. Carlos reached over to an end table, plucked a tissue from the box, and handed it to Annie.

"Thanks," she said.

"During the deafening cacophony, a bullet came from the balcony and pierced his right temple, and it lodged somewhere in his cranium."

"Oh, God, no!" She wrapped her arms around her own shoulders and recoiled into a shriveled ball. "But what's happening now, Carlos?"

"The doctors are working to remove the bullet and see what damage has resulted. So now we just wait and see. It's been a little over two hours since they took him into the OR."

The waiting part would be almost more than she could bear. She whispered a prayer. Carlos said "Amen" and placed his arm around her shoulders.

"What about the gunman?" Annie asked.

"Or gun woman," Mike corrected. "We have some evidence that the shooter could possibly be a woman. There was a woman's broken shoe heel near the balcony steps. That does not prove anything, of course. But it does open up the possibility."

"But how did the guy get away?" Annie was not interested in whether the perp was a man or woman. *Guy* would do for her now.

"After the shooting, the perp apparently ran down the balcony stairs and escaped into the dark alley through the north narthex door. The door had been standing wide open. That in itself was highly unusual."

"I know."

"There's reason to believe it's the same person who killed Basil."

Carlos reached for another tissue. Annie grabbed it quickly and wiped the moisture from her face. Annie felt a tap on her shoulder.

"Ms. Richey," Nurse Sharon said. "Are you okay?"

Annie abruptly awoke from her trance. "Sorry. I must have drifted."

She watched the nurses complete their assignment. Mike had been lying there sedated for nearly four days with tubes, multicolored wires, needles, and all sorts of accoutrements attached to his body. At least he was there—and not in the columbarium niche. At least he was partially awake—and not in some kind of coma. At least he could still speak—sort of.

"Ms. Richey, Doctor Ranhaji will be here shortly. He's on his way from the sixth floor. He'll answer any questions. But, Ms. Richey, I believe Father Mike is going to be okay."

"Thanks, Sharon."

Dr. Ranhaji had, of course, talked with Annie immediately after the surgery, but now was the real test. Now she would know. Now she could relax—at least for the moment. As Sharon and Amy started to leave, the doctor swept into the room with an entourage of nurses and young residents. He nodded to Annie, spoke to her briefly, and then rushed to Mike's bedside. He took Sharon's report and greeted the priest.

"Hello, Father," he said with a Mid-Eastern accent.

Mike greeted the doctor with a mumble. Before saying anything else, Dr. Ranhaji did a series of his own tests, many of which the nurses had already performed. He pored over Nurse Sharon's notes to see if he had been able to replicate the results of her examinations. The enormous amount of waiting time put Annie on edge.

"I believe I've got good news for you, Father." He turned so he could include Annie.

Ranhaji explained in physicianese what had occurred in Mike's head and then translated himself into more understandable language. "In other words, you're going to be okay. The bullet entered the left occipital region and it passed into the periphery of the right temporal lobe, where it lodged."

Mike frowned and started to speak but decided against it.

"The surgery was successful, and with a bit of rehab, you'll be just fine. I'm giving you a lighter sedative now. You really need to rest for two or three more days. I've given Officer Ruiz permission to visit you for a few minutes, but after that you must sleep."

After some further instructions, Dr. Ranhaji and his retinue moved on to another room and another patient, and Annie rose from the chair, crossed to the hospital bed, and caressed Mike's face. He reached up and touched her hand.

"I love you," she whispered.

"I love you back," Mike smiled. He still sounded as if he had a mouth full of sterile cotton balls, but Annie understood him clearly.

She pecked him on the lips.

Mike grinned. "My clerical collar is off."

"But I didn't see you take it off, now did I?"

"Is that a prerequisite?"

"'Fraid so." She kissed him again.

Mike reached up and touched Annie's arm. "Where's Tim?"

"Mom and Dad came up from Sumter. They're keeping him for us at the Hotel Bentley. The police have stationed a uniform in the hotel corridor. He's been in to see you several times, but you weren't awake enough to know."

"I think I remember hearing his voice. I need to see him. Just to know he's okay."

"I'll ask Mom and Dad to bring him up this afternoon. He'll be so happy to see you awake."

"It's great that I'm going to be okay. But I still don't know what I'm okay for." The door from the corridor opened a crack. "I don't know what happened, except I was shot in the head."

"Perhaps I can answer that," Carlos said, pushing the door open further and coming into the room.

"Hi, Carlos," Mike greeted. "Hey, hey, hey. Tell me what all this is about."

Carlos came in and crossed to the bed.

Annie interrupted, "Hi, Carlos." She turned to Mike. "The bishop stayed for the duration of the surgery. She asked me to call her when you woke up. I'll go on and do that now." She gave Mike another peck on the lips and left the room.

✝✝✝

SO?" MIKE questioned as he took Carlos's hand and squeezed it for a moment.

Carlos began at the beginning and told Mike everything from the moment Mike was shot—where the shot came from, what kind of gun the bullet came from, how the shooter escaped, and even about the broken shoe heel.

Inez? Mike thought but didn't say anything. Then his mind turned to the narthex door. "That door the shooter escaped through is seldom open. Jake never opens that door except to air out the narthex."

"There's something else I reluctantly tell you," Carlos continued.

Mike put his hand to his bandage and then took it down again. "Tell me. I guess there's not much that can shock me now."

"We found Jake dead on the upper flight of the balcony stairs. A bullet through his head."

"Jake?" Mike crossed himself. "My dear Lord, take him unto yourself."

"He apparently had heard some sort of noise in the balcony stairs and went up to investigate. If that is true, then we are pretty certain the perp had planted himself—or herself—in the balcony before the congregation started arriving for the funeral. Jake apparently surprised the murderer and got himself killed."

Inez did come in late and leave early. Mike confided his thoughts about Inez to Carlos.

"That's something we'll need to look into."

"Thought you had been taken off the case."

Carlos smiled—sort of a quirky kind of smile. "Back on now."

Mike raised his eyebrows.

Carlos put his hand on Mike's shoulder. "Since somebody put a bullet in your skull in front of Jerry's eyes, he had no choice but to reach the conclusion that you're not the killer."

Mike tried to smile but couldn't quite make it. He just closed his eyes. Then he opened them quickly. "Basil! Basil's ashes! What happened to Basil's ashes?"

"The bishop. Bishop Michener took charge of the ashes. She saw to it that the ashes were inurned in St. Christopher's columbarium."

"Thank God."

"One more thing, Mike, I need to ask you," Carlos said.

"Yup?" Mike opened his eyes.

"Where was your sermon manuscript before you processed into the church?"

"It was in a binder open to the first page and lying on the pulpit. I always place it there before every service."

"How long had it been there before the funeral began?" Carlos queried.

"A couple of hours, maybe. I had to run an errand just before the service began and decided it would be better to go ahead and put it in place. That way I wouldn't have to worry with it immediately before the procession. Why is all this important?"

Carlos sighed. "Between pages three and four someone had inserted a note."

The proverbial pregnant pause permeated the room "The sins of the fathers," they said in unison.

Carlos continued. "The perp probably expected you to find the note during the delivery of the sermon. More than likely he was intending to shoot right after you made the discovery and paused or turned green or whatever he was expecting you to do."

Mike grunted and his lips turned up slightly at the ends. "He was that deliberate?"

"When you closed the manuscript to speak impromptu, it discombobulated him, and he had to revise the plan. So when you moved to the urn and the reverberant applause interrupted the service, he considered it a propitious moment to pull the trigger without the congregation hearing the report."

Mike yawned. The sedative had begun to do its work.

"When you dropped to the chancel steps, nobody had heard the shot. The congregation, including the cops who were present, thought you had simply blacked out from all the pressure. So they didn't react as they might have if they had heard the shot. This gave the perp a few more seconds to get out of the balcony and escape through the north narthex door without being seen."

Mike yawned again. "So that's the saga, is it?"

"*Sí*. Is there anything you can remember that might be useful to know?" Carlos asked.

Mike paused a moment. "I certainly can't think of anything." He yawned again. "If anything comes to me, I'll give you a call."

"I'll let you get back to your napping. Tell Tim I said *hey* when he comes up to see you, okay?"

"Will do," Mike slurred.

Poor Jake. He never had a...

TWENTY-SIX

ERE, PUT this on." Annie handed him his rabat and clerical collar. Mike had always worn the traditional black rabats—clerical vests priests wear over the fronts of their shirts—but on a whim he had purchased the tartan plaid vest he sometimes wore on celebratory occasions. Mike had slipped on his jeans and was unfolding his Polo shirt from the bag Annie had brought from home.

"My collar? What do I want my collar for now? This is a hospital, not a church."

"So you can take it off when we get home, silly."

Mike grinned. "So you've got an ulterior motive there, Annie Leigh Richey?"

"So I do." Annie pecked Mike on the cheek. "So I do." She leaned up against his bare chest, placed her arms around his back, and felt his prominent, firm pecs against her breasts. Then she gently reached up and touched his surgical scar—the large head bandage had, over the past three weeks, devolved into a small gauze patch. She placed what would have been a slow, prolonged kiss on Mike's lips—but— there was a brief knock on the door and it eased open.

"Harrumph." Carlos cleared his throat. He grinned and pulled the door back between him and the lascivious scene before him. "Anybody home? Hope we're not interrupting anything important."

"Stay out," Mike yelled. "Can't you see when a man is busy?" He continued to hold on to Annie for a couple of seconds, but she pressed her index finger against his lips and smiled as if to say, *I'll be back later.*

"Come on in." Annie turned to them. "Just getting him ready to go home."

The two detectives trudged into the room with no further apology.

"Wow!" said Carlos. "What a send-off!"

"Good morning, Reverend." Jerry ambled over to Mike. "How's the rehab going?"

"Great. Last three weeks in rehab have been a snap. Should be ready to hit the Y again soon."

Jerry scowled briefly and immediately changed the subject. "Sit down for a moment. We need to talk." He turned to Annie. "The doctors have been having a field day making sure we didn't come in here and disturb the reverend."

"Here you go." Carlos pulled up a chair for Mike.

Mike laid the rabat aside. "I'm not an invalid, Carlos." But he took the chair anyway.

Jerry shifted his mouth slightly and pressed his lips together. He paused a moment longer. "'Preciate your prayers in the hospital, Reverend. They meant a lot to Maureen."

Mike noticed that Jerry did not include himself, but he knew how difficult it was for him to say this much.

Mack, he told Mike and Annie, was now at home and under the care of Dr. Wyla Matthews, one of Madison's leading psychiatrists. He should be going back to school tomorrow.

"Thank God."

Jerry quickly changed the subject. "All this shooting business—"

Carlos interrupted. "We have a couple of things to talk about, and then we'll let you get back to, harrumph, whatever you were busy doing."

Mike rolled his eyes. "Thanks a lot, Carlos."

"Annie," Carlos continued, "sorry to have to tell you this, but you've got to take Tim away. As you know—and I won't beat around the bush—the killer is serious about taking Mike's life. And we're certain he's also serious about taking Tim's. So Tim's got to remain out of danger."

Annie clinched her eyes shut and reached over and took Mike's hand.

"Mike and I will take him to—"

"No!" Jerry stopped her.

Carlos held up his hand to Jerry.

Mike had never seen Carlos interrupt his superior officer before, but, other than a brief grimace, Jerry didn't seem perturbed. They must have had a prior understanding as to who would do the talking.

"What Chief Detective Majors is saying, Annie, is that you must take Tim alone with you. If Mike is with Tim, we're going to have double trouble. They'll both be in the same place, and the perp—the killer, whoever he or she is—will find it a lot easier to do his job."

"But Carlos…"

"It's got to be this way, Ms. Richey." Jerry interrupted.

Mike looked at Annie as if to say, *Everything's going to be okay, Annie. We'll get through this.*

'Reverend, you're not to correspond directly with Ms. Richey or Tim in any way until we give you the go-ahead," Jerry said. "That includes e-mail, postal mail, telephone, telegraph, text-messaging, or whatever. And if the perp is in any way technically savvy, the communication will be easy to track."

Annie shrank back as if to say, *Okay. If we must, we must.*

"As you know we've had uniforms stationed outside your hospital room ever since you've been here." Jerry's brow arched. "It's been nearly a month now."

Mike squeezed Annie's hand.

"We pressured the doctors to keep you here for longer than really necessary," Carlos said. "Mike, we wanted you to have your strength back—or most of it at least—before you got back into the world—basically alone."

"The only way you can correspond is through us." Jerry looked intently at both of them. "When either of you contacts the department, we'll be sure and get the message to the other. We have a special, secure telephone line set up for just such a purpose. Here's the number." He handed them each a card. "Memorize this number—now. Give absolutely no one this number."

Annie sighed. "Okay, Detective."

"Good," Jerry said. "Now you decide where your hideaway is going to be. And when you get there, Ms Richey, give us a call at that number on the card."

The two looked back at the cards and nodded.

"And do not go back to your parents' home, Ms. Richey. The killer will find that easily enough."

Annie winced.

"You will not drive. Officer Takesha Crimmsey will take you there. She knows how to lose a tail in the event one shows up," Jerry said. "Mrs. Richey, your parents, of course, have been keeping Tim with them at the Hotel Bentley so you could take care of the reverend while he was cooped up in this place. It was easier for us to place a guard there than at the rectory. When you leave here, go directly home. Do not go by and get Tim. I don't want you to undergo any unnecessary exposure. Officer Collins, the young lady who took care of Tim the day you arrived, Ms. Richey, will go by the hotel and bring him to your house around six this evening. Your parents will go directly to their home, and you will not see them till all of this is over. We will keep them informed as to your well-being. You will have several uniformed guards surrounding your house tonight, and Officer Crimmsey will pick you and Tim up at around 8:00 tomorrow morning."

Annie started to sigh—then caught herself.

"Now, Reverend, get your shirt on and get Ms. Richey on home." Jerry crossed over and slapped Mike on the back and grinned. "I believe you have some unfinished business to take care of." He left the room.

Mike had never seen Jerry so informal.

Carlos shook Mike's hand with both of his and then turned to hug Annie. He walked to the door, paused for a moment, and turned back. "I'll be praying for you guys."

Mike's heart was strangely warmed. "Thanks, Carlos." He raised his hand in a so-long salute.

When the cops were out of the room, Mike reached for his shirt, crossed to Annie and held her close to him. Then without warning, the Pink Lady volunteer, wheel chair in hand, knocked and shoved the door open. "Hey, I'm Georgie. Ready for the ride down?" she asked, oblivious to the scene immediately before her. Mike quickly put on his Polo and sat down in the wheelchair. Annie gathered the bags and placed them in Mike's lap, and they were off. The Pink Lady drove like Jeff Gordon.

Annie ran ahead of the chair—she had to run to get to the entrance ahead of the breakneck driver to retrieve the recently repaired Camry—and left Mike a captive audience. It had taken Georgie about three months to get over her gall bladder surgery. She had been afraid Dr. Greene had left a surgical gadget in her gut. But x-rays showed nothing. When she got home from the hospital, she had tried to pick up her twenty-four pound great-grandson. And speaking of her great-grandson—and on and on with a barrage of personal data Mike could have lived without hearing.

Officer Crimmsey stood by the Camry. "Ms. Richey? Father Mike? I have orders to follow you home, if you don't mind. Chief Detective Majors doesn't want you to be alone at any time."

"Fine, Officer" Annie said. "We'll be on our way, if you don't mind."

"Certainly, ma'am." The officer got into her patrol and waited for the Richeys to pull out.

On the way home, they said nothing and held hands like two teenagers in a movie theater

‡‡‡

ANNIE DRAGGED Mike—blindfolded—through the doorway. She ushered him into the den and turned him around to face the hallway door and gently slipped the blindfold off. *Welcome Home, Father Mike.* The swagging sign over the doorway greeted him with fervor. Multi-colored balloons, branded with quite colorful wit, hung from every available protrusion. Smaller and somewhat irreverent gags, calligraphed on unlined index cards, leaned against every lamp stand. Mike beamed. He knew the work of June Ellerbe, the diner manager, when he saw it. He strode through the house grinning at each one.

Annie sent Mike with the bag upstairs to the bedroom to unpack while she went into the kitchen to prepare lunch. She opened the fridge and discovered it packed with fried chicken and salads and ready-baked potatoes, and cheeses. The note read, *From your people at St. Chris's.* She smiled. *Well, at least he won't starve while I'm away.* She and Mike and Tim would have a good dinner this evening. But now they were eating tuna salad with Pringles and dill pickles, so it wouldn't take her long. She went about her work with dampened eyes.

"Mike, come on." Annie called. "Lunch is ready." She heard nothing. She called again, "Mike!" No answer. A mass abruptly accumulated in her throat. Her stomach reeled. Annie ran upstairs to the bedroom, flung the door open, and there Mike was, lying on the bed unambiguously naked, except for his clerical collar, which he immediately reached up and slowly removed.

"You beast!" Annie shouted. "You wretched beast!" She ran over to the bed and grabbed a pillow. "You scared me to death!" Annie climbed onto the bed and began pounding him on the backside with the pillow.

"Alas! You smote a wounded man," Mike emotically moaned. So he grabbed his own pillow and gave Annie a whack on the derrière.

"Ow! If you were any kind of a man a-tall you wouldn't strike a helpless little woman, now would you?" Annie's assumed Irish brogue, learned from her grandmother, Colleen, always appeared when she was in the mood to make love.

Mike responded in kind. "So that's the way you would have it, Annabel Leigh Richey, now would you?"

And tumbling they did, in spite of the hole in Mike's head. Carefully from top to bottom, from side to side they roughed the covers and the sheets and the blankets. And Annie delivered the fervid kiss she had promised him—which led to kisses on the breasts, which led to strokes of the buttocks, which led to caresses of the inner thighs, which led to the crashing of the walls of Jericho. It was three o'clock before they had their tuna sandwiches.

Annie stopped eating and looked directly into his eyes. "I love you, Michael Basil Richey," she said.

"I love you, Annabel Leigh Richey," Mike replied.

✝✝✝

IT SEEMED forever until six. Annie packed for herself and Tim, and by the time Officer Collins brought Tim home, she was ready to go. They had grilled steaks, baked potatoes, and cole slaw for supper, watched a couple of television shows together, and Mike and Annie took Tim to bed.

"Let's say our prayers."

"Okay."

"You first."

"Okay."

The family knelt beside the bed together. Routine for the Richey family, the bedtime prayer was a sacred occasion for them. It had been a long time since they had been together like this, and they cherished it.

"Dear God," Tim began, "thank you for Mom and Dad. Please keep my dad safe while Mom and I are away. And help me to be a man, just like my dad. In Jesus name."

Mike and Annie looked at each other with raised brows before they said their *amens*.

"Our Father," continued Mike, "thank you for Tim and what he means to his mother and me. Keep them both safe while they're away." And in the familiar words of *The Book of Common Prayer*, he continued, "Keep watch, dear Lord, with those who work, or watch, or weep this night, and give your angels charge over those who sleep. Tend the sick, Lord Christ; give rest to the weary, bless the dying, soothe the suffering, pity the afflicted, shield the joyous; and all for your love's sake."

And they all said, "Amen."

They finished their devotions with the Lord's Prayer, and Tim crawled into bed and drifted off to sleep. Mike and Annie kissed him good night and tucked him under the covers. They held hands in silence for what must have been a half hour. The two quietly went into their bedroom, undressed, lay down, and caressed each other. They held each other tightly until their eyes closed.

TWENTY-SEVEN

MIKE SAW Annie and Tim off at the appointed time. His heavy heart pressed deeply into his chest. Now he had to put Annie and Tim out of his mind and get back on the case. Finding the killer was the only way to get Tim out of trouble. It must be sooner than later. But where should he begin now? He couldn't let Carlos know what he had in mind. Then suddenly he remembered that he had reneged on his—sort of—appointment with Jimbo in Masters Park. It had been a number of weeks since he had talked to Jimbo at the river, but the intervening circumstances had erased the old man from his mind.

He grabbed the Camry out of the garage and headed down to Massey Alley, where Jimbo usually pitched his tent. He knew Jerry would set an officer—a coyote, as he called him—on his tail, but Mike didn't care now. Whatever made the MPD happy. He glanced in his rear-view mirror. *Yep, there he is.* But Mike moved on as if he hadn't noticed.

The alley was barren, so he headed toward the Tyrone Street Bridge to see if he could find the old man. But Jimbo wasn't there. Most of the hobes didn't come in to the conclave until around noon, but there were Marty and Jo sipping their brunch.

When Jo saw Mike, she suddenly had business behind a makeshift lean-to on the other side of the bridge and beat a hasty retreat. Mike crossed over to Marty and told him his business with Jimbo and asked him to relay a message. "Tell him I'll be in Masters Park near the back Dumpster. He'll know what I'm talking about." Mike allowed a couple of dollars to fall from his pocket as he turned to leave. Marty would never take money directly from Mike. He was too proud. But if Marty found the money, it was an entirely different matter. Mike traversed three or four yards and heard the scramble for the big bucks, but he pretended not to hear and kept on walking.

‡‡‡

THE CLOUDS hovered over Masters Park. The rain could come any minute now, but Mike was determined to keep this appointment. He sat on the park bench nearest the back Dumpster, which in turn sat about ten yards or so from Shelter #3. He didn't know whether Marty would deliver the message, or whether Jimbo would come after getting the message, or whether Jimbo would say anything once he got here. But he believed it was worth the wait.

Mike unfurled the *Madison Times* he had picked up from his walkway as he left the rectory and read about a murder on the north side of town, terrorists in Iran, and two bank robberies in Greenville. He continued with the letters to the editor—a couple that made him cringe. He read a column by Clarence Page with whom he often agreed, a column by Cal Thomas with whom he often disagreed, and an article on similes and metaphors by Jack Kilpatrick, who often made him smile. He went to the funnies and had a pleasant time with Snuffy, Baldo, and Zits. He checked out Gary Trudeau's "Doonesbury," that, on the whim of some editor or other, had been relegated to the classified ads section. He removed his pen and worked on the cryptogram and the word puzzle, both of which he conquered without a great deal of trouble. And finally the crossword puzzle, ending up stuck with one open space he couldn't seem to fill. He folded the paper to put it in the park's recycle bin, and just as he let it go down the chute, he remembered the missing letter from the crossword. *Ha!* He had won after all. But there was no Jimbo.

He would wait another half hour before giving up on the old man. In the far corner of the western sky a black cloud cover drifted in his direction. The wind thickened, and Mike pulled his jacket just a bit tighter. He felt the first drops of rain on his head and decided to call it a day. He stood and headed toward the park exit.

"Hello, Father." Jimbo seemed to appear out of nowhere.

"Jimbo! I was about to think you weren't coming."

Jimbo said nothing.

He placed his hand on Jimbo's shoulder. "Let's go over to the picnic shelter and get out of the rain."

The two slugged toward the shelter as fast as the old man could make it. They settled down in the dry pole-barn structure and let the rain fall where it may. The spatters on the shelter's tin roof grew stronger, the noise almost overpowering their voices.

"It's great to see you, Jimbo."

Jimbo said nothing.

Mike waited several seconds before he went on. "I apologize for not making our appointment last time."

Jimbo had been at Sir's funeral and had witnessed the shooting. "'S all right, Father."

"You told me"—Mike tried to talk above the rain—"when we talked last that you might've heard something unusual on the night of Juice's murder."

Jimbo said nothing.

"Jimbo, can you tell me what you heard on the night of Juice's murder?"

"Bang."

"Bang? You heard the shot?"

"Two."

"You heard two shots?"

Jimbo nodded.

"What did you do when you heard the shots?"

Jimbo said nothing.

"Did you go over to see what was happening?"

Jimbo nodded.

"What did you see?"

"Somebody ran away."

"Man or woman?"

Jimbo shrugged. In spite of the cool rain around him, sweat drops formed on his forehead. Mike figured Jimbo knew a heck of a lot more than he was telling.

"You don't know whether or not the person was a man or woman?"

Jimbo shrugged. The sweat drops turned into dirty, brown streaks.

"Jimbo, I'm not going to turn you in to the police. I'm on your side of this thing. I'm just trying to keep anybody else from being murdered."

Jimbo said nothing.

Mike asked probably a dozen other questions, and all the answer he got from Jimbo was a shrug.

"Jimbo, people are dying. Your friends are dying. I might be dying. My son might be dying. Is there anything at all you can tell me about that night?"

"Black cape."

Mike raised his eyebrows. "A black cape? Could you tell anything else about him? Was the person tall, short, ugly, old, young?"

Jimbo shrugged. The brown streaks trickled down the deep, age-produced crevices of his face.

"When the person left the alley, did you go into the alley to see what had happened?"

Jimbo said nothing.

"Did you go into the alley, Jimbo?"

The sweat rolled down his cheeks and drained from his chin, and Mike let him be. The old man reached into his coat pocket and dragged out a faded bandanna and mopped his face. But the handkerchief was not alone. A long, slender object flipped out of his pocket and rolled under Mike's feet. Mike leaned over and picked up a gold Cross fountain pen. The old man quivered like a leaf in a storm. On careful inspection Mike detected *18 k* etched into the clip.

The sweat drenched Jimbo's clothing. "I didn't steal it, Father! I didn't steal it, Father!" The rain escalated, and the patter on the shelter's tin roof grew louder. "I didn't steal it, Father!"

Mike took the old man's hand in his. "I believe you, Jimbo." A couple of minutes of silence and the rain slowed to a sprinkle. "I do believe you, Jimbo. But can you tell me where you got it?"

Jimbo said nothing.

"You will be helping me out a great deal if you will tell me where you got the pen."

"I found it, Father."

"Where did you find it?"

"In Slocum Alley."

"The night Juice was killed?"

The rain had all but stopped now.

Jimbo nodded.

"I'll give you ten dollars for the pen, if you'll sell it to me."

Jimbo hesitated and then held out his hand for the money. Mike reached into his wallet and laid an ATM-crisp ten-dollar bill in the old man's hand.

"Can I go now, Father?"

Mike paused. "Of course, Jimbo. Thanks so much for your help." Without a moment's hesitation, Jimbo scurried off.

Mike sat there appraising the pen. An expensive pen, the type often given to retirees at their final send-away bash. On the gold lid of the pen was engraved the word *MAVIS*.

And the storm came.

MIKE SAT at the picnic table under the shelter to wait out the downpour.

"Reverend!" The James Earl Jones voice boomed forth, sounding like the voice of God belting out the Ten Commandments on Mount Sinai.

Mike knew he wasn't Moses, but he froze. Dead still. He did not bother to turn around—perhaps hoping that the voice would dissipate in the surrounding rain.

"Need an umbrella, Father?"

Only then did Mike allow himself to turn and face the man. In front of him stood a uniformed police officer the size of the Colossus. *The coyote. He's been here the entire time.* What had he heard of his conversation with Jimbo? What had he seen?

"Officer," Mike answered.

"Sorry I startled you, Father."

Mike stood and held out his hand. "Hi, Officer. I'm Mike Richey. I don't believe we've met. Are you new to the force?"

The young man had a kind face. In spite of his quarter-back build and his blond burr cut, he looked as if he missed his mother terribly. His penetrating blue eyes met Mike's own, and he smiled. "Hi, Father. I'm Officer Gerald Ford. No relation to the president, I'm afraid. I just transferred in from the police academy three days ago. This is my first real job." He gripped Mike's hand with a confident firmness.

"That's why we haven't met. I'm chaplain at the downtown station house. Or was, until this whole mess came up. It's good to meet you."

"I've heard a lot about you, Father."

Mike didn't bother to ask him the banal question that often accompanied that statement. He just studied the young man for a moment. "That voice. Do you sing? We could use another bass in St. Christopher's choir."

Gerald grinned. "I'm afraid I'm already spoken for, Father."

"Aha."

Gerald snapped open a golf-sized, black umbrella. "I'm here to offer you a dry walk back to your car."

Mike sighed and took the coyote up on his offer.

MIKE FASTENED his seat belt. *The pen.* He reached into his pocket to retrieve the pen, but it was not there. He searched every pocket in his clothing, but the pen was not there. He must have dropped it back at the shelter. *I've got to find that pen.* The sky looked as if it would never give up. He looked toward the opposite side of the parking lot, and there was the coyote sitting in his patrol car waiting to escort him to his next stop. *What the heck!*

He got out of the Camry, pulled his coat up over his head and headed back to the shelter. He searched with all the thoroughness he could muster. The shelter table. Under the benches. The soggy grass and sand that surrounded the shelter like a moat. The pen was gone. Had Jimbo somehow gotten it back before he left? The coyote? To hand over to Jerry?

He sat on the bench, leaned back against the picnic table, and clutched his head in his hands. The pen. With *MAVIS* etched upon it. Inez had retired from MAVIS. Dozens of other people had also retired from MAVIS. Dozens of other people could have a pen like this one. Dozens of other people could have lost the pen for Juice to find and pass it on to Jimbo in death. A coincidence? Mike thought not.

He had to confront Inez about the pen. He, of course, couldn't show her the pen. Couldn't even prove he'd ever seen the pen. Yet he had to find some way of making her understand that he knew about it.

Mike struggled up and practically swam back to the Camry. Where was the coyote and his umbrella when he needed him? There he was, still sitting at the wheel in his patrol car. Apparently the coyote had been unwilling to give Mike a second chance. He put the Camry in drive and headed back through the city, turning every three blocks or so. The coyote followed his every move. He finally ended the journey at the rectory.

Mike immediately rushed into the house and picked up the phone. "Jerry," he said, "call off the coyotes, will you?"

TWENTY-EIGHT

*T*HERE'S SOMETHING *about that preacher.*

Jerry shoved the Crown Vic into drive and headed toward home. He was ready to be relieved of hunting down perpetrators. He saw the glaring yellow arches only as he passed and had to turn around to pull through the McDonalds drive-in lane. He had to get something for Mack.

There's something about that preacher. Jerry really didn't know whether he was thinking about the reverend or Brother Sam. It could have been either.

"How may I help you?"

At least Jerry hoped that was what she said. The young lady sounded as if she were speaking a dialect of some Martian tongue.

"Giant peanut butter McFlurry."

"Gi-mmpf bmmfph-ter McFmmm-ry?"

"Yes." Jerry thought he could fill in the *mmfph* blanks.

He pulled around to the first window and handed the cashier a five. He reached for his change, and the greatest of his pet peeves reared its ugly head. The teenager laid the one-dollar bills in his hand first and then placed the coins on top of the bills—a circumstance made for disaster. Two quarters immediately slipped off the paper money onto the asphalt below the car. With a boisterous grumble, he pulled the Crown Vic farther up the lane, got out, and walked back to pick up his quarters. The young lady was full of sincere apologies.

Jerry smiled at her—something he would not have done a few days ago. "Apology accepted."

The teenager smiled back at him.

"Hey," he said. "I've figured out a way to keep that from happening. If you'll put the coins in the customer's hand first and then the bills, that accident will almost never happen again."

"That's something I'll need to remember." The teenager smiled again. "Thanks, sir."

Jerry smiled for the second time that day and walked back to the car. He picked up the McFlurry at the second window and headed for home.

There's something about that preacher. He didn't know exactly what he was thinking, but there was something about that preacher.

When he pulled into the driveway, he noticed Brother Sam Argyle's car parked on the grass beside the pavement. Brother Sam had been faithful to drop by Mack's hospital room almost every day. But Jerry had noticed, to his distress, that the preacher had grown more and more distant. The first few days he would come in and say a prayer for Mack and linger awhile, speaking encouraging words. But then he began popping in, saying a prayer, and popping out. No encouraging words, no explanation for his popping behavior. No anything. Jerry was happy to see him here.

Mack met Jerry at the door. "Hey, Dad." He didn't seem to notice the McDonalds bag. "Come here. I want to show you something."

Mack galloped back through the hallway at gazelle-like speed. Jerry smiled for the third time and followed his son—at a somewhat slower pace—toward his room.

Maureen poked her head through the hallway door. "Brother Sam's here, Jerry. Come on in."

"Be there in a minute, sweetheart. Mack needs me right now." Jerry eased on into Mack's room. "Here, Son. I brought you something."

"Thanks, Dad." Mack peeled into the bag and brought out the McFlurry. "My favorite, Dad. Thanks."

Jerry looked at his son. Proud. He had always loved him. Truth be known, probably a bit more than the other two. But he had never been *proud* of him. He had been proud of Sissy. Among other achievements, she had pitched a perfect softball game last season. And of Jack. He had come in third in the hundred-meter dash in the Children's Olympics held at Bridgewater Church last spring. But now he was proud of Mack. Not from any sporting prowess. Not because of outstanding grades. But because of his courage. He had tried to kill himself—true. He had put his parents through many an anxious hour—true. But he had been brave. He had had the courage to survive.

Jerry reached over and hugged his son—at least as much as the teenage boy would allow. "I'm very proud of you, Son." If his own father had ever used those words to him!

Mack looked down at the still-bagged McFlurry and didn't—couldn't, perhaps?—acknowledge the compliment. "Dad, look what Brother Sam gave me." He reached down and picked up a beautiful red, leather-bound bible.

Jerry took the bible and looked at the front cover. *The Holy Bible*, it read. *The King James Bible for Teenagers.* "That's great Mack. It's a beautiful bible."

"Look down at the bottom, Dad."

"Your name's engraved. In gold, no less. Have you thanked Brother Sam?"

"Dad?" Mack flipped through the pages starting at Genesis and ending a couple of minutes later with the last page of Revelation. "Dad, I want to be a preacher."

Jerry's heart sank to the bottom of his stomach. He had always dreamed of his sons becoming outstanding athletes. If they made it to the pros—fine. And if they didn't—fine. But they at least could play high-school varsity and college. That ambition for Mack, of course, had been destroyed fourteen years ago. But certainly he could go to college in business and become a successful vice president of Microsoft or some such company. He wanted Mack to do a heck of a lot better than his old man.

"Dad?"

Jerry touched Mack on the shoulder. "I really need to go visit with your mom and Brother Sam. We can talk about this later. Say tonight—right before bedtime."

Mack's face drew back and his lips tightened. He wrinkled his forehead just as he always did when he was disappointed. He reluctantly relented. "Okay, Dad." Then he picked up his new bible again and held it tightly.

Jerry left the room and emerged in the den ready to shake the preacher's hand. "Brother Sam. Glad you dropped by."

The preacher's handshake was less than firm.

"I was just telling the preacher—" Maureen stopped in mid-sentence. The two men were staring blankly at each other.

"My time is very valuable, Brother Jerry." The preacher was clearly ticked because Jerry had not come in to see him immediately.

Jerry ignored the underlying accusation. "Brother Sam. Please. Please sit." The two men sat across the coffee table from each other. "Glad you came. Maureen and I want to thank you for your support when Mack was in the hospital."

Argyle looked down at the floor as if he were humbly accepting the gratitude of a thankful man.

"And thanks, too," Jerry continued, "for the beautiful, red bible you gave him. He's very proud of it. It was the first thing he showed me when I walked in."

Argyle looked up, almost as if he were about to ask for the bible back. "Brother Jerry. Mack. He's what I really came to talk with you about."

"Oh?"

"Could we go find some private place where we can talk alone?"

Jerry's eyes twitched. *What has Mack done now?* "Is Mack in some kind of trouble, Brother Sam?"

"Let's just talk, the two of us."

Jerry looked over at Maureen. She had her fists closed, her fingernails cutting into the palm of her hands. She shrugged. She didn't have any idea what Brother Sam was talking about.

Maureen stood up. "I'll just walk over and check on Sissy and Jack. They're at the ball park, and it's about time they got home."

Jerry pushed his palm toward her. "No, Maureen. You stay—right—where you are."

Maureen sat back down.

"But," Argyle said, "we need to…"

Jerry's blood pressure surged. "What is it that you want to say about her son that you can't say in front of her?"

Argyle frowned and raised his right hand, perhaps as a barrier to a perceived threat. "Brother Jerry, calm down now. It's just that, as a man, you're the head of the family, and the wife must be submissive to you in all cases. I just wanted to talk to you and then let you decide how to handle it with Maureen."

Jerry swallowed and took the time to allow his rapid breathing to ebb. "Sorry, Brother Sam."

The preacher nodded in acceptance of Jerry's apology.

Jerry looked directly into Argyle's eyes. He did not raise his voice. He spoke with the calm of a hurricane's center. "As head of this family, Brother Sam, I'm ordering Maureen to stay for this conversation."

The preacher appeared not to hear the sarcasm. "Very well. As you wish."

Jerry waited a moment, expecting the preacher to speak. "What is it, Brother Sam?"

"It pains me to say this, Brother Jerry." He continued to address Jerry rather than the both of them. "But I'm afraid Mack may have fallen into the clutches of Satan."

The air in the room abruptly grew thick.

"And he may," the preacher continued, "be in danger of losing his immortal soul. I gave the boy the bible so that, if he reads and inwardly digests it, he may be able to, with God's help, pull himself out of this gulf of evil."

Maureen opened her mouth to speak but apparently decided to say nothing.

Jerry felt his blood pressure rise. He could have yelled, he could have raged, he could have walked out the door. But somehow he withdrew from his bank of police experiences the knowledge that calm was usually better than rage. "Brother Sam, why in the world would you say such a thing?"

Argyle delivered his best Jerry Falwell smirk. "First of all, Brother Jerry, suicide, or even the attempt at suicide is always the devil's work."

Maureen burst into the conversation. "But that's over with. That's been forgiven. He's alive, and he will soon be completely well, thanks to—" She thought better than to complete the sentence.

"You do know, Sister Maureen"—the first time the preacher had looked at her—"that if Mack had died, he would have gone directly to hell. No questions asked."

"So you've told us before," Jerry said. "But that didn't happen, did it? He's strong and getting stronger every day. Does that sound like the work of the devil?"

Maureen exploded. "And Reverend Mike said—"

Jerry gave Maureen a shut-up look.

Argyle renewed his smirk. "And that, my friends, is the continuing problem." The preacher slipped easily into his preacher's voice—a tone above his normal range and singsong in delivery, as if he were Robert Preston chanting "Trouble in River City" from *The Music Man*. The smirk turned into a snarl. "All I hear is Reverend Mike. Reverend Mike. The man's a pagan. Evil, I tell you. Evil. A man who kills his own father is evil."

"Brother Sam!" Jerry managed to get in.

"A man that kicks his wife and son out into this evil world is evil. A man who spews pagan jargon over an innocent child is evil. I tell you he has that child in the grip of his hand, and it wouldn't surprise me if he were the devil personified."

"Just one minute, Sam Argyle." Maureen didn't have the police bank to withdraw from. She stood and held forth as only a mother defending her child could. "Reverend Mike did not kill his father, and it was, sir, the police who sent Mrs. Richey and Tim away for their protection."

"Protection from who-o-om, Sister Maureen?" The preacher turned to Jerry. "And that's what comes of letting a woman take charge. How can you let your wife, a woman, whom the Apostle Paul tells us should remain silent, say those words to a man of God?"

Jerry looked at the preacher, his eyes staring blankly into the man's face.

Argyle rose from his chair. His face changed complexions three times—from pasty white to pink to crimson. "Unless you agree with her, Brother Jerry."

Jerry stood to meet Argyle's eyes. "I think you've overstayed your welcome, Brother Sam. I'll escort you to the door. Say goodbye to Maureen."

The preacher looked at both his congregants, tears of dejection moistening his eyes. "Goodbye, Maureen."

The two men left the room. And Jerry heard his son cry out in terror, "Mom!" *Mack has heard all this!* He pressed his lips together into a tight, angry, straight line, gripped his fingers into his palms, and made two gigantic fists.

Jerry did not wave as Argyle pulled out of the driveway.

TWENTY-NINE

MIKE HAD never feared controversy. He had never been afraid to confront when confrontation was appropriate. But this was different. He would be facing Basil's wife—his own stepmother—and virtually accusing her of murder. So this trip to Charleston was even more difficult than the last one.

Inez expected him. Mike had called to make the appointment, and—in spite of her earlier hostile deportment—she seemed eager to talk. This would be a good time, Inez had insisted. Lorraine would be at work, and they would have some privacy. Maybe this was not going to be such a grueling experience after all.

Yet Mike could not help but feel a bit uncomfortable. Why was Inez so willing? If she were indeed the killer and the two of them were alone in the house—suppose this is a trap. A quiver shot through his body like an electric shock. But then it was over.

He pulled up in front of 2049 Renola Avenue and sat in the car for another five minutes before emerging from the Camry. He stood erect in his full-dress, clerical uniform and marched like a general to a rendezvous with the enemy.

Inez opened the door. Mike was surprised at her appearance. Her hair had been done up in a chic bun, and the gray had been turned into henna. Her mid-length green skirt and white blouse suggested she had just returned from high tea at the Middleton Place Country Club. She apparently had removed the jacket and had replaced it with a lacy, starched and ironed apron, of all things. Mike had not seen a woman in an apron since he was a child. Come to think of it, the woman he most remembered having worn an apron was Inez. What was she up to?

"Come in, Mike." Inez held the door open for him.

"Hello, Inez." Mike came into the now-familiar room. "You're looking lovely today."

Inez smiled. Probably the first time he had ever seen Inez smile. "Why, thank you, Mike."

Mike smiled back. He hadn't heard the word *why* used in that way for at least a couple of decades.

"It's good to see you again."

Those were the last words he had expected to hear.

"Come on into the kitchen, Mike. We can talk there." Inez led Mike into the hallway.

But Mike didn't follow her directly into the kitchen. There was that glass-doored gun safe that held the rifles and the six revolvers— and one revolver appeared to be missing from its assigned place. He stared at the gun case with the concentration of the most zealous student the night before exams.

"Are you coming, Mike?" Inez called.

"I'm on my way." Mike stopped again, just short of the kitchen door. There, on a Queen Ann console table, along with a couple of candlesticks and a vase of silk daisies, sat photographs of the late twins. He picked up the two pictures and examined them closely.

Inez stuck her head back through the kitchen door. "Ah, there you are. Thought I'd lost you for a moment."

"Just looking at these pictures of Clay and Marv. We look a lot alike, don't you think?" Mike returned the photographs to the table.

Inez said nothing about her sons.

He went into the kitchen where she had stationed a comfortable chair for him at the breakfast table. The aroma of slow-broiling fish penetrated the air. Small bowls of ingredients for sundry appetizers, side dishes, and desserts lined the tiled cabinet top. Inez went about her work.

She picked up a wine bottle. "A glass of Chardonnay while we chat?"

"No. No, thank you, Inez. Not today."

"Teetotaler for the day? I see. Uh, what about coffee?"

"Coffee, I'll take."

Inez reached for the carafe from the Mr. Coffee machine, poured the freshly brewed blend into a large pre-heated mug, and placed it in front of Mike. "I always like to indulge in a glass of Chardonnay while I'm cooking. Gives me the sting to help me deliver in the culinary arts department."

"Uh, Inez, I—"

"Oh, Mike," Inez said. "I do apologize. But we'll just have to talk while I'm cooking." Inez withdrew a sprig of rosemary from the spice bowl, and sprinkled the tiny leaves onto the broiling fish. "I've got a date this evening. In fact he's due here soon after you leave." This, Mike supposed, put him on some kind of notice. Inez would probably invite him to leave when the mysterious moment came.

"He wanted to go to that lobster chain place, and I said, *What? With all the great seafood places available in Charleston?* That's when I decided to let him come and taste some of my seafood cuisine."

A date? And Basil's ashes barely in the ground? But maybe that was a good thing. She couldn't very well leave a dead body lying around the house if someone were coming by to visit.

'Now, Mike. What is it you wanted to talk to me about?"

"I'm concerned, Inez. As I'm sure you're aware, my life is in danger."

Inez didn't turn toward Mike. She did not move. She stood there with the gigantic spatula in her right hand and gazed at the digital clock on the back of the stove. "My sons were in that line of succession too."

"But I'm still in that *line of succession*, as you call it."

"Yup. You got yourself shot during Basil's funeral. Better be careful. Next time you may not be so lucky."

Next time? "Tim—my son—is also in danger."

"The *children's children* part of the threat."

Mike nodded. "If you don't mind, Inez, I want to find out as much about Basil as I can—like people he hung out with, folks who had it in for him for some reason, or those who wanted him dead. Maybe something will pop out that'll give me a lead."

Inez pulled out a mixing bowl from the cupboard above and threw in a cup of brown sugar, a bit of salt, butter, and vanilla extract and whisked them together with inordinately quick motions. "The police have already asked me those questions." Inez added three eggs and whisked them vigorously. "Besides, what little I have to contribute, if it hasn't helped the police, will certainly not help you."

"Tell me about Basil's—first death."

Inez poured the mixture into a waiting pie crust. "What about Basil's first death?"

"Did you really believe he was dead?"

Inez added a measure of pecans and slipped the baking pan into the oven. "Of course."

Her answer sounded too pat for Mike. "How much *of course?*"

Inez checked on the broiling fish in the oven and held her breath. "I had my doubts."

"And you applied for the insurance money anyway?"

Inez's face hardened. She clenched both fists around the spatula. Mike thought for a moment she was going to use the potential weapon on him. But instead she relaxed a bit and placed it in a bowl on the side of the stove.

"Yes, I did. I figured the bastard owed me that much."

"But the insurance didn't pay."

"Nope. Said I'd have to wait seven years and then have a judge declare him dead before they'd pay a cent."

"Did you keep up the payments on the insurance policy after his disappearance?"

Inez took another pot from under the cabinet and held it in both her hands. She ran water into it and placed it carefully onto the left front burner. "And of what business is that of yours, Michael Basil Richey?"

"None. No business at all. I shouldn't have asked that question."

She ignited the burner under the pot. "Should you be here asking any questions?"

"Perhaps not."

A moment of silence. She reached into the cabinet for a can of tomato paste.

"Inez?"

She said nothing.

"Inez? Now that you know for certain that Basil is dead, do you intend to renew your application for the insurance money?"

Without warning, Inez grabbed up the pot of water and flung it at Mike. The pot fortunately missed him, but the water unfortunately didn't. His clothes were drenched.

Mike jumped up from his chair. "Dammit, Inez!" He grabbed a paper towel, and attempted to blot himself dry.

Inez left the room.

Mike worked on his trousers with two more swipes. He could hear Inez scrambling around in the hallway, and he suddenly remembered the missing revolver. "Inez, what in the hell are you doing?" Then he heard the front door open.

"Inez, I'm home." Lorraine called from the living room. "I got off early today to tend to some business. Is that Mike's car outside? Tell him I'll be down in just a minute. I have to change." She dashed up the stairs.

Inez reappeared in the kitchen—not with the gun but with a huge mop in her hands—and began swabbing the floor. Mike sighed and grabbed the mop from her and started to work on the water. Inez, without any sort of apology, grabbed a dishrag and swiped the spattered stove.

"Inez?"

Inez said nothing.

"May I ask you one more question?"

"Ask."

"Your pen. Your Cross pen. The one MAVIS gave you at your retirement."

Inez froze. "What about it?"

"When did you lose it?"

Inez went back to her wiping but said nothing.

"It was found at the crime scene." Mike saw no reason to tell her *which* crime scene.

"That pen? I haven't seen that pen in a long time. In fact, I haven't seen that pen since Basil disappeared."

"Was Basil in the habit of using that pen?"

"That's two questions."

"So it is. Was he?"

"Yes."

"Inez?"

"I think you'd better go now, Mike."

"Inez?"

"No, Mike. Just go. You can find your own way out."

"Please give Lorraine my excuses." Mike walked back into the hallway. But his eyes were not on the gun display. His eyes were on the console table with the candlesticks and the daisies and the pictures—and a Smith and Wesson .38.

‡‡‡

MIKE HAD left Inez still mopping up the mess she'd made and headed toward Hyman's Restaurant on Meeting Street for good Charleston nourishment. In spite of her madwoman display, Inez's pending dinner had whetted his appetite for some of the best seafood along the eastern seaboard. But he was not accustomed to eating out alone. He hankered for Annie and Tim and opted not to go. So he settled for Wendy's instead—chili, a baked potato, and a Diet Coke.

He spent the night on the tenth floor of the circular Holiday Inn on the bank of the Ashley River, but he couldn't enjoy the view. He pulled into 203 Pine Street around noon the following day and discovered Carlos waiting in the Crown Vic in front of the rectory.

"At your beck and call." Carlos grinned.

"Thanks for coming. Your cell threw me into voice mail, and I hoped you would get my message before I got back. Come on in for a bit of lunch."

"Come on into the kitchen and sit while I grab something out of the refrigerator."

Carlos grinned. "What? No menu?"

Mike smiled for the first time in three or four days. "The picture menu's on the lighted marquee." He opened the refrigerator door, and the light snapped on, displaying the array of food available for the choosing.

"What the…?"

"St. Chris's has been keeping me well stocked."

"And a goodly stock it is."

"Your order, sir."

Both men decided on a roast pork sandwich with Pringle's low fat potato chips. And a dill pickle.

"A Michelob, sir?"

"Nah, I'm on duty."

Mike threw down a Diet Coke for Carlos and a Heineken for himself and went about the business of constructing the sandwiches. "How're you and the girls? Everything okay?"

"Still in limbo."

"I'm sorry." Mike pulled the loaf of Nature's Own bread from the shelf and slapped mayonnaise and mustard on four slices. "You know— I think I know what I would do. I've had a lot of time to think lately."

Carlos raised his eyebrows.

"I can only imagine if Tim and I would have this sort of problem. I would be devastated, as you are. I think—no, I know—I would apologize."

"Apologize? But the girls were wrong to—"

"Yes, they were. But so were you."

"But—"

"No buts. You were wrong, Carlos. Now take a trip to Clinton and apologize to the girls. I can almost assure you that they will apologize in return, and you can get on with your lives."

The two finished building their sandwiches, said grace, and bit into the roast pork.

"I'll—I'll take that under advisement." Carlos ate half of his sandwich before he spoke again. "So—what's the deal?"

"Whatta ya mean *what's the deal?*"

"I know you didn't call me over here just to talk about the girls."

"But what if I did?"

"Mi-i-ike, don't play games. I know where you've been."

That statement didn't surprise Mike. Big Brother had been watching. The coyotes had apparently followed him all the way to Charleston. He looked at Carlos and shrugged. He told him about his meeting with Jimbo in the park, the MAVIS pen, and its lead to Inez.

"What became of the pen?"

Mike paused somewhat longer than Carlos apparently thought he should.

"Mike?"

Mike certainly didn't want to tell him about his ten-dollar purchase. "When I started to leave the park, the pen had disappeared. Jimbo must have taken it back with him."

"That pen is evidence, you know. It's got to be turned over to the police."

"I know it's evidence, Carlos. That's why I'm telling you about it now. But I don't have the pen, and I don't know where it is."

Carlos had never and did not now question Mike's veracity. But he knew Mike was not telling him everything. He left that subject alone—at least for a while. "What happened with Inez?"

Mike went over his visit with Inez step by step, the insurance questions—

"We already knew that."

—and the question that set off the temper tantrum—

"Hmmm."

—and the gun—the Smith and Wesson .38.

Carlos raised his eyebrows and took a bite of his roast pork. "Hmmm, delicious, Mike. You make a *magnífico bocadillo*."

Mike took a bite of his sandwich.

"Mike?"

"Yup?"

"Mike, I want you to stay away from Inez."

Mike chewed on a few Pringles and took a sip of Heineken.

"Ya hear me, Mike?"

"Yup." He took another bite.

"Do you really hear me, Mike?"

Mike continued to chew.

Carlos wiped his mouth with the paper napkin and sighed. "Mike, I tell you what I want you to do."

It was time now for Mike to raise *his* eyebrows.

"I want you to stay away from Inez, but I want you to go back into the hobe community and see if you can find anything else."

Mike looked up from his sandwich.

"We have a great deal of difficulty with the hobes. They won't talk to us, and I can understand why. But they'll talk to you. They trust you." Carlos looked straight into Mike's eyes. "Will you do it?"

"Yup." Mike finished off his sandwich.

Carlos stood. "I've gotta be going. Got a little work to do. *Gracias.* Thanks for keeping me apprised."

Mike walked Carlos to the door. "I'll do what I can." He didn't want Carlos to think he was too eager.

"Mike? If you run across that pen again, it's ours." And Carlos walked out the door.

THIRTY

TIM'S EYES flew open. He lay in the dark trying to remember where he was and how he got there. *The farm. Mr. Max's farm. The colonel's farm.* He'd been there many times before, when he was younger. In fact, Tim had been born in Wardell, and Colonel Mabry had been his dad's senior warden when they lived there. The farm lay a few miles out of town in the low country of South Carolina. It had a stream and a small pond. The stream was loaded with trout, and the pond contained plenty of catfish, crawfish, perch, and bass. The property also lay along side the Zephyr Golf Club, of which Mr. Max took full advantage. One of Tim's greatest pleasures when they came to visit was accompanying his dad and Mr. Max to the golf course. His dad would often allow him to play a few holes with them.

Now here he was, lying in this silly room, and he didn't know why. Why was everything such a secret? When his dad got shot, it had devastated him. But his dad was well now, and the cops were on the verge of catching the guy that did it. Why did he and his mom have to go away? It didn't make much sense to him.

He lay there a moment longer. The full moon sprayed a somber light through the large window, casting an eerie shadow of the gigantic, gnarled oak onto the floor. Tim had never liked this room, but he didn't have much choice. The room where he normally slept was under renovation as part of Mr. Max and Miss Pauline's plan for the restoration of this old house. The room was supposed to be finished some time next week. If he and his mom were here long enough, maybe he could move back into his old room. But in the meantime, he was stuck in this room.

Tim called the decor girly. It certainly was not intended for ten-year-old boys—especially ten-year-old boys who played with dumbbells and barbells and baseballs and basketballs and who swung on parallel bars and took Kodokan lessons. All the table legs curled up, for crying out loud. Even the daintily carved chair backs seemed as if they had just returned from the beauty shop. And the four-poster bed—with a pink canopy, no less.

Now with his eyes wide open, he didn't know how much time had passed. The gnarled oak shadow changed shapes and positions—slowly. He traced every branch with his eyes. Then he caught the face of the enormous grandfather clock staring down at him from the opposite wall. Its steady, every-second tick-tock had eased him to sleep, but now it sounded like the jackhammer breaking up the pavement on Church Street. 1:33—in the morning. Tim pushed back the cover, got out of bed, and walked over to the window. The moon had moved behind an elephant-shaped, cumulus cloud. He thought he could see something moving in the distance. He unlocked the sash, raised it gently, and leaned out the window. The outside air smelled green, and the weather was comfortably warm. A night bird—Tim couldn't recognize the class—trilled its not-so-gentle song. What? He again saw something move. Something glistened—briefly. The cloud moved quickly out from under the moon, and the creek that lay ensconced in a large circuit of pines reflected its light.

Tim looked at the old oak again. With a little effort he could reach that thick upper limb. He climbed onto the sill and sat with his legs dangling outside the window. He leaned forward and grabbed the limb with his right hand and then with his left and swung on to the limb with both hands. His dexterity and his gymnastic arms came in handy. He put one hand across the other and held tightly. He thought he heard a crack. He paused. A chill ran down his spine, and he looked down. The thirty feet that separated him from the stone-hard ground caught his attention. No—he couldn't think about that now. He waited half a minute more. He was beyond the reach of the windowsill now. He had to keep going. Then that crack again. Tim froze. The limb quivered. Tim's hands clinched the limb with the grip of a blacksmith's vise. His hands briefly felt as if a rasp file had scraped across his knuckles, and then the limb stopped quivering. Dead still. The squirrel that had scampered across his fingers charged to the bottom of the tree and scurried off to give high-fives to his partner in deception. It took another half minute for Tim to regain his composure. Then he put hand over hand and walked himself the necessary four feet to the trunk of the tree.

Tim made his way down the tree with little effort and stole through the shadows of the night to the creek where he had sat on the bank and played many times before. He really didn't want to think. He picked up an imaginary rod and reel and cast for trout after trout to fill his imaginary fish bucket. If only his dad were here. The fishing game had always been one of the happiest pleasures when he and his dad went camping at Table Rock or King's Mountain or Lake Kiawah. Three fish he had caught so far—five actually, he had thrown two back. Tim dropped his fishing rod into the creek and watched the current take it as far as the next bend. He leaned over and placed his face in his hands. *I need you, Dad!*

The soothing breeze calmed him, and he lay down on the bank with his head on a clump of Spanish moss ripped from the limb above him and drifted into the land of Nod. He dreamed of Quinton, his best friend. Of Kodokan and pecan pie. And of the red-haired girl who was new in his class but to whom he had never had the courage to speak—not even once. And of the nights under the stars with his dad. *I need you, Dad*, he dreamed.

Tim jerked and opened his startled eyes.

"What are you doing here?" The grizzly man looked vaguely familiar. Maybe like Tom-Tom or Marty or one of the hobes back home. No—Sir. He looked a lot like Sir. "My house is right back there." Tim pointed back to the Mabry's farm house. "I might ask you the same thing."

"Do you know what time it is?" The grizzly man sat down beside Tim. "Do your folks know where you are? Anything could happen to a little boy in the middle of the night like this." The man grinned, revealing yellow teeth with huge cracks between them. He wore ragged jeans, held up by olive drab suspenders, and a dirty, plaid, flannel shirt. He was a skinny man, but short—five-eight at the most—with a scraggly beard dripping with tobacco juice. His breath took Tim's own breath away. Rotten eggs. That's what it smelled like. Tim sidled a bit away from the grizzly man.

"Here," the grizzly man growled. "Whatcha moving away for? I ain't a piece of shit!"

Tim stopped moving. Why should he be afraid? He's just a hobe like Juice and Jo. "Where do you live?"

"My little friend—as the good book says, the foxes have holes…"

And the birds have nests, but the grizzly man has nowhere to lay his head. Sunday school was coming in handy now. *Jo.* "You sound like Jo."

"Jo?"

"Jo. A friend of mine. She likes to quote the good book." Maybe this guy was like Jo and Marty and Tom-Tom and—Sir. He couldn't forget Sir, perhaps his closest homeless friend. But Sir was gone now.

"I'm Tim." He held his hand out to the grizzly man. "What's your name?"

The old man took his hand—tentatively. "My name? Uh. You can call me Mr. Smith."

The old man's hand felt to Tim like the trout he had just thrown back into the creek. "Okay, Mr. Smith. You hungry?"

"What did you have in mind, my friend?"

"I could go back to the house. I didn't eat my dessert last night. I could get it for you." Tim started to stand.

"Ah—no." Mr. Smith's hand grabbed Tim quickly by the shoulder. "No. No—don't want to wake your parents."

"No problem. I can get it okay."

Tim got up quickly and turned to go back up the hill to the house. He stopped suddenly. A hand again had grabbed him by the shoulder—tighter than before—so tight it hurt—bad. Tim stiffened. Then he felt a blunt object jabbed into his back.

"You ain't going nowhere, my friend." Smith twisted the gun hard into Tim's ribs. "Except with me."

Smith grabbed Tim's hands and held them together behind his back until the pain was so great Tim had to wince. "Let's go, my friend. Do as I say and you won't get hurt."

Tim's whole body vibrated like a jackhammer and the sounds in his head were equally as violent. "Please, Mr. Smith. Let me go."

Smith's laughter, though subdued, was as wicked as the jackhammer's crushing sounds. He let Tim's hands go, grabbed him by the scruff of the neck, and marched him ahead like a criminal in custody. "You'll do as you're told, my friend."

"My dad's got a policeman friend. A whole bunch of policeman friends."

"Are you threatening me, you little bastard?" And Smith pushed him forward.

The trek took Tim, shoved along by the persistent Mr. Smith, around trees, over rocks, and through shrubs. Tim was afraid but he refused to cry. Even when he tripped and found himself struggling in the creek's frigid waters. Even when Smith reached down and jerked him up from the water like a fish hook snagging a bass.

"Get up, you little shit ass," the old man hissed. Smith crushed him up against a ragged boulder and lectured him on the etiquette of being a captive.

Then the old man briefly loosened his grip on the stone behind him, and Tim suddenly dropped to one knee. He grabbed the grizzly man behind the left knee with his right hand, latched onto Smith's other hand with his left, and flipped the old man over his shoulder, Kodokan style, and brought him down. The gun fell to the ground and spun itself into the creek immediately behind. Then Tim ran.

The last thing he heard as he charged back through the brambles: "I'll get you, you little shit ass!"

THIRTY-ONE

CARLOS HAD to find a stopping place soon. He had just come from a Charleston briefing session with the CPD. Now he had to squeeze in fifteen minutes of time to talk to Ellen. Three o'clock here, ten o'clock there. He couldn't wait too much longer or she would be asleep. Then his cell phone abruptly spit out a version of "De Colores," a Mexican folk song he especially liked as a kid.

"Hey, big man. Thought you were going to call me."

"Hi, sweetheart. Let me pull over here so we can talk." Carlos pulled the Crown Vic onto the shoulder of I-26. "Anything happening?"

"I think that's the question I need to ask. Got your voice mail at least three times."

The difference in time zones had been a bit tricky for Carlos. "First of all, I love you."

"And second of all?"

"I miss you."

"And third of all?"

"And third of all, I need your opinion on a couple of things."

"Aha! The real reason comes to light."

"It's the girls."

"A father-daughter conflict." Ellen had always been able to put her finger right on the sore spot.

"And a big one."

"Uh-oh." She waited a moment, but Carlos did not go on. "You there?"

"*Sí.*"

"Okay, what then?"

Carlos told Ellen everything. The girls' standing him up. The calls between them. His rushing over to the dorm room—yes, he confessed to his tough-guy attire to scare the shit out of those boys— to bring the girls home. Rita and Laura's flight back to college. "I am devastated."

Ellen said nothing.

"I need you to…" Carlos paused.

"Are you okay?"

"I'm fine."

"Good. Now, could you call them up and—" Ellen paused for far too long.

"And—and what?"

"Apologize."

Carlos said nothing for several moments. His mind swung back and forth a dozen times.

"Carlos?"

"That's what Mike said."

"Then?"

"Yes. Yes, Ellen, I will."

✝✝✝

ITA? DAD."

"Hi."

"Hi, sweetheart."

Rita said nothing.

"What's your last class this afternoon?"

"Biology lab."

"When's it out?"

"Four-thirty."

"Laura's too?"

"Yes. We're in the same class."

Carlos's heart foundered. Rita's usual exuberance was gone, and her normal chattering with Dad about any and every thing had shriveled into monosyllabic statements. Sweat seeped down the tiny wrinkles of his face. "*Venga en*, sweetie. We can't allow this stupid spat to come between us."

Rita said nothing.

"I'm coming through Clinton from a work assignment in Charleston, and I'd like to see you. Could we meet at Whteford's this afternoon about five?" A pause left Carlos waiting—afraid to say more.

At length Rita responded. "Can—can we make it Señor García? It's Laura that likes Whiteford's."

"*Por supuesto. Por supuesto. Por supuesto.* But I want Laura to come too."

"I'll tell her. But I think she has something after lab."

"Tell her I'd really like her to be there."

"I'll tell her."

The sweat didn't stop when he hung up but haunted him throughout the rest of the afternoon. It drenched his body as if he had just completed a heavy workout. It was a good thing he always carried a change of clothing. His profession sometimes insisted that he search under houses or in Dumpsters or the like. He pulled into the rest stop at mile post 62 between Newberry and Clinton. He refreshed himself, threw on the fresh clothing, and got back on the Interstate.

Carlos parked in the Señor García lot at five minutes of five, but neither Rita's nor Laura's car was there. He waited in the Crown Vic until five, and then decided to go on into the restaurant. He requested a table in the small private dining room. The tortilla chips and salsa instantly hit the table. The *garzón* returned shortly with the requested Diet Coke.

At five after the hour, Carlos looked at his watch. At ten after, he looked again. At fifteen after, he buried his face in his hands. *This cannot be happening.* At twenty after he grabbed his cell and punched in Rita's number. He didn't realize until he heard a slight, feminine, throat-clearing sound that she was standing beside him.

"Hi," she said.

Carlos closed his cell. "Hi, sweetie. Where's Laura?"

"Oh, some sorority stuff."

Rita offered no explanation for why she was late, and Carlos ignored the omission. He glanced at Rita and then closed his eyes. Tears wanted to come, but he managed to hold them in check. The sweat came again.

"Dad?"

Carlos flitted back to sanity. "Come on! Let's eat something."

Rita sat in the chair across from her dad. The *garzón*, like the materializing of a genie, suddenly stood beside them.

"*Mi tomo su orden?*"

Rita looked up and smiled. "*Hola, Antonio.*" She looked at her dad. "*Salami garzón favorito,*" she said. "*Voy a tener la cálida tortillas de harina con queso derretido, verde cabollas, y guacamole.*"

"*Y usted, señor?*"

Carlos weighed two or three choices and then settled. "*Voy a tener la misma cosa.*"

Antonio nodded, took the menus and magically disappeared.

The two of them searched each other's faces, both trying to decide what to say.

Before they could eat the first tortilla chip dipped in spicy hot salsa, tears came hurtling down Rita's face. "Dad? Dad, I'm so sorry. I'm so sorry."

Carlos gently squeezed her hand.

"I'm so sorry," she repeated.

"When I called you," he said, "my intention was to come here and tell you how sorry I am that this thing got so out of control."

Rita fiddled with her uneaten tortilla chip.

"It was wrong of me to come bursting into the boys' room like a bully. I've never been a bully in my life." Carlos reached over and took Rita's other hand. "I'm sorry too. With all my heart, I'm sorry."

"Dad, Laura and I were just being shitty teenagers."

"If you had just called me. I was worried like hell about you. Anything could have happened to you. Believe me. I'm a police officer. I've seen too much."

"Dad?" She looked down for just a moment and then back into his eyes. "Dad, if we had called you and told you where we were, would you have made us come on home right then?"

Carlos gave that question some serious thought. "I would have been highly disappointed."

"But—but what would you have done?"

"I would have wanted to tell you to get your little you-know-whats home right then. Not later, but then. Whether or not I would have gone through with that, I really don't know. I just know that I lost you once—to the Great State of Montana. And I certainly didn't want to lose you again. I might have questioned you—maybe even interrogated you—about the boys and what you were going to be doing. But I like to think that your answers would have been good ones and that I would have eventually said okay."

Carlos paused and looked into the beautiful young woman's eyes. "You're a woman now, you know, and should be able to make your own decisions. But I still worry about you because I still love you. And I hope you would make wise choices. And considerate choices. Considerate of others. And," Carlos smiled, "especially your old man."

Rita squeezed her dad's brawny hands with her very feminine ones. "I love you, Dad."

"And I love you, sweetheart."

A long silence ensued.

"What about Laura?" Carlos eventually asked.

"She's not ready yet, Dad. Give her time."

Carlos suddenly realized that the *comida* had already been laid before them, perhaps minutes earlier. "Let's eat," he said.

THIRTY-TWO

GIN-GIN TURNED away from Mike. He had often encountered hobes who refused to speak but very few who turned away.

Mike had searched three different alleys and Masters Park and then decided to go on to the Tyrone Street Bridge. The hobes usually didn't come to the river this time of day. This was patrol time for most of them. But he found Gin-Gin alone sorting her loot on the near side of the bridge. Interestingly enough, there were several other hobes, mostly men, clumping themselves together over on the far side of the bridge, staring at a strange hobe a distance away washing a pair of boxer shorts in the river's edge.

Mike walked over to Gin-Gin and sat down on a protruding rock. "Who's your new friend?"

Gin-Gin shrugged.

Mike suspected she had come to the river to check him out. The hobes were particular about whom they chose as their friends. Just any hobe wouldn't do.

"May I talk to you, Gin-Gin?"

She didn't move.

He walked around her and sat down on a concrete block so he could see her face. "Gin-Gin?" Still no brooch. The vision of a small white object under the edge of Juice's body popped into his head. That *aha* moment raised his eyebrows. That was Gin-Gin's brooch.

"Gin-Gin?"

At length she looked up at Mike. Her spotty old brown face with its burned-in wrinkles revealed years of smoking and drinking cheap gin.

"Gin-Gin, I've got to find out who murdered your friend Juice and your friend Sir."

The old woman leaned over to peruse her pile of booty and picked up a rather large doll she had scavenged from a trash bin somewhere in the city. It had been a beautiful doll, Mike noticed. If it only had hair and an untorn dress, it would be the pride of any little girl in town.

"Will you help me?" Mike asked.

Gin-Gin ran her fingers over the doll's balding pate, undoubtedly wishing that she could provide the silky, black, corn-rowed hair that had once been the doll's pride. "'Merican Girl."

Mike ran his fingers through his hair, swallowed, and clinched his teeth briefly. "American Girl?"

"'Merican Doll. Chicago."

At some point in her life Gin-Gin must have lived or at least spent some time in Chicago. Mike recalled some years ago, while doing graduate work at the University of Chicago, he went with Annie to the American Girl Doll Place on East Chicago Avenue to get a Christmas gift for Annie's niece Betty. The dolls were beautiful—and expensive, especially if the shopper purchased the required accessories. But how did Gin-Gin know the doll came from the American Girl Doll emporium? And how did she know the doll came from Chicago? American Girl Doll shops could be found in other cities.

But they both were digressing. Mike zoomed in on where the brooch was once located. "Gin-Gin, have you lost your brooch?"

The old woman shrugged again, reached down in her booty bag, pulled out a piece of baby blanket about the size of a hand towel, and unfolded it carefully.

"I'd like to try to help you get it back." Mike fingered his hair. "Do you remember where you were the last time you had it on?"

The old woman said nothing. She took the blanket and wrapped it cape-like around the doll to cover the ragged dress.

"I can't help you if you won't help me."

She took the top end of the cape and shaped a hood to go over the balding head. "M' mum's."

"It was your mother's brooch?"

Gin-Gin nodded.

"Did you lose it the night Juice died?"

Gin-Gin cradled the brown-faced doll in her arms and rocked it back and forth to get her to sleep. Then to Mike's surprise, Gin-Gin started singing—loudly—as if to drown out Mike's horrible questions. No words, just *dums*. Brahms's "Lullaby." *Dum dum dum— dum dum dum—dum dum dum dum dum dum dum*. She stroked the doll, perhaps in an effort to comfort her for her hair loss. Gin-Gin kissed the doll on the forehead.

"Have you named your doll?"

"Shanika."

"Shanika's your doll's name?"

Gin-Gin nodded.

Mike observed Gin-Gin closely and a lump burned itself into his throat. "Gin-Gin, do you have a daughter?"

Gin-Gin shook her head vigorously—no. Too vigorously, Mike thought. She cuddled the doll more tightly and brought her into her ample bosom. She stroked the doll's cheek with her right thumb as if she were wiping away a tear.

"Did you once have a daughter?"

Gin-Gin froze and Mike knew he had hit a nerve.

"What happened to your daughter, Gin-Gin?"

"Dead."

"Your daughter died?"

Gin-Gin nodded vigorously.

Mike's heart went out to her. He touched her gently on the shoulder. She drew the shoulder into a knot, but at length she relaxed and Mike reached down and took her hand. Tears appeared on her cheeks and eventually inundated her face. The doll fell from her arms and Gin-Gin leaned over and put her face against Mike's chest and sobbed. It occurred to Mike that these must have been the first tears she had shed since the loss of her daughter. Mike said nothing. It was a long time before either of them spoke.

"Shanika," she muttered between sobs.

"Shanika's your daughter?"

"Shanika killed. Shot."

This was getting close to home for Mike. He held Gin-Gin tighter.

"Gangs. Chicago. In the projects."

And Mike understood. That was all he needed to know. He would not press her further now. At length Gin-Gin loosened her grip on Mike and picked up the doll. She quickly dried her eyes as if she were ashamed of having been so weak. She reached down and pulled out various items from her booty bag—two tennis balls of different colors, a five-dollar bill, a toy truck, a half-eaten apple, and a host of other odds and ends Gin-Gin would find a use for. She surveyed each item carefully and sorted them into three piles. Mike didn't ask what the three piles were for—there must be a logic there somewhere. But he was just as interested in her loot as she was— although for different reasons. He yearned to know Gin-Gin's history, but that was another story for another time.

Mike stood to go. "Gin-Gin, my son—my son Tim—is in danger of being murdered—much like Shanika. If there's anything you can remember about Juice's and Sir's murders. I beg you—please let me know."

And Mike left the Shawnee River, his head bowed and his heart aching.

♯♯♯

THIS MORNING'S workout was just what Mike had needed to refresh his weary brain. Carlos had unfortunately not been able to make it this morning—some police business or other. But Mike really didn't miss him much. He had his mind on other things and really didn't feel like talking or arguing or whatever the two of them had been doing with—or to—each other lately. So he walked out of the Y door and began his jog back to the rectory.

Mike spotted a hooded figure sitting on the curb in front of the rectory. This location had become a favorite haunt for the hobes when they needed him. He slowed his pace and eyed the person meticulously. He—or she—sat with feet in the street gutter, hands around the knees, and face buried between the thighs. Mike approached cautiously. "May I help you?"

The figure lifted the hood—a small baby blanket—and turned slowly. "Hello, Father."

"Gin-Gin! What a surprise." Mike sat down on the curb beside the old woman. "What've you and Shanika been up to?"

The old woman snuggled Shanika up against her right breast, almost as if she were nursing the doll. "I ain't had no breakfast yet."

Mike figured it would be better to drop the Shanika subject. "I'm a bit hungry myself." He had had his breakfast before he left the rectory this morning, but what the heck. "Come on in the house and let's get us a bite." Mike rose from the curb. Gin-Gin didn't move. "Come on." He bounded up the steps to the porch and looked back at Gin-Gin. "Will you come in with me for a bite of breakfast?"

"I ain't going inside no house with no handsome man."

Gin-Gin's interesting compliment made Mike smile. "Then we'll have our breakfast out here," he said and disappeared into the house. He went to the well-stocked refrigerator and removed a homemade peach pie—more than likely from June—and cut two generous pieces, put them on two of Annie's Wedgwood dessert plates, and heated them in the microwave oven. He removed the pie, decorated each piece with a liberal dollop of Blue Bell vanilla ice cream, and warmed up two mugs of his usual coffee blend. He carefully placed everything on a serving tray and headed out the door balancing it on one hand like a stereotypical French waiter.

Mike's heart fell to his stomach. Gin-Gin was not there. He laid his tray on the stoop and stepped out onto the sidewalk. He spotted Gin-Gin about a block up Pine, headed in the direction of St. Christopher's. He sprinted toward the old woman and caught up with her just as she turned the corner onto Church.

"Gin-Gin, wait up."

The old woman at first feigned not hearing and kept walking. She had gone halfway from the corner of Pine to St. Christopher's before she thought better of it and stopped. She waited for Mike. "What can I do for you, Father," she said, pretending she had forgotten that she had initiated the visit.

"You can come back and have breakfast with me on the porch. You won't have to come into the house."

Gin-Gin said nothing. She stood there for what seemed to be a full sixty seconds before turning and heading back toward the rectory. Mike set his pace by hers. The two spoke not a word as they retraced their steps to 203 Pine.

Mike joined the old woman on the top step and spread two linen napkins between them, upon which he carefully set the Wedgwood plates bearing the rich desserts. Mike said a blessing and the two dug into their breakfast with gravity.

Gin-Gin finished her pie long before Mike did. "Father," she said.

Mike laid his spoon on his plate and set it down on the napkin. He was eager to listen.

"I lied to you yesterday, Father Mike."

Was this to be a sacramental confession? Perhaps not. Perhaps just a one-on-one conversation between friends. Mike stared at Gin-Gin. "About what?"

"About the brooch. I ain't never lied, Father. But I lied to you about the brooch."

Mike took her disclaimer with a grain of salt, but he took her confession seriously. "As I remember, Gin-Gin, you said nothing about the brooch."

"I know I didn't say nothing, Father. But it was still a lie."

Mike waited for the old woman to continue.

"I did lose my brooch."

Mike waited again for her to go on, but she seemed not to want to confess any further. Perhaps she needed a prompt. "Where did you lose it?"

Gin-Gin hesitated only slightly before answering Mike's question. "In—Slocum."

Mike certainly was not surprised at the content of Gin-Gin's answer, but he was surprised at her readiness to answer. "When did you lose it?"

"I ain't saying no more."

Gin-Gin, in spite of her earlier pang of conscience, apparently was getting cold feet. And cold hands as well, for she grabbed her mug of luke-warm coffee and held both her hands around it, apparently to attract whatever heat the mug continued to hold.

"Why were you in Slocum Alley, Gin-Gin?"

To his surprise, Gin-Gin started chattering. She had heard the shot—actually two shots—from a couple of alleys away and went to see what they were all about. She had loved—implying love in the erotic rather than the phileotic sense—both Juice and Sir. Mike had never thought of the hobes as being anything but asexual, and it was a bit of a jolt to discover otherwise. But Gin-Gin had felt it necessary to alleviate his ignorance. He listened.

When Gin-Gin went to the alley, she saw a person—it was too dark to tell whether the culprit was a man or a woman—running from the scene, gun in hand, dressed in black. A "booger man," she called the perp. He ran to the next block and got into a car and "flew away."

"What kind of car was it?" Mike asked.

"Don't know."

"What did it look like?"

"Just a car."

"What color was it? How big was it?"

"Black. Definitely black, Father. A little car."

All the black Ford Escorts he had seen danced through Mike's head. He paused a moment. "What did this person look like?"

"Like you, Father," she said.

"Like me?"

"Tall like you, Father. But big."

"Big?"

"Fatter than you, Father."

"Can you remember anything else about this person you can tell me?"

Gin-Gin hesitated long and hard. Then she ignored the question entirely. "I hid behind that old hedge. You know, Father Mike, that old piece of a hedge there on the corner."

Mike nodded.

"Thought he was going to find me there for sure."

"What did you do next?"

"After this killer was gone?"

"After the killer was gone."

"I went into Slocum and everything was topsy."

It took a moment for Mike to realize she meant *topsy-turvy*.

"Ain't nothing where it's 'posed to be. Went to look. Juice was deader 'an a doornail. Bleedin' all over the place, he was." Gin-Gin stopped and wiped her eye with the tattered doll blanket.

"What did you do then?"

Gin-Gin composed herself. "Went to see Sir."

He was surprised she had called Basil *Sir*. That was a name he'd come by at the diner, and Mike didn't know the hobes had picked it up. He didn't question Gin-Gin about it. "What did you find?"

"His tent was still there. He was still asleep. Probably too drunk to hear the shots. Could tell he was still breathing. Didn't see no blood." Gin-Gin stopped as if she didn't want to say anymore.

"How long were you in the alley?"

"Long time, Father. Went back down to where Juice was and held a wake for him."

"A wake? Did you pray for Juice?"

"Yeah, I prayed. And then I moaned. I prayed and I moaned. And I waited. Gone to heaven, you know."

Mike was impressed by Gin-Gin's sincerity and her simple faith.

The old woman continued. "Then I heard somebody coming, and I skedaddled. Thought it was the killer coming back to get me. Ran out of Slocum and hid behind the bush again. That musta been where I lost my brooch, though." And Gin-Gin stopped talking.

No matter how many more questions Mike asked, Gin-Gin refused to say anything. But what she had said was a lot more than Mike had expected her to say. All he really knew now was that the perp was a tall, fat homosapien who drove a small black car. He didn't know what else he could glean from Gin-Gin's narrative. He thought he would try one more time. "Did you see anyone else in or near the alley when you were there?"

"Yeah."

Mike sat up straight. Did she mean what Mike thought she meant? Was there really somebody else in the alley that night? "A hobe?"

Gin-Gin leaned forward and hugged her knees again but said nothing else.

When Mike was convinced Gin-Gin had clammed up for good, he thanked her profusely, and stood to go back into the house.

"Father?"

Mike turned back, hoping for another burst of conscience-clearing. "Yes?"

"Can I have another piece of that peach pie?"

Mike smiled. Perhaps Gin-Gin's conscience had been cleared enough for today.

THIRTY-THREE

JERRY FOUND Mack—naked, except for his boxers—lying on his bed, his face buried in his down-filled pillow. The bedroom looked as if a thief had plundered the room looking for booty. Mack's clothes, pulled from his closet and his chest-of-drawers, cluttered the room. A pair of Levi's and accompanying tee-shirt lay at the foot of the bed, along with a large duffel bag, wide open, filled with underwear and jeans and tees, and many of Mack's favorite things.

"Going somewhere?" Jerry asked.

Mack said nothing.

Jerry's mind returned to another time and another place. He himself had lain on his bed, his mother urging him to go downstairs and apologize to his father. It frightened Jerry. "Mack?"

Mack again refused to answer.

Then something else quickly caught Jerry's eye. On the floor beside the bed, lay the remains of Mack's new bible—the gift from Brother Sam—shredded like confetti. Jerry knelt down, picked up several pages, glanced at them briefly, and tossed them to the side. Then from under the leather cover, he picked up a page wadded up into a small ball. Jerry carefully opened the wad and discovered a verse from the first epistle of Peter highlighted with a yellow marker.

> *Be sober, be vigilant; because your adversary the devil, as a roaring lion, walketh about, seeking whom he may devour.*

Jerry folded the page the best he could and slipped it furtively into his trousers pocket. "Mack. Son."

Mack did not stir.

"Why did you tear up your new bible?" The sobs Mack attempted to muffle in his pillow caused Jerry's heart to leap into his throat. "Turn over, Son, and let's talk.

The sobs grew louder.

The memory of Jerry's belting from years back flashed through his brain. "Son, I'm not going to punish you. Just turn over and talk to me."

Mack's crying gradually subsided. Slowly he scrambled over but did not look at his dad.

Jerry waited.

"Dad," Mack eventually said, "I don't think I believe in God anymore."

Jerry's veins tightened. He had undergone many terrifying experiences in his childhood. He had witnessed many appalling situations, such as abused children, murdered mothers—a son attempting to kill himself—in his adulthood. But never had he questioned the existence of God. "What do you mean, Son?"

"I dunno. If there's a god, why did he create the devil?"

Jerry had never thought in those terms. His mother had taught him that there was a god—the good guy, sort of like the cowboy in the white hat—and a devil, sort of like the cowboy in the black hat. There was good and there was evil, nothing in between, and he had never questioned that. In fact, that philosophy had greatly influenced his entire life, both personal and professional.

Mack hugged his pillow—tightly. "Did the devil make me shoot myself?"

Jerry hesitated and pressed his lips together. "I don't know, Son."

Mack turned over into his pillow again, his body convulsing like a dying dog. "I don't want to go to hell, Dad."

Jerry's own body convulsed. His eyes closed. His fists clenched. *No! No! No! No!* His suffering burgeoned into pain he couldn't shake off. He had to calm himself for Mack's sake. He couldn't let his son see him this way. He reached over and touched Mack on his forehead and quickly took it away. That would have been too much like putting the reverend's holy oil on Mack's head. He lay down and placed his own body against Mack's. He hadn't done this since Mack was a toddler. He whispered, "Now what makes you think you're going to hell?"

Mack's body slowly eased its pulsing. His eyes lost their tears. His voice lost its tremolo. "Brother Sam said so."

Jerry closed his eyes and raged inside. *That bastard.* It took him a moment before he could return to any kind of articulate speech. "What exactly did he say?"

Mack turned back over and looked at his dad. "He said if I died I was going to hell. No questions asked."

"But you didn't die. You lived." Jerry could answer this one. "So stop your fussing. You're alive and you're not going to hell."

"But he said I was in the clutches of the devil."

Jerry didn't want to go there. This muck was getting too deep for an old mind to swim in. "That was just Brother Sam's opinion."

Then out of the mouth of a young teenager came questions that his dad would never have dreamed of asking. Why did Brother Sam get mad at you and Mom? Why did Mom get so upset with Brother Sam? What did Brother Sam mean about the clutches of Satan, the gulf of evil, the grip of the devil's hand? What's pagan jargon? Did God or the devil heal me? The boy had heard everything. Hardly a pause crept between any of Mack's questions.

"Dad?" Mack continued. "Did Reverend Mike really kill his own father?"

"Son—"

Before Jerry could answer, Mack sat up in bed and looked his dad straight in the eye. "Dad? Dad—is Reverend Mike the devil?"

THIRTY-FOUR

THE *DAY-MARES*, as Carlos called them—a day-time reliving of the horrific nightmares he had had since Laura didn't show up for his meeting with Rita—hit him in the head like a baseball from the bat of Sammy Sosa. Laura. Juice. Laura. Sir. Laura. The killer. Laura. Most of the time all of them mingled together, like the numbered ping-pong balls at a bingo game. Sometimes the dream would zoom in on a tall black-clad man with long god-awful hair and a long black beard that touched his belly. Blue-Beard Brunson. He walked with a limp. He soared into the dark sky like Superman, but he always made a heavy crash landing, driving Juice and Sir and Laura into the ground with something like a double-sized sledgehammer.

Carlos sat at his desk and stared like a zombie at his computer. He shook his head vigorously to get his mind back on the case. He was trying to piece his bits of seemingly unrelated evidence together. He checked file after file. His evidence list had grown, but integrating the pieces was another jigsaw altogether. Some avenues petered out. Others seemed promising, but many of these faded away because he had very little to build on.

One route did seem as though it might lead somewhere. Judy's and Lorraine's description of Inez's son Robert—whom Inez refused to discuss. The two Richey women had seen Robert only once, when he had shown up on the Richeys' doorstep to beg Inez for money.

The visit lasted no more than half an hour, as Inez had summarily turned him down.

The Richey sisters-in-law described him as tall, overweight—a big man with fat where muscles should have been—and scruffily groomed, with short black unkempt hair and a pointed black goatee. He said he had recently been released from a three-year prison term for robbing a convenience store and promised to go straight if Inez would give him the money.

But where was this Robert—or Bobby, as Mike had called him? The old law-enforcement grapevine had last placed him in Kansas. He had been released from a court-ordered mental hospital stay in Topeka, and no one knew where he had gone after that. That was too much to think about right now.

His mind kept shifting back to Laura. It had been five days already since his trek to Clinton to see the girls. Carlos had left message after message, but she wouldn't return his calls. Rita told him that Laura had been acting uncharacteristically strange lately. She hardly spoke to Rita, except out of necessity. She went to class, then to the library to study, and after that Rita didn't know. Often she wouldn't see Laura until after she had gone to bed. Laura would sometimes come into the room after midnight, stumbling into bed, and waking up the next morning with a horrific headache.

Carlos had called Dorothy on several occasions, and the one time she had answered the phone, she had placed all the blame on him. She told him that if he hadn't gone over to those boys' dorm room half drunk and acting like Rocky Balboa, none of this would have happened. *I know that!* She finally dismissed it as "college girls will be college girls, you know."

A fat man—no, it was a woman this time—Queen Victoria?— floating like a helium-filled balloon, passing over the city, popping down from time to time to nab Juice and Basil and Laura. Laura again? And the woman's beard and long tangled hair swung down to brush stains of blood onto Juice and Basil and Laura. No matter what, Laura would always appear in these dreams one way or another. Carlos would wake and wash the crumbs of sleep from his eyes, hoping to wash the dreams from his brain. He couldn't.

How did Laura get into all this mess? She was his daughter. A daughter he loved dearly. A daughter he was sure loved him. A daughter he would fight any Bluebeard Brunson or Queen Victoria to save.

Here he sat at his office desk, trying to sort out the real from the unreal. The beard and the hair were real. He was almost sure of that. How much of the rest was real. Then he sat up straight. *I've seen him.* The tall, bearded, fat man with the acne. Now why would a fortiesh man have acne? Nobody—no informer—had said anything about acne, but some how or other Carlos knew he had acne. *I've seen him.*

Carlos got back on the computer and typed for about five minutes. *He almost fits the description.* He had pulled up the data on the accident—the one that stopped their progress the day he and Mike hopped the Harley and left the Y for the Wells Fargo building to identify Basil's body. He typed some more. ID, Barry Brunson. Driver's license in good order. Address, 203 Camus Street, Camden, South Carolina 29020. Carlos picked up the phone. "Murdock? Find Barry Brunson for me." He gave Murdock the vital information and hung up.

His cell vibrated.

"Hey, big man." Ellen's voice sounded so real, so clear—almost as if she were standing next to him.

"Hi, sweetheart. What's up?"

"Hate to call you at work. Can you talk now, or should you call me back later?"

Carlos sat up with a start. "I have a few minutes. Let's talk now. Is anything wrong?"

No lover-type pleasantries. Ellen got down to business immediately. "What's happened with you and the girls?"

Carlos sighed. He told her the story—at least part of it—the trip to Clinton, Rita's apology to him, his apology to Rita, the new relationship they were building with each other.

"Rita?" Ellen said. "And what about Laura?"

Carlos sighed again. A long, loud sigh.

"That tells me everything," Ellen responded. "Seems like you need me."

The tingling started in his groin but quickly radiated in all directions until it reached the uttermost extremities. *Si! Si!* Then he relaxed for just a moment. "Are you proposing anything serious?" Carlos could feel her smile through the cell phone.

"I'll be there next Monday. Meet me at 4:32 p. m. at GSP."

"*Si! Si!* 4:32. Flight number?"

Ellen ignored the question. "Carlos?"

"Uh-huh?"

"Carlos, Laura will call you."

"What do you mean? How do you know…?"

"Just mark my word, sweetheart. Laura will call you to apologize. But listen to me now. You apologize first."

"But how do you kno…?"

"No buts. I love you, darling. Bye." And Ellen hung up.

Carlos was elated and worried at the same time. How could Ellen be so sure about this? Has she been tampering with—?

His cell vibrated again.

"Hi, Dad," Laura said.

THIRTY-FIVE

TIM WATCHED through the large window of his newly renovated room, hoping to see the Kershaw County sheriff's patrol car come up the driveway. Maybe his new deputy friend could walk with him. He had been cooped up in the farm house for a long time now, and he was wishing for some freedom. Freedom to explore the acreage. Freedom to walk down to the pond to fish. Freedom to hike down the country roads to see where they led. And freedom to play in the old red barn he had enjoyed so much on previous visits.

But it was not to be. He vividly recalled his escape from the farm house and the trouble he got into. His mom had called the sheriff, and, when he finally got back to the farm, the place was surrounded by law officers. The Mabrys and his mom paced the floor in great anxiety. Of course, he told them everything.

The sheriff and, it seemed to Tim, his entire crew were there. The sheriff himself had questioned him for at least a couple of hours. And then there was Deputy Judge. He was especially kind to Tim during the whole process. After the ordeal was over, he sat and chatted with Tim, not about him and Mr. Smith, but about ordinary things. They shared interests in the outdoors and in sports—the same sorts of things he and his dad shared. And, he found out, that the deputy was also pretty good in school, like he was.

After the officers had left, the panic subsided, and Miss Pauline immediately went into the kitchen and made bacon and eggs and grits and biscuits. Tim ate as if he had never had breakfast before.

He never would forget what his mom did next. She left him at the breakfast table and went upstairs to her room. By the time he had finished eating, his mom returned, and the Mabrys mysteriously disappeared from the kitchen.

His mother sat down at the table across from him. "I've just talked with Dad."

How Tim wished his dad were here.

"We've both agreed," she continued, "that I should tell you something that you need to know. You remember when Dad said we would tell you something when the time was right?"

Tim nodded.

"The time is right."

Tim looked at her, his eyes wide open, as if he were seeing an apparition. "What?"

"This may frighten you. It frightens Dad and me too." His mom took an extraordinary amount of time to clear her throat. "You need to know that Dad's life is still in grave danger."

A sharp pain hit Tim in the gut. "The bully?"

"Yes. The bully."

Then she told him about Sir. She told him Dad had discovered that Sir was his own father—and Tim's grandfather. For some unknown reason the killer wanted to kill Sir's son too. "You and I," she said, "had to get away from home so that Dad and the police could—"

Another pain swept through Tim's body like a bolt of lightning. "Mom, does the bully want to kill me too?"

Now he had to be brave—just like his dad. He certainly *could* be brave. His Kodokan experience with Mr. Smith had taught him that. The bully was after his dad, and his dad was brave. The bully was after him too, and he would be brave. He would be just like his dad. He would be a man now.

The window answered Tim's hope. *There he is!* Deputy Judge—Tim's protection—drove up to the farm house. Tim ran down the stairs and out to greet him. When he had first met the deputy, he thought that *Judge* was a funny name for a deputy sheriff, but he got over that soon enough. The two had met only twice before but had become fast friends.

Tim had been amused that a funny-looking face had accompanied his funny-sounding name. The deputy parted his blondish hair right down the middle and had a long nose with freckles dangling off the end. He had a great big smile—sort of like his dad's smile, but more twisted at the corners of his lips. But his funny looks had evolved into wit and a sharp and friendly demeanor, so Tim had forgotten all about his first impressions.

"Hey," Tim said.

"Hey." The deputy smiled, got out of the patrol car, and shook Tim's hand.

Tim liked that. It meant that maybe Deputy Judge trusted him as a friend now. "What's up?" He had inherited his dad's informal greeting style.

"I've gotta make a patrol run around some neighborhoods a mile or so down the road here. Thought maybe we could get your mom's permission for you to tag along with me on patrol. Sheriff says it's okay."

Tim didn't delay. He took off into the house, and within a few moments his mom came tagging along, Tim pulling her every step of the way.

His mom waved. "Hello, Deputy."

After the necessary pleasantries, Annie got down to business. "Tim told me you had a proposition for him."

"I'd like to take him on patrol with me. He'll be very well taken care of," the deputy added. "He'll be safe because he'll be with me in a marked patrol car."

Annie hesitated. "Why are you doing this?"

"Because I like Tim. He reminds me of me, when I was his age. And because he needs to get out—off the farm. A young man his age and with his energy and his circumstances needs a friend."

Tim was elated that the deputy had called him a young man instead of a child. But his mother seemed very hesitant. What was she afraid of?

Then his mom looked at the wedding band on the deputy's left hand. "Do you have any children, Deputy?"

"Oh, yes ma'am. Peri and I have a son four and a daughter two. Dick and Jane."

A funny smile, Tim thought, crept onto his mother's face. "And by any chance do you have a cocker spaniel named Spot?"

The deputy grinned. "As a matter of fact, we do, ma'am."

His mother's funny smile grew funnier.

Deputy Judge laughed. "Go ahead and laugh, ma'am. I think it's funny too."

He and Tim's mother laughed for the better part of a half-minute.

"Do you mind if I talk to the sheriff about this?"

"Not at all, ma'am."

She bolted into the house and was back shortly. "The sheriff gives you the highest of recommendations, Deputy. When do you propose to be back?"

"In a couple of hours, ma'am."

Annie sighed. "Okay. Be off with you." She gave Tim a peck on the cheek, which he almost declined for fear of being thought of as childish, but at the last moment conceded.

And the two took off down Route 404. After a couple of minutes of wit and small talk, Tim settled down with his eyes glued to the vista beyond the windshield, looking at everything the deputy looked at and hearing every sound the deputy heard.

Then the questions started rolling. Tim asked all about the deputy's life as a law enforcement officer. What he did when he got a call to a crime scene. How he went about discovering evidence. How he tested the evidence to see if it was any good. How he decided to use the evidence.

After that day, Tim went on patrol with Deputy Judge almost every day, unless the deputy had been called to an emergency. He questioned the deputy on each patrol, and the deputy seemed pleased that Tim was so interested in his work. He learned about the grid search at the crime scene, physical evidence, circumstantial evidence, interviews, and interrogations.

When Tim was alone in his room, he would play questions and answers—or interviews and interrogations, as he preferred to think of it. He would ask the questions as if he were the police officer, and then he would answer as if he were the suspect. Often his mother would play the game with him. She seemed pleased that Tim was no longer bored. He was happy too. He was a man now.

THIRTY-SIX

MIKE PARKED the Camry on the street and descended the rugged bank to the hobes' hangout under the bridge. He chose the shortest rather than the easiest path and found himself virtually skiing down most of the steep trail. He made it into the conclave without injury and looked around to find some friendly faces. He heard a single "Hello, Father," and it took him a moment to see Jimbo sitting over beside a wobbly pine sapling.

"Hi, Jimbo."

It surprised Mike that the others hadn't greeted him a bit more amicably. He walked over to Jimbo who was alone, sipping his after-dinner cordial, and sat down beside the old man. Jimbo didn't look at him. An ash-like substance smeared his face, a far cry from the generally sharp image Jimbo liked to project. "What's up?"

"Nothing, Father."

Mike looked around at the gathered body. Everyone was acting rather peculiarly today. Something eerily strange was going on. There were no women present. Almost as many women as men usually populated the place. Being down and out was an equal opportunity circumstance. "Where are all the women tonight?"

"Don't know, Father."

Mike realized he was going to get nothing more from Jimbo, so he stood and strode into the midst of the conclave. "Hey, men! I need to talk to you all about something really important."

The men froze in place. A field of statues. They didn't look up at Mike, and neither did anyone say anything. Mike had never seen them like this before.

Mike shouted to be heard throughout the conclave. "I really need your help."

He looked to the back of the crowd and repeated his plea. Strange. He looked again. The new hobe—the same hobe who was here with Gin-Gin when he came here earlier—sat in an inconspicuous shadow on the periphery. He stared at Mike—the only man in the entire group who looked at him. Mike perused him more closely. He was dressed in black, a white synthetic carnation on his lapel. But it was in a very odd place—the point at the bottom of the lapel. Mike would have been willing to bet the carnation camouflaged a serious moth hole.

"What, Father?" Jimbo called out.

Mike stirred. He could hardly keep his eyes off the black-clad man. He stuttered back to reality. "Uh, uh, er, gentlemen," he addressed the group again. "I need your help. *You* need your help. Two of you have been murdered within the last few weeks, and one of you has committed suicide. It's very possible that more could die. My life and my son's life are at stake." Suddenly a vision of the pregnant Lorraine Richey flashed through his head. "And very possibly a little baby's life is at stake." Was it his imagination, or did he see the black-clad man start when he mentioned the baby? He immediately rued that last sentence, but he couldn't take it back, so he grimaced and plowed on.

"Is anybody here who can tell me anything he saw or heard on the night Juice was killed or the night Sir was killed? Anything you know, no matter how unimportant you may believe it is, could be of some value in helping me find the murderer." He had long since forgotten that the police were the real detectives. It was his show now.

Mike waited as one by one and two by two the hobes dropped their heads and said nothing. Were they recalcitrant? Or were they afraid? Mike still wouldn't give up on them. "Gentlemen, if anybody knows anything about these murders or the evil person who committed them, I beg of you, please talk to me. I promise you that whoever contacts me, his name will remain completely confidential."

Mike waited for just a moment longer. "Thank you, gentlemen." And he turned to leave.

"Reverend!" someone called from the group.

All the hobes here called Mike *father*. This break with normal protocol worried him. Not because he insisted on being called father—he didn't—but because the word came from a man who was not a regular part of the conclave. The new guy.

"I saw somebody run from Slocum Alley on the night of—Juice, did you call him?—Juice's murder. Dressed in black."

This was consistent with what Gin-Gin had said. The man didn't appear to catch the irony of his description and his own wardrobe. But then—maybe he did.

"It was a woman, Reverend."

The hobes murmured louder. And then louder.

Mike raised his hand and the rumble gradually subsided. "Where were you that you could see this woman?"

"Never mind where I was, Reverend. But I got a very good look at her." He described the woman carefully—her nose, her hair, her gait, and, with a lascivious grin, her boobs. Then the black-clad man sat down and said no more.

Mike thought for a moment. The description might characterize any number of women. But the woman who fit the description the closest was Inez. But where could he have seen Inez? Perhaps he hadn't. Perhaps any resemblance to Inez in the description was strictly coincidental.

"Thank you. I appreciate your help." And Mike turned and walked away. He moved through the group and headed back toward the riverbank and the Camry. Then he heard a familiar voice.

"Hi, Father!"

Mike didn't see Marty at first, but at length he discovered his hiding place against one of the concrete bridge pilings. He was sitting next to Tom-Tom and sharing an apple he probably had brought from the diner and a bottle of Thunderbriar. Mike walked over and sat with them.

"What's going on?" he asked Marty.

Tom-Tom replied for his friend. "Nothing, Father."

Marty said, "That hobo was lying."

"How do you know, Marty?"

"I just know."

"But I need to know how you know."

"He weren't here the night Juice was killed. Ain't seen him around nowhere till yesterday."

The day Mike had seen the hobo with Gin-Gin.

"I make it my business to know things like that, Father."

Mike abruptly changed the subject. "Where're the women tonight?"

"The women? You mean the *femules*?" Tom-Tom said.

Marty let out a boisterous laugh that, in a couple of seconds, the whole conclave joined in. They could not have heard Tom-Tom's pun, because the two men were sitting too far away from the others. But they did hear the laughter. It was as if they were laughing on cue—when one hobe laughed in that raucous way, everyone was expected to laugh. It reminded Mike of his short stint as a substitute teacher. The class included a coterie of mischievous boys who stuck together like glue on glue. When any one of the boys said anything contrary to protocol, no matter how insignificant, all these boys would explode in riotous laughter—whether the young man's comment was funny or not.

Mike felt like scolding Tom-Tom for the sexist remark, but this was neither the time nor the place. So instead, he said, "The women. Why aren't the women here?"

Tom-Tom was ready with another answer. "They stayed home to primp, Father."

"To primp?"

"Yeah, to primp for the prom tonight."

Upon which Marty engaged in another round of vociferous bellying. And the others again accompanied him with belly laughs of their own.

Mike couldn't ingest this teenage behavior any longer. *There's bound to be something terribly wrong. They're not themselves tonight.* "Let's be calm a minute, guys. Tell me seriously why the women aren't here."

There was no answer. At first. Then Marty started to speak. When he opened his mouth, Tom-Tom jabbed him in the ribs.

This infuriated Marty. "Keep your elbows to yourself, bastard!"

Tom-Tom squeezed his body together, creating a cocoon with his shoulders and arms. He was duly chastised.

Marty hesitated a moment and then whispered—or at least he thought he was whispering. "They're scared, Father."

"Scared? Who—or what—is scaring them?"

"Don't know who. But what…"

Tom-Tom came out of his sulking. "Been raped, Father."

"Raped?" Mike was enraged, and he almost yelled the word. Then he realized it would not be helpful to bring any of the others into this conversation. "Who? Who's been raped?"

Marty took over. "Gin-Gin."

Mike stood quickly. "Oh, my dear heavenly Father, no. No!"

He could almost feel the eyes staring up at him, but he looked around him, and the other hobes had apparently not heard. He folded his arms tightly against his chest, the anguish spilling forth from him like a great waterfall. His biceps bulged, almost breaking his shirtsleeves.

He turned back to the two men. "When? I just talked to Gin-Gin this morning. At my house." Mike knew he would not get an answer to this one unless he softened his voice. He sat down again, put his hand on Marty's shoulder and said. "Please, either one of you. Can you tell me when this happened?"

Marty took a moment and then spoke—hesitantly. "Just before supper tonight. That's the reason she weren't at the diner."

"Is she okay? Where is she?"

No answer.

"How do you know this?"

Another bout of silence.

"Marty—Tom-Tom—I've got to know how you know this." He didn't intend for his words to sound as fierce as they probably did. It was just that he felt so—so—foiled.

Marty shrank back and opened his mouth to say something, and Tom-Tom elbowed him for the second time. But Marty was not to be bullied. "Jo."

"Jo told you about Gin-Gin?"

No one said a word. Then Marty again screwed his courage to the sticking place and said, "Jo told us. She took Gin-Gin back to her place. The guy must've thought she was dead when he left her. She was bleeding bad, Father."

A bulge thickened in his gullet. He blamed himself for this catastrophe. If he had not questioned Gin-Gin, this would not have happened. Whoever was after her did this because she talked. Whoever was after her knew that she had talked to Mike this morning. Then he thought back. Yesterday when he talked to Gin-Gin here at the bridge. The new man.

Mike stood up and immediately took off at breakneck speed, climbed the bank on all fours, and drove immediately to Bosham Alley where the three alley mates lived. He called Jo's name several times but got no answer. He came into the alley throwing tents around as if they were trash. And then he threw over Jo's tent. Jo was nowhere to be found. But Gin-Gin was.

Gin-Gin was dead.

‡‡‡

MIKE'S FIRST reaction was to kneel down beside Gin-Gin, anoint her with oil, and pray—which he did. But then he wept. If he had only left Gin-Gin out of this, she wouldn't be lying here now. What about Marty and Tom-Tom? They talked to him at the bridge this evening. "Why, God? Why, God? Why, God? Lord Jesus Christ, Son of the living God, have mercy on me, a sinner."

He grabbed his cell and dialed 911. Then he turned around. He needed to look for evidence. Since he couldn't touch anything or walk around lest he corrupt the evidence, he stood where he was and scanned the body and the surrounding area, and perhaps something would pop out at him like Gin-Gin's brooch had in Slocum Alley. *Hmmm. No Shanika.* Either the killer had taken her or Jo left her behind when she moved Gin-Gin. Jo had done everything she could to make Gin-Gin comfortable. She had pulled her torn clothes back on her. She had placed Gin-Gin on an old air mattress that had very little air and had covered her up with a ragged piece of red-checkered vinyl tablecloth. She had even placed an old cushion under her head. And there he spotted it—a red fake carnation entangled in Gin-Gin's hair.

He was not surprised. The hobo's carnation had been white. But in all likelihood he had a stash of fake carnations of assorted colors to insert in his lapel. He started to reach over and pick it up, but then thought better of it. The police would be upset. So he sat back down and placed his face in his hands.

No sooner had he touched the concrete block than the blue flashing lights of the caravan of police vehicles screeched to a stop on Church Street. The officers charged into the alley and headed straight for him. They made Mike step aside while they examined the body and the surrounding area. And then the questions began.

Within five minutes Jerry and Carlos arrived in their usual style. They stormed over to Mike, told the interrogating officer that they would take over from here, and pulled him aside and took him to the far end of the alley.

"Now, what's this all about, Reverend?" Jerry questioned.

"It's what you see. Gin-Gin was raped somewhere—I don't know where—and left for dead." Then he told Jerry and Carlos what he knew from his conversation with the hobes. He refused to reveal their names. "When I came here to find her, this is what I found."

"Uh-huh!" Almost as if Jerry didn't believe a word Mike was uttering.

"Apparently when Gin-Gin died, Jo fled. Probably thought she would be accused of the murder."

"Uh-huh!" again.

The two questioned Mike further, and he told them about the hobo and his carnation and the carnation found attached to Gin-Gin's hair.

"Detective Ruiz will take you to the station house and take your statement, and then he will escort you home. And you will stay there. Is there anything about that last sentence that you don't understand, Reverend?"

Few things perturbed Mike more than condescension. "No, Chief Detective."

He did his duty at the station house, and when they arrived at the rectory, Carlos offered several words of reproval.

"But you said...?"

Carlos held his index finger up to his lips.

Mike read the sign. *We still need your help with the hobes, but do it ve-e-ery discreetly.*

Carlos saw Mike into the rectory and left him there.

Exhausted, Mike lay down on the sofa, and in a moment he dropped off to a troubled sleep. He woke up about midnight and sat up with a start. He jumped off the couch and headed straight to the front door and charged out onto the porch. He opened his arms wide, as if taking in the entire city of Madison. "I will find you!" he shouted. "I *will* find you!"

THIRTY-SEVEN

THE SUDDEN clamor of the alarm clock startled Mike awake. It wasn't until he slammed his hand on the cease-and-desist button that he realized the clamor was not from the clock at all but from the telephone. He grabbed the receiver and tried to read the Caller ID screen, but his sleep-encrusted eyes prevented him. "Hello." He tried to sound chipper but hardly succeeded. But chipper was not the mood for this time of night, because no one would call unless the message was bad news. "Hello."

It was the small hours on Saturday morning, nine days after Annie and Tim had left home for the Mabry's farm. This night Mike had been particularly restless. He could not get Gin-Gin out of his mind—the drawn face, the dried blood, the tortured eyes. He got out of bed twice, once to make himself a midnight sandwich and again around two o'clock to read in his recliner. He hurt. He could not get the agitating lump out of his stomach. At length he dozed, rousing and napping and then rousing and napping again.

"Hello," he said again.

Annie apparently made no attempt to sound chipper. "Hi, sweetheart."

"Hi, baby, what's wrong?" Mike didn't wonder that she didn't contact him through the police. He knew something was out of kilter. "Are you okay?"

"I couldn't sleep." That was reason enough to call. He had missed her inordinately, and now they had something to share that defied any police prohibition against talking.

"Me either." Mike had the sudden sensation that lack of sleep was not the only thing Annie needed to talk about. "Is something going on?"

"I think we're being stalked."

The knot returned to Mike's gut. "What?" If the killer was not after him at the moment, he must be after Tim. How did he discover that Annie and Tim were there?

"I think we're being stalked," she repeated.

The lump grew larger. "Say that again." He wanted to be certain he was hearing right.

"I said we're being stalked. Somebody's been watching us with binoculars. He's standing across the road now. I've closed all the curtains."

"Have you contacted the sheriff?"

"No, I haven't. I wanted to talk with you first."

"Wake up Max, and let him know what's going on."

"He's not here. Just Pauline. Max had some overnight business in Columbia. He won't be back until about two o'clock this afternoon."

"Wake Pauline up. I'm sure she'll want to call Max. Then call the sheriff. Make sure all doors and windows are locked and stay out of sight. Make sure Tim is with you at all times," Mike ordered. "I'll be there in three hours. And all of you stay in one place together until the sheriff gets there. Love you, darling."

Mike hung up and immediately dialed Carlos's home number. "Come on, Carlos." He said under his breath. "Come on, come on!" It took forever for Carlos to answer.

"Yeah," Carlos growled.

"Carlos, it's Mike."

"Yeah," Carlos growled a little less grumpily. "You okay?"

"Not really." Mike told Carlos what was going on in Wardell.

"I'll alert Jerry and pick you up in fifteen minutes." Before Mike could protest, Carlos hung up the phone.

Mike hurriedly donned jeans and a sweatshirt and twiddled his thumbs for a good five minutes before Carlos arrived.

Annie and Tim continued to convulse in Mike's head. The night Tim was born had been a wonderful night. He and Annie had had a difficult time getting pregnant. She had miscarried twice, and they were afraid they would lose Tim. When he was born, Mike was in the delivery room and took him in his arms directly from the obstetrician. He had never been this happy in his life.

Mike's cell phone interrupted the trance.

"Mike." Annie sobbed uncontrollably. "Tim's not here."

"What? What do you mean he's not there?"

Mike turned to Carlos. "Tim's not there."

Carlos flicked on the blue light and the siren and shoved the accelerator to the floor. He alerted Jerry of the new development and charged forward.

"After I talked with you, I made sure the windows and doors were all locked. Then I went to check on Tim. He's gone, Mike!"

"Where's Pauline?"

"She's been up with me ever since I discovered Tim was gone. She's called Max, and he's on his way home right now. He should be here shortly."

Before he returned to Annie, he said to Carlos, "Tim's been kidnapped."

"Jerry has radioed Sheriff Tucker and he's getting the SCBI there as quickly as he can."

Mike turned back to the cell.

"Annie, are you okay?"

"I'm scared, Mike."

"Me too, sweetheart. I'm scared too." Then he turned to Carlos. "Can't you drive any faster?"

"Just hang on!" Carlos said, and he did.

✝✝✝

WHEN THE Crown Vic reached the farm, police were swarming everywhere, plowing through the wooded areas on both sides of the road, going in and out of the house at will—blue lights, yellow tapes, and loud sirens. Carlos jumped out of the car, and Jerry screeched to a halt immediately behind them. Carlos consulted with Jerry for a moment and then charged inside the house to consult with the South Carolina Bureau of Investigation agent in charge.

Mike moved quickly toward the house but stopped at the long, yellow tape. Baldwin, the officer in charge of stopping folks said, "Sorry, you can't go in there. There's a crime investigation going on." As if Mike didn't know that.

"No reporters allowed," shouted Parks, Baldwin's eager colleague.

"But I'm not a reporter. I'm…"

"Yeah! Sure! Now back off, buddy."

Mike needed Carlos to vouch for him, but Carlos was already in the house. But he would get in! He ducked under the tape with the agility of a teenager and immediately stopped—dead still. Baldwin and Parks had grabbed him under his arms and held him—tight.

"No, you don't, my friend." Baldwin smirked.

"I've got to get in," Mike yelled. "I'm the boy's father. My wife is in there."

Parks snarled. "Yeah, right."

Baldwin checked him over twice. "Now—where's your camera?"

"I'm not a reporter, Officer. I'm a priest. I'm his father."

This priest thing confused Baldwin even further. "Sure you are, Fa-a-ther!" The syrupy sarcasm drooled from both ends of his mouth.

"Priests ain't supposed to have kids," Parks said.

"Do you have a son?" Mike slowed down the conversation a bit.

"Nah, I've got girls. Two girls," Baldwin said, as if he were about to pull out his wallet and show pictures.

"None of your business," shouted Parks.

But before the cops could say anything further, Mike twisted his torso toward the right and then toward the left and threw the two cops one by one to the ground before they knew what was happening and sped toward the house. He knew his Kodokan black belt would be good for something some day. He started up the steps and abruptly felt the barrel of a police revolver between his shoulder blades.

"Don't take one step more."

Mike halted. This was a new one. He looked up and saw Baldwin and Parks charging toward him, guns out. The three of them wrestled Mike to the ground.

"You're under arrest for assaulting officers of the law, trespassing, and probably several other high crimes and misdemeanors I'll think of later," declared Remington, the new officer.

Another cop appeared on the porch eying the situation carefully. Before Remington could finish the handcuffing, the large, beefy batter stepped up to home plate. "What's the deal, guys?" Jerry asked.

"This reporter was trying to get into the house, sir," Baldwin said.

Jerry moved down to the sweat-drenched Mike, whose cheek was buried in the grass. "Officers," Jerry said. "This man is not a reporter. He's the boy's father. Let him up." He turned to Mike. "You know better than this, Reverend."

Mike struggled up with the aid of the repentant hands of Baldwin and Parks.

"There'll be no arrest for officer assault. Get back to your posts. And next time, make sure you know who you're dealing with."

"Yes, sir!" they replied in unison.

Jerry reached out and touched Mike on the shoulder. "Sorry about that, Reverend."

"Thanks, Jerry. I appreciate your help."

"Come on in. Ms. Richey needs you right now."

Jerry ushered Mike into the living room, where he found a tear-streaked Annie sitting on the couch. Pauline sat beside her, doing what she could to provide some kind of comfort. Mike sat down beside Annie and kissed her with all the passion the current situation would allow.

"Oh, Mike, I need you," she said.

Mike felt a tap on his shoulder. He stood up and greeted Max with first a handshake and then a hug.

"Mike!" Max said, "I'm sorry I wasn't here. Maybe I could have done something…"

For the first time tears welled up in Mike's eyes.

"Father Richey," a voice spoke behind him. Mike turned. "I'm Detective Mosker of the SCBI. So sorry about your son."

"Thanks, Detective."

Mosker gave Mike a pair of plastic gloves. "Put these on, Father."

Mike complied, and Mosker handed him a crumpled up piece of paper. "This was found on the front steps of the house, weighted down with a rock. Do you recognize it?"

Mike looked reluctantly at the note. "Yes, I do."

"What do you think it means?"

Mike looked directly into Mosker's eyes. "It means Tim's dead."

THIRTY-EIGHT

THE LONG, vicious night had engulfed Mike and Annie in its dragonish claws. The SCBI had grilled them as only the SCBI could grill. They were tired, they were hurting, and they were angry. They had returned to Madison with Carlos at around noon the following day. They both headed for the bedroom and tried to get some sleep, but the sandman eluded Mike.

He eventually rose from the bed, easily and carefully so as not to disturb Annie, and eased his way down the stairs. He paced a track in the rectory carpet as formidable as the track at Churchill Downs. Nightmares were not confined to sleeping. With each step came a malignant demon, with each demon, malignant despair, and with that despair everything that had occurred, from the time Annie had called until they had left the Mabrys' farm, labored before his eyes in horrid intensity. He especially recalled gazing at the killer's crumpled note, as if it were writ large on hell's expansive walls. *Tim's dead*, he thought. The killer had left notes only for dead bodies or—in Mike's case—those he assumed would shortly be dead. That could be the only meaning of that demonic ledger page.

He recalled Jerry walking over to them. "Reverend? Ms. Richey?" His greeting resembled that of a funeral director. Jerry—the nothing-ever-fazed-him detective—had been fazed.

Mike and Annie were barely able to look up. After the shock into some semblance of consciousness, Mike said, "Thanks for your intervention with the cops."

"No problem, Reverend." Jerry grimaced. "I'm sorry the SCBI detective felt it necessary to call your attention to that note, but he said he had to do it."

"Tim's dead," Mike declared.

Jerry hesitated a moment and rubbed his nape briefly. "Not necessarily. In fact, it's very possible that the perp took Tim and is holding him hostage. We should find out soon."

"And he wants me in exchange?" Mike asked. "Okay, he can have me!"

Annie cringed. "Mike!"

Jerry paused again, as if he didn't want to say what he was about to say. "Not in exchange."

Mike knew exactly what Jerry was about to say next. "He wants me to come looking for Tim so he can get me first. Following his screwed-up logic, he needs to get the children before he gets the children's children."

"I'm afraid so. I'm afraid that's exactly what he wants."

Annie clutched Mike's arm so tightly that his fingers began to tingle. Mike reached over and placed his hand gently over Annie's.

Jerry continued, "I want you and Ms. Richey to go home with Detective Ruiz. He will take you to your house, and you are to stay there. Do not go out of the house for any reason. If you do, you will be opening yourself up to a bullet in your head. Do I make myself clear, Reverend?"

This hit Mike like a Richter-seven earthquake. Now he had a double mission—to find Tim and to find the killer-kidnapper. He had to get out of the house to do that.

"But what about…?" Mike almost let it slip—the permission Carlos had given him to interview hobes. He wouldn't betray Carlos.

"What about what?" Jerry said.

Mike quickly changed the subject. "Am I under house arrest?"

"I prefer to call it protective custody. At this point, that's the only way we can keep you from being murdered." And Jerry walked away. It was a done deal then. No negotiation, no—anything.

After the SCBI was through with them, Carlos came in and said he was ready to drive back to Madison. When the three had arrived, Carlos went through the house making certain windows and doors were locked and shades were down. He programmed the telephone so they could signal the police with the push of a button. He assured them that officers in patrol cars would be constantly patrolling the street.

"You told us once to call off the coyotes. We did. But now we're calling them back again—full force." And Carlos walked out the door.

He had to stop this pacing now or he would go crazy. Mike went into the kitchen and put on a carafe of Cajun Coffee, the strongest he could find in his stash of coffee tins. He pulled out an English muffin and threw the halves into the toaster. In a moment he sat down at the kitchen table with a charred muffin—no butter, no jam, no cream cheese—and a mug of Cajun so thick his stirring spoon almost stood erect. The first mug didn't faze him, so he poured a second.

He slugged the Cajun down and beat the tips of his fingers against the table. He had another problem he couldn't seem to get rid of. He loved Annie with all his heart. He did. But somehow he couldn't help but blame her for Tim's abduction. If she had only taken him into her room when she realized the stalker was there. If she had only locked the doors as soon as she realized the stalker was there. If she had only... If she had only... He clenched his teeth and abruptly stood. He could sit there no longer. He charged back into the den. The walls trembled, the furniture danced, the lights flickered. His pacing became an uneven run. His arms wrenched, his head jerked, and his legs withered. Mike's heart was about to burst, his head was about to split, and his firm muscles turned to mush.

He suddenly dropped to both his knees, and he prayed, "My God! My God! Why have you forsaken me?" And then he thundered, "My God! My God! Why have you forsaken me?"

Mike slumped down prone onto the floor, his right cheek flat against the carpet fibers. In spite of his Cajun intake, he lay there in a solid stupor, dazed from the events of the last twenty-four hours. His left hand twitched once, and he closed his eyes.

ANNIE OPENED the bedroom door slowly, tiptoed onto the stair balcony, and stood watching Mike, envying his ability to sleep now. Her restlessness had been as troublesome as his. She knew when he got out of the bed, but she did not follow. He needed his time to grieve alone as did she. But now she needed him, even if she could not speak to him.

Annie stepped down the stairs and into the kitchen. Finding the coffee already made, she poured a mug full. Making her way back to the den, she sat on the couch and stared blankly at her husband. It was her fault that Tim had been abducted—if she had only... She should have been more careful with the doors and windows. She should have searched the house before she put Tim to bed. She should have made Tim sleep in the bedroom with her. The guilt prods kept coming one after the other until she melted into a deep, dark funk. She could not think about that anymore.

Annie took her first sip of coffee—and winced. She caught herself and looked over at Mike. Her stirrings apparently had not fazed him. She set her mug of coffee on the end table and lay back on the sofa. She glanced at Mike again. Her heart skipped a beat. *How I love that man!* was the last thing she remembered thinking.

MIKE JERKED awake. A gunshot. He held his breath and lay deathly still—for two brief moments. He exhaled easily and slowly. The nightmare again. He raised himself from the floor and sat dazed for a dozen minutes before he tried suppressing the pictures of Tim riding in the airless trunk of an old Ford Escort. The picture of Tim being manhandled by a pair of crudely warped hands. The picture of Tim being sexually assaulted by a perverted creature, using his power to intimidate a ten-year-old boy. Mike ran his fingers through his hair. He couldn't erase those images from his brain.

He rose from the floor and spotted Annie on the sofa. He was glad she could sleep now. Mike walked into the kitchen for another cup of coffee, but the empty carafe told him that he had had enough. He fixed himself—probably because he didn't have anything else to do—a peanut-butter and fig-jam sandwich and sat down at the kitchen table to consume it. After the third bite, he leaned forward and grimaced. *I can't sit here!* If Tim was still alive, which he sincerely doubted, he was God-knows-where being raped by God-knows-who, and Mike winced. He had never felt as helpless in his life. *I can't sit here!*

Mike sneaked back up into the bedroom. He opened the third drawer of his chest—the drawer squeaked—Mike thought shrieked—and he retrieved a warm-up suit and pulled it on. He threw on his running shoes and tiptoed back down the stairs.

He scribbled a note for Annie and left it beside her coffee mug on the end table. He strode to the bay window and searched the streets for phantoms, for killers, and coyotes. But he saw no one.

He closed the front door as quietly as he could manage, walked down the steps, and searched again. A shadow here, a shadow there, but again he saw no one. Then he ran. He didn't know where he was going—he just ran—he ran like a gazelle down Pine Street.

The last thing Mike heard as he charged down the street was Annie. Annie—dear Annie—calling. "Mike! Mike, come back!"

THIRTY-NINE

TIM'S EYES opened to the darkest dark he had ever seen. His head burst with the most severe pain he had ever felt. His skin tingled as if his whole body had fallen asleep. He tried to rub the golf-ball sized knot on his head, but his hand wouldn't move. His shackled wrists and ankles kept him wadded up in a position his body had never been in before. The car moved rapidly down some road or other. He could feel every bump, every jiggle, and the stale, tire-odored air in the trunk made it difficult for him to take an easy breath.

Tim cried. His head hurt. He needed his mom. He needed his dad. A sense of sadness swept over him like the sheet over the ghost he had seen at last year's haunted house. The guy that had grabbed him—what was he going to do with him? He started—suddenly remembering his death sentence. He gasped for breath and quivered. He tried to remember. What could he remember? The pain removed all clear thoughts from his head. *Children and children's children.* That's what he thought he remembered. The guy was taking him to be— murdered. His body stiffened. And if the guy planned to murder him, then his dad must already be dead. He thought he remembered something about his dad having to go first. He sobbed until he had no more tears to shed.

It was his fault—this mess. He acknowledged that. His mother had tucked him snugly into his bed, but he had lain there with eyes wide open. Unlike the other room—the girly room—this newly renovated room appeared manly enough. Col. Mabry had made certain of that. All the furniture was covered with leather—even the headboard on his bed. On the side walls hung photographs of rhinos and hippos. And two bison. Tim had never seen a bison—only pictures. But on the wall directly in front of his bed hung a huge taxidermied sword fish. He would have to ask Mr. Max where he had caught it. Then he remembered that his room had been the colonel's son's room—the son killed in Iraq. And Tim grieved for the Mabrys.

Then his body lurched. That bang on the roof. *A squirrel.* He relaxed, but after that he heard every squirrel that pounced on the house top. He heard every shift of the mild wind outside. Then he heard something else—a car door. It shut—softly, gently—but he heard it nonetheless. The person closing that door didn't want to wake the sleeping members of the household. Tim didn't believe it was Deputy Judge—he never came at night. It might be Mr. Max—but he wasn't due back home until sometime tomorrow afternoon. His heart raced.

Tim now heard all sorts of sounds. He heard his mother's bedroom door close. Her voice, muffled though it was, saying something like *talking* or *stalking*—he couldn't decipher it. *Must be talking to Dad.* He heard another noise outside—he couldn't tell what. His toes began to freeze, and a sensation of horror inched up his body until it penetrated the hairs on his head. He said a prayer—a prayer his dad had taught him years ago and one he said frequently. *Lord Jesus Christ, Son of the Living God, have mercy on me, a sinner.*

His fears abated momentarily. He couldn't be a baby now. He had learned to be a man. He *had* to be a man. A man just like his dad. He eased out of the bed and, still in his pajamas, sneaked quietly into the hallway between his room and his mom's. He listened at her door for a brief moment. She was still talking—still on the phone with his dad. He tiptoed down the stairs. He hesitated a moment, then unlocked the front door noiselessly, and slipped out.

The night enveloped him. There was no moon, and the only lights visible were two security lamps on the outer edge of the lawn. He thought he could make out the silhouette of an automobile parked across the road. He kept his eye on the car and sneaked down and sat in the shadows on the front steps to watch for something to move. He wasn't sure what he would do if he saw something, so he crawled back up the steps to be ready to fly back through the front door, if necessary.

Then he heard a noise he had not counted on. His guts wrenched. Someone in the house relocked the door he had just come through. He ran to the door and started to yell for his mom. But that's all Tim could remember.

A car horn suddenly jolted his consciousness. Here he was—locked up in the trunk of a stranger's car. The car was doing a lot of stopping and starting. Other cars whizzed by every second or two. Traffic lights? It was clear he was in some city or other. Then he saw a tiny shaft of light reflected off the inside of the trunk door, and he twisted his body so he could find the source. He spotted a small ragged hole about the size of a nickel in the floorboard. It was light outside. It was morning.

Then another sound rang out. He had heard the unmistakable sound of St. Christopher's carillon calling the faithful to the Daily Office, a prayer service held every morning at eight. Tim relaxed slightly.

He was home. Maybe the driver had had a change of heart. Maybe the guy would stop and let him out. But the car didn't stop. The anxiety resurged in his body when he heard the sound of the carillon fading in the distance. They were getting farther and farther away from St. Christopher's. Where was the guy taking him? And then what?

Tim suddenly forced himself into a moment of truth. He deliberately shut off the tears. If dad had been killed already, he *had* to be a man now. He had to stand up to this guy. He had to take dad's place. He would bring this killer to his knees—like he had Mr. Smith. He knew he could.

He felt the car dancing again—even greater than before. The driver had apparently turned off onto a rough, graveled road. He could hear the small stones popping against the underside of the car. Tim had difficulty measuring the time, but at some point the car stopped. He could hear people walking and talking and laughing. Car doors slammed and cars drove away.

Then the driver turned left and slowly made his way up a rougher road. The road curved and bumped. At one point Tim bounced halfway to the roof of the trunk and then down again. The car turned right and stopped. A driveway, perhaps. And Tim heard nothing else.

Time passed. Half an hour? An hour? Tim couldn't tell. Then he heard a key slip into the trunk door socket. The key turned slowly, and the door popped open a crack. He could see the light under the door's edge, and he was afraid of what he might see next.

Then the door flew open, and a hideous face behind a hideous grin forced its way into the trunk. And a hideous raspy voice spoke: "It's time, you little son-of-a-bitch. It's time."

FORTY

"M IKE! MIKE, come back!"

But Mike ran faster. The heavy morning fog slapped him in the face. He couldn't see where the street curbs were, but he plunged ahead. He turned right and continued on Church Street for a block or so. And then Mike suddenly felt indescribably weird. His body stiffened. His heart raced. His head swirled. Somebody was following him. He glanced back quickly and through the fog saw the dim shape of a large man running after him. He reached Downing Street and forced himself to look back. A dark-clad man closed in on him, and he ducked inside the Y.

Without stopping he climbed onto the Cybex abs machine and began his repetitions, slowly at first. He finished his first set before he noticed someone in dark clothing working out on the machine next to him. Ignoring the man, he did his second set of ten reps. The man beside him did eleven. Then Mike did twelve, and the man did thirteen. Mike stopped and Carlos stopped. Mike started again. Carlos was the last person he wanted to see, but he determined to best Carlos at the abs game. He didn't.

At last he stopped. And Carlos stopped. But neither of them left the machine.

"You're not supposed to be here, you know," Carlos panted.

Mike did not look at Carlos. "Are you the coyote on me now? Thought you'd leave the dirty work to the peons."

"What do you have to say for yourself?"

Mike wanted to run like hell. "Carlos, I can't do it. I cannot stay holed up in my own home, when my son has been kidnapped by a mad man."

"So doing reps on the abs machine is going to find your son?"

Mike didn't try to answer that question.

"I understand your feelings, Mike. But—"

"No, you *don't* understand, Carlos. Your daughters are safe."

"*Touché.*" Carlos paused. He vividly remembered the confrontation with Rita and Laura and winced. He thought for certain he had lost them forever. But he couldn't think about that now. "The best way to help your son—"

"If he's still alive," Mike interrupted. He had never been a pessimist, but the weight of this ordeal had created an unwanted shift in his spirit. The killer had seen to that.

"If he's still alive," Carlos conceded. "The best way to help your son is to keep you safe so that he will have a father when we find him."

That's a low blow.

"And we will find him. Make no mistake about that. And you've got to be alive for Tim to come back to."

This hit Mike hard. "I've got to find him myself, Carlos." There. He had finally said it. Annie would be upset. The MPD would be enraged. His bishop would be furious.

Carlos extracted himself from the abs machine and towel-dried the sweat from his face. "You can't do that, Mike."

Mike grabbed his towel and sat down on the bench. "I've got to, Carlos. I hate every moment I stay in that locked-up house. There's no light to see, there's no air to breathe, there's no music to hear. My energy all goes to my stomach."

"You've got to be there for Annie."

"Annie. Carlos, I have had a great deal of difficulty forgiving Annie for not protecting Tim. She shouldn't have left him alone in that bedroom, even to go checking the windows."

"You know better than that, Mike. It could have just as easily happened on your watch," Carlos scolded.

"Intellectually, I know that, Carlos. But my gut says something else. I haven't said anything to her."

"Then don't! She's hurting as much as you are." Carlos looked directly into Mike's eyes. "She needs you."

Mike grabbed his towel, and headed for the showers. Carlos followed. When they emerged, they said nothing.

Finally Carlos spoke. "Mike?"

"Mike what?"

Carlos creased his lips. "Mike, I can't let you do this. You aren't going to do this!"

"Watch me."

"Damn you, Mike Richey. There's going to be blood, and you'll be right in the middle of it." Carlos didn't say another word. He threw on his clothes and left the Y.

FORTY-ONE

THE ONCE proud Reverend Michael Basil Richey walked like a beaten man. He stepped out of the Y into a fine mist that held the faint odor of the Reicher Paper Corporation, a paper mill located about three or four miles outside of town. On heavy days like this one, the pungent smell permeated the hazy air like diesel exhaust on Church Street. The clouds grew darker. Lightening splattered the heavens but shed no light. The ensuing thunder reinforced the dread in the recesses of Mike's heart. The blatant drops of water made him droop like Quasimodo.

Mike opened the front door and came face to face with Annie, still in her night gown, standing there holding out a towel for him to blot the water from his sodden face. After a perfunctory "thanks, darling," he dashed into the master bedroom and in ten minutes returned wearing jeans and a fresh sweatshirt.

Annie languished on the couch as if she were in the last throes of life. There was little love in the room this morning. Mike ambled over and sat down on the sofa beside her, put his arm around her shoulder, and kissed her briefly on the cheek.

Annie did not look at him. "Where have you been?"

"Out." Mike was having difficulty formulating the words to explain what had happened to him this morning.

She squirmed. "Out where?"

"I couldn't sleep. I finally got out of bed and paced the floor. I paced and I prayed. I prayed and I paced."

"And I didn't?" Annie interrupted. "I am just as hurt as you."

"I know you are, sweetheart." Mike said as heartily as he could manage. He leaned over to kiss her, and Annie responded mechanically. "But I had to get out of this detention camp. I could not stand the constraint. I had to leave."

"Without telling me?" Annie responded.

"I wrote you a note, sweetheart. I left it on the end table." He looked and the note was gone.

"Which I might or might not have found."

"I am sorry about that, sweetheart. I wasn't thinking clearly. I knew if I stayed here I would explode."

"Where did you go?"

"To the Y. I wasn't intending to go to the Y. I just wanted to run. I ran, probably harder than I've ever run since Sewanee."

"What made you stop at the Y?"

"Someone was following me. Every turn I took, he took. My escape was the Y. I ran in and got on the abs machine and started pumping. All of a sudden someone appeared on the machine beside me. I tried not to pay him any attention, but then we got into competitive action."

"Carlos?"

"Yeah, Carlos was tailing me. We had a fight." This was the first time in their years of friendship that the two had had cross words. It was hard even for Mike to make sense of it now.

"You and Carlos fought?"

"Verbally. He insists that I stay in this house and leave the policing to the police. I can't do that, Annie. I've got to find Tim."

Annie reached up and caressed his cheek. He leaned over again and the mutual kiss was more genuine.

"Annie," Mike began, "I love you. You know that." What Mike was about to say was difficult—not because he didn't need to say it, but because he might hurt Annie even more than when he had walked out of the house. "I have wronged you."

"Wronged me?" Annie winced. "Wronged me how? What have you done, Mike?"

"I blamed you for losing Tim. If you had just not left him in his room alone. If you had only—if you had only—"

Annie slumped back against the couch, and her tears soaked the tissues she grabbed from the end table. She brought her legs onto the sofa and doubled up into a sitting fetal position. "Oh, Mike," she cried. "The guilt I've had to harbor since Tim's abduction was unbearable enough, but for you to—"

Mike quickly interrupted. "Carlos helped me to understand that I was wrong." He reached over and gingerly took her hand. "That I was totally wrong. I understand clearly that I was totally wrong."

They sat there at length, Annie's sobs the only sound.

"Carlos tried to dissuade me from telling you this. He knew this would hurt you." Mike folded his arms around Annie and pulled her close to him. His heart was bounding. "Annie?"

It was a long time before Annie was able to answer. "Yes?"

"Annie, I had to tell you this because I want your forgiveness. I need your forgiveness. I was wrong and I am sorry. I need your forgiveness."

Again there was a lengthy nothing, except for Annie's convulsive shudders. Mike waited with his face adjacent to Annie's face and his chest heaving against hers.

At length Annie's breathing eased. She gently touched his face and looked into his eyes. "Of course, Mike." She gripped him harder. "I think I would probably have felt the same way if I had been you."

"Thank you for loving me," Mike said, meaning it.

They held each other for an eon.

"Sweetheart?" Annie said.

"Yes?"

Annie reached over and pulled a wrinkled scrap of paper from the pages of her prayer book on the coffee table. "Sweetheart, I discovered this piece of paper under the cactus pot on the front steps." She handed it to Mike. "I found it when I went out to call after you. You didn't see it when you rushed out."

Mike stared at the paper for a good two minutes. Mike slowly opened it and froze. The paper was the same, the backside of what appeared to be an old invoice form of some sort. The writer had begun the note in the strange child-like manner of the other notes. *Sins of the fathers,* it said, and stopped there. But Mike could not believe what he saw next. The note no longer pretended to be written by a child. *Want to see your son again?* the note continued.

Come to Nob Hill at 2:00 today. Bill's Garage. Any signs of cops or guns and the boy will die. Death.

Mike crumpled the paper.

"He's alive, Annie. He's alive!"

"It's a trap!" Annie said.

Mike unwadded the paper and read the note again and then a third time. "I know."

"What are we going to do?" Annie held her breath. "We've got to give this to Carlos."

"Can't do that, Annie." Mike came back quickly. "If Carlos or Jerry either one gets this note, they will swarm the place with cops. We can't take that chance." The fear that had gripped Mike earlier reappeared with a vengeance. If Tim was alive, and Mike had some hope now that he was, the last thing Tim needed was the attention a bunch of cops would bring. The killer had murdered several times before, and he would murder again as he chose.

Annie gripped Mike's hand. "What'll we do then?"

"I've got to go."

"No, Mike. It's a trap." Annie's voice reached almost hysterical proportions. "He'll kill both of you."

"There's nothing else I can do. If I don't go, he'll kill Tim. Look at the note again." He handed her the crumpled paper. "If I do go, maybe, just maybe, I can talk him into letting Tim go." Mike understood that the chances of accomplishing this mission were slim, but he could never live with himself again if he didn't give it his best shot.

"Mike!"

"I know. I know there's a chance he could kill me. There's a chance I could get hit by a car on the street tomorrow morning. But there's also a chance of saving Tim. And there's probably no chance of saving him if a swarm of cops goes buzzing into Nob Hill."

"That is insane!" She hesitated, her eyes teared, and she touched her hands to his unshaved face. "I know I can't stop you. Go, if you must. I'll pray."

The morning was a long one. Two o'clock seemed days away. Neither Mike nor Annie spoke. They tried to eat a bit of lunch but couldn't. The time passed somehow. At about a quarter after one, Mike said, "It's time."

He took out the note to look at it once more. For no particular reason, he turned the paper over and looked at the front side—the invoice side—and there in the upper right hand corner was a piece of a symbol of some sort. Apparently a bit careless, the killer had torn through what appeared to be a logo of some sort. He had left a trace of what seemed to Mike to be a capital H, perhaps with a circle around it. He had seen that logo before somewhere—maybe on an old warehouse of some sort. But he couldn't really remember. He said nothing to Annie about this discovery.

Mike surged to his feet. "Gotta go, sweetheart."

Annie rose and held Mike tightly, as if she could never allow this to happen. And then suddenly she let go. "Whatever you have to do, do it now. Go on, darling. God go with you."

"I love you, Annie." He turned quickly and charged down the garage stairs.

FORTY-TWO

MIKE TURNED right on Church. Dark clouds drooped heavily from overhead, but he drove on to Route 27 for the six-mile trek to Nob Hill. He smiled—briefly. Whatever comparison there had ever been between this Nob Hill and San Francisco's famous Nob Hill had long since disappeared from the memories of its citizens.

Mike had been there to visit parishioners on numerous occasions, and the tiny town had always saddened him. The village had at one time been a thriving community. But when the Parsons Textile Mill closed a decade ago, the people left *en masse* to find other methods of supporting themselves. The only businesses left in the town were Brown's Market—a mom-and-pop grocery store—Rhetta's Café that dated back from before World War II, and Bill's Garage. The garage/service station was so dilapidated it was hard for Mike to see how Bill Seberg, the eighty-year-old owner, could attract any kind of business. But he was always there at seven in the morning and stayed until about five or until he felt like going home, whichever came first.

Mike sped on. He needed to get there before the kidnapper arrived. He decided to stake out a hiding place to spy out the territory—and the kidnapper. He hadn't driven more than a couple of miles before he noticed a black Ford escort some distance behind him. *The killer!* He left the Nob Hill route and drove toward Monder, a small town a couple of miles south. He slowed down a bit to see if the car would follow, but the Escort continued on Route 27 toward Nob Hill.

Mike allowed his breath to expire slowly. *Not him.* He eased on down to the next right turn and made his way back to twenty-seven in an angled short cut. He couldn't see the Escort either behind or ahead, so he continued on to Nob Hill. When he reached the old town, he saw no one. Padlocks gripped the doors of Bill Seberg's garage. *Wonder if the old man died?* He saw one car—not the Escort—parked between the café and the Mom-and-Pop. A Chevy Aveo. He couldn't tell which business had the customer.

He drove the Camry around to the back of Bill's Garage and hid it between two junked cars. Mike got out, closed the door quietly, stealthily moved to the far corner of the garage, and found three rusted, steel drums he used to conceal himself among. He thought he heard a car squeal out, but he eased his head above the drum enough to see the Aveo still there.

He remembered the old garage well. He had stopped there for gas on several occasions. The building looked as if it would fall to its knees at any minute. It had once been painted white with blue trim around the doors and its single plate-glass window. But no more. The paint had cracked and crumbled, so that just about any good storm could probably wash away any vestiges of pigment.

In front still stood two once-orange gasoline pumps. One was an ancient, electric pump that used to ding every time a gallon of gas spewed through its nozzle. The other was the more remarkable of the two. It was a ten-foot-tall, round, metal structure with a glass tank at the top. Bill would pump the gas from an underground container up into the glass tank, using a long pump handle attached to the side. Gravity then allowed the gasoline to rush through the conduit hose into the car's tank. *Gulf,* the sign read, proving the age of the pump.

The mist crept back into the atmosphere. The sky grew darker. Mike looked at his watch and had to engage the backlight to see the time. A quarter of two. The rain suddenly pounced on his head like a cat on a mouse. Mike squatted there, soaking up the surging water and peering again over the top of the drum.

Mike started. A small noise, like a chain against an empty steel drum. He looked down toward the other end of the long storefront and thought he saw something move. He craned his neck to see if he could see more. Then a huge figure, ignoring the rain, trudged toward his end of the garage, flashlight waving in the air, and water splashing from every puddle he stepped in. The figure stopped for a moment and pulled his raincoat tighter. Mike's heart fell into his stomach. The deluge blocked his clear view of the man—at least he thought it was a man—clearly. He was getting too close for Mike's comfort.

As the figure approached, Mike's heart lurched from his stomach to his throat, and he looked for a way to escape. If he moved, he would certainly draw the man's attention—something Mike wanted to avoid at all costs—but he had to do something. The rain slowed up briefly, and he could hear the man's feet plodding closer. Mike stood and quickly jumped to the opposite side of the steel barrel, hitting his knee against the metal and sounding an alarm less piercing only to the sound of a police siren.

"Hey!" the man yelled, and he headed directly toward where Mike had been hiding.

Mike turned to run back to his car, and within three strides he caught his foot under a wheel rim and tumbled head first into a small gorge filled with hubcaps and chrome bumpers. He found himself prone with his face lying on a spinner wheel cover. A gooey substance of some sort oozed around his ears. His dazed mind halted his thinking.

The footsteps grew closer.

Lord Jesus Christ, Son of the living God, have mercy on me, a sinner.

Mike could barely make out the beam of light moving back and forth. He held his breath. After what seemed a year, the footsteps stopped and the light steadied.

"What in the hell are you doing here!" the man shouted.

Mike cringed. He thought he knew the voice, but the buzzing in his head kept him from distinguishing clearly. He could not say anything. His left leg throbbed like an elephant's heart. He managed to turn over and sit upright, and he found himself staring directly into the barrel of a huge gun. He sweated but said nothing.

"Like I said, Reverend," the man shouted, "what in the hell are you doing here?"

"Jerry!"

Jerry slapped his revolver into its holster, put his flashlight into his police belt, and reached down and grabbed Mike's hand. "C'mon, Reverend, get out of there."

Mike reached up and took Jerry's hand, but he couldn't get his left leg to work.

"Are you okay, Reverend?"

"My leg. It's caught."

Jerry cautiously crept down into the pit. "Sit still for a minute." He eventually extracted Mike's foot and ushered him out of the pit.

"Thanks, Jerry."

The rain mercifully had stopped and the clouds were beginning to break up.

"Come on. Let's go to my car. We need to talk." Jerry ushered Mike forward.

"So *this* is your car?" Mike could not believe he was sitting in the passenger seat of an old black Ford Escort.

"Yep," Jerry replied.

The shock almost made him lose his composure. "Why have I not seen it before?" *Could Jerry be the killer?* Mike found his hands doubling into fists.

"I'm sure you have. I've been using it to keep an eye on you."

"I mean—why had I never seen it before that?"

"I seldom use it. I drag it out from time to time during hot cases like this one so I can really be unobtrusive. Very often criminals can detect a patrol car even when it's unmarked. I've solved several crimes using this old clunker."

Mike clenched his teeth. "I see." He was still uneasy. "Why didn't you tell me about the Escort? It would have saved me many days of anxiety."

"It wouldn't have been as effective, now would it?"

Mike ran his fingers through his hair but said nothing.

Jerry waited a moment. "If you had known that this was my vehicle, it would have given you too much freedom—freedom to get yourself killed."

"We're sneaky now, aren't we, Detective?"

Jerry hurried around to the driver's side and got in. They both sat there in silence for a couple of minutes. Jerry was a strong, rough, tough, and straight-talking cop, but Mike had always been able to hold his own with him—until now.

"Now tell me, Reverend" Jerry said. "What are you doing in Nob Hill?"

Mike sighed. He slowly reached into his pocket and pulled out the damp, crumpled paper and handed it to him.

Jerry poker-faced his way through the note. "Why didn't you turn this over to me or Detective Ruiz immediately?"

"You saw what it said about the police. I was afraid the guy would kill Tim."

"We could have worked it so that the killer would not have known we were here. And we wouldn't have put you in danger either."

"But why didn't the killer show himself?"

"He left. When he saw me drive up, he left. He spun out of there like a drag racer."

Mike broke out into a cold sweat. "What? You mean you let him drive off? Just like that?"

"I didn't have the benefit of your crumpled note. I had no reason to believe at the time that he was the killer. So he left."

Mike, for the first time in his life, was speechless.

Jerry said nothing for a couple of minutes. "Reverend?" He finally broke his silence. "It's apparent that I can't stop you from doing this your own way, short of locking you up in a cell." Jerry reached into his glove compartment and drew out a revolver—a Smith and Wesson .32 Magnum, one just like his own. "So I'm going to lend this to you for protection."

"No, Jerry."

"Yes, Reverend. From here I want you to go directly home. Do not pass go. Do not collect two hundred dollars. Tomorrow morning at six I will meet you at the police academy shooting range, and I'm going to let the folks there teach you how to use this thing. You're going to spend all day shooting. You just might learn enough to save your own skin, and you might just be in a position at some point to save your son's."

Mike turned and looked in the opposite direction.

"Do I hear an okay?"

"You know how I feel about guns, Jerry."

"Do I hear an okay?"

A long pause. "Okay." Mike surrendered. And then he shuddered.

✝✝✝

BEFORE MIKE got to the door, it swung wide open. Annie stood there, her face blanched. She folded her arms around him.

Annie placed her lips next to Mike's ear. She whispered. "Did you see Tim?"

Mike shook his head. "But I believe he's still alive."

"Thank God." Annie didn't hesitate. "How do you know?"

Mike brushed his fingers gently across her lips as if to say, *Sh-h-h. No crying. No talking. Let's just savor this moment.* And he held her tighter.

At some point or other, they broke apart, and without words Annie led Mike into the kitchen. The table had been laid with a virtual feast that Annie had put together from the generous food gifts of St. Christopher's church family. "Had to do something while you were gone. So—here we are." She placed the entrée on the table.

Except for the blessing, not a further word was spoken until they had sated themselves.

Mike reached over the table and took Annie's hand. "Thank you, sweetheart."

She gripped his hand tighter and a small grin—not a happy one—conquered her lips. "I slaved."

Mike returned the grin and nodded. It took him a moment or two before he could talk further. "The killer is keeping Tim alive to entice me into jeopardizing myself." He swallowed hard. "When he gets me, he'll get Tim."

Annie wasn't consoled. "What happened?"

Then Mike told her tales of steel drums and scrap metal, of screeching cars and intruding detectives, of Ford Escorts and loaded guns.

Annie winced. "The gun, Mike. You don't like guns."

"I really don't intend to use the gun." He told her about Jerry's demand that he train for a day at the police academy. He frowned for a couple of moments. "I think I'll take the gun."

Annie tightened her grasp on Mike's hands. "What do you plan to do now?"

Mike struggled with the question for several moments. "I don't know, sweetheart. I don't know."

FORTY-THREE

JERRY STEERED the Crown Vic toward home. There was a time when he would have steered it toward church. He and Maureen had seldom missed the Wednesday evening prayer meeting. But the family had not been to church since Jerry's row with Brother Sam. So he headed home.

He drove into his circular driveway and immediately drove out again. Jerry picked up his cell and called Maureen to inform her of his change of plans. He pulled into the Bridgewater Church parking lot half an hour early, ran up the steps of the portico, and in through the gigantic front doors. The congregation had not arrived yet, so he sat down in the back pew to be alone in his agony. His eyes drifted over the pulpit and past the choir, and he stared incessantly at the large wooden cross behind the baptistery.

He placed his hands on the back of the pew in front of him and slipped onto his knees, landing on the hardwood floor below the pew. He prayed for forgiveness. Forgiveness for the fight with his pastor, forgiveness for summarily dismissing his son's desire to become a preacher, and forgiveness for treating the reverend like a fiend. The cross from the baptistery seemed to float toward him. The more urgently he prayed, the closer the cross came. At the end of his prayer, the cross hovered over him like a hummingbird over its nectar. He bowed his head, and, when he looked up, the cross had removed itself back to the baptistery.

Jerry didn't join in the hymns that followed. Apprehension loaded his anticipation. He had to talk to Brother Sam. He had to apologize for his part in the spat. When the service was over, he remained seated until the congregation left the sanctuary. He struggled out of his pew, walked out into the vestibule, and offered his hand to Brother Sam.

Argyle let his right arm dangle at his side. "I can't take your hand, Brother Jerry."

Jerry pulled his hand back. "Why not?"

"The bible teaches us to heed the preacher's admonishments. If a person refuses, he should be treated as a heathen and a publican. In other words, he is to be shunned. The last time I looked, Brother Jerry, you were unrepentant."

Jerry had seldom been at a loss for words. Now he all but stuttered his way into asking, "Brother Sam, what sins have I committed?"

"You really don't know? Do I have to enumerate them for you?"

"I wish you would, Brother Sam."

Argyle motioned for Jerry to sit on one of the two short pews in the vestibule, pews usually reserved for latecomers waiting to be seated in the sanctuary. He sat down beside Jerry and placed his hand on Jerry's shoulder. Jerry felt the condescension.

"Brother Jerry, I hate to have to reiterate the list of the evils you are guilty of."

Jerry removed the preacher's invading hand. "No apology is necessary. Now go on."

Argyle turned toward Jerry and positioned himself to send down his pastoral wrath upon this weak brother. "Let's take them in order, shall we?"

Jerry stared into Argyle's eyes. "By all means."

"Firstly, you encouraged your son to commit suicide, the greatest sin a person can commit."

Jerry dropped his head. This was a low blow. He had asked himself numerous times what he might have done to have prevented Mack's action. He began to shake, as if his soul were freezing over.

"Secondly, instead of calling in a man of God to deal with the boy's sin, you called in a psychologist. A psychologist, mind you. Oh, the hoaxes those so-called psychologists have pulled on unsuspecting Christians!"

Jerry retrieved his gumption and looked again into Argyle's eyes.

"Thirdly, you let a woman—nay, you encouraged her, you urged her—to take over as head of your house. It would have been far better to have grabbed the most pimple-faced, teenage boy off the street to come in and do your job for you than a woman."

Jerry stood, his rage swirling through his bosom. His fists doubled. "That woman was my wife!"

Argyle was not to be intimidated. He stood and the two confronted each other like two Clemson and Carolina football players on the gridiron. "And the worst sin of all was questioning a man of God's authority to speak for God." Argyle smiled—the Jerry Falwell smirk, as any good preacher should be able to do. "And tell me. Are you still in league with Reverend Satan?"

Jerry said nothing more. He turned and walked out the church door and headed for home. He looked back through his rear-view mirror and spotted Argyle standing on the portico, exulting in his victory over the sinner of the year.

Jerry walked into his home, ignored the other children and Maureen, and walked directly into Mack's room. He sat on Mack's bed watching him complete an algebra problem. *He needs no help with algebra, that's for sure.* And Jerry smiled at Mack.

"Hi Dad. What's up?"

"Set your algebra aside for a moment, Son. We need to talk."

Mack looked up, his fear-filled eyes about to burst into tears. "Have I done something wrong, Dad?"

Jerry looked at Mack carefully—and loved him. "No. No, of course not." He took Mack's hand in his. "Son, do you remember asking me if the reverend was the devil?"

Mack nodded.

"Son, I can assure you with every ounce of my strength, Reverend Mike is *not* the devil."

FORTY-FOUR

TIM LAY on the dank, wooden floor and opened his eyes. The expanse of the open loft seemed endless. He turned his head as his position would permit, but all he could see was empty space all the way up to the tin roof with tiny nail holes that allowed some sunlight to seep in. All the window panes had been painted black, either to keep the sunlight out or to keep nosy-nellies from seeing in. Then he saw the stockpile of weapons lying spaced out in orderly fashion on the floor. He froze momentarily. *Will one of those guns kill me?* But he chose not to think about that now. Other junk decorated the floor. Empty tin cans, bits and pieces of clothing, and half-full, plastic grocery bags all suggested the kidnapper had lived in this old building for awhile. He turned his head again. There was another side of the warehouse. He couldn't see in there very easily. All he could see was a part of an old forklift of some sort.

The building had a bit of an odor—not an obnoxious one—like oats, maybe. The smell reminded him of Col. Mabry's barn at the farm. Maybe the building had once been used to store animal feed. He turned his head again and made out wooden pallets—mostly broken ones—and another old yellow forklift somewhere in the distance.

He felt a sharp jab against his thigh.

"Wake up, kid," a strange voice said.

That was one thing he had had a great deal of difficulty doing. His head hurt—probably from the punch the bully had given him. Yes, *bully* was the right word for this evil man—this savage, this monster. Tim suddenly understood his conversation with his dad, when he told him a bully was after him. *This is that bully.* Tim's head hung over, as if he had been given some kind of drug or something.

"I said, wake up, kid."

Tim looked at the bully for the first time. He was a tall, big man—mostly fat—not muscled like his dad. The scowl on his face, the red in his eyes, and the long hairs growing out his nose made him look like the monster he really was. Tim felt a sudden kick in his side.

"Ya hear me, you little bastard? I said, wake up!"

He tried to answer but couldn't. His mouth had been duct-taped shut—along with his wrists and his ankles. The only maneuver he could make was a flip from side to side. But his Kodokan and gymnastics-induced agility allowed him some movement that others in his condition might not be able to execute.

"Wake up! I've gotta keep you alive for a little while longer." The savage opened a can of pork and beans. "Let's see if I can make you fart." The weirdest laughter issued from the bully's mouth, like the rasping clatter of a box of metal bolts dumped onto the floor.

The bully's hand reached for the tape that locked his lips together. It paused there for a moment, and Tim steeled his body to take the agony of the tape-pull. "Won't do you any good to holler, kid. Nobody for miles around." And the hand ripped off the tape.

Tim jerked. The rip stung his cheeks like sandpaper scraping against the skin. He wanted to reach up and sooth his face. He couldn't, of course, but he emitted the loudest yelp he could muster.

"Sorry, kid," the bully said. He sounded almost as if he meant it.

Then Tim's mind shifted to more important things. "Are you going to—to—murder me?"

The monster was taken aback. He apparently had not expected such a blunt question from a ten-year-old boy. "My, aren't you the odd one." He looked at Tim and grinned—an eerie sort of grin like Tim had last seen on Glen Mables behind the school building. "In time, kid. In time. But murder is such a strong word. Execute. Now *execute* is a more appropriate word."

"When? When are you going to execute me?"

"Don't know yet. Gotta get rid of your old man first."

This frank announcement hit Tim, like a fist, right in the forehead. Inside his body the tears welled up from his stomach through his esophagus into his head—but they never reached his eyes. He was a man now, and he had to behave like a man. "What are you...?"

Before Tim could finish the question, the bully stuffed a spoonful of pork and beans into his mouth. He almost gagged, but he couldn't allow himself to do that either. He took a deep breath and swallowed the beans. Another spoonful came and then another and then another. "Water," he managed to say between bites.

The savage paid little heed to his plea and finished the beans off himself. Then he took the empty can over to a plastic grocery bag, reached in and brought out a gallon of water, and poured some into the bean can. He brought the can of water over to him and gave him a few sips. The water missed his mouth and splashed onto his pajama shirt. Laughter again came in the same shrill rat-a-tat voice.

Then the monster's hand grabbed the duct-tape roll and ripped off a twelve-inch strip. "Here, kid. Gotta stuff that ugly mouth again."

"Do you have to do that? I promise I won't yell."

The hand paused for a moment. "I can't trust you, you little creep."

"Maybe. Maybe not. Are you afraid to take that chance?" The moment Tim said this, he wished he had kept his mouth shut.

"Smart ass little brat." And the tape sealed Tim's mouth with a vengeance. The bully apparently didn't like assertive—much less obnoxious—kids.

Tim turned over on his right side and drew his legs up into the fetal position. The tears he had forced himself to keep inside now flowed in abundance.

"Whatcha crying for, kid?"

Tim buried his eyes in his left arm, and then he felt the flow of warm liquid oozing out from between his legs. Try as he might he couldn't stop the seepage. The embarrassment almost overcame his fear.

The bully laughed again. "Can't hold it in, huh? Little babies have to let it go, so they say."

Tim pulled his knees tighter toward his stomach. How could he be a man now? Men didn't pee in their pants. Men didn't cry. It was hard being a man. He stopped his crying and lay there with his eyes closed, not wanting to look at this bully.

"Ya know? I've been good to you, kid." The savage stopped talking as if he were expecting Tim to answer him. "Ya know?" the kidnapper started up again. "If I was a different kind of person…"

Tim felt stenchy breath on his neck. He squirmed but thought better of it and stopped.

"If I was a different kind of person—an evil person, say, I would reach over and pull your pants down and…"

Tim's pajama bottoms suddenly slid down to his knees. He winced.

"Goddamn! Now see what you did, kid? I'm going to have to waste your drinking water washing the piss off my hands." But that didn't stop the bully from going further. "You've got a little dick, kid. You'll never get to be a man with that little twig. Come to think of it, you'll never get to be a man anyway. Not after I'm through with you." The savage laughed again—the raucous jeer.

Tim felt a rough scaly hand reach into his groin.

"Now, if I wasn't a decent person, you would feel me playing with that little dick. But I am a decent person, so I won't do that."

Abruptly, with all the strength he could muster, Tim turned over rapidly and his fetaled legs sprang forth and rammed the savage in the belly. The bully fell to the floor and rolled from side to side screeching in sheer agony. He finally settled down and lay there in quiet repose. Tim lay quietly for a couple of minutes, dreading the moment the savage decided to move.

At length the monster stirred. He suddenly bellowed raucously, and Tim turned quickly to see the savage charging toward him like a wild bull. He jerked his bound wrists up to his head to shield his face from any forth-coming injury. Then he heard a sudden loud noise, like wooden boards clattering to the floor. The bellowing abruptly stopped, the charging abruptly ceased, and the monster made a bee line to the gun stash.

The savage quickly picked up a pistol—Tim didn't know one from the other, so it was just a pistol to him—and turned and charged back toward Tim. This was it. He would never see his mom and dad again. But he had to be brave. He had to be the man he wanted to be. He had to be like his dad. *Lord Jesus Christ, Son of the Living God, have mercy on me, a sinner.*

But the savage flew past him and charged into the other side of the warehouse. He heard voices. Then someone—a man, he thought—screamed. And then a pistol shot. The noises stopped.

A million years later, Tim heard the savage coming back toward him. He braced himself for another shot, but that shot did not come.

"Kid," the savage said. "Kid, we gotta get out of here."

FORTY-FIVE

CARLOS DROVE the fire-engine-red BMW convertible back onto I-85. The Delta Connection flight from ATL to GSP had been fifty minutes late. It took twenty more minutes to efficiently fill the trunk with bags and to tuck odds and ends into every available cranny.

Ellen grinned. "Thought you might come to get me on your Harley. In your, hmmm, muscle shirt?"

Carlos returned the grin and stroked the dash. "Thought I should put this baby to some good use."

The BMW was Ellen's. He took it out from time to time for a pleasure spin and to show off a bit to the poor guys on the streets of Madison who didn't own a convertible. This afternoon he was showing off not only the BMW but its owner as well.

The temperature was a bit cool to put the top down, but Ellen insisted. So they tightened their jackets, and the top came down. She closed her eyes and laid her head back onto the head rest, her wind-reddened cheeks highlighting the smile she kept on her lips. Her ravishing, dark, shoulder-length hair flew back into the wind like the tail of a kite. Carlos looked—no, gazed—at her beauty. In spite of her ten-hour international trek covering seven time zones, Ellen looked sexy—awfully sexy.

"Keep your eyes on the road, Mr. Policeman."

Carlos had never understood how Ellen could tell what he was doing with her eyes closed, but he grinned and obeyed.

"Just wait until we get home," Ellen said. "And then you can ogle me to your heart's content."

Carlos stepped on the accelerator with the gusto of an Earnhardt. "Consider us there."

"Whoa, Mr. Policeman." She put her hand on Carlos's shoulder. "Who do you think you are, a teenager?"

Carlos slowed down to ten miles-an-hour above the limit and reached over and touched her hand.

"And besides, I'm famished. I want a welcome-home dinner before we start the billing and cooing. Has our chef prepared us a seven-remove banquet? Or did you do it yourself?" Ellen smiled and touched his knee.

"Damn." Carlos snapped his fingers. "I almost forgot." He picked up his cell phone and dialed home. "Is this Jeeves, the butler?" He waited for a butlerly reply.

Ellen held on to his right arm.

Hell. How could he drive, listen to the butler, and become sexually aroused all at the same time? But he tried. "Jeeves, tell James, the chef, that the two of you can have the evening off. The mistress and I will have dinner at the Down East this evening."

Carlos hung up and within fifteen minutes, he pulled into the restaurant's parking lot.

Ellen looked around at the dozens of automobiles that littered the lot. "I see you got here for the Early Bird Special."

"As a matter of fact," Carlos checked his watch, "I did. Let's go."

The properest of maitre d's, dressed like Paul Revere with a feather in his hat, summoned the properest of waiters, dressed like Paul Revere, Jr., without the feather. "Mr. Ruiz and Ms. Scott have reservations at six in the Boston Tea Party Room."

Ellen shifted her eyes toward Carlos and muttered, "You had this already planned, didn't you?"

Carlos simply looked smug and said nothing.

Then Mr. Revere, Jr. showed them through the magnificent and densely filled Mayflower Dining Room and led them toward the back.

"Surely not next to the kitchen!" Ellen rolled her eyes and feigned disgust.

"I love you too," Carlos mouthed and grinned.

The Boston Tea Party turned out to be a small private dining room, the décor like the deck of a seventeenth-century ship, far away from the madding crowd.

"I love you, Carlos Ruiz," Ellen mouthed even before Paul Revere, Jr. left the room.

"I love you back," Carlos said aloud, and Paul Revere seemed to hear nothing.

And by romantic candlelight and the music of Mozart—yes, the waiter knew Mozart was an Austrian, not a New Englander—the two lovebirds drank wine like Henry Fielding's Tom Jones, ate lobster like Molly Seagram, and talked of love.

FORTY-SIX

TIM STARED at the bully's ashen face.

"We gotta get outa here," the savage said again and charged to one of the blackened windows with a broken pane that allowed him to look outside. "Arrgh. The cops." He watched the road outside for the next five minutes. He stepped back and flitted like a moth around the vast space. Then he abruptly stopped his violent wings and turned to the boy.

Tim leered back at the distressed man. He seemed smaller than usual. Perhaps it was his sagging shoulders. His scraggly black beard made his bluish-gray eyes appear dull and hopeless. His obese torso and balloon-sized arms almost made Tim feel sorry for him.

Until he spotted the guns. Three pistols and three rifles. Which one of these guns had shot his dad? What about Sir and Juice and Jake and the other "collateral mishaps," as the savage had called them? These guns had killed them. And Tim lowered his head in grief.

The savage reached over and grabbed a black jacket, collected his cache of guns, put them in the proper traveling cases, and swung them over his shoulder. "We gotta get out of here," he said. "Somebody must have heard the shot, and the cops drove by. But they'll be back. You can count on that." He took one more anxious look out the window. "You stay here, little creep, while I go get the car." As if Tim could go anywhere. The savage took his shouldered guns, grabbed his duffel bag, and lunged out of the warehouse at double speed.

He was back within five minutes. He gathered the food items, packed them in two plastic Bi-Lo bags, and stuffed whatever clothing he had into another. He crossed over to Tim, unwrapped the tape—excepting his mouth—and shoved the two grocery bags into his hands. He ordered him to grab the bedroll and head on out to the car. "I'll be right behind you, little creep, so don't try any funny stuff."

Tim did as he was ordered. The murderer came immediately behind. They got to the door, and a grocery bag abruptly broke open. Goods of all sorts rolled in every direction.

"Stay where you are, little creep."

But Tim didn't stay where he was. He dropped the bedroll and charged out the door like the wind of a Category 5 hurricane. The savage was right behind. Tim was far faster than the savage, and he ducked around the Escort and ran straight toward the highway. Another football field and he would be where he could get some help from a passing driver. But the savage sprang into the Escort and headed after him. The car came up close behind him, Tim rolled into the right-hand ditch, and the Escort passed him. Screeching to a dead stop, the savage leapt out of the car and headed back toward the boy. Tim left the road and circled through the brambles, moving through them as quickly as the briars would allow. He came out on the other side and discovered a revolver staring him in the face.

"Stop right there, little creep."

Tim did.

The bully grabbed Tim by the arm and shoved the pistol against his ribs. "You're going with me, you little asshole." The two marched in tandem to the Escort and the savage shoved Tim in on the driver's side, the revolver still trained on the boy. "Move over, asshole."

Tim moved on over to the passenger's seat, the savage got into the driver's seat, and the Escort headed out. After five minutes or so, the savage stopped the car, grabbed the always-available roll of duct tape, and retaped Tim's wrists and ankles. He reinforced the mouth-gag and wrapped the tape around Tim's eyes and head. "No sight for you, little creep." The savage grabbed the boy, forced him out of the car and into the back seat, and ordered him to lie down on the floorboard. "Little creep, if you ever want to see your daddy again, you'll stay right where I put you. You understand that, little creep?"

Tim did not move.

"I said do you understand that, little creep?"

Tim nodded.

"That's better." The savage grabbed something out of the trunk and got back behind the wheel.

Tim's only source of intelligence now was his ears. He heard the cars roaring by, but very little else, except the savage's singing—off key. A hymn, no less. "There is power, power, wonder-working power, in the blood..."

Then he smelled the smoke. The monster had lit up again. The odor was bad enough in the openness of the warehouse, but in this closed-in car the stench created a nausea that he didn't know how he could handle, if worse came to worst. Then the sound of rushing wind. The savage had apparently lowered his window to allow the smoke a way of escape. His tummy eased a bit. Then he heard the sounds he knew. The traffic rush. A siren or two. St. Christopher's bells. The car eased its speed to blend with the city traffic.

The monster ceased his warbling and slowed down almost to a stop. "Hey, little creep. Here's the alley where that old woman witch met her maker."

Tim didn't know which woman witch he was talking about. But he worried.

The savage sped up and then slowed again. "And here's the alley where that juicy bum got his due."

The nausea returned. Now Juice, he knew.

And again the savage sped up and slowed down. "And here, little creep. This is where your grandpa got it. Splat." He laughed a hideous and raucous laugh. "Right in the head." Then the savage started singing again—"When I see the blood, when I see the blood…"

Sir. Tim's heart jumped into his throat. Sir. He prayed to keep the pork and beans in his stomach.

The savage had slowed down at each shrine as if he were praying the Stations of the Alleys.

"Shit!" The monster suddenly braked the car. "The bedroll. Little creep, what the hell did you do with the goddamned bedroll?" He made a block and started back in the opposite direction.

He must be going back to get the bedroll. His heart leapt with perhaps a modicum of joy. If he went back to the warehouse, the police might be there now.

But then the savage slowed and stopped again. "Hey, old man."

He must be talking to somebody on the sidewalk. Tim didn't hear an answer.

"I said hey, old man."

Again Tim heard nothing.

"Old man, how would you like a fresh bottle of Thunderbriar?"

Tim still heard nothing.

"I'll buy you a bottle of Thunderbriar if you'll come do something for me."

"What?" the old man finally said.

"I want to hire you to run an errand for me. I'll give you a bottle of Thunderbriar for your trouble. Come on. Get in the car."

Apparently the savage had touched the old man's heart, for Tim heard the old man start to open the door to the back seat. And Tim's heart leapt.

The savage stopped him, his voice harsh and raspy. "No! No, not the back seat. Come on up front where the rich folks ride. Sit beside me."

Tim heard the old man get into the front seat, and the Escort started rolling. A few minutes later the car stopped again. He heard the savage get out of the car. Tim waited a moment and then made as much noise as the gag would allow. The old man let out a bloody scream and leapt out of the car. Tim sighed. The old man couldn't help him.

A moment passed and the car door opened again. "Get back in here you mother-fucking sot."

Tim heard the old man scramble back into the car. A door closed.

Several minutes later the driver's door opened, and the savage crawled back in. "I've got your Thunderbriar here, you goddamned drunk. And I'm putting it in the glove box. You won't touch it until you've earned it." He paused. "You got that, old man?"

The old man said nothing.

"I said, you got that old man?"

The old man muttered something Tim couldn't understand, and the car peeled out.

They drove around awhile before the savage talked again. "Here, take this flashlight." The savage told the old man his errand.

The old man grumbled something, but Tim couldn't tell what.

The Escort eventually came to a stop, and the old man got out of the car.

"If you're not back here in ten minutes, I will not be here. No Thunderbriar for you, my friend."

The gravel crunched a gritty sound as the old man staggered up the road.

The savage turned the Escort around and waited. Tim could sense the savage growing more and more tense as the minutes passed.

"Okay, you goddamned bastard, get your ass back here—now." He made no attempt to soften his voice. He shouted, "Okay, you asshole, get back—now!"

Tim cringed at the cursing. Then he heard some kind of racket—sounded like a scuffle of some sort—and a couple of voices.

Something about one of the voices sounded familiar to him. Tim was stunned. *Dad! That sounds like Dad!*

"Goddammit," the savage cursed under his breath, and he put the car in drive and shoved out. He said nothing as he rumbled back through town. Then a half-hour later, as best as Tim could guess, the monster pulled into what Tim thought must have been a driveway of some sort. He heard bushes scraping the sides of the car. *He must be hiding the car.* Then the car came to a stop.

The savage got out, and Tim heard him walk away. *What is he doing now?* A minute or so later, Tim heard some loud voices, and then a woman screamed. Tim cringed. It seemed a long time before he heard the monster walking back toward the car.

The back car door opened. The monster dragged Tim out of the vehicle, untaped him—except for his mouth—and shoved the duffel bag into his hands along with another grocery bag full of stuff. He wrapped his fat hand around Tim's nape and marched him into an eerie looking old house.

The savage pushed Tim up the stairs—the widest staircase Tim had ever seen in a house—and threw him on the floor. "Okay, you little asshole." He took the flashlight and began pounding Tim's face and head. The tape wouldn't allow him to scream, but he made horrible agonizing noises—and cried. The savage's blows seemed measured. "This one," he said, "is for thinking." *Pow!* "This one is for running." *Pow!* "This one is for making me run after you." *Pow!* These are for leaving the bedroll. He opened his hand. *Slap. Slap. Slap. Slap. Slap.* The bully bound him again, dragged him across the floor, and attached his feet to a post of some sort.

In a moment he heard the savage leave the room. Then the car crunched out of the driveway. He was alone.

FORTY-SEVEN

AFTER HE finished the day of shooting, Mike walked back to the Camry, started the engine and abruptly turned it off again. That note. That logo—or piece of one at least—had to be a clue of some sort. A store, perhaps. A warehouse, maybe. It had to be a warehouse. He'd seen a logo—the piece seemed to fit—on an old abandoned warehouse somewhere. *I've got to find that warehouse.* His cell phone rang.

"Hey, Mike."

"Hey, Carlos. What's up?" Carlos often called when the MPD needed the services of the chaplain, but Mike hadn't been doing much chaplaining lately.

"I've got to talk to you about yesterday morning. We've been friends too long to let egos come between us. I'm off duty now, so how about meeting me at Sarah's place for a couple of beers?"

Mike was relieved. He had sorely regretted that row. But first things first. "Can't do it right now. Can I meet you there in a couple of hours?" Mike had to find that warehouse.

"Yeah, sure. That'll be okay, I guess." Carlos sounded disappointed. Maybe he thought Mike was not as eager to make the peace as he was.

"See you there." Mike pressed the END button and quickly called Annie to let her know he'd be late. He started the engine again, pulled out of the parking lot, and traveled down Myers Street out to Route 12. He sped out of town toward Shiloh. The sun was going down, and he knew what he had to do—and fast—before dark finally came.

Warehouses—some busy adjuncts to city stores but several, deserted and lonely—lined the road. Mike drove slowly, scrutinizing each one. Nothing looked familiar. Then he noticed an abandoned side road that he recalled led to a couple of old buildings that had at one time been inhabited by several hobes until the police had ushered them out. Mike recalled this place well.

The brush had grown up all around the old structure, and the broken sign that hung from the front eave verified the logo. He barely made out *Houston Feed Company*. The piece of the H was of the same font style as the piece of a logo he recalled from the note.

He pulled the Camry up about a tenth of a mile beyond the warehouse and parked it in an unused driveway. He sat there a couple of minutes, debating whether or not to take Jerry's revolver with him. Believing that guns easily obtained were often invitations to murder and other high crimes, Mike had always been a proponent of strict gun control laws. Yet—he had taken it. Mike reached into the glove compartment, retrieved the revolver, and tucked it into his belt. Despite today's balmy weather, he reached into the back seat, grabbed his overcoat, and put it on to cover the gun.

Mike emerged from the vehicle and walked stealthily back up the road to the old warehouse. Before he got to the driveway, he peeled off the road and brambled his way through the brush. He cautiously pushed the last painful branches aside, and there it was.

He approached the building. Everything was still. It was growing dark, and he could see the moon and a couple of stars. No one in sight. No car, no person, no noise, no anything. He made out some recent footprints etched into the drying mud. He measured them against his own shoe size—a pair of elevens—or so—and a pair of eights—or so—Tim's size. He reached into his coat pocket for his flashlight to examine the tracks more closely, but the flashlight was not there.

Mike reluctantly and carefully drew his gun and stole up to a broken window to spy out the structure. The warehouse was dark inside and Mike could see nothing. Then he heard footsteps crunching up the graveled driveway. He froze. With each step he visualized the killer closing in. The gait seemed unsteady, as if the person were either drunk or carrying a heavy load. Mike held his breath and prayed the heavy load was not a dead body. The moon hid itself behind a dark cloud. He waited.

Mike sneaked his way back toward the front of the building and craned his neck to see a dim light bobbing up and down and moving furtively toward the building. Without further thought, Mike dove back into the brambles and waited. He hardly breathed. He got *veins in his legs*, as Tim called it.

The wobbly flashlight moved closer. Mike waited. His veins grew tighter and tighter. The figure approached the door, staggered up the steps, and fumbled with the door latch. No luck getting the door open. He stepped back to get a good look.

Then the man brusquely fell to the porch floor. Mike straddled his frame and rammed the gun under his chin. The man looked up at Mike, and his eyes stretched like an inflating balloon.

"Father!" he cried. "Don't shoot! Don't shoot!"

"Tom-Tom!" Mike pulled the revolver away. "Tom-Tom, what in the heck are you doing here?"

Tom-Tom was the hobe who lived in Bosham with Marty and Jo. For a flashing moment it occurred to Mike that Tom-Tom could be the culprit, and for a flashing moment a pulse of rage swept over him. But then reason set in. Tom-Tom was in the congregation when Mike was shot. Tom-Tom didn't have the means of transportation to get to the sites of the crimes. Tom-Tom was too weak to carry out such a mission.

"Father, I didn't mean anything bad."

Mike relaxed, his veins pliant again. He eased the revolver into his overcoat pocket. "I know you didn't, Tom-Tom."

Mike reached out and gently struggled Tom-Tom up to a sitting position on the steps and sat down beside him.

"Now, Tom-Tom, tell me what you are doing here."

"The man."

Mike wanted a name, although he really didn't have any hope of getting one from Tom-Tom. "What man, Tom-Tom?"

"I dunno, Father. Just a man. He saw me in Bosham and made me get into the car with him."

"He abducted you?"

"You mean like kidnap, Father?"

"Yes, like kidnap."

"No!"

"You mean he didn't kidnap you?"

"No."

"Why did you get into the car with him then?"

"He promised me a bottle of Thunderbriar if I went with him."

"Aha!" Cheap wine or cheap gin could bribe most of the hobes on almost any occasion. *A man. The killer's a man.* "Did you know the man? Was he someone you had seen before?" If the man knew where Tom-Tom lived, if he had found Juice and Sir, surely Tom-Tom must have seen him snooping around in the hobes' hideouts at some point.

"Didn't know him, Father. But I've seen him around."

"What did he look like, Tom-Tom?" Perhaps he was camouflaged as another hobe.

"Just a man. Black clothes. Eerie face."

"What kind of eerie face?"

"I dunno, Father. Just an eerie face." Mike knew he wasn't going to get anymore out of Tom-Tom about the man's appearance.

"What kind of car was he driving?"

"Oh, I don't know. Old one, maybe black."

"Do you know what kind of car it was?" Mike figured he was going to run into a dead end here as well.

"No. Never paid much attention to brands. Don't even know what kind of potted meat I eat for lunch."

"Did he bring you here?"

"Brought me here and let me off at the road."

"You mean the driveway here, or the road from the main highway?"

"Not the driveway."

"He let you out back at the road?"

"Back on the road."

"Just now?"

"Yeah. He wanted me to go inside the warehouse and bring him a bedroll." The man was apparently using Tom-Tom to collect something he had forgotten. But why?

"A bedroll? Why didn't he come in and get his own bedroll?"

Before Tom-Tom could answer, Mike suddenly jolted at the squeal. A car, apparently on the highway, burned rubber peeling out into the road and shagging out at ninety miles an hour or thereabouts.

"That's him," Tom-Tom said. "That's the man. He told me he would wait for me. Told me he'd leave me if I wasn't back in ten minutes."

Mike suddenly had the urge to rush to his Camry and chase the man. But just as suddenly he had the urge not to. He would never catch up with him now. Apparently the man was afraid of coming back to the warehouse for some reason, so he sent a surrogate. "Tom-Tom, that man's a bad man. That's the man who killed Juice and Sir. It's a good thing he didn't wait for you."

Tom-Tom's face contorted and his entire body trembled. "But I want my Thunderbriar. I *need* my Thunderbriar." Tears appeared in the hobe's eyes. "The man gave me a brand new bottle of Thunderbriar, if I'd get his bedroll for him."

"Where is the Thunderbriar now?"

"In his car."

Mike asked the question that he dreaded the answer to. "Did he have anybody else in the car with him?"

"No."

"Are you certain?"

"Yeah, I'm certain, Father. I swear I'm certain, Father."

Mike's throat tightened. "Like a little boy?"

"I swear I'm certain, Father."

"That man stole a little boy, Tom-Tom."

Tom-Tom mopped his face with his sleeve. "Not a little boy, Father!"

Mike's throat constricted again. "I'm afraid so, Tom-Tom. He stole my little boy, Tim." It was all Mike could do to say Tim's name.

"No, Father! Not Timmy." The tears welled up in Tom-Tom's eyes. "I love Timmy. He was always good to me at St. Chris's. He's a good boy, Father." The tears erupted. "I love Timmy, Father."

Mike was moved. "So do I, Tom-Tom, so do I." It was at that moment he knew he had to get back to St. Christopher's and the diner as quickly as possible. These men and women needed him, and they needed Tim.

"Tom-Tom, I really need your help. I need you to remember as much as you possibly can about that man. I've got to get Tim back."

Tom-Tom stopped sobbing. "To hell with the Thunderbriar, Father. I wanna help you find Timmy."

"Thanks, Tom-Tom. I tell you what you can do right now—what you can do to help me find Tim."

"Sure, Father," Tom-Tom agreed. "I'll do anything to help you find Timmy, Father."

Mike's silence was so long, it appeared to make Tom-Tom nervous.

"Where did you get that flashlight, Tom-Tom?" Mike reached over to pick it up from the step where Tom-Tom had dropped it during the tussle.

"The man gave it to me."

Mike stopped his hand in midair. The flashlight would have the killer's fingerprints on it. He felt around in his overcoat pocket and pulled out a pair of well-worn gloves. He slipped them on and reached back for the flashlight. "I need to use the flashlight, Tom-Tom. I've got to go into this warehouse and look around. I have to know if there's any sign of Tim in there. What I want you to do is to stand watch here by the door. I want you to let me know if anybody comes into the driveway or if you see or hear anything strange. Can you do that for me?"

Tom-Tom quivered. "By myself, Father?"

"Yes. I'll be just inside. I'll be able to hear you."

"But he's a killer, Father. He likes to kill hobes."

"Remember Timmy, Tom-Tom."

Tom-Tom averred in the strongest voice he could manage, "I'll do it, Father." After a moment he seemed to relax a bit and reverted to Tom-Tom meek and mild. "Can you get me some Thunderbriar, if I do it?"

"Of course I can. Now you stay right here. I'll be back out as quickly as I can." Mike turned and went to the door.

"Good luck, Father." Tom-Tom sat down next to the door, leaning his back against the wall.

Mike quickly opened the door and immediately stumbled over the bedroll Tom-Tom apparently was after. He took the flashlight and went, having to wade his way through several empty cans and other assorted rubbish, in search of what he could find. Mike walked into the huge empty space and stopped to get his bearings. He swirled the flashlight about the warehouse. He flashed the light into the rafters above, revealing enormous cobwebs and darkness. A bat fluttered from one beam to another.

Mike moved uncertainly around the borders of the space, searching corners and crevices among once-stacked wooden pallets. Then he stopped—dead still. An odd object—looked like a body— lay between the pallets and leaned against a rusted, ancient forklift. The lumps in Mike's throat tripled as he moved closer and—he hesitated—thrust the beam of light directly onto the face of a bloody corpse.

The flashlight worked its way up and down the length of the body. Despite Mike's uneasiness, he knelt down beside it. And that's when he saw the dried-blood bullet hole in the body's forehead. He looked closer. He did not recognize the face, but then he spied an empty Bowie's Farm bottle clutched by the neck in the corpse's right hand.

"A hobe," Mike muttered aloud. Or more likely a hobo. Poor guy. Wrong place at the wrong time. He signed the cross over the man and said a prayer.

Mike stood up and continued his investigation. On the other side of the room he discovered the camp, apparently where the killer had set up housekeeping. There were the discarded empty tins that had once contained Vienna sausages and various and sundry other canned goods. He sat down on what used to be a chair, without its slatted back, and surveyed the space with the flashlight.

Then something of interest caught Mike's attention. He walked over to the pile of cans and raked through them like his schnauzer making a place on the rug to lie down. A doll. Quite a large doll with its head buried beneath the cans. *What?* He reached down, picked it up, and examined it under the ray of the flashlight. A grimace crossed his face. A balding head, leaving just a few strands of black wavy hair. A ripped floral dress. He winced. Gin-Gin's doll. He quickly tucked Shanika back into the position where he found her. Mike said a quick prayer for Gin-Gin. Then before he could move away, he spotted something else right beside where Shanika lay. Another doll—a tiny one. *What is this guy? A doll collector?* Mike picked up the doll and looked at it carefully. His lips spread slightly apart, and he exhaled slowly. Then without further thought, he tucked the doll neatly into his pocket and continued his inspection of the warehouse.

And there they were—the pads of invoice forms that had apparently been left behind when the business had closed. He picked one up and examined it carefully. *Yup.* Then suddenly he dropped the pad. A dirty pajama shirt clung to the base of an erect, weight-bearing post. Mike knelt down and grabbed it. But the dirt was not dirt. "Oh, my dear God!" It was blood.

Mike dropped the shirt and ran to the door. Tom-Tom was nowhere to be seen. "Tom-Tom!" he called. Tom-Tom didn't answer. He called again and again and again.

Mike dashed to his Camry and pulled the car out of its hiding place. He turned it around, not gingerly at all, and sped down the road toward town. Within a quarter of a mile he spotted the form of a hobe on the right side of the road. He pulled over and got out of the car.

"Get in, Tom-Tom," Mike commanded.

"I can't Father! I'm afraid, Father."

"Get in, Tom-Tom. I won't let you get hurt. Just get in."

Mike escorted Tom-Tom to the Camry and put him in the passenger's seat. They spoke not a word on the drive back into town. Mike dialed Carlos's number. No answer. He tried again and the voice mail's narrator announced Carlos's unavailability. He had momentarily forgotten. A cell usually had difficulty picking up a signal in Sarah's Café—something about the building's structure.

He spotted Carlos's Crown Vic and pulled into Sarah's parking lot. "Tom-Tom, I want you to go with me."

"Where, Father?"

"I want you to go with me into Sarah's. I can't trust you to stay out here by yourself. And I promise, on our way out, I'll stop by C-Mart and get you a bottle of Thunderbriar. Just go with me."

"Will I get into trouble with the police, Father?"

"No, Tom-Tom. I'll see to that. Trust me."

Tom-Tom got out of the car, and Mike escorted him into Sarah's Café. Somehow the cafe didn't seem as cold as usual, but he didn't linger on the thought.

The table was already set up with his favored Heineken, Carlos's Michelob, and a couple of frosted Pilzner beer glasses.

"Tom-Tom, how about sliding into the booth. I'll sit on the outside. Detective Ruiz, you know Tom-Tom from the diner?"

"Yes, of course. Tom-Tom, you're the gentleman from Bosham Alley, right? You and I have had some discussions from time to time."

"Yes, Detective. That was when you were a plain old cop. You've always done right by me, but that other cop…"

Sarah popped by to see if they needed a sandwich of some sort. "Hi, Father. Something else I can get you?"

"Don't believe so. Thanks, Sarah."

Carlos turned back to Tom-Tom. "What brings you here?"

Tom-Tom started to tremble as if he were afraid the detective would slap cuffs on him at any moment.

"Carlos," Mike interrupted, "we're not going to have time for the beers. I tried to call you on your cell, but I forgot you can't get a signal in Sarah's." He told Carlos about the warehouse.

"We've gotta get up there now. I want you and Tom-Tom there so you can help us make some sense out of this situation. You take Tom-Tom in your Camry, and I'm going to whip by and pick up Jerry."

"I'm not gonna get into trouble, am I Detective?" Tom-Tom's voice shook like Katherine Hepburn's in her last years.

"Just the opposite, my man, just the opposite. That is, if you cooperate and tell us everything you know." Carlos threw a ten-dollar bill on the table, and Mike and Tom-Tom followed him out the door.

Tom-Tom sat in the passenger's seat quivering. "F-f-father?"

"What's the matter, Tom-Tom?"

"What about my Thunderbriar, Father. You promised."

"Of course, Tom-Tom. You've got it!" Mike drove over to C-Mart and parked the car. "You stay here, Tom-Tom. I'm going to lock the car from the outside, so if you try to get out, the Camry will sound its theft alarm. You don't want that to happen, do you, Tom-Tom?"

"No, Father."

"Good, I'll be right back." Mike was gone about two minutes and returned with a bottle of Thunderbriar in a brown paper bag and thrust it into the glove compartment. "You can't open this until we get there, Tom-Tom. It's against the law to have a bottle of Thunderbriar open in the car while driving. You wouldn't want me to get arrested for breaking the law, would you?"

"No, Father."

Mike got on the cell to call Annie. "You be careful, darling," Annie said. "I love you."

"Love you too," Mike hung up.

It seemed all Tom-Tom could do to keep from reaching into the glove compartment. But he finally settled back and waited.

Mike pulled up behind Carlos and Jerry at the Houston Feed Company warehouse.

"You wait here, Reverend," Jerry ordered. "And the hobe too. I don't want either one of you to get shot in the event the killer has returned to get his bedroll. I've called for backup. They should be here any minute now."

Jerry and Carlos pulled their guns and slithered through the brush.

Six agents in three SCBI vehicles pulled up silently and parked on the highway. They alit from the cars without speaking. They spread apart and gradually encircled the warehouse without making noise.

"Oh, Lordy!" Tom-Tom sighed.

"It'll be okay," Mike whispered. "Here's your Thunderbriar." Mike reached over and retrieved the wine from his glove compartment and handed it to Tom-Tom.

"Thanks, Father." Tom-Tom placed the bottle neck into his mouth and inhaled the potent liquid.

After half an hour or so, Mike spied Carlos walking toward the Camry. "What's up?"

Carlos placed his hands on the base of the car window. "It's been cleaned out—apparently since you left here. Everything's been cleaned out of the warehouse, including the bedroll, and no one is about. The perp did well in cleaning up, so we're going to have to get as much information as we can from what signs are left."

"Did you find the body?"

"Yes. The ME'll be here in a few minutes."

Mike sighed. "What about the bloody shirt?"

"Gone. No longer here."

Mike sighed again.

"Jerry's going to stay here with a couple of the guys to lift a few fingerprints and do the things that cops do when something like this happens. In the meantime, I want you and Tom-Tom to follow me back to the station. We need to get down in writing in minute detail everything that happened this evening involving the two of you."

"Am I in trouble?" Tom-Tom asked.

"No, Tom-Tom. I just need you to tell me everything you know. See you at the station house."

Carlos got in his Crown Vic and pulled out into the highway with Mike and Tom-Tom immediately behind.

Mike's eyes teared. *Where's Tim? What has he done with Tim?*

FORTY-EIGHT

TIM ROLLED over on the hard, wooden floor and gradually opened his swollen eyes the best he could. He recognized very little. He searched the room over for the savage but saw no one. He was surprised, however, at what he did see. In contrast to the starkness of the warehouse, this room had tall, elegant walls, with once-attractive wallpaper, covered almost completely with portraits of men with long beards and women in long dresses. The ceiling appeared to be made of painted, tin squares with decorative swirls etched upon them. The large chandelier in the center of the ceiling drooped precariously, one of its three base-bolts completely gone. Tim had seldom seen furniture this old. Then he looked through the gigantic French window. He definitely was on the second floor, because he could see nothing but treetops and sky.

Tim tried to move again. His limbs ached, and his back felt like somebody had kicked it with the rhythm of a redheaded woodpecker. The savage had slept in his newly retrieved bedroll, which he had placed carefully on a long couch he had shoved in front of and up against a glass-paned, double door on the wall behind Tim. Tim barely remembered all the commotion last night, when the monster had thrown Tim down on the floor while he rearranged the furniture. Tim guessed the savage had moved the couch there to better keep an eye on him during the night. He made Tim sleep on the floor with only a ragged and reeking blanket for a bed, and he had slept fitfully.

Tim tried to pull his legs up, but they stopped abruptly, halfway to their destination. The kidnapper had tied his ankles to the leg of a ancient-looking grand piano with a slim Manila rope—the kind with itchy grass stuff sticking out from its surface. He and his dad often used this kind of rope on camping trips. Fortunately, he had a bit of leeway on the rope and managed to screw himself into a slightly less awkward position and lean back against one of the other legs.

Tim looked around for the monster, but he was nowhere to be seen.

Now what? In the warehouse the savage had sometimes left him tied up and alone for several hours at a time, but he couldn't afford to wait hours. He had to loose himself quickly—before the bully got back. Fortunately, the bully had left his eyes untaped. He had to get his hands undone. This guy believed in duct tape. His feet. His hands. His mouth.

Lord Jesus Christ, help me do this. He pushed himself into a kneeling position and began sawing his wrist tape against the sharp corner of the top of the square piano leg. Several times he tried, but the tape wouldn't budge. After a quarter of an hour or so, he had made no progress whatsoever.

Then Tim had a brilliant idea. His mouth tape didn't go all the way around his head. He sat back down and surveyed the piano carefully. The piano leg itself caught his eye. He guessed the square, massive leg to be at least six inches thick. It started small at the top and then gradually ballooned to its full thickness before it tapered slightly back to four inches or so. The leg eventually came to rest on a decorative caster, similar to the caster on his mom's baby grand at home.

The caster's brake lever was used to keep the piano from rolling. When he was younger, he had often created a hideout under the piano at home and was well-acquainted with brake levers. He wriggled his way over to one of the levers and lowered his face to the floor, scraping his cheek against the sharp end of the lever over and over again. A dozen scrapes later, he heard a slight rip. *The tape—it's coming loose.* With heightened energy, he kept scraping. Blood oozed down his chin, but Tim didn't care. He scraped on and eventually felt the tape loosen. He had managed to get the lever between the tape and his cheek and had worked his face up and down until the tape began to tear.

But Tim's mouth still wasn't free. He moved his face up the piano leg several inches and leaned his cheek against the leg. The adhesive side of the torn tape latched onto the wooden leg, and Tim began to pull. It hurt—hurt like crazy—but he didn't stop. He suddenly jerked his head back and—*phew*—he was free of the tape. He could move his lips. At some point he was able to yell.

And yell he did. He didn't know whether the bully was in another room, whether he was outside doing something with the Escort, or whether he had gone into town to find someone else to murder. He didn't care. He could make a noise and somebody might hear. If the savage did come back, he couldn't kill Tim yet, not until he had killed his dad. All the bully would do was shut Tim up and kick him around a bit. He had learned to expect that by now.

His screams wore his voice to a rasp, and he sat back against the piano leg and let his chin drop to his chest. He didn't cry—he was beyond that now. He was a man. Tim sat back on the floor and began working on his wrist tape with his teeth. He heard a sudden, loud bang from somewhere down stairs. He stopped. He was not alone in the house. He had to hurry. He had to get out of there before the savage came back into the room. He worked even harder. Another five minutes. No real progress. Surely, there was a better way.

Tim looked around the room. Wide, glass-paned French doors led into another room of some sort. A hallway? A foyer? A balcony? That must be where the stairs are.

Tim moved back to the roped piano leg, stood up the best he could and pressed his back against the belly of the piano. He knew he couldn't budge the piano up with his back, but he tried anyway. Of, course, nothing happened.

He sat back on the floor and looked again at the brake lever and then at the other two levers. In a split second he knew what he had to do. Tim had gotten into trouble more than once for pushing his mom's piano out of place. He reached his tethered hands down and with labor pulled on the lever until he had the brake unlocked. And then the other two.

He pushed forward, but the piano refused to budge. He pushed it to the right—it moved. He pushed it to the left—it moved. The rear leg was still braked. He left his post and scuttled himself back to examine the brake. There. Tim got it and scrambled back to the roped leg and pushed. It moved!

Then he froze. A loud clatter, like books falling from a high bookshelf. Tim held his position. Two gun shots in rapid succession. He held his breath. He remembered the savage shooting rats at the warehouse. So he's here. Maybe shooting rats here. Or maybe, God forbid, another hobe. He had to hurry!

Tim pushed the piano one inch—two inches. The piano was difficult to push. It must be bigger than his mom's. The creaking noises the casters made as the piano moved gave him pause. If he just had some WD-40. Then he heard it again. The clatter. It was a bit different from the other one. He couldn't tell exactly how. He stopped—waited—and waited some more.

He hunched his back up against the belly of the piano and started up again. Because of his taped ankles, he gingerly hopped along as he pushed. Tim inched the piano on its casters over to the French doors. The left door swung open handily. But not so, the right door. It was latched at bottom and top. He twisted the piano so that he was next to the bottom latch. He sat down with his back against the door and managed to pull the latch up from its resting place in the floor receptacle.

Now the top latch. Tim sat on the floor for a time contemplating his next move. There it was. Why hadn't he thought of that before? A broom stood leaning against the corner of the mantel. Tim again pressed his back against the belly of the piano and maneuvered it over to the fireplace. He somehow managed to reach with his tied-up wrists and nudge the broom until it fell to the floor. He worked to grab the broom head between his legs and scrambled the piano and the broom back to the French doors. He was in luck. The broom-handle end had a triangular, metal loop for hanging the broom on a hook. Tim straightened the loop, lay on his back, and, clutching the broom between his forearms, reached the broom handle up. It took him several tries before he was able to snag the latch knob with the loop.

Tim turned with a sudden jerk. The footsteps came slowly but deliberately, as if the monster were carrying a heavy load up the stairs. Not these stairs, he could tell. Must be stairs in the back of the house. The noise grew stronger. He had to hurre-e-e!

Tim jerked on the latch knob and the latch slid easily out of its receptacle. He pushed on the door, and it swung open. He lay on the floor. *Phew!* He wanted to quit—badly. He wanted to cry—badly. But, like his dad, he refused to do either. He had gone this far. He couldn't stop now and still call himself a man.

The heavy steps appeared to be reaching the top. Tim cringed briefly but got himself up and began rolling the piano through the French doors. The formidable, curved stairwell gaped wide before him. He continued to push the piano toward the stairs. Inch by inch it moved. At last he made it. The noises suddenly stopped. *Where is the savage?*

He worked even faster, now. He crawled to the right rear leg and tightened the brake—not completely tight, but tight enough. He had watched his dad do this sort of thing on their numerous camping trips to keep a small wagon or other small-wheeled vehicle from moving down a hill too fast. He crawled to the front and gave the piano several more hard tugs. The piano moved. He pushed it up against the newel post. Then he wheeled the piano around so that the piano leg he was tethered to dropped off the edge of the top step and hung suspended between the top step and the next step down. The other two legs and the newel post held the weight now, and the piano sat there and didn't move. He slipped his rope knot down the leg, over the caster, and off the end. Free at last. Well, not really free. He had to manage to get down these stairs and out to the road so somebody would see him.

"You stupid kid! You sorry son-of-a-bitch!"

And Tim felt the sharp toe of the savage's foot jab him in the back. Not once. Not twice. It felt like an arrow thrust deep into his flesh. He tumbled forward bumping hideously down each step to the bottom of the stairs. He remembered no more.

♯♯♯

THE SLAP was hard, but Tim felt only a quick pressure on his cheek. He lifted his head from the nap he had crumpled into, and he opened his eyes wide enough to see the savage staring him in the face. If the bully would just let him sleep. Tim had been vaguely aware of the light and of the dark—but very little else. His head hurt, his back hurt, his legs hurt. Not a single inch of his body was without pain.

"Wake up, you little horse shit!"

Tim tried to open his eyes wider.

"That's it, buddy boy. Open those fucking eyes."

Tim tried to shift his body a bit to wake up his tingling arms and legs. But the attempted movement made him aware of his shackles—his limbs tied together more securely than before—back to the piano leg. A different leg, of course. The other one was still dangling off the top stair step.

Fortunately, the bully had not retaped his mouth. "Water!" Tim's raspy, whispered voice could hardly rouse a napping mite.

"We're getting a bit impolite now, are we? Did I hear *please*?"

"May I have some water, please?"

"Water? What do you need water for?" The savage chuckled his interpretation of a wild hyena. "Won't be long till you'll be dead." The monster waited for a reaction but got none. "Yes, sir. Deader than that piano leg you're tied up to."

Tim almost wished the bully would quit threatening and just go ahead with what he was going to do. Then he remembered his dad. His dad had to be murdered first. For the first time in a long time tears formed in his eyes and dripped down his cheeks like rain. He wanted his dad. He needed his dad. He was a little boy again, and it felt better that way.

The bully held out a bottle of Evian, ostensibly for Tim to reach out and take. "What? Thought you wanted some water." The savage grinned, showing his mouth full of black and white teeth that almost matched the piano keys. "Oh, I forgot." The bully held the mouth of the bottle to Tim's cracked lips, pouring half the water down his shirt and into his crotch to mix with the urine Tim had been forced to emit.

The bully pulled the bottle away. "Goddammit, kid. You're wasting all the water." The bully screwed the cap back on and threw the bottle across the foyer.

Tim said, "Thanks."

"Ah. We've rejuvenated our etiquette, have we?"

Tim said no more.

"Ya know, baby blue eyes, your da-da is coming."

Tim's eyes widened. "When?"

"He's coming today. Are you eager to see him?"

Tim almost said *yes*. But then he remembered that he might be coming to his death, and Tim's eyes closed and then tightened.

"That's right, kid. He's gonna come and get himself knocked off."

Tim squirmed but said nothing.

"Gotta get ready for our guest."

Tim watched the savage, through the open French doors, move around the huge room with deft efficiency. Placing used tin cans into a plastic bag. Straightening the gun collection. Vacuuming the carpet. Sweeping the floor. Almost as if his dad were being invited to dinner.

"Your da-da is welcome, kid. First class."

The savage charged toward him and Tim cringed. He passed on by and headed toward the piano leg that dangled from the top stair step. "Sorry you had to act like a turd, kid, and shove this piano off the edge." He turned to Tim. "Gotta get this piano back where it belongs. Don't want nothing out of place for your da-da."

Tim squirmed again.

"Guess you'll have to help me."

The bully untied Tim from the piano and untaped his ankles. *Boy, that feels good.* He stretched his legsw as much as the monster would allow.

"Now I want you to show me how you did this, kid. Get under the piano and lift it up enough to get this fucking piano leg back on the floor."

Tim moved—slowly, painfully—up to the front of the piano. He strained. He hurt. He pushed. He could not budge the piano.

"Never mind, kid. Come on back here."

Tim carefully moved back to the rear of the piano.

"You grab this leg and pull backwards. I'll push up from the front." And the bully took his place on the top stair in front of the piano. "Now pull."

But Tim didn't pull. He suddenly remembered the half-braked caster, reached down and released the lever, and pushed the piano.

The piano lunged forward, throwing the bully onto the stairs, and the leg landed on the next step down. But it stopped there.

Before Tim could give the piano another shove, the bully got up from the stairs, with no apparent hurt, and charged up to him, pulled him away from the piano, and shoved him down on stairs. "You stupid shit ass. Thought you could pull one over on me, did you?" He backhanded Tim a half dozen times on both sides of his head.

Then he sat down beside Tim and placed his arm around Tim's shoulders. "Open your eyes, kid. I want you to see something. You see this grand staircase?"

Tim nodded and allowed his eyes to wander down the once-elegant staircase, stairs fit for the grand entrance of a king or a prince or something like that. The stairs widened before his eyes and curved like the stairs on Royal Caribbean's *Majesty of the Seas*, a ship he and his parents had once cruised on.

"Behold, you little shit ass. Behold your da-da's final resting place."

FORTY-NINE

SINCE YESTERDAY'S ordeal, Mike had not ventured from the rectory. He had neglected his morning workout. He had even ignored his parishioners' food gifts that packed the refrigerator. He and Annie sat at the kitchen table holding baloney sandwiches—half eaten. Mike dropped his sandwich onto the paper plate in front of him—as if to say *to hell with baloney—ever again*. His eyes and his shadowed look suggested perhaps that he himself had slept in Slocum Alley the night before. He ran his fingers through his hair, jammed his elbows onto the table, and leaned his face into his hands.

Annie reached over and picked up the phone, its shrill screech pelting the air like an owl screaming after its prey.

She looked up at Mike. "It's Carlos."

Mike shook his head. Vigorously. *No! No! I don't want to talk to him.*

Annie turned back to the phone. "You need to talk to Mike?"

Mike shook his head again.

"Okay. Here he is."

Mike sighed heavily, shot Annie a nettled look, and grabbed the receiver from her hand. "Hey, Carlos."

"Missed you at the Y."

Mike rolled his eyes and then closed them—tight.

"Whatcha been up to?"

"Oh, nothing." Mike's soul swirled in an eddy of emptiness.

"You okay?"

Mike pulled the receiver away from his ear a moment and clenched his eyes again before he replaced it. "Okay? Depends on what you mean by *okay*."

"Is that anything like saying it depends on what the meaning of the word *is* is?"

Mike managed a weak smile. This Clintonism from the Monica Lewinski affair had always amused the two men.

Annie frowned, left the table, and wandered into the den to comfort Mr. Craggles, whose low, gurgling growls suggested that he sensed the injustice of the situation as much as Mike and Annie did.

"What can I do for you, my friend?"

"Oh, nothing. I was just worried about you. That's all."

Mike said nothing. He just doodled on his napkin with his finger.

"Once again, Mike. As a friend to a friend. Are you okay?"

After assuring Carlos he need not worry, the two men began rehashing the evening before. That was the last thing Mike wanted, but he couldn't help himself. The warehouse. Tom-Tom's visit. The dead body. The debris. The pad of blank invoice forms. And Tim's bloody shirt! Perhaps this conversation filled a therapeutic need in Mike.

When the conversation ended, Mike jumped up from the table and, with a streak of energy he had not felt all day, headed upstairs into the bedroom. Half an hour later, he came out clean-cut and buckling his jeans belt.

Annie's eyes flicked open. "What are you doing? Where are you going? You're not leaving now are you?"

"No. Not yet. Just going out to get the newspaper."

He appreciated the *Madison Times* for trying to stay on top of Tim's story. The more Tim could be in the public eye, the better chance of getting him back.

Mike turned toward Mr. Craggles, who ran the household. "Wanna go porch?"

Immediately the four-year-old schnauzer jumped at the opportunity to go out onto the front porch to see if he could find anything worth barking at. Mr. Craggles got to the door first and bossy-pawed it until Mike got there to open it. The energetic dog apparently had difficulty understanding why Mike was so slow getting there. He let Mr. Craggles out and retrieved the paper from the walk. Highly disappointed, Mr. Craggles had unfortunately found nothing to bark at, so he slunk back into the house and curled up on the sofa, buried his nose under his paw, his eyes looking—as Jane, Annie's closest friend, would say—'umble. But Mike called it *pitiful*.

Mike opened the *Madison Times*, and his heart quickened. A scrap of paper dropped to the floor. His adrenaline surging, he grabbed up the note and forgot the *Times*. This time the note wasn't written on the invoice paper, and the kidnapper didn't bother to print in the childish scribble of the earlier notes, but Mike had no doubt that it was authored by the same person. He stopped in the foyer. *Follow the Solo Road.* Mike's heart quickened again.

"Annie!" he yelled. "Come here."

Annie rushed down the stairs, his very urgent voice daunting her, and she immediately broke into tears.

"Look!" Mike handed her the note.

She read it several times before she dared say anything. "What does it mean?"

"I don't know—yet." He really didn't know what the words literally meant, but he believed he recognized the metaphor. His heart quickened again.

"You've got to call Carlos," Annie said.

"Yeah." Mike reached over and picked up the receiver and started to punch in the numbers. He stopped in mid-dial. He couldn't call Carlos. This was personal. Very personal. "Can't do it!"

"Can't do what?"

"Can't call Carlos." Mike paused a moment. "Come with me."

Mike led her to the coat rack in the foyer, reached into his overcoat pocket, and brought out a tiny doll. Annie immediately understood. It was an effigy of Darth Vader.

‡‡‡

MIKE HAD sat on the sofa for half an hour contemplating the doll. "Annie?"

Annie raised her head from his shoulder.

"Annie, I think I know how to find him."

"How? What are you going to do?"

"Gotta follow the Solo Road."

Annie looked at Mike and raised her eyebrows. "What's the Solo Road?"

"Not sure. I'll have to find it."

"Okay. I don't know where you're going, but I do know one thing. I'm going with you."

"You can't go with me, Annie, it's too dangerous."

"I'm not asking your permission, Mike. I'm making a statement. I am going with you."

"Why do you want to go, Annie? You'll just put yourself and everybody else in danger."

"Because," Annie answered, "if you find Tim at the end of this Solo Road, I want to be there. I want to see Tim. I want to talk to Tim. And if this mad man does kill Tim, I want to see Tim alive before he does it. Please Mike, don't stand in my way of this. My heart is breaking. I have to go."

"Suit yourself." He agreed reluctantly, but deep down he understood her heart clearly.

They gave Mr. Craggles his customary treat, and went down the stairs to their basement garage.

They had driven about a mile or so, and Annie broke the silence. "Where are you going, Mike?"

"I seem to remember a billboard out on Route 17 that may have something to do with that note."

"What? What kind of billboard?"

"Can't remember exactly, but I'll know it when I see it."

Mike drove about eight or ten miles on 17. "Not where I thought it was." Then he made a U turn and headed back to Madison. At Hollandale he crossed over to Route 23 and headed away from town once more. He drove another three or four miles scrutinizing every billboard that came into sight.

"Look!" Mike commanded. He pulled over to the side of the road and stopped.

"What?" Annie looked up where Mike was pointing and inhaled sharply. Beside a scraggly, peeling image of a cartoon-like operatic tenor in the midst of an aria, the large unkempt billboard read *The Solo Café, Half Mile.* An arrow pointed to the left.

Mike turned left. Then he noticed the name of the route—Hanvey Solo Road. Hanvey Solo, if Mike's memory served, had been a well-respected pioneer in early Madison County. He probably deserved a better road than this littered country route. *Hanvey Solo. Han Solo? The Star Wars guy?*

"I've been here before, Annie. The Esso station. The dilapidated restaurant will be just before we get to Floyd's place."

The required mileage did indeed disclose the promised restaurant. Down and out. Kaput. Probably out of business for at least ten years. Then about a tenth of a mile or so past the cafe, he spotted the Esso service station.

Mike pulled up to the old station and stopped. Floyd was nowhere to be seen. "Look, Annie."

"Oh, a house," she said.

"Floyd's house. The grand proprietor of this awesome station."

"Big house." Annie squirmed. "The Bates house."

Mike turned his attention to the Esso station. The door. Unlocked. Standing ajar. "Wait here, Annie."

Mike got out of the car and went up to the door. The huge Yale lock was gone. He pushed the door further open and looked inside. Nothing appeared to be out of place. At least nothing any more out of place than Floyd might have left it. He came back to the car. "Something's wrong."

"What?"

"I don't believe Floyd would have left the door to his business open. When I was here before, he made a big point of unlocking the padlock. Now the lock's gone. I don't like this."

"What're you going to do?"

"Dunno."

Mike pulled the Camry around the station and parked it among a couple of briary bushes, camouflaging it the best he could. "You stay here, Annie."

"Don't go, Mike, please."

"I've got to Annie. Just think about Tim."

Mike tightened his coat and felt for Jerry's gun. Unfortunately, it was there. "If I'm not back in half an hour, call Carlos."

Mike crept furtively up the hill from shadow to shadow, and tree to tree, at least a half a football field's length, and made his way around toward the back of the house. Everything was still. Stiller than it had to be. Frighteningly still, like a two-year-old when he's getting into trouble.

Mike sneaked farther toward the back of the house to look for a back entrance of some sort and stopped—dead still. There, tucked into the brush, an old, black car stood—grazing in the brambles like a hungry ibex. *The Escort.*

FIFTY

FROM THE time Mike had had to deal with his father's defection and his own subsequent life journey, he had seldom been afraid of anything. He had sworn to himself, with apologies to Scarlett O'Hara, that, as God was his witness, he would never be afraid again. And yet here he was. Afraid. Not for himself, but for Tim.

He looked around at the back side of the old house. Only one door—presumably locked from the inside. He dared not touch it lest he alert the killer. He paused for a moment and then crawled under the back porch and poked his head through the scuttle hole that issued into the crawl space under the house. He paused to allow his eyes to adjust to the darkness. He could make out piles of junk—a piece of an old bicycle, broken sets of Venetian blinds, a rusted wheel barrow, and an olio of odds and ends that Floyd might have put there.

And then—a shaft of light. Three or four floorboards appeared to be missing, and light shone through from the room above. The space looked to be two or three feet long—perhaps barely large enough to compress his broad shoulders through. For a moment, he thought about doing just that. But, even if he could, he would not be able to protect himself from the insane man who roamed the floor above and who had his son constantly in his grasp.

Mike slowly backed out of the scuttle and snaked his way back from where he came. He lowered himself into the bushes and settled down to collect himself. A slight rustling erupted in the bushes behind him, and then a sudden paralysis swept over him. "Annie!" he almost shouted but reverted to a whisper in the nick. "I told you to stay in the car." He gathered Annie up behind him. He didn't have the option of showing his irritation at this point. He could not afford to alert the killer to their presence. "Stay right here."

"Mike," Annie whispered, "I called Carlos as soon as you left the car. They should be here any minute."

Mike clenched his teeth. Now he had to work faster. He had to get the job done before the cops arrived. "Shhh!" he whispered.

That uttered sibilancy must have scraped up the scum from the floor of the old house, for an eerie noise that perhaps substituted for laughter echoed and re-echoed from an upstairs window. "I knew you'd come, Reverend!"

Annie grabbed Mike's arm and squeezed. It was all she could do to keep from screaming.

That voice! The man in black under the bridge. Mike faltered for a moment to collect himself. *Lord Jesus Christ, Son of the living God, have mercy on me a sinner.* He settled Annie onto the ground and flung himself forward behind the trunk of a fallen oak. A bullet rammed into the other side of the tree. Mike gave in to an apoplectic jerk. "Where's Tim?" Mike yelled.

The disappointment in missing his target evidenced itself in the killer's voice. "That's for me to know and you to find out!"

Now Mike was angry—no, livid. He slowly pulled his gun from his coat pocket.

"Mike," Annie whispered.

Mike held his palm up in the hush position.

"Mike," she whispered. "That gun. What are you going to do?"

"Stay here."

"Don't Mike!" Annie cried out.

Mike looked for another large tree or some other shelter closer to the old mansion. There. The oak next to the nearest window.

"You brought the little lady with you, I see. Somebody else for me to sight with my trusty Winchester."

Mike dove behind the tree. *Lord Jesus Christ, Son of the living God, have mercy on me a sinner.*

"Goddammit!" the killer shouted. "Pardon my Latin, Reverend. Too bad you didn't go down at the funeral."

"What do you want from me?"

"I want *you.*"

The words bounced around in Mike's brain like tennis balls at Wimbledon. "What have you done with Tim?"

"Dad!" Tim cried out from somewhere behind the window.

"Tim!" Annie shouted.

"Mom!"

A scramble erupted inside the old mansion, the killer apparently getting Tim under control. From the ground it looked as if the killer were stuffing him down into a hole with his foot.

Lord Jesus Christ, Son of the living God, have mercy on me a sinner. Mike's heart pounded incessantly. "You used Tim as bait to get me, right?"

"You're sharp, Reverend."

Mike ran his fingers through his hair. "When you get me, you're going to get Tim, right?"

"God, Reverend. You're really sharp. And you'll be down within the next five minutes. Mark my word."

"What have you done with Floyd?" Mike yelled.

"Now how would you know Floyd, Reverend?"

Then suddenly a new voice Mike easily recognized yelled out, "Hey, Mr. Death! We've got you surrounded." Jerry and his backup crew had so stealthily positioned themselves that Mike had not heard them take their places. "If you want to stay alive, why don't you drop your gun and come out with your hands up?"

The killer shot into the brush. "Not likely. And who might you be?"

"I'm Chief Detective Jerry Majors, Mr. Death. We've got sharp shooters stationed all around this house. You'll never get out of there alive."

Another shot. Another miss. "Goddamn!"

"Cool it, Mr. Death."

"What's with the Mr. Death business? My name is Robert Grover."

Yes. It's Bobby, Mike confirmed to himself.

"My bad, Mr. Grover. You signed all your notes *Death* if I recall."

Deafening laughter rattled from the house like a 1920s Tommy gun. "Let me see your face, Detective."

"Put your gun down."

"The hell, I will!"

"Can you let us in on your little joke?"

And suddenly Mike realized that Jerry was stalling for time. The backup wasn't there after all. He was still waiting for the SCBI. Mike had seen Jerry and Carlos do this once before when he was on a call with the police. The house was not surrounded at all. Mike knew this was his only chance. He ducked down and took advantage of Jerry's distraction and snaked his way quietly toward the back side of the old mansion.

"My little joke? Har. Har. Har."

"Yeah. What's so doggoned funny?"

"Never been to grammar school, Detective? Your readin' ain't right."

"Then correct me."

"Bobby sounded almost as if he were singing under his breath. "That was *Darth*—not *Death*."

"Aha! The Vader guy."

"Ya got it, Detective."

"You're a hoot, Bobby," Jerry said.

Another shot cracked through the brush. "I'm a man, Detective!" Bobby screamed. "Why can't you take me seriously?"

"My bad again, Mr. Grover. Sorry."

"Robert!" The voice came from the opposite side of the house.

"Who's that?" Bobby shouted. For the first time his voice seemed to show a bit of nerve strain. "I got my gun trained on the boy now. I swear I'll kill him. I swear I'll kill him if you make one false move."

Carlos. The great negotiator. The SCBI must be here now. Mike was under the house, glad he'd made it before the rest of the police arrived. He could hear every word.

‡‡‡

I'M DETECTIVE Carlos Ruiz, Robert. Can we talk?"

"What do you wanta talk about, Detective?"

"You can call me Carlos, Robert."

"I ain't got nothing to say to you, Detective."

"Robert, I'd like to try to be your friend."

Bobby gave no immediate answer.

"Robert, what can I do for you?"

"What do you mean, what can you do for me?"

"I need to know what you want from us so we can end this thing without anybody else getting hurt."

"Got my gun on the boy, Detective."

"I know you have, and that's why we've got to talk."

Another pause. "Why don't you show your face, Carlos?"

Maybe Carlos was making some headway. "Perhaps—in a minute. Now, how can we help you?"

"You can't help me with a fucking thing."

"What do you want?"

"I know what *you* want. You want me to stick my head out so you can crack it off. That ain't gonna happen."

"We don't want your head, Robert. We don't want any more killing. We want to know what we can do for you to stop the killing—not get somebody else killed. Not even you."

Again Bobby was silent.

"What do you say, Robert?"

"I want that prick of a preacher you got running around here."

"Is that all you want? Just the preacher?"

Robert paused for a moment. "I reckon I'd be satisfied with the preacher."

Carlos questioned Bobby over the course of the next half hour or so. The killer's obdurate answers never wavered, but he did ease off his visceral, emotional outbursts.

Carlos's heart beat faster and he decided to take the ultimate gamble. "If I come out, Robert, will you come out where we can see each other face to face?"

Bobby said nothing.

"Robert, will you give me your word that you'll hold your fire on Tim if I come out to talk with you?"

"I don't have nothing against you, Carlos. Even if you are a Mexican."

On any other occasion Carlos would be perturbed by the racist remark, but now was neither the time nor the place to correct the man.

"I don't want to kill nobody but that preacher," Bobby said.

"But what about the others who died while you were trying to get the preacher?"

"They got in my way, Carlos. Collateral damage, as they say in the army. You ain't planning to get in my way, are you, Carlos?"

"I don't plan on it."

Carlos braced himself. He had faced many dangerous criminals before, but even now his veins tightened in his legs, his heart beat into the hundreds, and his stomach brusquely rolled into a knot. *Lord Jesus, give me strength.* At that moment the symptoms of fear eased their way out of his body, and he stood straight. "Is the little boy okay?" Little boy. Not Tim. Not young man. Little boy. He wanted to keep the emphasis on Tim's innocence.

"See for yourself." Bobby reached down, jerked Tim around in front of him, and stuck Tim's head through the window opening.

"I'm here for you, Tim."

"I didn't give no permission to talk to the boy, Detective."

Carlos's gut wrenched. Tim's face looked raw and blood ridden, his ripped shirt laden with dirt. The tape was stretched across his mouth like the tape-strapping around a UPS parcel, and Carlos wanted to heave.

Bobby held Tim directly in front of himself, apparently using the boy as a human shield. He yelled out, "If any of you wise guys get any smart ideas, you'll get this little boy, as you call him, smack dab in the face."

"I read you, Robert, loud and clear."

Carlos paused briefly. "Robert, is there anything I can do—or any of us can do—to get you to release Tim?" He had at last given the boy a name. That made him a person.

"Yes!"

Carlos wasn't certain he heard right. He surely hadn't expected such a blunt assent. During his years of dickering with criminals, he had never experienced anything like it. "Yes?"

"Yes."

"What are your terms?"

"Turn the reverend over to me."

Carlos had expected something of the sort, but he knew that even if he should meet Bobby's demand—which he was certainly not going to do—there was surely no reason for Bobby to keep his promise once the demand had been met. Bobby's word was worth nothing. Carlos talked and listened. He spoke about Tim—his youth, his vulnerability, his kindness to the homeless. Then he heard Bobby's rebuttal. He recounted all the hurts and perceived hurts he had endured during his lifetime. He was now the victim, and he laid the fault directly at Basil's feet. During the next half hour, the conversation became highly intense.

Suddenly Bobby's rifle appeared in the window and Bobby cocked the gun.

"Look out!" Carlos shouted.

"It's time for you to go, you mother fucker!" Bobby shouted back. And then the shot rang out.

♯♯♯

M IKE HAD made his way through the floor hole and wandered into the lower level of the old house. A bedroom, he surmised. Strange. Painted red. A dull, faded, eerie shade of red. The room probably hadn't been used in a quarter of a century. Dust. Dirt. Grime. Cobwebs. Two closed doors led to somewhere. He picked the door to the right. He had to find his way to the stairs.

Holding the gun in front of him, he moved furtively toward his chosen door. He carefully reached for the knob and abruptly fell against the door casing. *Shit.* He had tripped on a loose floorboard. He caught himself with his hands, and the gun fell to the floor. He righted himself, and in a moment of distraction inadvertently kicked the gun through the floor hole. *Shit, shit.* Then—*Good*, he thought. *I really didn't want the gun anyway.* He hoped the clamor hadn't been heard upstairs.

Mike reached for the knob and stepped inside. The library, he guessed. The room boasted floor-to-ceiling book shelves covered with cobwebs and filth and vintage books. But that one bookcase, the one to the left, had apparently lost its tomes to the floor. This was a recent disturbance, because the space where the books had been was free from dust.

Then he stopped—dead still. Half covered under a pile of books lay Floyd and his wife, bound and gagged—and dead. An ugly red blotch appeared in both their foreheads. Collateral damage! Mike crossed himself and said a brief prayer for the couple.

He went back into the previous room and carefully tiptoed his way around the other floor holes to the second door. He had to get upstairs. He opened the door. Before him lay a huge foyer. And the stairs. He rushed over to the steps and tiptoed up them as quietly as he could manage. *A piano!* A grand piano blocked the way at the top of the staircase. He stopped for a moment. All Bobby's intended victims had been found on steps. He looked around at the once-resplendent, curved flight and grimaced. He couldn't afford to allow these stairs to become his death steps. But he couldn't think about that now. He had to think, *Tim, Tim, Tim*.

So he carefully crept around the piano legs, under the piano, and finally up to the second-floor foyer. Glass French doors. He could see into the great room beyond. Blue—the kind of putrid blue Mike had often seen in surly seascapes. Bobby. Tim. Tim stood in front of Bobby at the window, and Bobby held a rifle of some sort to his shoulder. Electricity shot through his heart like a bolt of lightning. Mike had to get in there somehow.

Then a yell of some sort issued from the outside. Mike gripped his fingers into a fist. Bobby raised the rifle and shouted. "It's your time to go, you motherfucker." And he took aim and shot out the window. "Damn, I'm good!"

Mike flinched. It had to be Carlos. He almost charged through the glass doors to pummel Robert through the floor, but he, thankfully, restrained himself. He couldn't allow himself to think about Carlos now.

The clatter from outside rose heavily. Mike took advantage of the commotion and found his way from the foyer into an adjacent room. A dining room. This was more than likely the room in which Floyd and his wife had been eating when he had stopped for gas. Three doors—one locked—lay ahead of him. Floyd's padlock. The hasp on the locked door must have been there at least a century. It had been painted over probably a dozen times. But Bobby had taken advantage of it and used Floyd's gas-station lock. Mike clinched his teeth. He didn't want to think about what might be behind that locked door. Another door appeared to open into a corridor on the far side of the dining room. Then the third door. A glass-paned double door that issued into the great room where Bobby kept Tim hostage. Bobby had apparently pulled a couch of some sort up against it on the other side. Bobby was still holding Tim in front of him at the window and from time to time tossing profane epithets to the police below. If Bobby had suddenly turned around, he could have easily sent a lead pellet through the glass and into his flesh. He had to move.

Mike inched his way back to the foyer door and braced himself. "Bobby!" Mike yelled.

A small silence. "Reverend!" Bobby guffawed. "Reverend. So you got in the house now, did you?"

Mike gripped the doorknob. "Bobby. Good to hear from you again."

"And you, Reverend."

"One question. Before you murder me, Bobby. One question."

"Murder? Such a harsh word, Reverend."

"One question."

"Make it only one, Reverend."

"One question: Why?"

"Why what?"

"Why did you kill my father?"

Bobby didn't hesitate. "God told me to, Reverend."

Mike heard Bobby lumbering toward the French doors and to him, so he closed the foyer door quietly and headed quickly back into the dining room and to the door to the corridor. He could hear Bobby breathing laboriously on the other side of the door he had just left.

"You have a gun, Reverend?"

"What makes you think I'd be up here exposing myself to almost certain death, if I didn't have a gun?"

"You've changed in your old age, Reverend."

Carlos called from the ground again. "I've got a deal for you, Robert."

The shot—it wasn't Carlos then. Thank God. But who?

Carlos again. "If you'll let the little boy go, we'll—cut you a real good deal."

"You hear that, Reverend?" Bobby called out. He laughed again. "They wanna make me a deal. You think I should take that deal, Reverend?"

"Bobby, I—"

"You've got some crazy friends out there, Reverend."

Bobby kicked the door, and it flew open. Instantly, Mike slipped neatly into the adjacent corridor. He eyed Bobby briefly through a small crack in the ancient door and then quickly moved aside. Bobby had apparently exchanged his rifle for a handgun of some sort. He stood there pointing the gun into empty space. "We're sly now, aren't we, Reverend?"

Then Mike spotted another door—another glass-paned door leading from the corridor back into the great room. He shifted over to the glass door quickly and could see Tim scrambling around the floor. Tim reached the sharp edge of a wrought iron flower-pot pedestal. It looked as if he were attempting to scrape the tape from his mouth.

Mike quickly turned his attention back to Bobby. "Why are you trying to kill me and my little boy?"

"That's two questions."

"Okay, that's two questions. But I need to know."Mike moved tentatively back toward the door he had just come through.

"You know, as a reverend you are acquainted with the bible."

"Of course, I am." *Lord Jesus Christ, Son of the living God, have mercy on me a sinner.*

"You know about the sins-of-the-fathers verse in Exodus."

"You've bombarded me with it enough."

A shot. A pellet of lead blasted through the door and whizzed by Mike's ear.

"Just had to keep you on your toes, Reverend."

Mike heard something fall downstairs.

"Your friends coming in too?"

Mike could hear Bobby gasping for breath.

"Where are you, Reverend?" Bobby chanted.

It sounded to Mike as if Bobby were doing a poor audition for a Gregorian choir.

"You know it's just a matter of seconds."

"What did you have against my father?" The proposal of only one question had long since dissipated into thin air.

"You want the long answer? Or the short answer?"

"I want an answer."

"I guess the short one will do."

"Okay, the short one then."

"Your daddy stole my mama."

"Bobby? I, I..."

"They call me Robert now, Reverend."

"Okay, Robert, then."

"I'm glad you're a reverend now, Reverend. You'll understand."

"Understand what?"

"I got religion when I was in prison."

Lord Jesus, deliver me from maniacal religion getters. "I'm glad you got religion, Bobby. Good religion makes you save people—not kill them."

"Not if you live by the bible. The bible says..."

"I know what the bible says," Mike snapped. "But Bobby, that verse doesn't mean vengeance is in your hands."

"My bible teacher said it did. He was a cell mate of mine, and he was a preacher. He knew the bible from Genesis to Revelation."

"But Robert."

Another shot, and Mike dodged through the glass door into the great room—the room where Tim was. Tim had almost succeeded in scraping his mouth-tape off. Mike latched the door from the inside, though dubious of its efficacy, and dodged quickly behind an ancient, upright, oak wardrobe.

"And then, when I was in Camp Marshall, God told me so."

Mike knew Camp Marshall. While he was still at Sewanee, he had worked for a summer as a chaplain in the state's largest mental institution. "God spoke directly to you?"

"God told me if I didn't do what the verse said, I'd go to hell."

"But the innocent people? Tim certainly did nothing to harm you."

"God told me to."

"I was left in the same situation you were, Bobby, and I'm not out mowing folks down."

"But God told me to, Reverend."

That mantra again. "Call me Mike, Bobby. We were buddies. We played together. We went to the movies together. Do you remember *Star Wars*?"

"Why do you think I'm here on Han Solo Boulevard?"

Then the apocalypse descended. The glass door rattled like a thousand diamond-backs, and suddenly the glass shattered into a thousand pieces. Bobby charged through the broken door, grabbed Mike, and shoved the barrel into his face.

Mike's hands shot up.

"Ha! You don't have a gun! Mark one up for you, Reverend."

"Bobby!"

"And mark two up," he cocked the hammer, "for…"

"Dad!" Tim cried. "Dad!"

Bobby's eyes flitted quickly to Tim, and in the split second of distraction, Mike grabbed Bobby with his powerful arms, wedged his foot between his ankles, and threw him to the floor, the killer's gun sailing across the room.

At that moment the SCBI agents charged into the room from every direction.

And Mike embraced his son. The long, long nightmare was over.

FIFTY-ONE

THE HOSPITAL was quiet. On Sunday morning only a few nurses and nurses' assistants wandered the halls, slipping in and out of patients' rooms performing necessary duties. Nurse Greta strode the corridor like a woman on a mission. She barged into Room 306 in a blaze of puppy-dog personality, opening the blinds, and greeting Tim with the energy of Mr. Craggles bossy-pawing the front door.

"Good morning, young man."

Tim looked up and grinned. He'd been awake about a half hour now, anticipating this very moment. He glanced about the institutionally-green walls, lit up now—not just with the outside sun but also with every fluorescent bulb in the room. "Hi. Where's Mom and Dad?"

"Who?" the nurse queried with a grin.

"Mom and Dad."

"Oh, them? They sneaked out a couple of hours ago to go home and freshen up. They'll be back in a little bit to collect you and get you out of this dull place."

Tim beamed. "Did they spend the night?"

"You'd better believe they did. Do you think they'd leave you here at night with all the boogers under the bed?" She grinned.

Tim wasn't sure that was funny. There had indeed been boogers under the bed—and over the bed—three nights ago when Tim had slept here for the first time. The fiendish nightmares he had dreamed kept him miserable throughout the night. The monster had stolen him from Col. Mabry's farm, tied him up, and dragged him into that eerie warehouse. He would toss a bit of cheese on the floor, the rats would scurry in, and he would shoot them dead with a potshot pistol. Then he would laugh hideously as he leered at the blood spitting forth from the holes in the rats' sides. He really couldn't always tell what was real and what was nightmare. Maybe it was all nightmare.

But the most horrible nightmare of all was yearning for Mom and Dad, calling them in his sleep, only to be waked up by the savage and punched in the face with the handle of a pistol. Then he would cry himself back to sleep only to repeat the ordeal.

Tim was better now. The violent dreams came less and less often and were not quite as intense as they were. The doctor—psychiatrist—told him the two of them would visit together from time to time over the next several months to help get rid of the nightmares completely. He wanted that. He wanted to get rid of those terrors—fast.

"Here're the clothes your mom wanted you to wear this morning." Nurse Greta laid them on the back of the visitor's chair.

"What? Huh?" The nurse's voice had shaken Tim out of his reverie. Then he drove himself back into his thoughts. The most important thing he remembered, though, was the moment his dad had thrust his arms around the man and brought him to the floor in three sleek Kodokan motions. *What a dad!* Tim could almost grin again now.

"You might want to sit up now." The nurse pulled over the breakfast tray—littered with congealed oatmeal, hard-fried eggs, a couple of burned toast slices, and two cold bacon strips—that a nurse's assistant had placed there a half hour ago.

"No thanks, Miss Greta. Think I'll just take a shower."

"Never known of a boy to turn down food."

He jumped off the bed, his youthful exuberance on its way back to normal. "Gonna have pancakes after Mom and Dad get here." He grabbed his robe and ensconced himself in the bathroom.

When Tim returned, his hair slicked down like Hercule Poirot's, the nurse was gone as was the tray of inedible food. In the nurse's place a new set of visitors had appeared. "Hi, Mom. Hi Dad." The boy ran over for exuberant hugs.

"You're awfully dressed up. What's the deal?" Tim had seen his dad in clericals almost every day of his life, but this morning was different. He always looked sharp, but this morning he looked cool— really cool. "And Mom. You're gorgeous, Mom. Again, what's the deal?" It had been so long since Tim had noticed anything but dark and drabness and guns and rats. He was eager to see life again—and happy dads and proud moms.

"We're going to church," she said.

"But we always go to church on Sunday."

"Today is special," his dad said. "*You* are going to be the guest of honor."

"Me?"

His mom reached and pressed her index finger on his cold nose. "Yes, you."

"What about you?"

"We all are. Now get your clothes on and let's head out. We've got a couple of stops to make before we get there."

✝✝✝

MIKE HELPED his son with the last-minute chores, and in five minutes flat—with Tim in a wheelchair, because the hospital required it—they boarded the elevator on their way to the sixth floor. They went to Jerry's room but discovered it empty. The nurse told them that he had been released around 6:00 this morning. "At his own persuasive insistence," the nurse added. He had not been scheduled for release for another couple of days.

"Sounds like Jerry," Mike interjected.

Jerry had also apparently pulled rank on the nurse when she had offered him a wheel chair. He had insisted on walking—though with the aid of a walker—out of this *hell hole*, as he had put it.

The Richeys left the hospital and pulled into the Broad Street Denny's parking lot. Original Grand Slams were the order of the day, and Tim ate his way through four fluffy pancakes and bacon and sausage and orange juice and everything else that had appeared on his plate. The hell the three had traversed was conversationally off limits—and would be for some months to come. But Tim's return to school was very much a conversational target.

They drove into the church parking lot a half an hour before the service was scheduled to begin. The three walked over to the columbarium, where Basil's ashes had been inurned. Mike placed his hand on Basil's face stone, signed it with the cross, and prayed. He thanked God for God's forgiveness—both for him and for his father. Then he ended the funeral he had begun weeks ago:

> *Rest eternal grant to him, O Lord;*
> *And let light perpetual shine upon him.*
> *May his soul, and the souls of all the departed,*
> *Through the mercy of God, rest in peace. Amen.*

✝✝✝

THE BISHOP was preaching and celebrating Holy Eucharist this morning. She had especially wanted to be here to welcome Mike back as rector of St. Christopher's and head of St. Christopher's Diner. The Richeys walked into the church during the magnificent organ prelude, Bach's "Jesu, Joy of Man's Desiring," to Mike's mind the most spiritually stirring of all musical pieces. It pleased him that the organist had remembered him in that way. They reverenced the altar and took their seats toward the back of the church among a large contingent of diner denizens. The noisy welcome of these wonderful homeless folks in response to the Richeys presence was heart warming. And the organist burst into a thundering introduction to

> *This is the feast*
> *Of victory for our God.*
> *Alleluia! Alleluia! Alleluia!*

The service continued with prayers and the reading of the scriptures. Appropriately, June Ellerbe, the diner's manager, read the lesson from Isaiah, and the choir rendered the Psalm in beautiful, flowing Gregorian Chant. And then the reading of the Epistle. The reader was apparently taking his or her time getting from the congregation up to the lectern. Mike craned his neck to see a large man with his arm in a sling hobbling down the center aisle on a walker. Mike caught his breath.

The man announced the Epistle of the day. "A reading from Paul's first letter to the Corinthians." Chief Detective Jerry Majors. The man who had constantly looked askance at Mike's expression of his faith, the man who would never darken the door of an Episcopal church, but the man who had taken a couple of bullets—one in the shoulder and the other in the thigh—for Mike and Tim. This man opened his mouth and read, saying,

> *If I speak in the tongues of mortals and of angels,*
> *But do not have love,*
> *I am a noisy gong or a clanging cymbal.*

He continued St. Paul's thoughts on the qualities of love. *Love*, the writer said, *is kind and patient, is not proud and resists egotism*. And then Jerry ended the reading:

And now faith, hope, and love abide,
These three.
And the greatest of these is love.

Mike was moved. He knew that Bishop Michener must have invited this Christian man from a different tradition to lend his presence and his strength in welcoming Mike and Annie and Tim home. And Mike was pleased.

But probably the most moving moment of the service was the Passing of the Peace, the point in the liturgy, after the congregation's Confession of Sin, at which the people normally stood and with the shake of the hand or a gentle hug shared God's peace with those near them. But today was different. Today the bishop called the three Richeys to the altar and invited the congregation to come down to share God's Peace with them. The people lined up, and, one by one, offered the Richeys their hands in the name of Christ.

And Jerry, the man who was most familiar with this Evangelical-style approach to greeting others, offered his hand to Annie and Tim and then to Mike. "God bless you, Mike." Mike gripped both his hands around Jerry's. This was the first time Jerry had ever called him anything but *reverend. Mike.* It was good to hear. He lightened his grip and said, "God bless you, too, Jerry."

Jerry moved on, but the approach had been made, the deed had been done, and the friendship had been sealed. And Mike repeated, "God bless you, Jerry."

Mike looked down the row and spotted two more friends holding hands and making their way toward the Richeys. Carlos and Ellen embraced Annie and Tim and Mike in a kind of group hug, and Carlos whispered into Mike's ear, "You think you can put a wedding on your to-do list?"

Mike's eyes glowed. "You got it, man." Then he reached over and gave Ellen a kiss on the cheek. "You got it, Ellen." And his extravagant grin lasted throughout the long line of peace-sharers.

Then the bishop continued with the service. She intoned, "The Lord be with you."

The congregation responded, "And also with you."

"Lift up your hearts."

"We lift them to the Lord."

"Let us give thanks to the Lord our God."

"It is right to give him thanks and praise."

And The Great Thanksgiving had begun. The bishop consecrated the bread and wine, and all who received the body and blood of Christ said, "Amen."

✝✝✝

JUNE AND other members of the congregation had prepared a covered-dish luncheon in St. Christopher's Diner as a welcome-back reception for the Richey family. A large Thunderbriar or Bowie's Farm bottle, holding a couple of hand-picked flowers, probably from the beds of Masters Park, stood on each table. Mike knew at once who had contributed those beautiful bouquets. A knot rose up in Mike's throat as he reached out to caress the bouquet nearest him. A scrawled message caught Mike's eye: *To Father Mike from Tom-Tom.* Then he noticed other bouquets with similar notes attached. And then there were those that had no notes. Tears emerged in his eyes and lingered there. He held his hands out over the bottles, and he prayed, using the hallowed words of *The Book of Common Prayer:*

> *Almighty and most merciful God, we remember before you all poor and neglected persons whom it would be easy for us to forget: the homeless and destitute, and all who have none to care for them. Help us to heal those who are broken in body or spirit, and to turn their sorrow into joy. Grant this, Father, for the love of your Son, who for our sake became poor, Jesus Christ our Lord.*

And the people answered, "Amen."

And for the first time ever, the homeless men and women of St. Christopher's dined together with the entire congregation. Surely the Lord was in this place.

After the sumptuous meal, the people began to drift away. Mike turned to Annie and told her to take Tim on home, that he needed to meet with the bishop for a few minutes.

"Sure," she said and gave Mike a peck on the lips. "We'll be waiting."

The bishop wanted to assure Mike that he and Annie and Tim had regularly been in her prayers and the prayers of the entire diocesan family. She pledged her own help and that of the diocese in restoring his mission at St. Christopher's and in the diocese.

The meeting lasted no more than half an hour. When the bishop rose to leave, Mike knelt before her and she blessed him. He signed himself with the cross and felt a spiritual relief he had not felt in many weeks. He prayed silently. He prayed for Annie and for Tim and especially for Jerry. And then he prayed for Bobby—for his mental health and for his salvation—and for himself that he may be able to minister effectively to his childhood friend in great peril. When he looked up, the bishop was gone. Mike stayed there a moment longer to revel in the aroma of the flora that surrounded him.

Mike left the church and walked down to Pine Street and turned right. He entered the rectory and looked to see Annie sitting in the corner of the sofa, her eyes closed and a smile on her lips.

"Where's Tim?" Mike asked.

Annie didn't open her eyes. "He was tired. He's taking a nap."

"Good."

"Good?" Annie opened her eyes just in time to see Mike reach up and remove his clerical collar.

About Dale Osborn Rains

✝ WAS BORN in the town of Marthaville, Louisiana, whose metropolitan area consisted of a population of 250 souls. I had the distinct honor of having my great-great grandfather found the town and name it after his wife Martha. That, of course did absolutely nothing for my financial situation or my social status.

I was usually considered the kid who would never get into much trouble and who would go to seminary and pastor Southern fundamentalist churches for the rest of my life. Probably my two greatest acts of rebellion were majoring in theater (that took care of the first of these assumptions) and becoming an Episcopalian (that took care of the second).

I spent over forty years of my life teaching, acting, playwriting, and directing theater. Somewhere in that forty years, my wife and I found the time to build—much of it with our own hands—a geodesic dome home. But I found very little time to write.

Now I take up my pen to write a murder mystery--my favorite genre. I've always admired the pens of Poe, Christie, Doyle, Kellerman—both of them—Follet, Grafton, Eco, and scores of others. Here's hoping that someone somewhere will enjoy my humble contribution to the genre.

www.DaleOsbornRains.com